I0612663

SHADOW MAGIC

THE DIVINE KEY TRILOGY BOOK 1

JAMES E WISHER

SAND HILL PUBLISHING

CHAPTER 1

Sultan Vilos the First approached the walled city of Kira's Oasis riding at the head of a double column of one hundred cavalry. The sun beat down on them without mercy. The light reflected off the white sand of the desert with such intensity it could drive a man mad. And the less said about the heat, the better.

The sultan had left his normal robes of state at the palace in favor of warrior's garb. Magnificent leather armor engraved with sand lions covered him from neck to toe. On his brow he wore a gold circlet shaped like a coiled cobra, the symbol of his office. At his side hung Heat's Bane, his enchanted shamshir. Even sheathed, the blade's magic lowered the air temperature around him ten degrees, making the desert heat more bearable. His men bore equipment similar to his, though less ornate. They all rode the hardy, two-humped war camels that served the royal cavalry.

Behind the cavalry trudged eight massive warriors. The eight who walked felt no resentment toward those who rode. In fact they felt nothing at all, for these were the sultan's stone soldiers. Seven feet tall and weighing nearly a ton each, the golems looked like armored warriors carved from granite. The stone soldiers formed the heart of the sultan's royal guard. Numbering twenty in total, a dozen remained behind guarding the White Palace.

Kira's Oasis sat at the very edge of the High Kingdom and provided the only shelter for many miles. The city also served as an important rest stop for the many caravans that criss-crossed the desert.

Beyond the city walls, the nomad tribes roamed much the same as they always had, herding their camels between small oases that dotted the landscape. Sometimes, in a bad year, the tribes would raid a passing caravan. Never had they dared attack one of the kingdom's walled cities.

Until now.

At the sultan's approach, the city gates opened with much creaking and grinding of metal on metal. The gates shut as soon as the last golem had entered. Vilos spotted Tarik Yin-Nasir, the town's governor and an old and loyal friend. A small man, even among the natives of the High Kingdom, Tarik stood only five foot two. He had the typical dark hair and eyes of his people, and his skin had baked dark brown under the sun's angry gaze.

Vilos dismounted and approached his old friend. Tarik had received the governor's position in Kira's Oasis several months after Vilos's coronation, as thanks for his support during the Crown War.

Vilos clapped a hand on Tarik's shoulder and smiled. "So, what kind of trouble have you gotten into now?"

Tarik looked up at his lord, a definite necessity as Vilos stood well over six feet tall. "A large group of nomads attacked the city eight days ago. They breached the fortress's defenses after a short but brutal battle. My family and I used the escape

2

portal to flee along with two score soldiers. Archers now surround the walls, preventing the nomads from escaping. After the battle, we didn't have enough men left to retake the fortress. We've maintained the siege since requesting help."

"Doesn't sound too bad," Vilos said. "How many nomads survived the initial assault?"

"At least a hundred and fifty plus their camels."

Vilos nodded. "Let's go take a look."

The two men walked together down the street. Along both sides sat adobe and sandstone buildings. A few small shops had two stories with a living area above and a work area below, but the majority of the buildings had only one story. These buildings, with a kitchen and living space, housed the majority of the people in the High Kingdom.

Many people now crowded in doorways to watch Vilos pass by. He smiled and waved to everyone. Vilos knew he made quite a sight with his long blond hair, blue eyes, and pale skin. He appeared the polar opposite to the people he ruled.

A few steps behind Vilos, his stone soldiers stomped along ready to crush anyone foolish enough to attack their master. Vilos noted with pleasure that no one stopped cheering or cringed in fear when the golems appeared. It meant the people didn't fear him.

His smile broadened as he remembered the day his father had taken him and his twin brothers, Nord and Kent, aside and told them the secret to ruling well. He'd said the people should never fear their lord. He should represent a source of pride for his people. *Make them love you and you can sleep safe at night knowing they won't take up arms against you. Become a tyrant and you'll never know a moment's peace.*

In his nineteen-year rule, not a single city had turned against him. Even the merchants kept their complaints to a minimum. His daughter would inherit a rich and content land.

"Majesty, we have arrived," Tarik said.

Mostly content, he amended, as he looked up at the fortress. Its design mirrored that of all the fortresses around the kingdom. It was surrounded on three sides by twenty-foot stone walls with the city's wall on the fourth.

A heavy wooden door provided the only way in. The yard where the soldiers trained separated the keep from the walls. Four small outbuildings dotted the yard: two barracks, a smithy, and a storage building. A second wooden door allowed entry into the keep proper. The keep consisted of a great hall, kitchen, and servants' quarters downstairs and living quarters for Tarik and his family upstairs.

Along the top of the wall, a number of nomads with bows stared down at them. Tarik's remaining soldiers glared right back.

Satisfied with his survey Vilos said, "This shouldn't take long. Captain, would you join us please?"

The commander of the sultan's cavalry approached the two men. Dark skinned and wiry, his sharp eyes were surrounded by a mass of wrinkles brought on by a lifetime of squinting in the desert sun. The ride had left his off-white uniform dusty and plastered to his back and chest with sweat. The captain looked more like a bandit chief than a soldier in the elite cavalry.

But looks counted for nothing. Captain Yosef had served in the cavalry since Vilos's father's rule and his loyalty was beyond question. "Majesty?"

"Captain, I want you and your men to form a semicircle around the front of the keep in case anyone tries to flee. Keep well out of arrow range."

"Are we not going to attack, Majesty?" Yosef sounded almost disappointed.

"The stone soldiers will deal with those in the keep. Your job is to protect the people should any escape."

"Majesty, the golems would be much better at defending the people. Let my men and me attack the fort." The captain's face had tensed and his eyes narrowed to slits as he argued his case.

"Captain, the golems move too slowly to catch a man mounted on a camel, and if your men attack they'd get slaughtered. Everyone has a job to do, now get your men in position so we can do it."

"Yes, Majesty." Yosef retreated back to his men and Vilos could hear him shouting orders.

"Rather presumptuous of him arguing with you like that," Tarik said.

Vilos shook his head. That had been just another skirmish in a long-running battle he'd been having with Yosef. He thought Vilos relied too much on his golems. He was probably right, but Vilos just couldn't stand the thought of risking men's lives without need.

"I encourage my men to speak their mind. Better to listen than to let pride do the enemy's work for him. Don't worry. Yosef will do his duty."

Tarik nodded. "Now what?"

"I'll give them one last chance to surrender."

"They won't," Tarik said, his voice grim.

"I know."

Vilos walked, calm as a desert morning, right toward the front gate. The cavalry had taken position a hundred and fifty yards from the walls. They parted to let Vilos through.

He stopped about fifty feet from the walls. "Hear me!" he shouted. "You have one last chance to surrender. Anyone leaving the fortress, unarmed, in the next two minutes, will be spared."

One of the nomads on the wall drew back and fired an arrow right at Vilos's head. Six inches from his face the arrow shattered. The magic of the golden cobra would allow no mundane weapon to touch him.

So be it.

"Come to me," he said.

Six camels moved aside as the stone soldiers marched forward.

"Kill everyone inside." Vilos pointed toward the fortress.

Arrows filled the sky as he walked around behind his cavalry. Most of them clattered against the stone soldiers, as useless as the curses hurled down by the archers.

Safe behind the cavalry, Vilos turned to watch his soldiers work.

The golems had almost reached the gate. Nomad archers continued to pelt them with arrows, though Vilos couldn't fathom why.

When they reached the gate three golems stood side by side and raised their arms up over their heads. Like a battering ram, they struck the gate, smashing fist-sized holes in it.

Again the massive arms went up only to come down with even greater force.

With two blows they had reduced the top of the gate to splinters. Vilos could see spear shafts poking through the hole only to snap off against the unyielding stone juggernauts.

The top of the gate lay in ruins, so the golems reared back and kicked the bottom. The gate burst in, knocking half a dozen nomads to the ground.

Before they could recover, the stone soldiers walked over them. Weighing over a ton each, the golems pulped the nomads like a winemaker crushing grapes.

The stone soldiers had moved out of sight, but Vilos could still hear the shriek of steel on stone.

The sound set his teeth on edge.

A few minutes after the golems had entered the fortress a score of nomads came racing out on camelback. They appeared eager to take a run at flesh-and-blood opponents and charged straight at the cavalry.

Half the soldiers rode forward to meet them while the rest closed the gaps in their formation in case more appeared.

The loud ring of steel on steel filled the air as the two forces came together.

The nomads had the advantage of momentum from their short charge and they forced the sultan's men back.

His royal cavalry gave ground absorbing the initial burst then began pushing the nomads toward the keep wall.

The nomads hacked at their opponents with wild abandon while controlling their mounts with an ease and precision born of a lifetime in the saddle.

A pair of cavalrymen fell from their mounts. The sight of their comrades falling seemed to galvanize the others and they bore into the nomads with renewed fury.

One on one, even the finest cavalryman was no match for the superior skill of the nomads who were basically born in the saddle, but fighting as a unit they soon dropped a few of the warriors. Superior numbers and equipment finally decided the day and the last of the nomads fell.

The uninjured cavalrymen rejoined their fellows while the injured, including the two that had lost their seats, retreated behind the line. No more nomads appeared and soon the sounds of battle within the fortress faded. Vilos allowed another five minutes before he stepped up to the demolished gates. "Stone soldiers, to me!" he yelled.

Thundering steps heralded the stone soldiers' arrival. The golems bore a red coat of gore from the battle but showed no damage. Vilos nodded once and waved Tarik and Yosef up to join him. "Tarik," he said, "have some of your servants clean the golems. In this heat it won't take long for them to start stinking."

"At once, Majesty." Tarik hurried off to find his servants.

Vilos turned to Yosef. "The golems did well, did they not, Captain?"

"Yes, Majesty, they did."

"Then why were you so keen to send your men into a battle they couldn't win?" Vilos asked.

Yosef grimaced. "May I speak plainly, Majesty?"

"Please."

"I'm getting old. I served your father and fought in many battles. Since you defeated your brothers in the Crown War, there hasn't been a battle worthy of the name."

Vilos frowned, not understanding where this was going. "You consider that a bad thing?"

"No, Majesty, it just... ahh. Someday you may have to fight a battle in which the stone soldiers will be of little use. If that day comes, may heaven forbid, you'll have no core of battle-hardened warriors to call upon."

"What type of battle could my stone soldiers not win?" Vilos asked. He could truly think of no battle the mighty warriors would lose.

"It seems to me, Majesty, that in a running battle in the open desert they would be of little use. As you said yourself, they couldn't keep up with a running camel."

Vilos looked thoughtful. Perhaps there was more to what Yosef said than he'd thought.

"I admit my men wouldn't have done well invading the fortress," Yosef said. "Still, I beg you to consider my words."

Vilos laid a hand on Yosef's shoulder. "I shall, Captain, I shall. Now you had best see to your wounded."

T he night after the battle, Vilos joined Tarik and his family for dinner at their temporary home. Though he wished to return to the White Palace as soon as possible, he would never dishonor his friend by refusing to join him for a meal.

Vilos currently rested on a large pillow at the head of a large, low rectangular table. Along each side sat Tarik's twenty children and four wives. His friend sat at the far end facing him. The table bowed under the weight of the food placed on it. Steaming tureens of bean soup and plates of fresh dates and figs sat beside slabs of roast camel meat and a tower of baklava. Vilos hated the bean soup that was a staple of his people's diet, so he contented himself with fruit and baklava.

As he sat munching Vilos said, "I see a new addition to your family since you last visited the palace."

Ever the doting father, Tarik took his little girl out of his youngest wife's lap and held her up. "Beautiful, isn't she? My little Sasha."

Vilos grinned at his friend. "Takes after her mother." He'd said it more to tease Tarik than anything, but as he looked at Tarik's youngest wife he could see the truth in his words. Blessed with the ample curves common to women of the kingdom, Tarik's wife also had long dark hair down to her waist and deep-brown almond eyes. She looked so much like Ayia, his late wife, that it made him ache to look at her and at the same time he didn't want to turn away.

Vilos realized his friend had continued talking and that he'd been staring. "I'm sorry, old friend. What did you say?"

"I said has your daughter found any suitors to her liking yet?"

Vilos chuckled. "No, that's why I've invited every eligible

prince I could think of to her birthday party next month. Eighteen years, by heaven, where has the time gone?"

The meal finished, Tarik and Vilos went to the lounge to finish their coffee. Soft camelhide chairs welcomed the weary men. Vilos sipped his coffee and sighed. Strong but sweet, just the way he liked it. "What do you think prompted the nomad's attack?"

"I haven't the slightest idea, Vilos. We've been trading in peace with them for years. Then, like a sand drake, they attack without warning."

"Whatever the reason, I don't like it. I have a few friends among the nomads. I'll contact them when I get home." Unable to stand it any longer Vilos said, "Tell me about your new wife."

Tarik laughed. "I wondered how long it would take before you asked. Tara certainly draws the men's eyes."

"I didn't think I was quite so obvious. She looks so much like Ayia when we first met…"

Tarik nodded. "I hadn't realized it myself, but now that you point it out the resemblance is obvious. I hope seeing her didn't cause you pain."

Vilos smiled at his friend's concern. Not the false worry of a nobleman who might have offended his lord but the genuine concern of an old friend. It made Vilos realize just how few true friends he had. "Don't worry, seeing her was a surprise, but a pleasant one."

"You know, Vilos, if you ever thought of remarrying, Tara isn't really my wife."

Vilos raised an eyebrow at this. "Oh?"

"She's the daughter of another old friend, a merchant. His wife wanted to arrange a marriage to a nobleman in the north known to beat his wives. When my friend heard he claimed he'd already promised Tara to me. His wife wasn't pleased, but since I outranked the other nobleman she agreed. I learned this by messenger three days later. I didn't really want to marry her."

Vilos thought of the beautiful young woman and offered his friend an incredulous look.

"Truth. I swear I was quite content, and it seemed strange, after all I have a daughter two years older than Tara. Still I wished the young lady no harm, so I agreed. We haven't even consummated the marriage. That was two years ago."

"But the child."

Tarik smiled. "My granddaughter. We pretend she's Tara's when we have guests, just to keep up appearances."

"Quite a story. Tara is a lucky young woman. Plenty of men would have taken advantage of her situation."

Tarik nodded. "Another reason her father chose me. So you see, if you wished to remarry, I would give her up. Since the marriage never really began there would be no dishonor. I saw how you looked at her."

Vilos smiled but shook his head. "I may have looked at her but I didn't see her, I saw a ghost. I appreciate your offer, but it wouldn't be fair to Tara. The comparison to Ayia would always be there and it wouldn't be a fair one to make. Better for all if she stays here."

"As you wish. Now, speaking of family tell me of yours. Where are Nord and Kent?"

"My brothers? Last I heard Nord had joined a mercenary band fighting in the duchies to the north. That was five years ago. Kent I hear news of almost weekly. His merchant company operates out of Port Haydrien. He's gained a great deal of wealth and now sits on the merchants' council."

"Haydrien, that's about as far as you can get from the White Palace and still remain in the High Kingdom," Tarik said.

Vilos sighed, feeling the familiar sadness as they spoke of

his brothers. "They both hate me. I fear my family will never be restored."

"There's still Shara," Tarik said.

Just the mention of his daughter brought a smile to Vilos's face. "Shara's a good girl."

Tarik returned his friend's smile. "Didn't her alchemy tutor once call her a thrice-damned hell spawn?"

Vilos winced. "She isn't that bad. He just got angry because she blew up his lab."

"Twice," Tarik crowed.

Vilos shot him a pained look. "Twice."

He hoped he'd find the White Palace still standing when he got back.

CHAPTER 2

Shara raced through the white marble halls that gave the White Palace its name. She still wore her black silk pajamas and old pink slippers even though it was almost midday. Her long auburn hair streamed behind her as she ran. Her best friend, Sarafin, squealed with delight as she tried to keep up. Soon they would reach her father's mosaic room. The entire floor was covered in bright, smooth ceramic tile. Her favorite pink slippers had long ago lost the rough bottom that her new ones had. That made them perfect for her favorite game, skating.

She hit the mosaic floor at full speed and slid into a graceful glide. Her arms extended to the side and, balanced on one foot, she coasted three-quarters of the way across the floor before running out of momentum.

She smiled as she held the pose. Shara still remembered the day six years ago when her history tutor had shown her the picture of northmen sliding across the ice balanced on a single steel blade mounted on their boots. There was no question in her mind that she had to try it. Pity ice didn't form in the desert. Sliding on the mosaic was the best she could manage.

Reality came hurtling back as she heard Sarafin approaching. Her friend hit the tile and tried to imitate Shara's graceful glide. Unfortunately Sarafin weighed about fifty pounds more than Shara and had the dexterity of a three-legged donkey.

It took only a moment for her to fall on her ample stomach, completely out of control. Shara groaned as she realized Sarafin was headed right toward her. An instant later Shara found herself sprawled across Sarafin's back and riding her friend like a camel for another ten feet. They finally stopped just short of the rear wall.

The two girls laughed for a moment then Sarafin said, "Heaven's mercy, I'm going to miss this, Shar."

Shara sighed and rolled off her friend. Sarafin was almost two years Shara's junior but she had already gotten engaged. Soon she'd leave the palace where the two of them had grown up like sisters and start a new life with her husband-to-be.

Sarafin's parents had arranged the marriage to seal a trade agreement. Shara had seen the fat old merchant in court a few times. He wheezed just climbing the steps to the throne room. "You deserve better, Sara."

Sarafin held up her hand to forestall Shara's argument. "I'm the youngest daughter of a minor noble family. An arranged marriage was my destiny. Besides, I'm homely as a mule. No prince is going to come sweep me off my feet."

Shara hopped up. She loved Sarafin like a sister, but had to admit her friend had a point. The two girls couldn't have looked more different. Shara was tall and slim with shoulder-length auburn hair. Sarafin was round and short with black hair and dark eyes that couldn't see ten feet in front of her. Roly-poly, her father had called Sarafin. The word seemed apt.

"It's lunch time, isn't it, Shar?"

Shara grinned. The next meal was ever on Sarafin's mind. "I'm the princess, my dear. Lunch is whenever I wish it."

Sarafin giggled at Shara's imitation of the noble ladies that inhabited the palace like sand fleas in a beggar's hovel. "I'd better get dressed first," Shara said. "Father would have a fit if he knew I spent the whole morning in my night clothes."

They walked back through the gleaming halls toward Shara's room. When they arrived she waved aside the stone soldier standing in front of her door. The golem took two steps to the left so she could reach the gold-inlaid door. As soon as she closed it she heard the heavy steps of the golem returning to its post.

Shara stripped off her pajamas and tossed them toward the bed. They stopped in midair about three feet from her target. The clothes flew toward the far wall where they vanished as her invisible servant passed through the wall on its way to the laundry. Shara walked over to her closet and regarded the many beautiful garments hanging there. After a moment's deliberation she selected a pair of billowy white pants and a sapphire top that revealed her flat midriff. She finished it off with a platinum tiara her father had gotten for her a few years ago.

She spun in a circle. "How do I look?"

Sarafin had sprawled on her huge feather bed. She sat up and smiled. "Beautiful as always, Shar. It's bad enough the men have to look at you every day without teasing them with a top like that."

Shara leapt through the air, spun a full flip, and landed on the bed beside Sarafin. "You know Father would never let me dress like this. He's due home tomorrow so this is my last chance."

"Don't forget what happened two years ago."

Shara lay back and sighed. How could she forget?

Two years ago, a few days after her sixteenth birthday, she had gone for a walk in the garden dressed much as she was now. A handsome young nobleman, about a year her senior, spotted her. Thinking she was out looking for a tryst he'd hurried over, eager to oblige.

Unfortunately for him, he'd gotten a little overeager and grabbed her arm. A stone soldier appeared a moment later—there always seemed to be one of those things nearby. Before she could stop it the golem ripped the young man's arm off. It took all the skill and magic of the palace healers to reattach it. The story soon spread through the palace and now most men wouldn't even look at her.

"I remember, Sarafin, don't worry. I doubt anyone would be foolish enough to try a stunt like that again."

They left Shara's room and headed downstairs. A sweeping white marble staircase led to the main hall. The kitchens were situated in the rear of the palace so the hustle and bustle wouldn't bother the nobles.

At the base of the stairs the two honor guards snapped to attention at the princess's approach. Shara noticed one of the guards, a young man new to the post, watching her from the corner of his eye. She winked to let him know she'd seen him. He immediately looked away. Shara smiled a sad little smile and turned toward the kitchen before Sarafin decided to go cannibal on her.

CHAPTER 3

Prince Nord surveyed the two score soldiers assembled before him. Raggedy and still smelling of smoke, most of the men had survived the sacking of Duke Gallow's keep. The survivors had a grim, hard edge to them. The remaining half dozen looked like boys taken straight from the fields. They held their war axes on their shoulders like they planned to go chop firewood.

Still, all of them cowered as Nord looked down at them. At six foot eight, Nord weighed over three hundred pounds—all of it muscle—without his armor. By far the largest of the three brothers that had vied for the crown of the High Kingdom, Nord still believed he should have won. Now he'd been reduced to a mere mercenary captain.

How the mighty had fallen.

The men assembled before him represented the latest recruits to the White Tigers mercenary band. The White Tigers numbered four thousand strong and many counted them among the most skilled mercenary bands in the Broken Kingdom.

This had not always been the case. When Nord had fled north after the Crown War, the White Tigers had amounted to little more than a miserable band of outlaws numbering perhaps twenty.

Nord encountered them first in the forest near their camp. He'd approached in peace, not wanting to fight an entire camp of armed men. The White Tigers had drawn steel and prepared to attack. He'd been forced to kill three of them before their leader, Dragen, had called them off.

Nord and Dragen spent the rest of the day talking and taking the measure of each other. He took a liking to the bandit leader almost at once and they'd struck a bargain whereby Nord would use the wealth he'd secreted out of the High Kingdom to buy better equipment for the White Tigers and to entice new recruits. In exchange Nord would get the rank of second-in-command.

Six months later the Tigers numbered over a hundred, including a sorcerer of middling power. Nord and Dragen decided the time had come to make their name.

A messenger had gone to the castle of Duke Cassius. Cassius was engaged in a fierce battle with his neighbor, Duke Ballin. Ballin had managed to construct a fort between two rivers. This fort overlooked the only ford for many miles in either direction. Ballin used the fort to halt all merchant travel heading toward Cassius's land. The White Tigers offered to sack the fort in exchange for whatever plunder they found.

Cassius had agreed with the understanding that if they failed, he wouldn't acknowledge them. The Tigers had accepted and managed to complete the mission. Well pleased, Cassius had hired them for several other missions. The wealth and fame gained from these efforts brought the White Tigers to prominence.

For eighteen years now Nord had fought with the White

Tigers. He'd more than doubled the wealth he escaped with and now controlled half the Broken Kingdom through puppet dukes.

Dragen died in battle four years ago and Nord now ruled alone. In another year or two he'd control all the Broken Kingdom and then he'd turn his sights south to his brothers and the High Kingdom.

Assuming he could turn these plow boys into soldiers.

. —※

Prince Kent sat unperturbed as his new business associate ranted about the unfair price Kent had offered him for his pearls. The eastern merchant, he called himself Yin, paced from side to side tossing his hands in the air. Kent's beautiful office had a spell of silence surrounding it, so Yin's ranting went no further.

"They're worth three times what you offered me!" Yin shouted for the fourth time. "Twenty-five gold pieces each is an insult."

Kent leaned forward and rested his elbows on the large mahogany desk that dominated the room. "You'll do no better elsewhere. Accept my offer or get out."

Kent's blunt ultimatum seemed to jar the merchant. He sat down in one of the small leather chairs in front of the desk. "It's just that my expenses ran a little higher than I anticipated. Couldn't you make it a little more?"

Kent smiled. He had his fish hooked now. "I'm not without sympathy, Yin. I'll make it thirty gold pieces each."

"I accept," Yin said. "Thank you, sir."

Kent rose from his high-backed chair. At just under six feet, Kent wasn't the most physically impressive figure, certainly not when compared to his brothers, Nord and Vilos. The runt of the litter, they always called him. That had rankled at the time, but he soon learned that his brain could often get him what his lack of size couldn't.

That was a lesson that served him well over the years.

He patted his belly and swallowed a sigh. The good life had taken its toll.

"My pleasure," he said. "We merchant men have to stick together."

"Indeed we do, sir." Yin bowed to his host.

Kent walked around his desk and escorted Yin out the door that led to his main warehouse. "Just tell the clerk what price we agreed on when you bring the pearls."

"I will, and thank you again."

Kent closed the door behind him and began thinking of a number of jewelers he knew that would be glad to offer one hundred gold pieces for each of those pearls. Kent had no sooner sat down than someone knocked on his door.

Kent touched a rune that had been engraved on his desk. Whenever he touched it the silence spell ended until he removed his finger. "Come in."

His beautiful assistant, Yaway, entered the office. Her flawless features were highlighted by a hint of rouge on her lips and a bit of sparkling crystal at the corners of her eyes. A loose, swirling robe covered her from neck to ankle, yet the thin silk clung just enough to give a hint of the perfection that hid underneath.

Not that her looks were the only reason Kent hired her. Yaway had a mind nearly as keen as his own. On those rare occasions when his business took him out of the city, he trusted her to handle matters in his absence. Given how few people he trusted, that was a rare honor.

"We received a sending from one of your ships, The Happy Mermaid," she said. "They'll arrive about a week late due to a storm. They've sustained some minor damage, but nothing that threatens the ship's safety."

"The Happy Mermaid..." Kent tried in vain to remember what cargo it carried.

"A variety of copper tableware," Yaway said as if reading his mind.

That's what he loved about the woman: besides a jaw-dropping figure she always seemed to know just what he needed. "No big deal. Anything else?"

"Your niece's birthday is approaching. Do you wish to send a gift?"

Kent thought about it. He hadn't spoken to either of his brothers since the Crown War ended. He didn't like Vilos, though more because they had little in common than due to any particular offense. Despite several magical conversations with his niece over the past few months, he hadn't yet decided if visiting the palace again was a good idea.

But perhaps the time had come to reach out to the Crown. "Pick out something nice and extravagant. I trust your judgement."

"Very good, shall I send it directly to the palace?"

"No," Kent said. I'll take it myself.

CHAPTER 4

Vilos smiled as he spotted the four gleaming towers of the White Palace jutting toward the sky. In another hour, Sultan's Oasis would be visible in all its glory. More than one hundred thousand people called the capital home. Most of the noble families also maintained a home there so they could live in comfort when at court. With his daughter's birthday fast approaching, the population would soon nearly double as nobles from many lands arrived for a chance to court the princess.

As they got closer to home the speed of their little column increased without them even being aware of it. Vilos glanced back at his fifty men and realized the stone soldiers had fallen behind. He held up his hand signaling the men to slow down so the golems could catch up.

Vilos had sent Captain Yosef and half the cavalry to look into the nomad trouble. Vilos was friends with several headmen who might know why the other tribes were so stirred up. The mission would also give the young cavalrymen some much needed experience.

Yosef readily agreed to the mission. He selected a mix of new recruits and veterans then headed into the desert as soon as they acquired the necessary provisions. Vilos expected Yosef to return about a week after Shara's birthday. He hoped the attack only represented one angry tribe and not a larger uprising.

Soon he could see the city walls and the main gate. The walls stood fifty feet tall and twenty feet thick. They had fallen only once to an invader, when Vilos's ancestor had conquered the city a thousand years ago.

Since then three sieges had befallen Sultan's Oasis. All three had been broken by winter sandstorms rather than the soldiers of the city guard.

They arrived at the gate, which swung open at the sultan's approach. Massive horns sang out to announce the lord's return. King's Way, a broad road through the heart of the city, went straight from the main gate to the palace. Along both sides throngs of people had gathered.

They cheered as Vilos rode down the street. About halfway to the palace a little girl in a dirty white smock darted out into the street. She carried a pair of King's Tears. The white flowers looked like daisies and grew wherever they could find a few drops of moisture. They were pretty, but most farmers considered them a nuisance.

Vilos dismounted and before the child's mortified mother could drag her out of the street he knelt and took the flowers. The girl wore a coat of dirt like a second skin. She smiled when Vilos accepted her gift. Vilos took one and broke the stem about four inches below the flower and tucked it behind the little girl's ear. The second flower he kept for himself.

"Consider that my personal invitation to you and your mother to attend my daughter's birthday celebration."

When Vilos got to his feet the people cheered even louder.

He remounted his camel and waved again. To the little girl he threw a wink. She beamed and winked back. This would certainly give her a story to tell her friends when she got home.

The rest of the trip down King's Way passed without event. As Vilos approached the white marble walls that surrounded the palace another set of horns sounded and the black iron portcullis clanked up. He had just entered the garden that grew around the palace when he spotted Shara running toward him. He just managed to dismount before she leapt into his arms. Vilos spun her around once then set her back down.

"I missed you, Father," she said.

"I missed you too, Shara." Vilos turned to his men. "I'll walk to the palace with my daughter. Take care of my camel."

The men saluted and one of them grabbed the reins of Vilos's camel.

Vilos linked arms with Shara and they started down one of the white stone paths that ran through the garden. Palm trees hung over the path providing shade to lessen the day's heat. "Anything interesting happen while I was away?"

"Sarafin's determined to go through with her marriage to the wheezer."

"I spoke to the man a couple times," Vilos said. "He didn't seem that bad."

"I know. I just think she could do better."

"If she's content, try and be happy for her."

"I'll try," Shara said. She still didn't seem convinced. Her face brightened. "I almost forgot. We received a sending from Uncle Kent yesterday. He's coming to my party."

Vilos looked dumbfounded. "My brother?"

"Yes, he said he's looking forward to seeing you again."

Vilos scratched his head. "I'll be damned. I wonder what he wants."

"I don't know." Shara's nose wrinkled up. "I think *you* want a bath."

· ·····✧

Vilos lay in bed that night thinking about his brother. In truth, he'd thought of little else since Shara had mentioned Kent. All through dinner he'd had only half an ear for his daughter and the small group of friends that had joined them.

Shara and Sarafin had debated endlessly about what Kent would be like. Shara had never met either of her uncles.

What could Kent want? In the nineteen years since the Crown War ended, Vilos hadn't heard a word from either of his brothers. When his wife had died he'd heard nothing. Now Kent decided to speak.

Vilos flopped over onto his back and stared at the silk canopy of his bed. What could he want? That was Vilos's last thought as he fell asleep.

· ·····✧

Vilos wandered through a tunnel. The dark stone walls pressed tight around him. A strange mist filled the air making it impossible to see more than a few feet in any direction. The floor of the cave was smooth so at least he had no fear of tripping on some unseen obstacle. Vilos shuffled along through the darkness and finally emerged into a huge domed cavern.

A creepy déjà vu feeling struck him. He swore he'd seen something like this long ago. Light filled the cavern as twenty torches ringing the perimeter burst into flame. The torches were held in the hands of twenty stone statues. The statues looked identical to his stone soldiers.

The far end of the cavern rose above the floor about ten feet. The raised portion still lay hidden in shadows.

Vilos knew where he was.

He didn't want to approach the dark corner of the cave, yet he found his legs wouldn't obey him.

Though he fought with all his will, Vilos continued to inch closer to the darkness. He stopped at the base of the platform and found a short flight of steps.

A blinding flash of light forced Vilos to raise his arm and cover his eyes.

When he lowered his arm he found a hooded figure seated on a throne of black volcanic glass. On either side of him stood a golden pole topped with a glowing crystal. The man wore a purple robe with black trim.

The dark figure beckoned.

Vilos had no desire to get any closer, but as before his body had other ideas. He climbed the steps and stopped ten feet from the throne. The man stood to face him. Though six inches shorter than Vilos and at least one hundred pounds lighter, the man radiated an aura of power such that Vilos knew if they came to blows he wouldn't get the better of it.

The dark figure threw back his hood, revealing the face that Vilos had feared for the last twenty years. Thin and hawkish with a bald head and icy blue eyes that seemed to look through rather than at you, the sorcerer hadn't changed since Vilos last saw him. Two tattoos resembling a skull surrounded by black flames, one on each cheek, decorated that strangely compelling face.

"What do you want?" Vilos asked at last. His voice sounded soft and weak in his ears.

"You know," the sorcerer said in a voice so deep it seemed to shake the cavern.

"No," Vilos said.

"I'm coming."

CHAPTER 5

"No!" Vilos sat up in bed screaming.

A pair of guards burst through the door.

"Are you all right, Majesty?" they asked in unison.

Vilos nodded as he tried to regain his composure. "Just a nightmare, I'm fine."

The guards saluted and returned to their posts. When they had gone Vilos rolled out of bed. He'd get no more sleep this night. He threw open the door to his balcony and stepped out into the cool of the night.

He loved looking out over Sultan's Oasis after dark. Even this late a few lights burned in the city. Saloons and gambling halls most likely. They never closed.

Vilos glanced up at the sky. The moon had passed its zenith and now hung low in the sky. At best he'd slept five hours. Tomorrow, make that today, would bring ten hours of open court.

A long ten hours.

A few strides brought him back to his bed. Vilos knew he should try and rest, but he kept on going, settling in front of his desk instead. At his touch, a small crystal globe in the center of the desk began to glow with a soft white light. Vilos smiled as he ran his fingers over the cracked surface of the desk. It was one of the few artifacts remaining from the first sultan's time.

He plucked the top parchment from a stack of fifteen on the corner awaiting his attention. Some people had sent a written complaint in advance of their court appearance. Since sleep seemed impossible, he might as well work.

When he finished reading all the complaints on his desk, the sun had risen and reclaimed the sky. His room filled with golden light and servants were moving around outside. Shara wouldn't rise for another two hours, at least, but he had to talk to her before court opened.

Vilos threw on his robe. Shara's room was just down the hall from his. Two stone soldiers barred her door. "Stand aside."

The two golems moved left and right and he rapped on the door. Shara must have heard the golems move because she answered the door after only a few seconds.

Disheveled and bleary eyed, her dark hair sticking up in every direction, she squinted at him. "Father?"

"We need to talk," Vilos said.

She stepped aside and Vilos went in. As soon as she shut the door the golems stepped back in place. Shara yawned and sat down on the edge of her bed. "What's wrong?"

Vilos told her about his dream.

"What a terrible nightmare," Shara said.

"It was more than a nightmare." Vilos stared pacing. "I know the sorcerer. Many years ago he did me a favor, probably saved my life. Now he's coming to collect his payment."

"So pay him." Shara said it like it was the simplest thing in the world.

"I intend to," Vilos said. "The problem is, the sorcerer can be a little unpredictable. You still wear the ring I gave you?"

She held out her left hand and showed him the silver ring with a moonstone setting. "You said I should never take it off and I haven't."

"Good," Vilos said. "You remember how to use it?"

She nodded. "Turn the moonstone three times to the right."

He nodded. "Good. If I tell you to use it, don't hesitate, and don't worry about me. Just use it."

"What kind of lunatic would dare attack me in the palace surrounded by guards, stone soldiers, and you?"

Vilos stopped pacing and sat down beside his daughter. "A dangerous one. Promise me you'll use the ring if I tell you."

She looked into his eyes, her lip trembling slightly. "You're scaring me, Father."

"Promise me."

"I promise."

He pulled her close.

"I love you, Shara."

CHAPTER 6

Daktari made his way through the streets of Sultan's Oasis. Throngs of people crowded the stalls. Merchants haggled with customers. The stink of livestock and unwashed men filled the air. All the noise and life set the purple-robed sorcerer's teeth on edge. How he longed to summon an acid fog to dissolve the flesh from their bones.

He forced the thought away. Always the demon's corruption tried to push him to violence. Unnecessary death and destruction was its way, not his. While he had no compunction about killing, he found mindless slaughter pointless and a waste of magic.

Grimacing, he pulled the cowl of his robe down lower over his eyes. Almost as unbearable as the people was the bright sun beating down on him. The heat didn't faze him, a simple frost aura kept it at bay. The light troubled him more. High sun would arrive soon and Daktari's eyes, accustomed as they were to the shadows of his underground home, complained with bitter tears of hate.

The miserable setting combined with the demon's influence almost pushed Daktari into a true rage. And when the shadow sorcerer was enraged, even demons steered clear.

He could easily have teleported directly to the palace. He'd been there several times and the feeble wards guarding it were no barrier to him. Unfortunately, he couldn't do so without alerting everyone inside and that would make his task more difficult. So Daktari endured and pushed his way through the crowd. The White Palace and his prize beckoned.

Near the end of the market he shoved a large man aside. The fellow stank of ale and vomit. No doubt that was from the stain on the front of his filthy tunic. Disgusting savages, the lot of them.

Before the sorcerer had taken two steps he felt a large hand clamp around his shoulder. The big man spun him around. "You'd best watch who you're shoving, little man."

That was more insult than Daktari would bear. He summoned a wisp of shadow magic into his right index finger and tapped the oaf between his beady eyes.

His head exploded in a red mist.

People ran screaming in every direction. Daktari let out a little sigh as the corruption and bloodlust that constantly haunted him backed off a fraction. It would be back of course. Like an addict, this fix would only keep the cursed feelings away for so long.

He hurried on toward the palace, no longer bothered by the unwashed masses.

The gates of the palace stood open and unguarded. Court day was the one day each month people could enter and leave the palace grounds at will, lucky for the guards—he was so close to completing his pact that any delay was apt to send him flying off the handle.

With barely a glance at the gardens surrounding the palace or the young lovers strolling through it, the sorcerer strode right toward the palace doors. Two guards dressed in leather armor and carrying spears stood on either side of the entrance. As Daktari approached they crossed their spears in front of him.

"Sorry, sir, court's closed after ten," the man on the right said, pointing toward a sundial sitting beside the steps.

Daktari's scowl twisted his lips. He didn't have time for this. "You're not going to let me in?"

"Orders," the man agreed.

"Pity for you."

Before the confused guards could figure out what he meant, Daktari pointed at the guard that had spoken, drew the ether around his extended hand, and infused it with shadow magic. A purple aura surrounded the guard and lifted him off the ground.

With a flick of his wrist Daktari sent the man streaking through the air.

The guard came to a sudden stop when he struck the palace wall. His body left a crimson streak down the white marble as it slid to the ground.

He turned back to find the second guard already had the door open. As he passed by he heard the fellow mutter, "Never wanted to be a guard anyway."

Daktari chuckled. The violence combined with his amusement to fully stabilize his mental state.

Once inside and out of the murderous light he let out a soft breath. The beautiful white floor and walls weren't really to his taste, but the shadows, at least, were welcoming.

He walked down the main hall. Along each side, a row of twenty pillars supported a high domed ceiling. Intricate carvings showed scenes from the daily life of the natives before the sultan's ancestors had conquered them. Daktari had no interest in any of this. He could sense his quarry straight ahead.

A pair of stone soldiers stood beside wooden double doors inlaid with gold. Daktari approached and flung the doors open with a gesture.

The court bore few decorations. A double row of ten benches ran three-quarters of the length of the room. At the front two chairs faced the sultan where he sat on a gold throne carved to look like he was sitting in the mouth of a cobra. Behind the sultan stood the remaining eighteen stone soldiers.

About a hundred people sat staring at Daktari as he entered. Vilos laid a hand on the hilt of his sword. Beside him, his daughter stared in apparent amazement that anyone would dare enter her father's court without permission. She looked beautiful in a conservative blue gown and silver tiara, so young and full of life.

Daktari smiled. At last he could complete the pact and free himself of the demon's malign influence.

"Court is closed," Daktari said. "Anyone who wishes to see tomorrow's dawn, get out."

No one moved.

They all stared at him, dumbstruck.

His recently sated rage came roaring back. He blasted the flesh from a fancily dressed man near the door. When the skeleton hit the floor it crumbled to pieces.

That had the desired effect.

People ran screaming past Daktari and out into the palace.

When the throne room had emptied of all save the sultan and his daughter, Daktari walked forward and sat in one of the chairs facing the sultan.

"Hello, Vilos. It's been too long."

"Twenty years. I thought you'd forgotten me. Until last night."

"No such luck." Daktari's lip curled into a serpent's smile. "I've come to claim my due."

He looked knowingly at the princess.

Shara started and Daktari laughed. "You never told her. My dear, you were promised to me before your birth."

The princess looked at her father. "Father? This madman is lying, isn't he?"

"Not now." Vilos stood up and faced Daktari. "I'm not the same weak boy you bargained with those many years ago. I am sultan now and I declare our contract void."

Daktari raised an eyebrow. "You declare?"

"As sultan my word is law. Now get out of my palace."

Daktari rose, eyes narrowed. "You presume much to speak so to me. Your word may be law, but only if you can enforce it."

Vilos looked at the nearest golem. "Stone soldier, throw this man out of the palace." The golem didn't flinch. He pointed at a different golem and repeated the order.

Nothing.

"You thought to use my own golems against me? Foolish."

"They've never failed me before," Vilos said.

"That's because I wasn't here to counter your orders."

"I have two hundred men on the palace grounds and five thousand in the city. You won't escape with my daughter."

Daktari shrugged. "Call them. They won't last long against *my* stone soldiers."

Vilos collapsed back onto his throne. Daktari had him and he knew it. The sorcerer had waited twenty years for this moment. Soon he would be free of the demon's yoke.

Vilos leaned over and whispered something in his daughter's ear, no doubt explaining that she'd have to go with him. With the princess in his possession, he could complete the ritual and complete the contract that bound him to his master. No longer having his body and soul linked to that lurking darkness would be welcome.

The girl fiddled with her ring and then she vanished.

No!

Daktari sent out a psychic probe.

He found nothing.

The girl wasn't cowering, invisible in some corner, she was gone.

He restrained a wave of murderous rage by the narrowest of margins. "What have you done?"

"I sent her away," Vilos said, triumph in his voice. "I knew this day would come, so I hired a wizard to enchant her ring. You'll never find her now."

"Fool!" Daktari screamed. "Ten minutes with a crystal ball and I'll have her."

"No. Once activated, the ring shields the wearer from magical scrutiny."

Daktari's eyes began to glow. "I'll rip her location from your mind."

Vilos grinned. "Go ahead. I have no idea where she's gone."

Red beams shot from the sorcerer's eyes and struck Vilos in the head.

The sultan screamed and tore at his hair.

Daktari riffled through his mind, shredding the feeble mental walls Vilos raised.

In less than a minute the light faded. He took slow, deep breaths. Killing Vilos wouldn't get him what he wanted, but the sultan may be of some use to him later.

"You hired Silvermane to send her to a safe location hidden even from you. Clever, I suppose. I'll just have to get Silvermane to tell me where she's gone."

Vilos had fallen to his knees but now forced himself to stand. "Good luck. Silvermane is the most powerful wizard in the High Kingdom. Binding, energize!"

The doors to the court slammed shut. Glowing runes appeared on every surface of the room.

Daktari snarled. He should have checked for hidden magic.

Vilos smiled. "I also paid her to build a magical trap. Now it's just you and me, and even if you kill me, the wards will keep you trapped in this room."

Oh how very wrong he was. Ether gathered around him and he charged it with shadow magic. As the power grew too great to fully contain, purple lightning flickered off Daktari's body. The jagged bolts of energy struck at random, sparking off the wards.

"If you think the old hag's magic can hold me, then you are sadly mistaken."

"We'll see." Vilos drew Heat's Bane.

The gleaming mithril glittered with a pale-blue aura. The temperature of the room dropped to near freezing.

Vilos raised the shamshir over his head and took two steps.

Daktari snapped his fingers and the blue aura vanished.

Another gesture and the blade slammed into the floor.

Vilos struggled until the cords on his neck stood out, but he couldn't budge his weapon.

"Did you learn nothing from my demonstration with the golems?" Daktari asked. "None of my weapons can harm me."

Vilos roared and charged the sorcerer.

Moron. Daktari was tempted to kill him simply to rid the world of his stupidity.

A tiny fraction of the gathered energy wrapped Vilos in a purple aura and lifted him off the ground.

Vilos hung upside down facing the sorcerer.

"You've accomplished nothing." Daktari had the beginnings of a plan now. That always helped keep the rage under control. "You only delay the inevitable. Now let me show you what I think of Silvermane's magic."

Daktari stepped to the center of the room. Purple energy grew so thick around him that it tinted everything. Daktari drew power from tiny portals linked to Heaven and Hell, weaving the antithetical power sources into a single whole through the ether. Few sorcerers could manage the subtle balance of light and dark, which was why shadow magic was the rarest and most powerful of all the fields of sorcery.

Like a storm building, more and more purple light filled the room.

Random blasts struck the wards and exploded like purple fireworks.

When the air thrummed with power, Daktari released it with a roar of anger.

Magic screamed in every direction.

The roof disintegrated.

Walls burst outward.

When the magic faded Daktari stood in a foot-deep crater. The court no longer existed as a distinct room. Rubble lay scattered around like a child's building blocks after a tantrum.

Overhead the noonday sun shone down, revealing the damage for all to see.

Daktari smiled at Vilos. The purple aura had protected the sultan from any harm. "So much for your trap."

"Just kill me and get it over with," Vilos said.

"I'm not going to kill you. No, I'm going to let you watch as your precious kingdom is torn apart. We had a deal, Vilos. When it comes to magic, there is only one unbreakable rule: never break a deal."

Daktari picked up Heat's Bane and held it up for Vilos's inspection. "This goes to Nord. He commands a small army to the north. It shouldn't be much trouble to set him against you. The stone soldiers will go to Kent."

"No, it will be the Crown War all over again," Vilos said.

"Correct," Daktari said. "Do you remember that conversation we had so long ago, when you came crawling to me, begging for a way to end the war? I gave you everything you needed and all you had to do was turn over your firstborn daughter when I came for her. How quickly you agreed that day. You'll throw away twenty years of peace and prosperity, the life of heaven knows how many innocents, all to save one girl."

"She's my daughter," Vilos replied as if that made an adequate explanation.

Perhaps it did, to him. Daktari despised children in general and certainly had none of his own. People did insane, irrational things for their children. Clearly the irony that many other people's children were going to die thanks to his efforts to save his own was lost on the man.

Vilos's glare held a mixture of rage and desperation. Both emotions as empty and powerless as the declaration that he'd betrayed Daktari for his daughter.

He levitated toward the opening he'd blown in the ceiling followed a moment later by the stone soldiers.

The sorcerer paused a moment beside Vilos. "You should have given me the girl." He rose up a few more feet then called down, "I'll send you Silvermane's head when I finish with her."

Daktari flew over the city. It looked like most of the soldiers had gathered around the palace. He stayed high enough to avoid arrows. He could have shielded himself easily enough, but saw no reason to waste the magic.

His home waited about fifty miles north of the city. Even flying it would take most of an hour to get there. Eager as he was to give the sultan's brothers their gifts, he had more pressing matters to attend.

The girl hadn't just disappeared off the face of the planet. She went somewhere and someone would find her. Daktari just had to make certain whoever did so brought her to him, unharmed. Should she be otherwise, he shuddered to think what his benefactor would do.

⊷❖

D aktari and the golems landed in the Chaos Hills outside the entrance of a cave. One of the few truly wild places left in the High Kingdom, the Chaos Hills deserved their name. Ogres, fire drakes, and worse called the hills home.

Daktari smiled. He was by far the worst. Just inside the cave, red glyphs writhed on the wall. A new skull lay on the floor, the remains of a goblin foolish enough to ignore his magic.

"Stay here. Kill anything that tries to enter the cave," Daktari told the golems.

Satisfied that nothing would disturb him, Daktari dispelled his wards with a wave of his hand. The burning in his eyes stopped the moment he entered the dim cave. He sighed in relief and descended deeper into the darkness. His lab waited about a quarter mile below.

As Daktari walked through the shadows, he had time to ponder his situation. For a hundred and sixty years he had languished under a cloud, waiting for his benefactor, the imprisoned elder demon Balthis, to name the task he needed to perform to fulfill their bargain. For all those years, this link between them poisoned Daktari's ageless body with demonic corruption, filling him with the rage and desire to destroy that defined the demon race. Freeing himself from that corruption was his highest priority.

The archangels had imprisoned Balthis several millennia ago for the crime of murdering a planet. They could have destroyed him. Even an elder demon was no match for an angry archangel.

But of course the angels knew that he would simply be reborn in Hell by the will of whichever demon lord created him in the first place. And once he was reborn, there was always the possibility that some other insane cult could summon him again to destroy a second world.

So instead, they trapped Balthis in a prison of stone reinforced by divine magic and set him adrift in the endless darkness between stars.

Balthis had drifted, forgotten, for millennia, until the day Daktari had contacted him.

The elder demon had been quite surprised when Daktari's sending reached him, though no more so than Daktari himself. It wasn't like he was seeking the imprisoned demon. The goal of that spell had been simply to see how far he could push out a sending.

Still, the chance to speak with a being of such knowledge and power wasn't one Daktari could cast away lightly. For a year they had conversed thus. Until finally a bargain was struck. Daktari would be told the location of an ancient book of magic, the Tome of Shadows, in exchange for a future task named by Balthis.

Not an ideal situation by any means. It was generally best to know the price before sealing a bargain, but after a decade of fruitless searching, he'd been desperate to find the tome.

The elder demon had kept his word and told Daktari where the tome lay hidden. It had taken the sorcerer over a year to find it as the landscape had changed a great deal in thousands of years. When Daktari had asked what he had to do in exchange, Balthis said he'd let him know.

Twenty-five years ago Balthis finally decided. Daktari had seen an image in his dreams of a blond-haired youth. Balthis explained that this young man would one day have a daughter that would be the key to his escape from his divine prison. The knowledge of the proper ritual had appeared in his mind.

Collect the girl and perform the ritual after her eighteenth birthday. Simple enough. Or so he'd thought at the time.

Daktari cared little if Balthis escaped or not. Certainly he was no demon worshipper. In fact, for the good of the mortal world, he'd prefer the elder demon remain imprisoned. But, as he told Vilos, a bargain was a bargain, and he had no intention of breaking his word.

Balthis wouldn't be pleased that Daktari had let the girl slip through his fingers, not that he planned to share that particular bit of information. He would find her again. It was only a matter of time.

Daktari sighed as he entered his lab. It was the only place in the entire world he truly felt at home.

Six tables decorated the sorcerer's lab. Two were covered with bubbling beakers and retorts. A sick-looking, viscous liquid dripped into a small vial. Daktari checked the progress of his work. The vial wasn't even half full. It would take at least a day before he had enough poison to foul the unprotected oases. That would certainly drive the nomads to attack the High Kingdom's cities, especially when his minion planted evidence that the sultan's soldiers had done the poisoning.

Word of the chaos in the High Kingdom would spread quickly. Hopefully, when the princess learned her father was in danger, she would rush back to his side in a vain attempt to help.

If she did, he'd be waiting.

He'd set this particular backup plan in motion on the off chance he failed to collect his prize. Granted, he hadn't considered that a particularly likely result of his visit to Sultan's Oasis, but here he was, empty-handed.

"Master." A black, bat-winged humanoid a little over a foot

tall fluttered down from its roost near the ceiling to land on Daktari's shoulder. "No girl?"

"I see nothing escapes the keen eyes of my homunculus. No, Bane, she vanished right before my eyes."

"The demon won't be happy."

"No," Daktari agreed. "But what he doesn't know can't hurt us."

Daktari rubbed his homunculus between its wings. Soon it started to trill. The sound resembled a cat purring only more high pitched. The trill was unique to homunculi and Bane's was the loudest he'd ever heard. Of course, everything about Bane was unique.

Any wizard worth the name could create a homunculus. The process involved some rare reagents and a blood sacrifice from the wizard. Once the material was gathered it took only a week of boiling and a few simple spells to produce the homunculus. The result was a pale-green humanoid about a foot tall connected to the wizard by a telepathic link. The creature couldn't speak or move more than one hundred yards from its creator. Most wizards used them as spies or lab assistants—their telepathic link let them know whatever their creator knew.

Bane's creation had taken almost a year.

Unsatisfied with the weak creations most wizards used, Daktari had infused Bane with shadow magic. The result was a stronger, tougher servant. Their link was strong enough that they could be half a world apart and still know what the other thought. Last, what pleased Daktari most was his creation's ability to speak.

"The poison's distillation is coming along well," Daktari said.

"Slow," Bane complained. "What will you do about the girl?"

"I'm going to put a bounty on her head." Daktari went over

to another table. This one held a crystal ball the size of his head sitting on a blackened silver tripod.

The sorcerer put his fingers against the crystal and it filled with purple mist. He pictured the princess as he'd last seen her, and then projected this image into the crystal ball. Next he attached a brief message with her name, a ten-thousand-gold-piece reward, and his location. Finally, he blasted the message through the ether with enough force to reach every magic user on the planet with a device capable of receiving it.

If the girl was out there, someone would find her. He cared not in the least if she returned on her own to help her father or trussed hand and foot in the possession of a bounty hunter. One way or another, he would claim her.

⸙

Vilos floated upside down watching the sorcerer fly away with his sword and golems. All the blood rushing to his head was making him dizzy. When the sorcerer had moved out of sight the purple aura started to fade. He just managed to tuck his head and roll through the fall as the magic ended.

Vilos staggered to his feet. His head still throbbed from the sorcerer's mind search spell. Looking around, he took in the extent of the damage Daktari had caused. He could see clear through to the other side of the palace. It would take months to repair, not that Vilos expected to have the chance.

He sighed. He'd felt certain Silvermane's wards would hold the sorcerer. The ease with which he'd torn through them only underscored how badly he'd underestimated his opponent. At least the ring had done its job. Wherever she was, it had to be better than here. Vilos only hoped there'd still be a High Kingdom for her to return home to one day.

A pair of guards poked their heads in what used to be the doorway. "Are you hurt, Majesty?" one asked.

"No," Vilos said. "Was anyone injured in the blast?"

"Many, Majesty, but no deaths."

"Thank heaven for that." Vilos picked his way through the rubble to stand next to the guards. "Round up everyone you can find and start searching for anyone buried under the rubble. Also send messengers to all the nobles in the city, the princess's party is cancelled."

"Yes, Majesty. Um, where is the princess?"

A big believer in honesty, Vilos said, "I have no idea."

He left the two guards behind and walked toward the garden. He needed to think.

CHAPTER 7

Shara sat on the cool ground, still dizzy from the magic that had whisked her away from the palace and that horrible wizard. Even without the aftereffects of the magic, her mind would have been reeling. In the last few minutes she'd learned a great deal that she wished she could forget. The most disturbing item being that her father had promised her to that hideous man.

Still, whatever her father had done twenty years ago, she knew he must have had his reasons. He was a good person and she loved him no matter what mistakes he may have made in the past. Now she had to get home and sitting here wasn't going to accomplish anything.

Shara got to her feet and noted with pleasure that her knees weren't shaking. She glanced at the sky hoping to get an idea of how much time had passed. The sun wore thick clouds like a veil, so she couldn't tell.

She looked around trying to get her bearings. Strange, tall trees with deep grooves in their nearly black bark surrounded the little clearing where she'd appeared. The trees didn't even have leaves. Instead they had long green needles. What had her tutors said about trees like these? Struggle as she might to remember, her mind refused to yield the information she sought. All she remembered was that needle-bearing trees didn't grow in the High Kingdom.

That little nugget of information almost caused her to collapse again. The ring had taken her farther from home than she'd first thought. Well, she'd just have that much farther to go to get back. The strange trees grew as far as she could see in every direction. The ground was rough and littered with needles that had turned orange.

That didn't bode well for finding civilization.

She smiled a little. One good thing about being lost was that it didn't matter if you went the wrong way because you couldn't get any more lost.

Without better options, Shara picked a direction and started walking. She hadn't gone far when thunder rumbled in the distance. If she didn't find shelter soon, she was going to get drenched.

A light drizzle had started to fall when she smelled smoke. She hadn't seen any lightning which meant a forest fire was unlikely. That meant someone had built a fire. Maybe a woodsman lived around here with a nice warm cabin like in the stories her nanny used to tell her.

Elated at the thought of finding another person, any other person, in this wilderness, Shara hurried as fast as she could manage toward the smoke. A short time later she found the source. Someone had built a small lean-to out of limbs and brush. Beside a boulder a few feet away they'd started a large fire.

She stepped into the clearing, all her senses alert for danger. What she'd do if danger actually showed up was another matter. No guards would come running if she screamed.

"Hello. Is anyone here?" she called out in the trade language used by merchants and travelers rather than in her native tongue. If anyone was here, they'd be most likely to speak that.

She felt something sharp stick in her spine.

"Yeah, I'm here," a deep, masculine voice said.

This wasn't right at all. Her rescuer wasn't supposed to stick a knife in her back. She started to turn around and offer a lecture in how to properly treat a princess, but the knife pressed harder against her and she changed her mind.

"I don't like people sneaking up on me," the man said.

"I wasn't sneaking up on you. I smelled the smoke and thought I could find shelter with whoever built the fire."

"You don't look too dangerous. All right, go sit by the fire. I'm not going to kill you right now."

Great, that was very reassuring. When he'd taken the knife away she walked slowly over to the fire. The side of the lean-to looked about six feet long and a single branch held up each end. There appeared to be just enough room to keep two people out of the rain.

She sat down under the lean-to by the fire and held out her hands. The heat felt wonderful. The strange man sat down beside her. He still held his weapon, a double-edged short-sword, she noted, not a knife.

Trying not to be too obvious about it, she took a look at her captor. He had dark eyes and a small, crooked nose. A few days' worth of stubble darkened his jaw. He wore his long black hair in a ponytail. The overall affect wasn't unappealing. His clothes left something to be desired. They didn't look like anyone had washed them in a year and a few holes revealed pale skin underneath. At least he didn't stink too bad.

Without warning he sheathed his sword and said, "I'm

sorry about the hole in your dress. There're bandits in these woods and it pays to be cautious. I was just talking before. I didn't really plan to kill you."

She sighed in relief. Maybe he'd turn out to be her savior after all.

"Apology accepted. My name is Shara, Crown Princess of the High Kingdom." She held out her hand for him to kiss.

To her surprise he just grabbed her hand and gave it a workman-like shake. "Robert Longridge." Robert released her hand. "That's a pretty ring."

Shara held it out so he could give the cause of her current predicament a closer look. The moonstone glittered in the firelight.

When Robert touched it a blue spark leapt out and struck his finger.

He jerked his hand away. "Son of a bitch, that hurt."

"It's a magic ring," she said.

He raised an eyebrow in her direction. "No kidding."

"Why do you believe me?" she asked.

"It just burned my finger. Jewelry doesn't normally do that."

"That's not what I mean. Most people would be a little more skeptical if a woman in the middle of nowhere said she was a princess from a distant land."

Robert smiled and leaned back on his hands. "When I was a kid I traveled a lot. My father was a merchant. I grew up on his ship. We hit every port worth mentioning including Haydrien in the High Kingdom. The style of your dress and the design of the ring proclaim your nationality to anyone paying attention. As for the princess thing, you're too tall and fair skinned to be a full-blooded native, so you must be a member of the royal family."

"When you say it like that it seems so obvious."

"It wouldn't be to anyone who hadn't visited your home,

which is most people in this neck of the woods. I'm more familiar with the High Kingdom than many ports because Haydrien was one of my father's favorite stops."

"Why was that?" Shara asked.

"One of his more attractive mistresses lived there. I spent quite a bit of time standing around in an alley outside her home waiting for him. Didn't have much to do but listen to the merchants haggle and watch the people walk by."

"Was she your mother?" Shara asked.

He gave her a curious look. "I don't think so. My father never said which, if any, of his mistresses was my mother."

Shara offered a wistful sigh. "That must have been an exciting way to grow up. Traveling the world and seeing strange sights every day."

"There were some good times," Robert said.

Shara didn't think he sounded like he meant it. "You sure?"

Robert laughed, rich and bittersweet. "I'm sure. Life on a ship isn't that great. Trapped in a space the size of a small house with thirty sweaty sailors can be an odiferous experience. My father never had much time for me. He was always working on the next deal. An old sailor named One-Eyed Clark raised me. He taught me the carpenter's trade and I helped him take care of the ship. He died in a storm when I was twelve."

"I'm sorry," Shara said, thinking about her own mother. "My mother died when I was born."

Robert nodded. "What about you? Living in the palace must have been nice."

"It was. I had everything I wanted and then some. The finest sages in the land tutored me. I never lacked for anything material. But the one thing I really wanted I couldn't have."

"What was that?" Robert asked.

"Freedom. Real freedom. To walk the streets without a

dozen armed guards surrounding me. To travel and see the world like you did." She looked away, astonished that she'd just told a complete stranger about her dreams.

As if he realized things had gotten too personal Robert changed the subject. "So how'd you end up here?"

Shara held up her ring again. "This stupid thing. Father had it made to transport me out of danger. It must be broken. One minute I'm standing in court beside my father and the next, poof. I'm in the middle of the woods."

She decided not to mention her trouble with the wizard. He might get scared and not help her. "So, where am I anyway?"

"The Vale," Robert said. "That's what we call it at least. It's a large forest separating the kingdoms of Umbria and Langton. Several trade routes pass through it, that's why the bandits lair here."

"Umbria and Langton, those names sound familiar." She tried in vain to remember where she'd heard the names before. "I give up, how far from home am I?"

Thunder cracked in the distance, an ominous sound, Shara thought.

"To get home," Robert said. "You'd have to walk due south for about a month. That'll get you to the Dread Sea. If you've got enough gold you can buy passage to the High Kingdom at one of the port cities. The trip will take about three months with favorable winds. Then it's just a camel ride to Sultan's Oasis."

She stared at him.

He shrugged. "You asked."

Shara closed her mouth and groaned. "I'll never get home."

Darkness was falling fast and the rain had just about stopped. "Listen, let's get some sleep," Robert said. "Things will look better in the morning."

She crossed her arms and looked at him. "What did you have in mind for sleeping arrangements?"

He grinned and Shara got a nervous quiver in her stomach. No stone soldiers would appear and save her if he had bad intentions. "Don't worry, I've sacked out with a woman before. Back to back seems to work best."

She sighed again. She'd worried he might try and take advantage of her. Though not cynical by nature, she knew some men wouldn't think twice about it. That he planned to be a gentleman was another point in Robert's favor.

"I'll sleep on the outside," he said. "If something nasty comes around in the night I'll be able to deal with it." He drew his shortsword and laid it on the ground beside him.

Nervous again, Shara asked, "What sort of thing?"

"Growlers are about the worst, other than bandits of course. Picture a mountain lion with a tail covered in spikes. They don't usually bother people. Growlers prefer prey that doesn't resist."

Shara swallowed the lump in her throat and lay down under the lean-to. She didn't know what a mountain lion was, but she'd seen a sand lion once and if they were similar she had no desire to meet Robert's growler. She turned on her side facing the wall of the lean-to. Robert settled down beside her, facing the fire.

His body felt warm and his broad back made a welcome wall between her and whatever might be out there. As she lay there trying to sleep she realized this was the first time she'd ever slept outside the palace. Her last thought before she drifted off was that it seemed strange that her first night out should be so far from home.

CHAPTER 8

Daktari awoke after about four hours' sleep. Even underground he had an excellent sense of time. He rolled out of bed and took a deep breath. The sweet scent of night drifted down to him. He could feel darkness spreading across the land. With the sun set, his powers had reached their apex.

Tonight, his work began in earnest.

Master?

His familiar's thoughts appeared in Daktari's mind. Due to their telepathic link, Bane knew he'd awakened.

Yes?

Poison's ready.

Excellent, Bane, I'll join you in a moment.

Daktari left his bedchamber and walked down the short tunnel that connected it to the lab. The distillation had finished sooner than he expected. Bane had taken the beakers off the heating stones and set them aside. With a thought Daktari disconnected the ether from the heating stones. The vial holding the poison rested on a small iron tripod. A wisp of steam rose from it.

"I got the last drop just before you woke up," Bane said in answer to his unspoken question. "What now?"

He blew out a sigh. Daktari had hoped it wouldn't come to plan B. "Now we sow the seeds of civil war. Come."

Bane flitted over and landed on Daktari's shoulder. The sorcerer walked to the center of the cavern where he'd carved a large pentagram in the stone floor. They stepped into the center of the symbol and Daktari spoke a word of power that activated the enchantment woven into the pentagram. The symbol blazed with crimson light. The glow from the protective spell made the cavern appear drenched in blood.

Satisfied with his protective spell Daktari began to chant the words of summoning. The ether swirled at his command and twenty feet away a small circle of darkness appeared in midair. As the strength of his spell grew, so did the size of the circle. When the spell ended the circle was big enough for an elephant to pass through with a foot to spare on each side.

Pleased, Daktari called, "Ulibo, come forth."

From beyond the dark circle a shifting form approached. The shadow demon oozed through the portal. When the last of it had entered the lab Daktari snapped his fingers and the portal shut.

Ulibo roared in anger at being trapped.

It flew toward the sorcerer slamming into the protective field that surrounded him.

Black claws ripped at the magic shield, sending crimson sparks flying.

Daktari waited, unperturbed, with his arms crossed. Bane huddled behind his master's head, appearing none too certain of the shield's power.

When its initial anger had played out Ulibo shifted its form into a vaguely humanoid shape. The demon looked closer at the human it couldn't reach. After a moment's study it fell to the ground on its knees.

"Forgive me, Master," Ulibo said. "I didn't know you at first."

Daktari smiled. Now that the shadow demon knew with whom it dealt, he could lower the shield without fear. The summoning spell, while causing the demon no actual pain, did leave it disoriented for a time. An angry and disoriented demon of Ulibo's power wasn't something Daktari took lightly.

The first time he'd summoned the demon over a century ago, he'd faced it without the benefit of the warding circle. He'd been eager to test the limits of his shadow magic. The battle had been ferocious, but Daktari succeeded in cowing the demon.

Now Ulibo recognized him as the superior force and obeyed without a fuss. He'd learned something else over the years of dealing with Ulibo and its lesser brethren: demons actually appreciated respect and a kind word from their masters.

Daktari stepped out of the pentagram and laid a hand on the shoulder of his most powerful servant. "No harm done. I know the summoning is unpleasant."

"Thank you, Master." The demon rose and glided along behind Daktari toward the table where the vial of poison waited.

"You recognize this?" Daktari asked, indicating the vial of poison.

Ulibo sniffed it and said, "Poison. You wish me to poison someone?" The demon sounded eager, like a child about to receive a favorite treat.

"Not someone," Daktari said. He could feel a wave of disappointment wash over him. "I want you to poison all the oases not protected by a village. Three drops of that poison will leave the water undrinkable for six months."

"What if the nomads try and stop me?" Ulibo had served him in the High Kingdom before and was familiar with the tribes that wandered the desert.

"What do you think?" He felt a ripple of pleasure from the demon. "In fact, if you kill a few that might work out even better. Can you make it look like soldiers with swords killed them instead of your usual talons?"

The demon held up its left arm and transformed it into the curved scimitar favored by the sultan's soldiers.

"Excellent," Daktari said. "You should also leave some camel tracks between several of the oases and the nearest village."

No fool, the demon said, "You mean to start a war between the nomads and the city dwellers."

Daktari smiled and handed the demon the vial. An even stronger ripple of pleasure washed over him as the demon accepted the poison.

U libo stepped into the nearest shadow and vanished. The shadow demon walked to the nearest oasis and dripped three drops of poison into the water. They vanished without a trace. Invisible and odorless, nobody would notice the sorcerer's poison until someone dropped dead. Ulibo wholeheartedly approved of its master's plan. It stepped into another shadow and emerged beside a fresh pool of water.

Of course, Ulibo approved of anything that fomented chaos and destruction. It poisoned the water and moved on to the next oasis. Over the millennia, Ulibo had served several masters. Few could control a demon of its power. When the sorcerer had first called it from Astaroth's Hell, a long time, even as demons reckoned it, had passed since the last wizard had tried to command it.

Ulibo had emerged from the portal eager to rend the flesh of a presumptuous wizard. Instead of some weak fool playing at magic, the demon had found a purple-robed sorcerer that threw off waves of power unlike anything it had felt in two millennia.

Ulibo had once been tricked by a wizard that could project an aura of great power but had little to back it up. Not one to fall for the same trick twice, Ulibo had surged forward to attack. The blast of energy that had struck the demon shook it to the very core of its essence. That one attack told Ulibo all it needed to know about the sorcerer. He wasn't playing at magic. This human was one of the three most powerful sorcerers Ulibo had felt in its eternal existence.

Still, the demon had attacked again, more to get a feel for the sorcerer's power than because it thought it had a chance of winning. Three times the demon had swooped in and three times the sorcerer had turned it aside. Satisfied that the sorcerer had true power, Ulibo had fallen to its knees and begun its fawning servant routine.

Most of Ulibo's past masters had liked a greater demon telling them how powerful they were.

This one didn't.

He'd flung Ulibo aside with a blast of magic to tell him so. Then he'd spoken the words that had filled Ulibo with joy.

"If I'd wanted a fawning slave I'd have summoned an imp not a greater demon. Now get up, we have work to do."

How those words had thrilled Ulibo. At last he'd found a master that didn't need constant praise and self-gratification. A master so confident in his power he didn't need to be told how strong he was. Perhaps he'd found his true master at last.

After that night the sorcerer had summoned Ulibo a dozen times more. Each time it had felt great pleasure at finding the purple-robed sorcerer waiting on the far side of the portal. The demon knew it would have real work to do. An assassination, sowing chaos among the sorcerer's enemies, something it could really sink its fangs into.

Now Ulibo was a part of the sorcerer's most ambitious plan yet, starting a war that would kill thousands. The demon was almost too happy for words.

It emerged without a sound at the twelfth oasis. The demon heard laughter and saw leaping flames. Oozing closer it found a small group of about thirty nomads. Filled with glee at the prospect of killing, the demon scratched the air, carving a small pocket dimension about a foot square. Ulibo set the poison inside then sealed the opening.

The demon formed six arms ending in curved scimitar blades. It circled the camp, blending seamlessly with the darkness. It found the first sentry facing north, away from the oasis. It crept up behind the man and stood looking down at him, delighted with his ignorance.

The guard must have sensed something because he turned just as Ulibo struck with a double slash. The guard fell in three pieces without a sound.

Barely able to suppress a giggle of delight the demon flowed on toward the next sentry. That man died as quick as the first. It had now made a complete circle around the camp. No guards remained to sound the alarm.

Unable to stand it the demon did giggle; a low, insane sound that carried on the wind toward the nomad's camp. A child cried in instinctive fear. Her mother tried to quiet her.

Don't worry, I'll quiet her soon enough.

The demon shifted into one of its more horrific forms, that of a giant warrior in jagged armor. It stepped into the firelight and before anyone could scream or draw a weapon it killed the two nearest men.

Chaos fell.

Men roared and charged with steel in hand.

The women and children ducked into a pair of tents to get out of the way.

Ulibo let the men get in two solid blows only to see their weapons pass through its body like smoke. It reveled in their fear as they realized how helpless they were.

Then it struck back, becoming a whirlwind of blades.

The battle, if you could call it that, ended in moments. The blood-soaked sand was covered with hacked corpses that used to be men.

The demon turned its attention to the tents.

It dragged the women and children out one at a time and ran them through. Soon the entire group lay dead.

Ulibo would have liked to take a little more time and enjoy the killing but if it wanted to complete its task before morning, then it couldn't waste time.

Remembering its master's order the demon scared off the camels then left a false trail leading to the nearest town. That done, the demon retrieved the poison and poured out three drops in the water.

Ulibo took one last look at its handiwork before shadow walking to the next oasis. It hoped there'd be more nomads waiting.

CHAPTER 9

Shara awoke staring up at a bright blue sky. The lean-to was gone. How had she slept through Robert taking it down? She must have been more tired than she thought.

Wait. Where was Robert?

Panic turned her insides to jelly. Her savior had abandoned her.

How would she get home? How would she survive the day without getting eaten?

Shara sat up. Her entire body shook. She was going to die alone in the forest without ever seeing the High Kingdom again.

"Good morning." She spun around just in time to see Robert emerge from a thick clump of bushes.

Relief flooded through her. He hadn't abandoned her after all. "Where were you?"

He cleared his throat. "Nature called."

Shara felt her cheeks flush. Of all the fool questions. She'd seen him coming out of the bushes. What else could he have been doing? She started to stammer an apology for her rude question but he cut her off.

"Did you sleep well?" he asked.

Happy to change the subject she said, "No. A stone jabbed me in the ribs and I kept hearing noises."

"The forest does leave something to be desired. On the other hand, sometimes breakfast wanders in all on its own." He pointed to something behind her.

Shara turned and saw a pair of small carcasses, skinned, quartered, and ready for cooking.

"Yuck. What are they?"

"Rabbits. Now that you're up I'll see if I can get a fire started."

Robert rummaged through the remains of the lean-to, finally pulling out some dry branches that crunched when he broke them. He also grabbed a handful of the dry needles they'd slept on. It took only a few sparks from a flint and steel to get a fire going.

Shara marveled at the ease with which he went about his task. She wouldn't have had the slightest idea where to begin, yet he did the job without a wasted motion.

Robert must have noticed her staring because he grinned and said, "Nothing to it. Hand me my pack, please."

She tossed him the leather satchel she'd been using as a pillow. He withdrew a small frying pan and set it on the fire. The rabbits went in next and they started to sizzle. The aroma smelled wonderful and she realized she hadn't eaten since the noon meal yesterday. She silently thanked whatever angel had placed this kind man in her path.

As the meat cooked she asked, "What happens next?"

He looked up from the pan. "What do you mean?"

"I mean after breakfast what are we going to do?"

"Oh, well, my companions are camped about eight miles

east of here. After we eat, we'll walk back to camp, then decide what to do about your situation. I figure we can at least escort you to the nearest port. From there you can purchase passage home."

"Were you part of a caravan?" Shara asked.

"Yeah, an axle on one of the wagons broke. While the others tried to fix it I went hunting. The storm came up in a hurry and I had to find shelter."

She smiled as she considered her good fortune.

"What is it?" he asked, giving her a funny look.

"Nothing," she said. "It's just that when my ring malfunctioned and brought me to this forest I thought heaven had abandoned me. Then I met you and you helped me. Now you're going to take me to join your caravan. I can't help but think I'll be home before very long."

"I wouldn't get too excited, Princess. The angels can be a fickle bunch of bastards and a lot can happen between here and the High Kingdom."

She wanted to ask what he meant by that but before she could he said, "Food's ready."

Robert took a two-pronged fork out of his pack, impaled a chunk of rabbit, and handed it to her. He repeated the procedure on a second piece, keeping it for himself. Not entirely sure how to go about eating the meat without a knife and plate she watched Robert. He tore a strip of meat off with his teeth and chewed it down.

Following his example she took a more dainty bite. Juice ran down her face and she burned her tongue on the hot meat. Embarrassment and hunger warred within her.

A princess shouldn't eat like a commoner. Hunger won out, however, and she attacked the meat with great enthusiasm. It had a wonderful, mild flavor, rather like grilled red-backed serpent.

When she finished, her hands and face were covered in greasy juice. She laughed.

"What's so funny?" Robert looked at her like she'd gone mad.

Getting herself under control Shara said, "I was just thinking what my etiquette teacher would say if she could see me now."

"I can imagine." Robert got up and stomped out the fire. "If we get going we should reach my friends before dark."

"I'll just be a second." Shara scampered over to the bushes.

When she returned Robert had his gear packed up and the fire covered with dirt. He held a small crossbow, cocked and loaded, in his hands.

"Ready?" he asked, shouldering his pack.

She nodded then asked, "Where'd you get that? I don't remember seeing it before."

"My pack."

She looked at the two-foot-long crossbow and then the leather satchel. "No way."

"It's a take-down model," he said. He must have seen the confusion on her face because he added, "It comes apart for storage."

"Why would anyone build a crossbow that comes apart?" she asked.

Robert set a north-northeast course and they started walking. "The first one I heard of was found on the body of a dead assassin. Apparently he'd snuck into the city posing as a merchant. When the city guards searched his wagon, they found the separate pieces scattered in with a number of other items. They didn't realize the parts combined into a deadly weapon."

"Did the assassin succeed in his mission?" Shara asked.

"No, he missed his target and the watch killed him in the

street. That's where a smith named Baren saw the crossbow. He got the idea that hunters and travelers might like a compact weapon that stored easily. He was right. The last I heard Baren had retired to a small island he bought with his profits."

"I'd never heard that before," Shara said.

"I'm surprised. Being a princess, I'd have thought assassins would be a large worry for you."

She thought she heard a little bitterness in Robert's voice but she didn't say anything.

The two companions walked through the forest shadows. All that remained of the previous night's storm were a few puddles. The ground was relatively level, making the walking easy.

Shara learned to her dismay that a dress didn't make the best outfit when traveling outdoors. Her skirt caught on every branch and bush she got close to. It wasn't long before it hung in tatters. She also learned in a hurry that the forest wasn't a quiet place. Birds chirped in the branches of trees. When they walked through a dense patch of brush something blasted out from under her feet in a rush of beating wings.

She scrambled over to Robert and grabbed his arm. "What was that?"

"Don't worry, it was just a grouse."

"Grouse?"

"A bird, about the size of a small hen. They make a lot of noise when they take off to startle predators. They're also very tasty."

"It certainly startled me."

He grinned. "The quiet animals are the ones you need to worry about. You won't hear most forest predators until they sink their fangs into you, except for tree rattlers. They let you know before they strike. They're nowhere near as tasty as the grouse."

She offered him an arch look. "Is there anything in this forest you don't eat?"

His grin broadened into a full-fledged smile. "Sure, if you see a small black critter with a white stripe on its back, that's a skunk. Nothing bothers a skunk."

"Why?"

"Cause they stink worse than a goblin's midden."

They continued on through the forest and Shara found she rather enjoyed the chirping of the birds. As the sun continued its journey through the sky, the temperature gradually increased. Shara still felt cold, but the warmer it got the more comfortable she grew, and the more this strange place felt like home. They paused only once more when a small furry animal with long ears popped out of a bush in front of them.

"What's that?" Shara asked.

"Breakfast."

"Excuse me?"

"I told you we had rabbit for breakfast. That's a rabbit."

She remembered breakfast less fondly now that she saw the adorable little creature they'd eaten. She took a few steps toward it hoping to touch its fur, but the rabbit scampered off.

"How could you eat something that cute?" she asked.

He shrugged. "You'd be surprised what you can eat if you're hungry enough. Let's get moving, we're almost there."

Shara followed along behind him and asked, "How do you know?"

He pointed in the air to the right. She saw a dark column of smoke rising into the air. "How can you be sure it's your friends and not bandits?"

"That's where I left them yesterday. I doubt they'd leave without me."

That didn't answer her question, but he started walking again so she followed. They couldn't have gone over half a mile before she heard the sounds of people talking and joking. She smelled something cooking and realized she was hungry again.

Robert slowed as they approached. In her eagerness to reach the food she moved past him and walked straight into the clearing. There she found six men and two women. They all drew weapons the moment they saw her.

It didn't take long for her to realize something was wrong. She saw no wagons or merchandise. The men in the camp looked at her with hungry expressions. She spun around to warn Robert that he'd taken a wrong turn and they'd stumbled into a bandit camp. He had his crossbow raised to his shoulder and at first she thought he planned to fight. Then she noticed he had the weapon pointed square at her chest.

"You're my prisoner," he said. "Behave and you won't get hurt."

CHAPTER 10

Vilos and his guards made camp in the garden around what remained of the White Palace. From the front, you almost couldn't tell the palace had been attacked. Most of the damage happened in the throne room and rear half of the palace. Inside, the truth became clear. All you had to do was look up at the giant hole in the roof.

The servants had gotten rooms in the city. They all had their eyes open for workers to start the repairs on the palace. The exodus of nobles had begun within hours of the attack. They'd come from near and far for the chance to court his daughter. Now that she was gone and the celebration canceled, they fled the city like rats before a torch.

Not that he blamed them. Things looked bad and weren't apt to get better soon. They needed to return home and tend to their own holdings. It actually came as a relief to have them out from underfoot.

Vilos had risen before dawn and now paced along the length of the wall that surrounded the grounds. The night watch said nothing, sensing their lord wanted quiet. They were right and Vilos appreciated the peace. He stared out over his city, still dark in the hours before dawn. Shara's birthday was today and heaven alone knew where she was. He felt some small comfort in the fact that the sorcerer didn't know either.

As dawn colored the city orange and red, Vilos spotted a short column of cavalry riding down King's Way. The lead rider carried the standard of his royal cavalry. It took a moment for Vilos to remember sending Yosef and his men to learn why the nomads had attacked Kira's Oasis. They were back much sooner than he expected.

Maybe that meant they had good news. He could certainly use some.

Vilos climbed down from the wall and headed toward the main gate. Now that the sun had returned to the sky, his men started coming to life. Soon the day watch would relieve the night watch. A few early risers had cook fires going. They'd have to make do with simpler fare until the kitchen was repaired. Those coherent enough threw a salute as Vilos passed. He nodded to each man.

When he reached the gate, the watch had it open and Captain Yosef's troops were streaming in. The captain glanced in Vilos's direction and he gestured for him to come over. Yosef nodded and dismounted. His camel followed along with the others and Yosef walked over to join Vilos.

Yosef began to salute but Vilos just waved his hand. "No need for that, old friend, it's just the two of us. What did you learn?"

"I spoke to two of the tribal leaders known to be loyal. They say someone poisoned an oasis and the tribe that attacked Kira's Oasis believed city dwellers were responsible."

"Ridiculous. Our merchants and patrols depend on those oases as much as the nomads."

"I know," Yosef said. "Most of the tribes agree that it was

unlikely any of us did it. It seems the tribe that attacked bore us ill will after we caught some of their warriors attacking a caravan."

"A revenge attack that used the poisoned oasis as an excuse?" Vilos asked.

"Looks like," Yosef said. "I asked the tribes to send someone here to alert us if anything else comes up."

"Good work," Vilos said. "I'm glad you returned so soon."

"Why's that, Majesty?"

Vilos filled him in on what had happened. When he finished Yosef asked, "You have no idea where the princess is?"

"None," Vilos said. "It's for the best. If I had known the sorcerer would have her by now. I hope she's all right."

"Shara's a smart girl. I'm sure she'll be fine."

Vilos smiled at his friend's attempt to reassure him. They both knew Shara had never traveled outside Sultan's Oasis before. If he ever saw his daughter again it would be a miracle. "Thanks, Yosef."

Yosef didn't smile. "Is this sorcerer really powerful enough to do what he threatened?"

"You haven't seen the palace," Vilos said. "Come with me."

They left the gate and walked toward the palace. As they approached Vilos heard Yosef gasp. Fallen chunks of marble littered the ground. They stepped through the shattered doors to survey the damage inside.

The sight stunned Vilos even though he'd seen it before. Rubble lay everywhere. The walls on the first floor had holes big enough to walk through blasted in them. The ceiling was cracked and sagging. It was amazing that anyone got out alive.

"I never imagined," Yosef said as he stared at the ruins. "When you said the palace was damaged…"

"Now you have an idea of the power we're dealing with."

They left the palace and walked down the steps. "I wonder why he didn't just kill me," Vilos said.

"I should think that would be obvious," a new but familiar voice said.

Startled, Vilos turned to face the newcomer. Kent stood surrounded by three guards with leveled spears. His brother had come home after all these years. With all the chaos Vilos had forgotten Shara mentioning Kent planned to attend her birthday celebration.

"As you can see I'm unarmed," Kent said, looking at the three guards.

Vilos nodded and dismissed the men. "So, can you offer some insight, brother?"

Kent smiled a mysterious smile. "Perhaps. Can we speak somewhere more private?"

Vilos led Yosef and his brother to his tent. It was made of strong, white cloth that kept out the wind without trapping the heat. On one side sat a table and half a dozen chairs and on the other a pile of silk pillows made a pallet for sleeping. Vilos threw himself into the first chair he came to and gestured for the others to do likewise.

When the two men had seated themselves, Vilos asked, "Either of you hungry?"

They both shook their heads. Vilos grunted and decided breakfast could wait. "Before you tell us your great insight, Kent, I've got to know. Why? After all these years, why come back?"

"You can thank your daughter for that. We've been speaking magically off and on for several months."

"How is that possible?" Vilos asked.

Kent smiled. "Apparently one of the apprentices to your court magician has a crush on her. She convinced him to contact me with his master's crystal ball."

Vilos ran his fingers through his hair. "She never mentioned the details."

"So I assumed," Kent said. "After we had spoken several times, I realized you mustn't have known she was contacting me. I asked her about it one day and she admitted not telling you. She said she wasn't certain how you'd take it."

"Probably thought you'd chew her up one side and down the other," Yosef said.

"Perhaps," Kent said. "However, I think she actually enjoyed doing something sneaky more than she might admit. Anyway, we talked for a while and eventually she invited me to her birthday celebration. I thought the idea a poor one but at her insistence I promised to think about it."

"Why'd you finally change your mind?" Vilos asked.

"Because, despite my intentions to the contrary, I did think about what Shara said. I did some serious thinking about why I was angry with you. At first I was angry because you beat me in the war. After a while I realized I no longer cared that I'd lost the war and that I was happier as a merchant than I ever could have been as sultan. My anger remained more as a reflex."

"If you never really wanted to be sultan, why did we fight the Crown War? With you supporting me no one would have backed Nord."

"I only realized my error in hindsight. At the time, I wanted to rule very much. Now I realize what I wanted was the trappings of the office, the wealth and power rather than the responsibility. When I came to that final conclusion the anger just faded away. That's when I decided to attend the party."

Kent cleared his throat and looked away from his brother. There seemed to be more he wanted to say but he couldn't quite get it out. Vilos remained patient, trying to absorb what Kent had said.

Finally Kent looked him in the eye and said, "I'm glad you won the war. You've ruled well, much better than I could have. And the less said about Nord, the better."

Vilos stared at his brother. He knew how hard it must have been for Kent to say that. Perhaps he really did want to put the past behind them. Vilos felt his throat tighten. To lose a daughter and regain a brother in less than a day was a lot to take in.

At last he said, "Welcome home, brother."

Yosef cleared his throat and Vilos decided it was time to get back on track. "What about this insight of yours?"

"Of course," Kent said. "The reason I believe this sorcerer left you alive is so you'll draw Shara back here."

"He said he wanted me to watch as the High Kingdom gets torn apart," Vilos said.

"Perhaps he does, but remember his main goal is to capture Shara. What better bait to draw her home than her father?"

Vilos nodded. It made sense. "Even if you're right, what can we do about it?"

Kent leaned forward in his chair and pressed his fingertips together. "I suggest we try and find her first."

"How?" Yosef asked. "We have neither the manpower nor the time to search."

"I have agents in every major city in the world. I can contact them and tell them to keep an eye out. She's bound to emerge somewhere and when my people find her they can deliver a message telling her to stay away from the High Kingdom until we find a way to deal with the sorcerer."

"You have agents?" Vilos asked. "Why would a merchant need a spy network?"

Kent smiled at his brother. "Do you know the secret to a successful business?"

"Gold," Yosef spat.

"Wrong," Kent said, "Information is the key. If I know more than my competitors, I can swoop in and steal away a deal before they're even aware of it. My network is the single biggest reason I'm the richest merchant in the High Kingdom."

"Why offer it to us?" Yosef asked.

Vilos said nothing but he'd thought the same thing.

Kent sighed. "Believe it or not, I've become quite fond of my niece over the past few months. I don't wish to see her harmed. If I can help, I will."

Vilos nodded. "Fair enough. There's one more thing you should know. The sorcerer is planning to visit you. He's going to offer you my stone soldiers."

"Why?" Kent asked.

Vilos grinned. "Because, like me an hour ago, he thinks you still hate me and will use them to attack me and my soldiers."

"Excellent, this could work to our advantage. If I control the stone soldiers we can use them against the sorcerer."

"I wouldn't try it unless you're contemplating suicide. Those golems won't obey any order he disapproves of."

"I see. Well, at least if I have them they won't be used against you."

Vilos nodded; again his brother had a point. "One last thing, he's giving Heat's Bane to Nord."

"No," Kent said. "With a weapon like that, Nord will turn his army south and attack the High Kingdom. He's nearly conquered the Broken Kingdom as it is."

"How do you know so much about Nord?" Yosef asked.

"A wizard in my employ checks up on him from time to time."

Vilos got to his feet. "All right, do what you can to find Shara. If you learn anything have your wizard do a sending." He held out his hand which Kent gave a firm shake.

"I should go," Kent said. "The sooner I get home, the sooner

I can start sending messages. It was good to see you again, Vilos."

Vilos smiled and clapped his brother on the back. "Likewise."

The three men exited the tent and Vilos waved as his brother walked toward the main gate.

When Kent had gone Yosef asked, "Do you trust him?"

"No," Vilos said. "But if he can help find Shara, I'll take my chances."

"Yes, Majesty. What now?"

"Go see to your men," Vilos said. "I'm going to get breakfast."

They parted company and Vilos headed toward the nearest cook fire. He hadn't gone far when he heard someone crying. The sound came from a small clump of trees. Curious, he walked around behind the trees and found Sarafin weeping softly.

"Sarafin?" he said.

She must not have heard him coming because she looked up startled then looked quickly away and wiped her eyes. "I'm sorry, Your Majesty."

"Don't be. You heard about Shara?"

She nodded. "They say she disappeared. That she was captured by a wizard."

Vilos groaned. He knew the rumors would fly as soon as someone noticed Shara was missing. "She wasn't captured. Can I trust you with a secret?"

Sarafin snuffled and nodded.

"A mission's underway to find her. It shouldn't be long before she's home."

Sarafin brightened. "That's wonderful, but she'll miss my wedding."

"Perhaps you can postpone it until she returns," Vilos said.

"I don't know. My fiancé is anxious to get married as soon as possible. I don't think he'd be willing to wait."

Vilos smiled and laid a reassuring hand on the girl's shoulder. "Perhaps if I asked him to wait, as a favor to the Crown..."

"Oh, Your Majesty, I'm sure he would."

"I thought so. Now, would you like to join me for breakfast?"

"Well, I've eaten once already, but, okay."

CHAPTER 11

The shadow demon returned to Daktari's lab before dawn. It emerged from the shadow of a small brazier near his crystal ball. Daktari had followed the demon's progress through the night. It had killed six nomad families and poisoned every oasis in the High Kingdom.

He should have been horrified at the atrocity, but all he felt was a cold satisfaction that his plan was moving forward.

When Ulibo had fully emerged from the shadow Daktari said, "Well done. I didn't think you could complete your task all in one night."

"I enjoyed it." The demon formed a smile on its blank face.

"I know," Daktari said. "I watched you work. Thank you for your efforts on my behalf."

"You're sending me back?" The demon looked crestfallen.

"I have nothing more for you right now. Still, if you'd like to stay and watch the carnage, you're welcome. I'm sure I can find something amusing for you to do."

"Thank you, Master. I have grown weary of Hell."

"As you wish. I must leave now and see to the next stage of

my plan." Daktari gestured and Heat's Bane drifted over to him. "Come, Bane."

His homunculus flapped over, settled on his shoulder, and they teleported away.

Daktari appeared in the Broken Kingdom, his arrival unnoticed by man or beast. Lucky for him he'd spent a fair amount of time in the Broken Kingdom and knew several secure places to appear. The sun hadn't yet risen, but Daktari and Bane had no trouble seeing their surroundings. They'd appeared behind a small clump of trees near a long fallow field. What remained of a farmhouse lay collapsed and rotten on the far side of the blackened earth.

"Find the mercenaries, Bane."

Bane leapt off his master's shoulder and flew through the night sky. He hadn't been gone a minute when a thought appeared in Daktari's mind.

Found them, Master.

Excellent, I'll be there in a moment.

Daktari left Heat's Bane floating behind the trees and teleported to his homunculus. Bane perched in a tree just outside the mercenary camp. Daktari glanced over his shoulder and could see the farmer's field. He'd gotten closer than he'd hoped. Turning his attention back to the camp, Daktari let his mind drift until he located the eight sentries posted around the perimeter. He felt them fall to the ground as his paralysis spell took hold. Content that they wouldn't be disturbed, Daktari sought out Nord.

He found the fallen prince asleep between a pair of whores in the center of camp. Bane fluttered down to his shoulder and they drifted silently through the darkness. It would have been so simple to kill them all, probably would have made the world a better place too, but these mercenaries had their jobs to do. Besides, killing useful pawns was a waste and he hated waste.

Halfway through the camp, Daktari felt a subtle probe from another wizard. Still half asleep, Nord's wizard had sensed his presence. Before he could fully awaken, Daktari mentally bludgeoned the weakling into unconsciousness.

He arrived at Nord's tent and found a guard sleeping in front of the flap. With a thought he wrapped the guard in a cocoon of purple energy and left him floating in midair. He stepped inside the tent then surrounded it with a dome of energy to keep out the excessively brave and loyal.

Inside, Nord lay snoring between a pair of naked women. The women looked ill-used judging from the number of bruises covering their otherwise exquisite bodies. Disgusted, Daktari hurled them through ethereal portals. He had no idea where they'd end up, but anywhere would be an improvement. Someone would get a nice surprise when those two beauties appeared nearby. He hoped it was somewhere warm lest they catch a chill.

Now that he had removed all the distractions, he woke Nord with a mental slap. The big man sat up and looked stupidly at his empty bed and the stranger standing before him. "Who the hell are you?"

"My name is irrelevant. However, your actions in the next few minutes will decide if I become your best friend or your worst enemy."

Nord snorted in contempt. "What could a little man like you do for me?" He rose to his full six-foot-eight-inch height. Daktari shook his head. This walking mountain outweighed him by a hundred and fifty pounds, at least.

"Get dressed," Daktari said. "The sight of you disgusts me."

"No one orders Prince Nord around." The fool raised his fist over his head, obviously meaning to crush Daktari with a single blow.

His fist came crashing down on Daktari's head.

It might as well have struck a stone pillar for all the good it did.

One of the score of magical defenses that surrounded Daktari at all times crackled to life. A jolt of energy passed through Nord and every muscle in his body contracted. He tried to scream but his jaw was clamped too tight to let any sound escape.

Daktari let him suffer for a slow ten count before negating the spell. Nord's muscles went limp and he collapsed into his bed.

"I trust you won't require another demonstration," Daktari said. "I do so hate slow learners."

Nord managed to shake his head.

"Excellent. I have other matters that require my attention, so I'll get straight to the point. I am the reason you lost the war twenty years ago. I made a deal with your brother. In exchange for the stone soldiers and Heat's Bane, Vilos promised me his firstborn daughter. He betrayed me and sent his daughter temporarily beyond my reach. He must pay for his betrayal."

Nord had managed to sit up by now. "So, what do you want with me?"

"I have chosen you as one of the instruments of my revenge."

Daktari's eyes blazed with purple fire. Nord scrunched down into the pillows. Daktari allowed himself a small smile. He had the idiot cowed now.

"I'm not stingy with my allies." He snapped his fingers and Heat's Bane appeared, floating in the tent. "Recognize this?"

"My brother's sword." The greed in Nord's eyes turned Daktari's stomach. Still, greed had its uses.

"You will march your army south and attack the High Kingdom. Destroy your brother's army and all those loyal to him. Do not harm Vilos. I want him alive to watch his kingdom fall apart. Should you get your hands on Princess Shara, you will turn her over to me, unharmed. In return, you may keep the sword and rule in your brother's place. Agreed?"

"What about the stone soldiers?"

Smarter than he thought. "The stone soldiers are for Kent. He will attack from the south and you from the north. Together you will smash Vilos."

"Two questions," Nord said. "What did you promise Kent? If I'm to rule, what's left for him? Second, I've nearly finished conquering the Broken Kingdom. If I leave now, all my efforts will have been for nothing."

"As for the Broken Kingdom," Daktari said. "There's no need for you to head south today. With Heat's Bane's power, you could consolidate your control here in a week or two of hard campaigning. As for Kent, I haven't offered him the golems yet, so I don't know what he'll want."

"Suppose I say no."

Daktari glowered and summoned the purple fire back to his eyes. "Then I hope you like pain."

Nord's laugh sounded a little hysterical. "In that case, I accept your generous offer."

"Splendid." They spent the next half an hour going over Heat's Bane's various powers and how to call them forth. When Daktari felt satisfied that Nord understood how the sword worked he said, "Know this. I will stomach no more betrayals. Cross me and yours will be a death to make demons quail."

With that he vanished in an inferno of purple flames.

Daktari appeared about one hundred yards outside the mercenary camp. "Do you trust this fool, Master?" Bane asked.

"No, I think it will be necessary to keep an eye on our would-be ally."

"Not me, Master, please. I couldn't stand following that oaf around."

Daktari scratched his homunculus between the wings. "No, Bane, not you. I wouldn't like to lose you for the months of observation necessary. I thought maybe a lava imp."

"Good choice, Master," Bane said.

Daktari drew a circle of flame in the air about two feet around. He spoke a word of power and a stream of fire flew from his left hand until the circle had filled and become a disk of flame. Daktari began the chant that would transform the disk into a portal to the elemental plane of fire. When the spell concluded he commanded, "Zin, come forth."

Zin was the name of one of half a dozen lava imps he knew. The minor spirits were useful for simple tasks like spying and carrying messages. Wind spirits were even better suited to the task, but he had always preferred servants capable of action should the need arise.

A ball of flame emerged from the portal and shifted into a humanoid figure about two feet tall with small wings and a barbed tail. "It's cold here, sorcerer, send me home or..." One look at Daktari's frowning face silenced the imp. "Forgive me, Master."

Daktari ignored the apology and conjured a foot-tall illusion of Nord. "Follow this man. Watch every move he makes. I will contact you for regular updates."

"As you command, Master. Where can I find this human?"

Daktari pointed toward the camp. Zin drifted off to look for Nord, using its magic to become invisible.

"That should do, Bane. Let's go home. Tonight we visit Silvermane."

CHAPTER 12

"What do you mean I'm your prisoner?" Shara was so angry she hardly even noticed the crossbow pointed at her.

"I mean," Robert said, "you'd better do as you're told or I'll start slicing at your toes and work my way up."

He said it in such a cold, unemotional voice Shara fell into stunned silence. She hadn't the slightest doubt he'd do just what he said.

One of the women disengaged from the group and slithered over toward them. Shara gave the woman a disdainful glance. As she got closer Shara realized how striking she looked with long black hair tied back in a ponytail and the most piercing blue eyes Shara had ever seen. Cords of muscle flexed on her bare arms as she approached.

Though lean and well muscled there was nothing masculine about the way she carried herself or the way she filled out the top of her leather armor. The only flaw Shara could see was a ragged scar on her right cheek and even that seemed to add to rather than detract from her beauty.

Robert dropped his crossbow as the woman approached. He seemed to think Shara wouldn't try and escape with all the others watching her.

The woman wrapped her arms around Robert's neck and purred, "Miss me, Bobby?"

Robert slid his arms around the woman's waist. "Every moment hurt, Blade."

Blade glanced over her shoulder at Shara. "Sure you didn't find some other amusement?"

Robert grinned. "You know the rules, Blade. Never play with the merchandise."

Shara's mouth hung open. That woman thought Robert had had sex with her. And what did they mean by merchandise?

She intended to ask but had to look away when they started kissing in a way Shara thought totally inappropriate considering the number of people watching.

She tried to ignore the rather wet smacking sounds they made. When she got up the nerve to look back Robert had Blade's breastplate half off and his free hand on her rear end. For her part Blade had her hand down the front of his pants. Heaven's mercy, were they going to do it right in the middle of the clearing with everyone watching?

The others seemed to think so as well because they started hooting and hollering, trying to egg the pair on, though they didn't seem to need any encouragement.

To Shara's relief, before they could get going someone yelled, "What the hell's going on out here?"

The others fell silent and Robert gently disengaged himself from Blade. Shara heard him whisper, "Sorry, Blade, business before pleasure."

A big man, most likely the one that had yelled, emerged from a tent. He stomped over looking like he wanted to break something. Shara put his height at nearly seven feet—he towered over Robert and Blade.

Ignoring Shara for the moment he said, "How many times have I told you two to keep it inside? The men can't think straight for a week after one of your performances."

Shara looked the newcomer over. His nose looked like it had gotten broken half a dozen times and his brown hair was hacked short like he cut it with a dagger. He gave off a rather brutal impression and she suspected that was intentional.

Robert looked properly chastised and said, "Sorry, Shale."

Blade didn't seem the least bit intimidated. She gave Robert one last long, lingering kiss then said, "See you later."

She shot a glare at Shale that made the big man flinch.

Robert's eyes burned as he watched her saunter off, hips swaying. What had she been thinking? A man like that couldn't be her savior.

"Well, Bobby, did you get 'em?"

"The driver bled to death before I could catch him. That fat little merchant was tough. He ran six miles before I caught up. I put a bolt in his back first chance I got."

"Good," Shale said. "No witnesses. Now what have we here?"

The two men turned to regard her. "This," Robert said, "is Princess Shara of the High Kingdom. She wandered into my camp last night."

Shale looked at Robert and raised an eyebrow. "You're kidding."

"Just look at her, the style of her dress and jewelry."

Shale grunted. "It's a wonder you didn't rob her before you brought her in."

Robert gave Shale a wounded look. "I'd never do that. I figured that ring in particular would be right up your alley."

What was Robert doing? He knew the ring was magical. As soon as Shale looked away from him Robert winked at her.

The scoundrel actually winked at her!

Shale grabbed Shara's arm, engulfing half of it in one massive paw. "Don't move."

The warning was unnecessary. Shara couldn't have moved if she wanted to. Fear held her immobile. The giant raised her hand up to get a better look at her ring. "Nice."

Robert sniffed. "Of course it's nice. I wouldn't capture just anyone, you know."

Shale reached for her ring. Just before he touched it a blue spark leapt from it. Shale yelped and dropped her arm.

He rounded on Robert.

"Did I mention it's magical?" Robert asked.

Shale's fists opened and closed like he wanted to wrap them around Robert's neck. "No, damn you, you didn't mention it."

Robert shrugged. "Must have slipped my mind."

Shale shook a warning fist in Robert's face. "One of these days Blade will get sick of you. When she does I'm going to break your scrawny neck."

"You've been saying that for a year and a half, Shale, and I'm still here. Now do you want to discuss our prisoner or what?"

"What's to discuss?" Shale asked, getting himself under control. "We'll sell her at the slave auction next week."

"Slave auction!" Robert and Shara said at the same moment.

"Are you nuts, Shale? Her father would pay ten times what we could get at the auction. I bet he'd pay a thousand gold pieces, easy."

"I'm still not convinced she's a princess. I say we sell her at the auction and be done with her."

"Get Scratch to do a truth test on her. That'll confirm it."

"No need." Shara spun toward the camp to see who had spoken. A man carrying a gray tabby cat was walking toward them. "She's worth considerably more than one thousand gold pieces. She's the one, Shale. I did a mind scan to confirm it."

"One what?" Shale asked.

"You forgot our conversation already? She's the one from the sending I received yesterday."

"What sending?" Robert asked.

Shara was curious as well. Perhaps the royal magician was looking for her.

She laughed at herself. She knew who was looking for her, she just didn't want to admit it.

"Come on, Scratch, fill me in," Robert said. "I wasn't here yesterday. Remember?"

"I received a sending from a powerful sorcerer, the most powerful I've ever encountered. He's offering ten thousand gold pieces to anyone bringing Princess Shara, unharmed, to some place called the Chaos Hills in the High Kingdom."

Robert whistled. "Wow, that's a lot of gold." A confused look crossed his face. "Why did the sorcerer send this message to you?"

Scratch sighed. "The message wasn't to me specifically. The same message went to every magic user in the world."

"Damn. Could you do a sending like that, Scratch?"

The wizard laughed. "There are less than a handful of sorcerers in the world powerful enough to do that. I'm certainly not one of them."

The three men looked at Shara. Scratch said, "He must want you bad."

"All right," Shale said. "After dinner we'll have a council and vote on whether we want to take her to this sorcerer or sell her here. Tie her up, Bobby, wouldn't want her wandering off."

Robert led her to a tree near the tents, picking up a length of rope on the way. He tied her wrists together first then tied the rope to the tree. Very efficient was her captor.

"Too tight?" he asked.

"It's fine," she said without looking at him. "Get a lot of practice tying up prisoners?"

He grinned. "Nah, just Blade. Speaking of whom, I'd better get going or she'll be upset. I'll see you for dinner."

Robert scurried off to find Blade, leaving Shara alone to contemplate her fate. Slavery or the sorcerer, neither option thrilled her.

When Robert returned darkness was fast falling. He carried a plate and mug and wore a big, stupid smile. No doubt he'd found Blade.

"Hungry?" he asked.

She turned up her nose but the growl from her stomach betrayed her. "Maybe just a little."

Robert set the plate and mug down so he could untie her. She picked up the plate. A joint of meat sat on it. She looked around but saw no knife or fork. Apparently the savages didn't use utensils. Shara took the meat in a delicate grip, careful not to burn herself, and took a bite. It tasted wonderful. She set it back down and took a drink. The liquid nearly gagged her, it tasted so bitter.

"What is that? It's disgusting."

"Beer. I'm afraid it's all we have."

"Aren't you having any?" she asked.

Robert shook his head. "I ate with Blade."

"Oh. What's going to happen to me now?" She tried to make the question sound nonchalant and failed.

"When everyone's eaten Shale will call a council and we'll vote if we want to take a chance on delivering you to the High Kingdom or if we'll just sell you here. Whatever the majority decides, that's what we'll do. Anyone who doesn't want to go can stay behind, except you of course."

She had to spit out some of his awful beer as she laughed. Heaven's mercy, the man was incorrigible. He was reminding her she was a prisoner and making her laugh at the same time.

She sighed. "I don't get you, Robert."

"What don't you get?" he asked. "Perhaps I can offer some illumination."

He seemed serious so she said, "I don't know. All this just doesn't seem like it fits. You don't seem like a bad guy."

"Once upon a time you would have been right. That story I told you out in the forest about growing up at sea with my father the merchant, all that was true. When my father retired he bought an estate about three hundred miles north of here. He also used his wealth to buy a title. That was the only bad deal he ever made."

"What do you mean?"

Robert leaned against the tree she'd been tied to. "Father might have bought the title but the other nobles would never accept him. A year later he was killed and I came into a lot of wealth with very little knowledge of the nobles. A group of them tricked me into helping in a plot to kill the king. The plan fell apart and I took the fall. The Crown stripped me of all my lands and my title. I escaped and hooked up with Blade and this crew. I used what knowledge I had of merchants and nobles to help plan attacks on the caravans that pass through the Vale. I took great pleasure in killing anyone that had anything to do with my former associates. I've killed three of those that betrayed me. There are only two left."

"I'm sorry," Shara said. She could hardly believe she'd said it much less meant it but she did.

"Don't feel too sorry for me," Robert said with a grin. "As

awful as it may seem out here, I wouldn't trade one day with Blade for the return of all my lands and title."

Shara shook her head in amazement. "You really do love her."

"More than you can imagine."

"Because she saved you when you fled the nobles?"

"Yes, though not exactly the way you mean. When I fled I didn't much care if I lived or not. Back then, I probably would have paid Shale to strangle me. Then I met Blade." He smiled as he remembered. "She lives life with such pleasure and abandon it's intoxicating to be around her. When we were together, I found I wanted to live. It helped that she fell for me almost as fast as I did for her. We started sharing a tent the day after we met."

Shara wanted to know more but before she could ask, someone struck a gong or something and Robert said, "That's Shale calling the council. Let's go."

He untied the rope from the tree and rebound her hands.

As they walked toward a large fire she asked, "How do you think the vote will go?"

Robert shrugged. "Blade and I will both vote for going to the High Kingdom. She's never seen the desert which is all the reason she needs. Most will probably vote with us. This crew's been together a long time. I doubt they'll want to split up now."

They reached the fire and found Shale and six others seated around it. Robert found a stump to his liking and plopped down. Shara sat on the ground a few feet away. The rest of the crew came drifting in. Blade appeared next. She came over and sat on Robert's lap. When everyone had arrived there were twelve bandits and Shara seated around the fire. That made thirteen, a very unlucky number.

"What did you bring her for?" Shale asked when everyone had taken a seat.

"I would have had to tell her what we decided anyway," Robert said. "I figured she could just as well hear firsthand."

"Fine," Shale said. "Fill everyone in, Scratch, so we can have our vote."

The wizard sat directly opposite Shara, his gray cat curled up in his lap. Scratch quickly brought everyone up to date. He made a point of emphasizing the ten-thousand-gold-piece reward.

When the wizard finished Shale said, "I call for a vote. All those in favor of going to the High Kingdom raise your hand."

"Wait," Shara said. "I'm certain my father would pay even more than the sorcerer."

"Shut her up, Bobby, or I will," Shale said.

Robert leaned down. "Keep your mouth closed or Shale will end this debate by caving in your skull."

Shara clenched her jaw tight. Robert was dead serious, no doubt about that. Some of the others started mumbling about what she'd said. Perhaps she'd gotten her message through.

"Maybe we could get the father to pay fifteen thousand," the other female bandit said.

"I'll have no part of a plan like that," Scratch said.

"Why?" Shale asked. He looked like greed might get the best of him.

"How long do you think it would take the sorcerer to find out who had returned her to her father? The minute he learned, he'd crush us, like that." Scratch snapped his fingers.

"All right," Shale said. "Let's vote. All in favor of taking her to the sorcerer raise your hands."

All but Shale and two others raised their hands. Shara's heart sank. She was going home, but not the way she'd hoped.

"Fine," Shale said sounding none too happy. "We leave in the morning. Morden, you're on guard duty."

A huge man, at least a foot taller than Shale, lumbered over toward her. He grunted and held out his hand. Robert handed over her rope and Morden led her away. She looked over toward Robert but he was speaking to Blade and didn't pay her the least attention.

Morden led her to the tree she'd been tied to before. He plopped down and stared off into space. Shara got as far from him as the rope would allow and lay down. She hadn't been there long when someone appeared. It was Robert and he carried a blanket over one shoulder.

Morden looked over but Robert just waved and said, "Relax, Morden. I just brought a blanket for our guest."

The giant grunted and returned to staring off into space.

Robert handed her the blanket. "It gets chilly at night."

Shara rolled up in the blanket. It felt heavy and warm. "Thank you."

He nodded. "Try and sleep. We leave early."

CHAPTER 13

The sun glared down on Sultan's Oasis. Vilos and Yosef stood on the outer palace wall and watched as the mob outside grew larger. There had to be at least three hundred people gathered around the gate. At the head of the mob stood three priests of The Binder, the archangel dedicated to the ideals of strength and obedience. Leading the way was their high priest, Saladin.

All the priests wore simple white robes without decoration. Seemed they were playing at being poor and pious. Having seen some of the decorations at the temple, Vilos recognized the act for what it was.

As if Vilos didn't have enough problems. Between getting the palace rebuilt, worrying about Shara, and trying to guess what the sorcerer might do next, his days were plenty full. He needed this distraction like he needed a boulder dropped on his head.

"What do you suppose their problem is?" Vilos asked. The crowd had been milling around for an hour and no one had said a word.

Yosef shrugged. "Shall I send one of my men out to see?"

"No, send a servant. We don't want to start any trouble. Tell him to be subtle."

"Right." Yosef left to find a spy.

Vilos watched as the mob continued to grow. If they had something to say, why didn't they just get on with it? He had no time to waste on this foolishness.

Yosef rejoined him after a few minutes. "I sent one of the stable hands."

Vilos nodded, watching as the priests put their heads together. That couldn't be a good sign. Before long someone came clambering up the steps. The scent of camel preceded him. This would be the spy.

The stable hand bowed. "Majesty, it seems they've had a vision."

Before the man could continue, Saladin spoke. His voice had been magically amplified so half the city probably heard it. "Sultan, The Binder has sent us a vision. He says you have become weak and the attack on the palace is proof. We demand you answer the challenge."

Vilos had never heard of a priest challenging the sultan. He looked at Yosef, who was quite knowledgeable about military history. "Any idea what he's talking about?"

Yosef hesitated then said, "Traditionally the priests of The Binder held the right to challenge the sultan if he showed any signs of weakness. They haven't issued a challenge in five hundred years. Usually, at some point in a sultan's reign, there's a war. The sultan either wins the war or dies trying. That was enough to satisfy the priests one way or the other."

Vilos massaged his suddenly throbbing temples. "Let me see if I understand. They're challenging me because I've done too good a job keeping the peace?"

Yosef winced but nodded. "You could look at it that way."

"What form does this challenge take exactly?"

"According to the stories, it usually involves single combat between the sultan and the local champion of the temple."

"The champion of a temple dedicated to the archangel of strength. Let me guess, large fellow with arms the size of tree trunks?"

Yosef nodded. "I've seen the champion and he's huge."

"Wonderful. Do I at least get to choose which form of combat I must endure?"

"That's the sultan's prerogative," Yosef said.

"Fine." Vilos turned to the stable hand. "Tell Saladin I'll fight his champion at his earliest convenience."

"Yes, Majesty." The stable hand hurried away.

"You have a plan?" Yosef asked.

"Perhaps. Go find my quartermaster and tell him I need my dueling staves."

A slow smile spread across Yosef's face before he went to find the quartermaster. Vilos turned back to watch his message get delivered. Saladin stared at the messenger then looked up at Vilos. He waved. The priest ran off to find his champion.

Vilos allowed himself a smile as he prayed he hadn't just made a huge miscalculation. His plan basically hinged on the idea that the priests held tradition in such high regard that they wouldn't have trained their champion with any weapons unfamiliar to the region.

The staff was a common weapon in the north where Vilos's ancestors hailed from. His father had insisted that he and his brothers become familiar with the weapon. Of the three, Vilos was the best. Nord always favored the sword and Kent didn't like fighting at all.

Yosef returned. "The staves have been found."

"Good." Vilos silently thanked his father for those lessons

years ago. Now he just prayed he could remember them all. "How long will it take their champion to arrive?"

"Not long, the temple is only ten streets away."

"I'd better get ready then." They left the wall and walked down to the gardens. The quartermaster was waiting with two six-foot-long iron-capped staves. Vilos took one and gave it a few experimental twirls. He grinned as the lessons came back. He spun the weapon around his body, moving it from one hand to the other, trying to get his muscles limbered up.

He had just about finished his preparations when the main gate opened. In paraded Saladin and two underpriests. They had changed into formal white robes and wore amulets featuring a crisscrossing chain design.

The priests formed a triangle around a dark-skinned native with more muscles than any three Vilos had seen. The champion carried a scimitar in one hand and a punch dagger in the other, the two most common weapons in the High Kingdom.

Perfect.

"In The Binder's name you are challenged," Saladin said. "I present the champion of our temple, Ukla."

The huge man stepped forward and flexed his muscles. They looked even bulkier than before.

Vilos managed to suppress a smile. With a body like that, Ukla would have neither the speed nor the agility to keep up with Vilos though the man was twenty years his junior.

"I accept your challenge. Your man won't need those weapons." Vilos nodded and the quartermaster carried the second stave over to Ukla.

"You expect mighty Ukla to fight with a stick?" one of the underpriests demanded.

"I have the right to choose my weapon, do I not?"

"Of course," Saladin said. "Your choice took us by surprise, that's all."

"If your man's afraid, I understand," Vilos said.

"I fear nothing," Ukla said. He handed his weapons to the priests and stepped forward to accept the staff. He held it at one end like a giant sword and swung it around over his head as hard as he could.

Vilos shook his head slightly; angry and incompetent, a perfect combination.

Ukla turned to bow to the priests. When he turned back, Vilos drove the tip of his staff into Ukla's nose. The champion staggered, blood gushing down his face.

"Bet that hurt," Vilos muttered.

Ukla came roaring at him, enraged beyond all reason.

He swung a blow that had it landed would have sent Vilos's head sailing over the outer wall.

Vilos ducked under it, letting Ukla's momentum unbalance him.

He staggered.

Vilos stepped in and struck with an uppercut blow to the groin that made every man watching wince.

Ukla's eyes rolled up and he collapsed.

Vilos took the staff from Ukla's limp fingers. "I'd say that's the end of the match, wouldn't you?"

Saladin scowled so hard it looked like his face might break, but he nodded and went over to help Ukla to his feet. The man came to just about the time they got him up.

"You have no honor," he roared and launched a vicious straight right at Vilos's head.

Before it could hit, Ukla's fist encountered the magic shield that protected Vilos from unenchanted weapons.

Every bone in his hand broke with an audible crunch.

Understanding dawned on the priests' faces.

Vilos nodded. "That's right, he never had a chance."

"The Binder doesn't approve of trickery, Sultan," Saladin said.

"I don't imagine he likes sore losers either. You challenged and you lost. I don't expect to see you again."

"You won't." Saladin spat on the dust and led the group toward the exit.

The priests and their battered, bloody champion retreated out the gates. Vilos ran up on the wall and raised his fists over his head. The mob roared. He pumped his fists again as the priests slunk away.

The crowd began to disperse, so Vilos climbed back down to the garden where Yosef waited. "Do think that was wise, rubbing their noses in defeat?"

"The people needed to see me. Now if the priests try and challenge me again they'll have less support."

"They don't take defeat well. They may visit the Reaper's Guild to buy some revenge."

"You think they'd stoop to assassination?" Vilos asked.

Yosef held out his hands and shrugged.

Vilos massaged his temples again. His headache was returning. "All right, have the temple watched."

"Yes, Majesty."

"Heaven's mercy, I hope Shara's doing better than us."

"She could hardly do much worse," Yosef said.

CHAPTER 14

Daktari woke at midnight. He rolled out of his feather bed, pulled on his purple and black robe, and strode out into the tunnel connecting his bedchamber to the lab. Bane waited for him outside his bedchamber. Daktari had never met Silvermane but she had a reputation as a skilled wizard, one of the strongest in the kingdom. Underestimating her would be foolish despite his own considerable strength.

"You won't accompany me tonight, Bane," Daktari said as they entered the main cavern.

"Why, Master?" Bane asked.

"It's too dangerous. Silvermane is wizard enough to attack me through our mind link. I can't be worrying about you while I'm fighting someone of her skill."

"What about me?" Ulibo oozed out of the shadows.

"You will remain here as well. I'll summon you if I need help."

Daktari went around to two of the stone tables, collecting a few minor items, the last and most remarkable of which was a black pearl the size of his thumb knuckle.

"Stay alert," he said. "I think I can handle her alone, but I'll be on Silvermane's ground. If I run into trouble, come at once."

"I'll be listening, Master," Ulibo said.

Daktari nodded then vanished into the ether.

When he reappeared, the first thing Daktari noticed was the ocean waves crashing against the shore. Silvermane made her home in a converted lighthouse on the southern tip of the High Kingdom. He could see it now, towering sixty feet above a rocky cliff.

Daktari had appeared about three hundred yards away from the lighthouse. He planned to approach on foot in case she had any shields that might interfere with magical travel.

As he approached he could sense the magic that bound a small fire elemental to the lighthouse, a much more efficient way to maintain the light than using oil.

The closer he got, the more pleased he felt at his decision to walk. Teleportation wards crackled around the lighthouse. He couldn't tell what they all did at a glance, but he doubted any of it would be pleasant for an intruder.

"Stop!" a voice thundered.

Silvermane stood on the balcony surrounding the glass top of the lighthouse. A slight breeze caused her long, silver-gray hair to swirl around her wrinkled face. A white robe with a high collar covered her from chin to ankle.

The aura of power surrounding her was strong, but nothing he couldn't handle.

He magnified his own voice with a thought. "Good evening, Silvermane."

"It was. There's nothing here for you, sorcerer. Leave, before I throw you out."

Arrogant witch. She must sense his power exceeded her own. Why did she sound so damn confident?

"I desire no conflict, Silvermane. Will you come down here

so we can have a civil conversation instead of yelling at each other?"

He blinked and she was standing ten feet away. "I have nothing to say to you, Daktari."

He smiled. The witch thought she knew his true name. That explained her confidence. Such knowledge in the hands of an experienced wizard would let their magic tear through an enemy demon binder's defenses. Pity for her that she only knew the name he'd chosen to use for the past several decades. That knowledge would gain her nothing.

And even if she did know his true name, he'd taken precautions when forming his pact with the demon to keep that particular weakness from ever being an issue for him.

"I want to know where your magic sent Princess Shara. Tell me now and you may continue living."

A shadow of doubt flickered across her face. She mastered it quickly though. "I'll tell you nothing."

She began to chant the words of a banishment spell.

"Stupid." Daktari raised his defenses with a thought. Purple fire blazed around him.

Silvermane completed her spell. "Be gone, Daktari."

He felt the spell wash over him. Silvermane was a powerful wizard, but without his true name the spell affected him no more than a night breeze.

Daktari stood, arms crossed, in the center of the flames. The look of horror on Silvermane's face revealed all. Any advantage she thought she might have had vanished.

"Last chance," Daktari said.

"Never. Solar Flare." She threw out her hand and a blast of searing white light shot out at him.

Daktari raised his hand palm out. "Eclipse." A beam of pure darkness struck the solar flare, negating the spell.

"You are overmatched, witch. Tell me what I want to know and I may have mercy."

"No." She looked to the heavens. "I call on the light. Aid me."

What foolishness did she intend now?

Daktari felt the power in her words. Another power answered. A point of light appeared in the night. It grew larger as it drifted closer.

Daktari snarled as it grew brighter than he liked. It was more than the brightness. Since he was contaminated by corruption, the holy light made his skin crawl and his eyes burn.

In the center of the globe of light a figure appeared. As it grew more distinct Daktari saw a tall being with a face to make women swoon and the wings of a dove. The angel wore archaic plate armor made of silvery metal and carried a longsword forged of the same material. When the angel had fully manifested it gave off a pure-white glow.

It appeared Silvermane had friends in high places. A celestial knight of Heaven's army was no weak opponent. With Silvermane's magic to back it up, their power equaled his and then some.

Daktari swore under his breath. Everything seemed difficult lately. "I see you need an angel to do your fighting for you, witch."

As he spoke he tried to get a feel for the celestial's power. It glowed in the ether just as it did in the physical realm. His best guess put it about midrank in Heaven's army. Not good for him, but far from overwhelming.

"This good woman is under my protection, evil one," the angel said. "You shall not harm her."

Daktari almost gave in to a powerful urge to flee. The angel's voice carried an otherworldly power. Still, though he shuddered, Daktari held firm. He also got a better feel for the creature's limits and smiled.

He was no match for Ulibo.

Daktari straightened and shot the pair a contemptuous look. "You aren't the only one with allies, Silvermane. Shadow demon, come forth."

Daktari's shadow stretched and elongated as Ulibo manifested. The shadow demon rose and took the form of a black, bat-winged angel sporting four arms that ended in long talons. Ulibo threw out an aura of darkness that surrounded and muted the angel's divine light.

Daktari felt immensely better enfolded in the darkness.

"You called, Master?"

"I thought you'd like to meet Silvermane's pet angel."

Ulibo's claws lengthened and he rubbed them together. Silvermane and the angel had their heads together. They seemed to be arguing.

He glanced up at Ulibo. "Do you suppose they've forgotten us?"

Daktari conjured an orb of black energy and hurled it at the pair. The angel leapt into the air with Ulibo right behind.

The orb shattered against Silvermane's personal shield.

Rather than retaliate as he expected, Silvermane's attention was directed up, toward Ulibo.

Daktari felt a spell building.

It seemed the witch meant to attack Ulibo, ignoring Daktari altogether.

Annoyed, Daktari struck her in the head with a telekinetic blast.

She staggered, her spell ruined.

Before she could start another one he encircled her body with three bands of shadow fire.

With her arms pinned to her sides she couldn't direct her magic.

Daktari strolled over. "Don't struggle. If those flames touch you, they'll burn your arms off."

Silvermane glared daggers but said nothing. They both turned their gazes skyward to watch the show.

Demon and angel circled each other. The celestial held its sword point out trying to ward off Ulibo.

The shadow demon charged straight in, counting on its superior strength.

Four clawed hands slashed and hacked, trying to get through the angel's defense.

To Daktari's surprise the celestial knight managed to fend off all of Ulibo's strikes.

They circled each other, making two full rotations before Ulibo attacked.

Claw and sword, shadow and light flashed in the night sky. This time the angel's defense wasn't good enough.

One swing made it through, smashing in the front of the celestial's armor.

Daktari looked over at his prisoner. Silvermane chewed her lip and cringed when she saw the dent in the servant's armor.

He understood now. The angel was more than a summoned ally. The creature meant something to the old woman.

Daktari got a nasty idea. He sped the thought to Ulibo who responded with delight.

They continued circling.

Ulibo feinted like it was going to charge in again.

As he did Daktari created an illusion of Ulibo pressing the attack. The demon circled around the angel.

When the celestial's sword passed through the illusion he realized his mistake.

Too late.

Ulibo crashed into the celestial knight from behind, forcing him to the ground.

His sword went flying on impact.

The pair landed about fifty feet from where Daktari and Silvermane stood. With a gesture Daktari dragged his prisoner over to where her ally lay. Ulibo stood triumphant. It held the celestial down with one taloned foot.

Daktari beamed. It seemed his hawk had caught Silvermane's pigeon.

"Now, Silvermane, before this foolishness began, I asked you a question. Where is Princess Shara? Now I ask again. This time, if you don't answer, my friend will rip chunks out of your pathetic guardian."

The angel looked a good deal less impressive now, lying in the dirt without his sword. Still, the fool creature had nerve. "Tell them nothing."

"Perhaps you doubt my sincerity," Daktari said. "Tear his wings off."

Gleeful, Ulibo repositioned his foot directly between the angel's wings. The demon reached down and grabbed the wings at their base. With one mighty effort Ulibo ripped both wings out of their sockets. The angel roared in pain.

Silvermane looked away.

Daktari gestured and a telekinetic force pulled Silvermane's face back and pried her eyes open. "You can end his suffering. Tell me what I want to know."

"I can't," Silvermane whispered.

"Pity," Daktari said. "Left arm."

Ulibo grabbed the angel's left wrist.

Silvermane screamed, "Wait!"

Too late.

Ulibo hauled back, tearing the angel's left arm out of its socket. A splash of pink blood came out with it.

"You don't understand," Silvermane said. "I can't tell you because I don't know."

"You take me for a fool? You must have chosen a destination when you empowered the ring."

"No. At the sultan's request I wove one hundred safe locations into the spell. At the moment it was triggered, one of those locations was chosen at random. The sultan insisted no one know her destination."

"Very clever." He turned to Ulibo. "End it. We'll gain nothing more here."

The demon seemed inclined to argue, but a glare from Daktari silenced him. Ulibo grabbed the celestial's head in two hands and ripped it off. The body vanished in a blast of white light.

Daktari turned to Silvermane and took a black pearl from his pocket. He held it up for her inspection. "Do you know what this is?"

"A pearl." Her shivering betrayed her fear. She knew its purpose. "Please, just kill me."

"Sorry, I may have more questions for you later." He tossed the pearl in the air where it hovered two feet from Silvermane's head. Daktari invoked the Soul Siphon. The pearl emitted a spiral of purple magic.

The spiral bore into Silvermane's forehead. After a few seconds it reversed course and came out with a ghostly image of Silvermane trailing behind it. Both were absorbed by the pearl.

Daktari caught the pearl as it fell and tucked it into his pocket. With the old witch's soul trapped, he could question her at leisure. Her body stood vacant, staring at nothing. Daktari snapped his fingers and shadow fire consumed it in an instant.

Ulibo drifted over. "Such fun, Master."

"Enjoyed that, did you?"

Ulibo nodded. "Many years have passed since I last battled an angel. Most flee when they see me."

Daktari nodded, brooding.

"You don't seem pleased, Master."

"I'm not."

Ulibo shied away. "I did something wrong?"

Daktari chuckled. "No, Ulibo, you did very well. The problem is, I came here looking for information and didn't get it."

"Ah, the location of this princess that obsesses you. Why do you seek her with such great zeal? I know several succubi that would be happy to entertain you."

Daktari smiled. A demonic matchmaker, how novel. "I don't seek her for myself. After two hundred years the pleasures of the flesh no longer tempt me as they once did. No, Ulibo, even as you serve me so do I serve a greater power. That power commands me to seek the girl."

"What power do you serve, Master?" Ulibo asked.

"I dare not name it before I am ready. To do so would invite questions I'm not yet ready to answer. Go now and fetch Bane. Perhaps the answers I seek await us in the lighthouse."

CHAPTER 15

Prince Nord sat on the floor of his tent trying to decide if his luck was good or bad. When he closed his eyes, he could still feel the heat of the sorcerer's flames. Heat's Bane lay on the floor a few feet from him. The blade was so polished it looked more like crystal than metal. How Nord longed to cut Vilos's heart out with it.

But that wouldn't do. His new benefactor had made it clear that killing Vilos was off the table and Nord wasn't fool enough to challenge the sorcerer. Not yet anyway. Should he get his hands on his niece, then maybe a new deal could be struck. For now, at least, he would toe the line.

Nord couldn't imagine what Vilos had been thinking to make such a powerful enemy.

Finally, Nord decided his luck was good. Any enemy of Vilos's was a friend of his. Best if he finished his business in the Broken Kingdom as fast as possible and turned south before the sorcerer lost patience.

Nord dressed and belted on his new sword. Outside, his

guard stood scratching his backside. Clearly getting ambushed had done little to improve diligence. "Morning, sir."

Nord grunted. "Rouse the camp. We march on Duke Aaron's castle today."

"Right away, sir." The guard ran off to wake the camp. At least he obeyed with alacrity.

Nord went to find his worthless excuse for a magician. His tent sat only forty feet from Nord's. When Nord pulled the flap open and stepped inside, he found his wizard face down in a groaning heap on the floor. Arkon wasn't the most impressive sight at his best and he clearly wasn't at his best.

Nord administered a none-too-gentle kick to his ribs. Arkon groaned and rolled over staring up at Nord. The sight of his glowering lord seemed to wake him.

"Get a good night's sleep, Arkon?" Nord asked.

"A sorcerer in camp," the wizard mumbled then shook his head. His eyes were black, bloodshot, and sunk deep in his skull. "I keep having the same nightmare."

"Your sleep habits don't interest me. I want to know how he waltzed through my camp like he owned the place. I thought you put protections in place. Why didn't you stop him before he reached my tent? What the hell good are you? You didn't even warn me."

Nord's voice grew louder with each sentence until he practically roared the last one.

Arkon struggled to his feet. He looked like a refugee from a famine. His ribs stuck out, his face had sunk in. The price of his magic, he claimed. The intruding sorcerer had looked considerably healthier.

"If you want me to battle that sorcerer, I'm no good at all. He overshadows my power like you overshadow an infant. I barely brushed his mind and he sensed it then dropped the psychic equivalent of a boulder on me. Yet I'm certain he could have turned my mind to pudding without batting an eyelash had he wished to."

"I thought as much. He wants me to attack the High Kingdom and bring Vilos down." Nord drew Heat's Bane. "He gave me this to help. Check it for traps. You were in no fit state to do it before."

Arkon took the sword and made several mystic passes over it. "Powerful, but I sense something hidden, buried in the enchantment. It doesn't seem to be a trap."

Nord nodded. "He told me the sword couldn't be used against him."

"That's probably it. As far as I can tell, there's nothing dangerous buried in the enchantment."

"Can you remove it?"

Arkon rubbed the bridge of his nose. "No. If I try there's no doubt in my mind the sorcerer will sense it. I expect he wouldn't be thrilled about me fooling with his magic."

"Probably not. He seemed a rather humorless fellow." Nord took the sword back and sheathed it.

"What now?" Arkon asked.

"Until I think of something better we'll do just what he wants."

"Wise decision," Arkon said.

Nord nodded. "Get ready. We march for Aaron's castle in an hour."

．—❊

The men had gathered and stood ready to march in under an hour. Good, that was the sort of efficiency he liked to see. The ranks of the White Tigers had swelled to five thousand strong. Though only a core thousand had much battle experience, the rest seemed eager for a fight and managed to stand in straight lines. That was more than a lot of conscript armies could say.

The army had arranged itself into standard battle formation. The front thousand carried pikes and long spears. Behind them were two thousand heavy infantry armed with single-handed arming swords and protected by mail and shields. Fifteen hundred crossbowmen brought up the rear. Two hundred heavy cavalry covered each flank, and the final hundred light cavalry rode ahead of and behind the main force to watch for spies and traps.

Nord rode a gray stallion at the head of the army along with a standard bearer. At the top of a twelve-foot lance flapped a black flag with a white tiger rampant. How glorious it would be when he swapped that white tiger for the High Kingdom's golden serpent.

Arkon rode with the scouts. His magic did a better job of spotting an ambush than a thousand men. Never one to take extra chances, the wizard dressed like an ordinary soldier and even carried the standard horseman's mace. Most enemy commanders tried to eliminate any opposing wizards as soon as possible. Nord could see no reason to give them an obvious target.

His scouts had gotten well on their way and Nord figured it was safe for the main force to move out. He drew Heat's Bane and called forth a cold aura. It glittered with a chill blue light. "White Tigers, forward."

—✣—

The White Tigers covered three-quarters of the distance to Aaron's castle the first day. The cavalry reported one ambush which Arkon had sensed and eliminated without losses. If the rest of the campaign went as smoothly as this first day, Nord would consider himself fortunate.

They set up camp two miles from Aaron's castle. After making sure a double guard had been posted, Nord went to talk to his wizard. He pushed into Arkon's tent without announcing himself. The wizard had shed his cavalryman's disguise in favor of a simple black robe. Arkon glanced up from behind his small folding travel desk when Nord entered.

"You did well with that ambush," Nord said. "They seemed to get discouraged awfully easy."

"Aaron's wizard sensed my presence," Arkon said. "Once they knew you had a wizard, there wasn't much sense bothering with another ambush."

"It figures he'd have a wizard." Nord dropped into a chair beside Arkon's desk. "How strong was he?"

"She," Arkon said, "was competent, but I could take her one on one."

"Good. Anything else I need to worry about?"

"Besides the ten-foot-thick, forty-foot-high walls surrounding Aaron's castle, I can't think of anything."

"Don't worry about the walls," Nord said. "We're going through the main gate."

"You seem confident."

Nord patted Heat's Bane.

. ⁓

The men were allowed an extra hour's rest before they broke camp. Nord planned to hit Aaron's castle by noon. The army marched as soon as they formed up. No ambushes troubled them for the remainder of the trip.

A small village situated about a mile from Aaron's castle

had been evacuated. It seemed they'd had plenty of warning as Nord's scouts reported nothing of value remained.

Their best find was an old wagon. For his plan to work Nord would need lumber, so he ordered two of the better-built houses demolished.

A hundred men with axes soon produced all the lumber he needed. Nord rode on toward the castle well pleased.

Duke Aaron's castle appeared quite daunting. Nord had heard reports of its size, but seeing it looming before him really brought it home.

The main keep towered thirty feet above the forty-foot-high walls. Every fifteen feet along the wall was a tower, no doubt manned by skilled archers. The main gate was barred by a foot-thick, iron-banded oak door, on either side of which stood a guard house lined with murder holes. Any enemy foolish enough to try and fight his way through that wouldn't last long.

Nord smiled. Heat's Bane would show them what their defenses were worth.

Large oak trees lined the road leading to the castle. Nord put some of his men to work building a ram. He signaled Arkon and the two of them rode to just beyond bow range.

"Can you amplify my voice so they can hear me?" Nord asked.

Arkon made a couple of mystic passes through the air. "Go ahead."

"Aaron." Nord's magically enhanced voice boomed like an earthquake. "Surrender now and swear allegiance to me and no one will be hurt."

The duke must have been waiting nearby because only moments later he appeared on the wall. Polished plate mail gleamed in the noonday sun and his long blond hair rippled in the breeze. Nord couldn't feel a breath of wind so he figured it must be a magic trick meant to inspire his men. Nord had to admit the effect looked good. Aaron reminded him of some legendary hero or maybe even Branik the Sword Lord.

Nord smiled a nasty smile. Too bad for Aaron he wasn't an archangel, because nothing less would save him today.

"It will take more than your pathetic little army to breach these walls, Nord," Aaron thundered down in an equally loud voice. "I'm feeling generous. Lead your men away and I may spare you."

"I don't think he's going to surrender," Arkon muttered.

"Remember I gave you this chance." Nord wheeled his horse around and went to rejoin his men.

Aaron's mocking laughter followed him.

The axemen had been busy in his absence. Four good-sized oaks had been felled, limbed, and bound together to make a ram. Two of his men had worked as carpenters before they joined up and they guided the others in mounting it to the wagon and building a mantle out of the old lumber. They did a passable job of cobbling it together.

It wouldn't win any beauty contests. To be honest, it looked rather like a diseased turtle, but the men wouldn't have to worry about arrows.

"I guess we're ready," Nord said.

His stomach churned and bile burned the back of his throat. It was finally starting to sink in just how much he was relying on the sorcerer's magic. He chose twenty raw recruits at random to push the ram. If they didn't survive, the loss would be minimal.

"Let's go."

Nord rode ahead of the ram and once more stopped just beyond bow range. He drew Heat's Bane and blue light blazed forth. He pictured a thin blue beam coming from the tip of the sword.

When he had the image firmly in mind he pointed the tip of the sword at the gate. "Now!"

A blue ray shot out striking the gate. It persisted until the whole thing carried a layer of frost.

"Charge!"

The men pushed the ram as hard as they could.

Nord watched as they drew closer and closer to the gate.

Time seemed to slow.

Every move took forever.

The arrows even seemed to hang in the air.

The ram struck the frozen gate with an astounding crash. Frozen iron banding shattered like glass and the whole gate collapsed inward.

His men fled the wreckage as fast as they could, dodging left and right to avoid the arrows.

Half made it back.

The remainder of the army advanced to join him. Arkon rode at their head.

He urged his horse up beside Nord. "That worked at least."

Nord grinned. He hadn't felt certain until the ram crashed through. "They'll send the heavy cavalry next."

In the broad field surrounding the castle it wouldn't do any good to advance the pike men. The cavalry would just ride around them to hit the flank. By deploying no defenses Nord hoped to draw them into a straight-on charge. If they took the bait, he had another surprise waiting.

It didn't take long for the cavalry to appear. Men and horses covered in heavy plate armor filed through the ruined gate.

What an awesome sight those knights made. Rumors Nord had heard said Aaron had spent most of his wealth buying the steel to outfit them. It was an absolute shame they all had to die. But they'd chosen to join the wrong side, so die they would.

All five hundred knights had assembled in two rows three hundred yards from Nord's army. Arrogant bastards meant to charge straight at them.

Perfect.

Aaron was a bigger fool than Nord had first thought. After the destruction of his precious gate, Nord thought he might show a little caution. It seemed he put great faith in the ability of his knights.

As the knights began their charge, it occurred to Nord that it was a good thing knights didn't make a living with their brains. The idiots had to know a trap awaited them, yet they charged anyway.

Perhaps wearing all that steel did something to your mind. Made you think you were invincible. Some lessons could only be learned the hard way.

At two hundred yards Nord began the mental exercises needed to summon another of the sword's powers.

As he felt the power build the sound of hoofbeats grew louder.

Too slow.

The power was growing too slow.

He'd underestimated the time he needed.

Thunderous noise.

They couldn't be more than a hundred yards away.

He wasn't going to make it.

They were going to reach him before the power was ready.

Seventy-five yards.

Almost there.

Fifty yards.

Now!

With a sweeping slash of the blade, Nord released Heat's Bane's magic.

A blue-white wave of force struck the knights.

Parts of men and horses went flying.

Metal shrieked and twisted.

In seconds, Aaron's prize cavalry lay dead or dying. The few men that survived moaned in pain. Nord plumbed the depths of the sword's power and found the well about dry.

He had enough power left for one last trick.

"Charge!" Nord cried.

His army surged forward with him in the lead. Mounted, he covered the distance much faster than his infantrymen. He had almost reached the wall before the archers recovered from the shock of seeing their champions fall.

Arkon rode stride for stride with him. If they could get in fast, the wizard could neutralize those archers in a hurry.

As they approached the shattered gate Nord saw a gleam of steel. The murder holes were manned.

Damn.

He called on the last of the sword's power and iced over the holes.

That was it. Heat's Bane had been reduced to a mundane, if fine, sword.

Inside a group of spearmen waited in the yard.

Nord leveled the sword at them.

They went diving for cover.

He grinned. Even without magic, the sword made a good bluff.

"The archers," he said to Arkon.

The wizard gestured and a fire sprang up along the top of the wall.

The archers either jumped or got roasted.

Most jumped.

The forty-foot drop didn't do them any good but a few survived. Arkon's fire took the last of the fight out of the defenders. All of the surviving soldiers threw down their weapons.

Nord brought in two hundred heavy infantry and put them to work searching the prisoners for hidden weapons. They'd checked out about a dozen men when Aaron came out of the main keep.

He walked at the head of a small entourage of ten people. Four were dressed in the stiff, fancy garb favored by the nobility. The other six wore simple servant's smocks. Aaron himself still had on the fine armor from earlier. He'd divested himself of all weapons. A wise move considering Nord's crossbowmen now manned the walls.

As they approached Nord whispered to Arkon, "Which one is the wizard?"

"The blond, second from Aaron's left."

A score of infantry had taken it upon themselves to act as escort to the duke's group. Good thinking that. Nice to see his men taking some initiative.

As the group approached Nord studied them, looking for potential trouble. The servants all walked while staring at their feet. Good, they looked whipped, no problems there.

Three of the nobles wore the bland, arrogant look most nobles preferred. Cowards one and all without an army to protect them.

That left Aaron and the wizard as potential problems.

The wizard looked this way and that, alert for trouble. The bitch looked like she had spirit.

Too bad. She was a looker.

Aaron wore the stunned, defeated expression of a man who didn't think he could be beaten. Nord saw no treachery there. Of course, he'd heard that Aaron had strangled his father to gain his current status, so he planned to take nothing for granted.

Aaron and his group stopped about five feet from Nord.

The duke dropped to one knee. "I offer my complete surrender."

"Generous of you considering I already control your castle."

Aaron sputtered and the nobles murmured among themselves. It seemed they weren't used to sarcasm. While they fluttered about Nord decided to give them something to think about.

He drew Heat's Bane and drove it into the wizard's chest. She collapsed, killed instantly.

A second swing took Aaron's head.

"He should have surrendered when he had the chance."

"What should we do with the rest?" Arkon asked.

"I'm certain they'll swear allegiance to me. Right?"

"Do we have a choice?" one of the men asked.

"Yes, the same choice Aaron had."

The nobles tried not to look at the headless corpse lying in the dirt beside them. Once they had sworn themselves to Nord he said, "I trust you will honor your word. I won't be as easy on a traitor as I was on Aaron."

With that admonition he sent the nobles on their way.

The servants stood quietly waiting for Nord to notice them. When he did he said, "As for you, I have no quarrel with servants. You may remain here and continue your work. I'll pay the same wage as your former master. Anyone who wishes to leave may do so now." When no one left he said, "You may go."

They scurried off to find something to clean. When they'd gone Arkon asked, "Can we trust the nobles?"

"No, but the first one that betrays me will die a slow,

terrible death while the others watch. I think that will make my point."

Nord flicked the blood off of Heat's Bane's blade and sheathed it. Only one duke remained. Once he'd been dealt with, the Broken Kingdom would be broken no more.

CHAPTER 16

Kent walked through his main warehouse. Judging from the number of still-damp boxes stacked everywhere, a new ship had recently arrived. Their contents were a mystery, one he had no time to explore. The clerks would have to manage on their own.

He'd pushed the men hard to get back to Haydrien in just three days and now he was anxious to begin the search for his niece. He entered his office in the rear of the building and found Yaway waiting for him. Just the sight of the beautiful woman washed away some of his worries.

"That visit didn't last long," she said. "Did you have trouble?"

"You haven't heard?"

"Heard what?"

Kent filled her in on his brother's troubles. "I offered to help find Shara."

She nodded. "Raven was jabbering something about the princess the other day. I didn't pay much attention but he seemed anxious to see you. We've had other problems. One of our caravans got wiped out twenty miles from the city."

"What happened?"

"I don't know. The official word is nomads, doesn't seem too likely though. They've never attacked a caravan the size of ours."

"That's all I need. All right, from now on all caravans get a double guard. Include a wizard if at all possible. Find Raven, I've got a job for him."

"Will do." Yaway sashayed out of the office. Heaven's mercy, he hoped she never found another job.

Raven must have been nearby because Yaway had only just left when the wizard showed. Tall and gaunt, Raven's long, black hair went every which way like he'd just gotten out of bed. He took his name from the ill-tempered familiar that rode on his shoulder. What his true name might be, Kent had no idea. Wizards tended to hide that particular detail.

The huge bird cawed at Kent.

Kent glared. "Didn't I tell you not to bring that damn bird in here?"

"Sorry." Raven opened the door. "Go on, Circe."

The bird offered a parting caw then took off up into the warehouse rafters.

"What's got you so worked up?" Kent asked.

Raven sat in one of the chairs opposite Kent. "There's a new sorcerer. He just made himself known a few days ago. He's powerful, the strongest I've ever felt." Raven went on to tell about the sending and the reward for Shara.

"The message is news to me, but I knew about the sorcerer already." Kent told him about the attack on the palace.

Raven shook his head. "Incredible, I'm afraid if this guy wants your niece he's going to get her."

"Why?"

Raven stared at him. "Because nobody with half a brain would dare oppose him."

Kent grinned.

"No," Raven said. "I refuse to believe you're thinking what I know you're thinking."

"He's after my niece. I have to help if I can."

"You've never even met this girl. Is she really worth your life?"

"My life?" Kent said, confused.

"That's right." Raven sounded grim, even for Raven. "If this sorcerer learns you're opposing him, I doubt all the legions of Hell could stop him from killing you."

"Relax. We're not going to oppose him directly. We'll be subtle."

Raven's expression softened. "What have you got in mind?"

"I want you to contact our agents. Tell them to keep an eye out for Shara. She's bound to show up in a city somewhere eventually. Tell our people to make contact and keep her under wraps. I hope, after a while, the sorcerer will think she's died or given up trying to get home. Once he stops looking for her, she should be safe."

Raven got up and started pacing. Good, that meant he was thinking.

"There's one obvious problem with your plan. A sorcerer of this magnitude would be able to learn for certain if she had died. Also, if he wants her as bad as it seems he does, there's no guarantee he'll ever stop looking for her."

"I grant you all that, but if we find her at least we'll know where she is and that she's safe."

"That's true. Your plan is also unlikely to get us all killed. I'll start contacting our people."

"Thanks, Raven." Kent offered a grateful smile.

The die was now cast. Hopefully he didn't come to regret his decision.

CHAPTER 17

Shara walked in misery. Three days ago they had broken camp and begun the long trip to the High Kingdom. The two men that voted with Shale decided to leave the group rather than make the trip. Both said they were too old to walk halfway around the world. No one seemed to think ill of them. Shale had gotten a small chest and counted out their share of the group's loot. Before they left, Scratch cast a spell to remove any memory of where the rest of them planned to go.

Of all the bandits, only Robert had ever been beyond the Vale and the two kingdoms that surrounded it, so the job of planning their route fell to him. Since they all had prices on their heads in both kingdoms, Robert chose a path that favored stealth over speed or comfort. Once they moved beyond the lands where they were wanted, they planned to steal some horses and step up the pace.

"Hey, kid. How you holding up?" Robert had wandered over.

Morden, her appointed guardian, ignored him. Of course,

Morden ignored everything except her attempts to loosen the rope around her wrists.

"I hurt everywhere. I think I've walked further in the last three days than the whole rest of my life combined."

Robert may have plotted their course, but Shale set the pace. It seemed to Shara that he wanted to get there by the end of the week. No one else seemed to mind though, so it might just be her.

"Don't worry," Robert said. "In a week or two you'll be fine."

"I'm not sure I'll live that long."

Robert laughed. "You'd be surprised what you can live through."

The leaders had stopped to let everyone catch up. Shara hoped they planned to take a break. She could stand to sit down for a few minutes. Or better yet a few hours.

"Wraith is back," Robert said. Wraith was the name of the other female bandit. Robert said she was so quiet she could walk across eggshells without making a sound. "Something must be wrong."

Robert left her to join the group gathering around Wraith. The discussion seemed quite heated from where Shara stood. It ended when Blade threw up her hands and walked away. Robert headed toward Shara, a concerned look on his face.

"What's wrong?" Shara asked.

Robert looked over at Blade who stood sulking a few yards away. He sighed and turned away. "Wraith stumbled across another crew."

"Crew?"

"Another group of bandits. Blade has a history with them and wanted to attack. They outnumber us about two to one and we have you to protect. She didn't care. Apparently the leader of this crew killed a friend of hers. Anyway, we managed to talk her out of it and she's pissed."

"How many bandits are there in the Vale?"

Robert shrugged. "Beats me. The way we kill each other off it's impossible to keep track."

Shale waved and Robert nodded back. "Time to go. Stay close to me and keep quiet. Blade says this crew is rougher than ours. Scratch doesn't think they have a wizard, so we shouldn't have too much trouble sneaking past."

Famous last words.

Still, when Robert started out she followed close behind, doing her best to avoid making any noise. With the forest still damp from the last rainstorm she didn't have too much to worry about.

They moved slow and easy for about ten minutes before the man ahead of them, Shara hadn't heard his name, signaled to stop. She strained to hear something, anything, but could only make out a faint rustling in the bushes.

Then a crunch.

Robert dropped to the ground and dragged her down with him. They lay behind some evergreen shrubs and a moment later someone walked by. She thought she could make out three distinct footfalls.

When they'd moved beyond her hearing she started to get up. Robert put a hand on her back and forced her down. She fell to her stomach again just as a fourth set of footsteps went by.

When the fourth person had gone by Robert helped her to her feet.

He whispered, "Sometimes they have a trailer like that to catch any overanxious soul who jumps up after the main group passes."

"I didn't know," she said.

"Don't worry about it. Just watch me and follow my lead."

They continued on at a much slower pace. Everyone seemed tense. Hands never strayed far from weapons.

They finally stopped when darkness fell. Shale ordered a cold camp and double guard. Robert wandered off, leaving her alone with Morden. He stood by her like a lump, saying nothing. Come to think of it, she hadn't heard Morden speak since she arrived in the bandit camp.

Curious, she asked, "Don't you ever say anything?"

He ignored her.

Shara shrugged, found a soft-looking patch of moss, and sat down to wait. Robert arrived a few minutes later. "I pulled first watch, Morden. Go get some rest."

The big man slumped with relief and gave Robert the rope. Morden trotted off in a hurry. "He seemed eager to go. What did you do to him?"

"Nothing, I just tried to get him to talk."

Robert nodded as though that made perfect sense. "I brought you some supper." He handed Shara three strips of jerky and a piece of day-old bread.

She gave the meat a dubious look then started gnawing. After giving her jaw a serious workout she asked, "What's his problem anyway?"

"Morden? Got his tongue cut out a few years ago."

"That's terrible. Why?"

Robert sat down with his back to a convenient tree. "According to Scratch, Morden had a thing going with a wizard's daughter. One day the wizard caught them in the hayloft. Morden had his tongue in her..." Robert cleared his throat. "Uh, let's just say the old man caught them having a slap-and-tickle session in the loft and got a little bent out of shape. The wizard zapped Morden and when he woke up he found himself in the Vale, sans tongue."

"How awful," Shara muttered around a mouthful of food.

"Could've been worse. First time I heard that story I joked to Scratch that Morden was lucky the wizard hadn't come along a few minutes later. He might have lost something more precious than his tongue."

Suddenly grateful for the darkness, Shara felt her face flush. Robert laughed and offered her a canteen of water. She washed down the last of her dry meal.

"Get some sleep, kid. Gonna be a long day tomorrow."

⸻⸺

S hara woke to screams and the clash of steel on steel. Heart hammering, she wiped the sleep from her eyes and tried to see what was happening. People were fighting in the dim light of the half moon.

Robert seemed to have vanished.

She tugged on her rope but found it secured to a small tree. "Damn." That represented her full complement of curses, though that complement grew every day she spent with her captors.

Behind her a bright white light filled the sky. That must be Scratch and sure enough when she turned she saw the wizard standing under a glowing orb of light. He had his sword drawn. Between his feet she saw the ever-present cat.

A loud snarl caused her to snap her head back.

A large black mastiff emerged from some nearby brush.

It saw her.

The dog barked, spittle flying from its lips.

Shara screamed as the beast charged her.

It leapt for her throat.

Shara squeezed her eyes shut and hoped the end would be quick.

After a few seconds when she didn't feel sharp fangs sinking into her throat she opened her eyes.

She was just in time to watch Robert drive his shortsword into the top of the dog's skull.

Nearby, someone let out a tortured scream. A man appeared from the same direction as the dog. He wore black leather and carried an ax.

Robert struggled to get his sword free. The newcomer stared at Robert as he sawed his sword back and forth, trying to rip it out of the dog's skull.

He let out another wail and charged, ax raised.

"Look out!" Shara screamed.

Robert rolled away, the ax missing him by inches.

The man recovered and brought the ax up for another blow.

Lucky for Robert, Blade appeared.

She lunged in and opened the ax wielder's throat with a slash so fast Shara couldn't even follow the movement of her sword.

The magical light revealed more people moving around the clearing. One man looked their way then shouted something to the others. Five more bandits joined him and they advanced toward them

Blade had just enough time to toss Robert a dagger before they arrived.

The poor fools must have thought the three of them looked like easy marks, two women and a man with a dagger.

They couldn't have been more wrong.

The one that had shouted advanced on Blade with a smile on his face.

As he raised his sword in a two-handed grip Blade darted in and carved a second smile below the first.

His life spilled down his chest.

The rest seemed to get an idea of what they faced but it was too late.

Blade waded into them, sword a blur.

Calling it a battle would be too generous.

It reminded Shara of farmers harvesting grain; she swung, and they fell.

While Blade was busy a seventh man tried to sneak up on her. Robert whipped his dagger into the man's chest dropping him in his tracks.

The battle was over in seconds. Shara now understood why Shale had flinched away from Blade the day she'd first come into their camp. As soon as the danger had passed Robert went to Blade.

"Are you all right?" they said at the same time. They laughed and embraced like the whole thing had been a game and their team had won. Blade left to find someone else to kill and Robert came over to her.

"You okay?" he asked.

Shara nodded, still a little stunned by the display. She'd never seen anyone killed before. "I see how she got her name."

Robert beamed. "She's something."

He walked over to the dog and put his foot on its head. With both hands he managed to jerk his sword loose. He cleaned it on the dead animal's fur and sheathed it.

Shara started to say something but he held up his hand. She looked around thinking he heard something approaching.

"Listen," he said.

"I don't hear anything."

"Exactly, the battle's over. Come on; let's go see if anyone got hurt." Robert untied her rope and they walked over toward Scratch.

Under the wizard's light was the brightest spot in camp and the others flocked toward it. A few had minor injuries but nothing too serious. About the worst was a deep cut on Shale's right bicep. Wraith was sewing it up when they arrived.

Blade was the last to arrive. She appeared none the worse for wear. Her sword dripped blood so Robert tossed her a rag. She cleaned her sword and threw the rag away.

That done she came over next to Robert and slipped her arm around him. "I circled the camp. Three of them got away."

Shale grunted as Wraith put the last stitch in his arm. "I doubt those three'll try anything more. What the hell happened, Scratch? I thought you said they didn't have a wizard."

The wizard held out his arms and the cat jumped up into them. "They didn't have a wizard. One of the dogs must have hit our track and led them back to us."

"Terrific," Shale said. "Next time check for wizards and dogs."

"Right, chief, whatever you say."

Shale glared and the cat hissed at him. "Bobby, watch the girl. Everyone else get some rest. We leave at dawn."

CHAPTER 18

Three days had passed since the priests of The Binder challenged Vilos. Perhaps the archangel had been pleased with his victory as heaven had blessed Vilos with peace and quiet. The laborers had the worst of the rubble cleared from the palace and they were now working on the roof. His chief engineer said the interior was still unstable so everyone was camping in the gardens. The groundskeepers had a fit when they saw the damage to their precious sod. Never mind that the palace lay in ruins.

High sun approached and the cooks had a dozen fires going to fix lunch for a couple hundred people. Vilos wandered around enjoying the sunshine and fresh air. It only distracted him from worrying about Shara for a few minutes, but he feared without that break he might go mad.

The hot season was ending and temperatures had come down to a more comfortable level. He'd heard nothing from Kent yet. That came as no big surprise. It would probably take at least another day for him to get home anyway. The royal magician had set up shop in the largest tent they could find and was once again able to perform the most basic of his tasks, the primary one being sending and receiving messages.

As if summoned by the thought, Vilos saw his magician approaching as fast as his stubby legs would carry him. Short even by the standards of the High Kingdom, Abin stood only a little over five feet at the tip of his bald head. In an effort to look more impressive, he wore a robe made entirely of cloth of gold. The bright sun made it nearly impossible for Vilos to look directly at him.

The little wizard bowed, his head coming about even with Vilos's knee. "I have troubling news, Majesty."

Vilos tried in vain to look through narrowed eyes. He finally gave up. "Can you do something about that glare?"

Abin looked around and realized what Vilos meant. "Sorry, Majesty." He muttered something and a small cloud appeared over him. "Better?"

"Much," Vilos said. "Now what's the problem?"

"I just received two messages. Black Moon Oasis and Zorn's Oasis are besieged."

"Damn. Nomads?"

Abin nodded.

"Find out how bad off they are and tell them we'll get help to them as soon as possible."

Abin bowed and trundled off.

Vilos started pacing. "Why would the nomads attack again?" he wondered out loud.

"I'll tell you." Yosef approached with a small man dressed in the loose white robes favored by the nomads. "This is Elder Rao. He is speaker for one of the two clans not at war with us. Tell him what you told me."

The elder nomad cleared his throat. "Several nights ago," he began in a halting voice. "Seven families were killed while camped near different oases. Also every wild oasis has been poisoned. Many of my people died before we realized what had happened. From several fouled oases camel tracks led back to your towns."

Vilos nodded, seeing the picture. "We wouldn't poison oases. We're as dependent on them when traveling through the desert as your own people. The other nomads must know this, Elder."

"We held a gathering and some argued as you do, myself included. Others spoke angry words. They blamed your soldiers and said we should fight. There was great anger and little sense in these words. When we explained our positions the rash ones couldn't change their minds without looking weak. We held a vote. All but my clan and one other chose war."

"I thank you for the warning, Elder," Vilos said.

"That is all the help you will get. We will not fight our own people."

"If we can find a way to purify the oases, will your people end the war?" Vilos asked.

"I don't know, Sultan. Many have died and others will want revenge. Even if the oases are made safe, I can't say what my people will do."

"I understand. Is there some way I can contact you if I need to?"

Rao held out his arm and let loose a shrill whistle. A falcon descended from the sky and alighted on his arm.

"Tie a message to his talon and he will seek me." Rao urged the bird away and it flew up into one of the garden palms. "I must go. My clan grows restless."

"Thank you again, Elder. Tell your clan that they can have as much water as they can carry."

Rao bowed and shuffled toward the gate. Vilos and Yosef watched him until the gate shut.

"What do you think?" Vilos asked.

"There's magic in this, no doubt about it. Your friend the sorcerer, perhaps?"

"No perhaps about it. Who else could poison every oasis in the High Kingdom so quickly?"

"What are we going to do about it?" Yosef asked.

"We're going to have to fight. How many men can we muster?"

"Five thousand can march tomorrow if needs be, and I can call up another ten thousand reserves."

"Call up half. We'll send them out to reinforce the other towns. You and I will lead the regulars north to relieve the besieged towns."

"If the oases are all poisoned, the nomads won't be able to last long," Yosef said. "If they can hold out a few days dehydration will take its toll."

"We can't count on that. I'll bet they have a secret source of water besides the oases."

Yosef nodded. "I'll start calling up the reserves."

Yosef left and Vilos went to check on Abin's progress. The wizard sat hunched over his crystal ball when Vilos entered his tent. Vilos stood quietly and watched as Abin weaved from side to side. He knew better than to interrupt a wizard at work. A couple minutes passed before the wizard shuddered and sat up.

"What news?" Vilos asked.

Abin started then turned to face Vilos. "Both towns' garrisons are holding. That attack last month might have been a blessing in disguise. The soldiers were extra alert and they got the gates closed in a hurry. No deaths reported on our side, yet. I also sent a short message to all the other towns warning them to keep their gates closed and barred."

"Good, that's better news than I feared. Now I've got

another job for you. Someone has poisoned the wild oases. I want you to find a way to purify them."

Abin frowned. The thought of actual work probably didn't appeal to him. "What about messages?"

"Your apprentice can handle it, can't he?"

"Yes, probably, but..."

"But nothing," Vilos said. "Find a way to purify the oases, now."

Vilos turned and left before Abin could think up any more excuses. When Vilos reached the soldier's camp he bellowed, "Quartermaster!"

The quartermaster, a grizzled veteran that had served Vilos's father before him, appeared as if by magic. "You yelled?"

"Yes, how much water would we need for ten thousand men for five days?"

"Marching through the desert you'll need a gallon per day each so fifty thousand gallons should do it."

"Very well, take whatever men and material you need, but get that water ready to go in three days."

"Three days? Why can't we just take the usual two gallons per man and refill at the Twenty Mile Oasis?"

Vilos frowned and briefly explained the situation.

"Damn me. Who'd be fool enough to poison water in the desert?"

Vilos offered a humorless smile. "My guess would be the same fool that flattened half the palace. Get that water ready."

The quartermaster saluted. "Will do, Majesty."

Vilos left to the sound of orders being barked. If anyone could get the job done, his trusty quartermaster could.

Two days passed in a hurry. The standing army had mustered in the central plaza of the city. A small crowd had gathered to watch, mostly family and curious children. Vilos walked down the ranks. Each man had his armor and weapons polished and in good shape. The archers had their bows restrung and a full brace of arrows. As he passed by Vilos heard several men grumbling about standing around out in the sun. He forced himself not to smile. If the soldiers were complaining it meant things were right about where they were supposed to be.

As he continued down the ranks he noticed some of the men had gotten a little round in the middle. Yosef was right; the men really had gotten soft during his reign. A few hundred miles of marching in the desert would take care of that. Vilos finished his review feeling pretty good about their chances.

The reserves wouldn't be ready until tomorrow and then they'd march to war.

Vilos sighed. After the Crown War he'd hoped he'd never have to lead men into battle again. A fool's wish he knew.

He shook his head; wishing was a waste of time. The battle needed to be fought and he would fight it. He left the troops under the watchful eye of his officers and headed to the palace to check on Abin's progress. If his wizard could purify the oases perhaps some bloodshed could be avoided.

The moment he started away from the troops a score of the palace guard fell in place around him. Now that the stone soldiers had gone, they took their jobs much more seriously. The people made a path for the sultan and his guards. Anyone that didn't move fast enough got a prod from the butt of a spear. He'd have to say something about that. Vilos couldn't have his guards striking innocent people.

When they reached the palace Vilos dismissed the guards

and made straight toward Abin's tent. The closer he got the fewer people seemed to be around. A nasty odor filled the air, rather like the time all the camels got that intestinal disorder at the same time. By the time he reached the tent his eyes had started to water. Vilos poked his head inside and immediately pulled it back out. He staggered a step as the stink overwhelmed him.

Abin must have seen him because the wizard's bald head emerged a moment later. "I'll be right out, Majesty. I just have one experiment to finish."

Vilos took a couple more steps to get further away from the stench. That turned out to be a wise move as a few seconds later something exploded and black smoke billowed out the flap. Abin staggered out a moment later coughing and spitting.

"I'm not encouraged, wizard," Vilos said when Abin had caught his breath.

"Neither am I. Things could be worse though."

"Explain."

"I don't want to get your hopes up so let me first say that I can't neutralize the poison. Whoever cooked it up really knew their stuff."

"Tell me something I don't know."

Abin winced. "The base poison is from an Abyssal scorpion. The demonic origin is one reason I can't neutralize it. The poison has been magically altered to make it exceptionally deadly to humans."

"I thought you said there was some good news."

"No, I said it could be worse." Seeing Vilos scowl Abin hurried on. "For example the water is harmless to animals."

"At least we can water the camels. Anything else?"

"Just one thing: this time next year the water will be fine."

"Explain."

"The nature of the poison will cause it to break down in approximately one year."

"Why?"

Abin shrugged.

"Very well, any news from the north?"

"None, Majesty."

Vilos nodded and left the wizard to his stink. One year. Maybe he could make a bargain. Vilos wandered through the garden lost in thought. The area seemed deserted, perhaps thanks to Abin's exploding tent.

Vilos spotted the nomad elder's falcon and held up his arm. The bird glided down to him. He took it to his tent, gathering more than a few curious looks as he passed through the more populated areas of the garden.

His guards moved aside as he approached his tent. Once inside the falcon hopped off his arm and onto the back of his chair. He rubbed his arm where its talons had scratched him. Vilos sat down and wrote a brief note asking for a meeting to discuss a possible solution to the hostilities.

Vilos tied the note to the bird's leg and took it outside. He held up his arm. "Take this to your master."

The falcon leapt into the air.

CHAPTER 19

Daktari swore in a language that no longer existed and threw the last of Silvermane's books into a pile on the floor. For nearly a week he and Bane had done nothing but read everything in Silvermane's lighthouse. They had stripped the bookshelves of her study and still they found no trace of where the princess might be.

Daktari rose from the soft leather chair and heard his back snap as he straightened. He'd sat hunched over that last book for two hours. "Bane, we're leaving."

His homunculus glided down from the bookshelf where he'd been resting and landed on Daktari's shoulder. "Sorry, Master. I'd hoped for better luck."

"As did I. You ever have the overwhelming desire to smash something?"

"Whenever you do, Master. Like right now for example."

Daktari snapped his fingers and they were outside in the darkness facing the lighthouse. A quarter moon hung low in the sky.

He raised his hands and purple fire blazed around them.

A few feet away a huge pair of purple hands appeared and began to mirror his every motion.

He reached out toward the lighthouse and squeezed. Purple fingers sank into the stone.

With one great effort he wrenched the lighthouse free of its foundation and flung it over the cliff into the sea. It crashed into the rocks and shattered into a thousand pieces. Daktari sighed with a mixture of pleasure and disgust at his lack of control and let the hands fade. He took deep breaths, trying to get his strength back.

"Is it wise to waste your power like that, Master?" Bane asked.

"No."

Like any exercise, using huge amounts of his power left him tired and weak. The more massive the effort the more tired he felt. On the upside every effort also increased his power once he recovered.

"But I needed that, Bane. I needed to vent the rage. Now my mind is clear, for a little while at least. Let's go home. In the morning we'll visit Kent and put the last player on the field." Daktari snapped his fingers.

When they appeared in the cavern Daktari said, "Use the crystal ball and check on our agents' progress. I must rest." He staggered off to bed leaving Bane to his work.

Daktari collapsed onto the mattress. A week of using magic to keep his body constantly alert had taken its toll. He was asleep before his head hit the pillow.

It seemed no time had passed when Daktari found himself drifting through a dark void. There was no up or down, no sensation of any sort. Daktari had used spirit projection enough times to recognize that his spirit now wandered free of his body.

The question was why.

In the darkness time had no meaning. He tried to will his spirit back to his body with no success.

After an unknowable time he began streaking through the darkness. He fought the pull but seemed powerless to affect it. Soon he found himself floating before a huge black stone statue. All around him bursts of random light and magical energy exploded. Swirls of pure ether appeared and disappeared. The chaotic energy gave away his location.

The dark between solar systems. Out here, with no sentients to impose their will on it, the ether reverted to its true, chaotic nature.

So if that's where he was, then the statue had to be...

"Daktari!" A voice of infinite depth echoed all around.

Balthis.

He'd forgotten to raise the spirit wards before he went to sleep. The elder demon must have dragged Daktari's spirit here. "How much longer must I wait? The girl is ready."

"Not long, my lord," Daktari said. "There were some difficulties we didn't anticipate."

"I grow impatient, sorcerer. I have waited millennia to escape this prison."

"I know, lord. But let us not rush now that we are so close. You will walk free soon."

"Do not cross me, Daktari," Balthis thundered.

Daktari grabbed his head as lances of pain shot through it. When the ringing faded he said, "I have never broken a pact, Lord Balthis. I will see the ritual completed as we agreed, you may depend upon it."

"Well enough, Daktari." Calm settled over the demon as quick as rage. "Besides, what is time to one who is eternal?"

With a mental flick Balthis sent Daktari hurtling back the way he'd come. Daktari sat up in bed. By the nine, their meetings never failed to overwhelm him. The elder demon's presence was incredible.

Master? Are you all right?

I'm fine, Bane. What time is it?

The sun is up. Beyond that I couldn't say.

Very well, I'll join you in a moment.

Daktari sat on the edge of the bed collecting himself. If Bane had felt the psychic shock of his visit to Balthis, then it must have unnerved him more than he'd thought. Served him right for not putting the spirit wards up.

Daktari stood and stretched. His muscles ached. He must have clenched up in his sleep.

He stretched the kinks out as he walked between the bedroom and the work area. Bane flew over and landed on his shoulder as soon as he entered the cavern. Like a cat seeking reassurance, Bane rubbed his head against his master's cheek. Daktari rubbed between Bane's wings until he started to trill.

When he stopped Bane asked, "Are you all right?"

"Yes, though more through luck than anything." Daktari related the details of his conversation with Balthis.

"We must make haste, Master."

"Yes, Bane, but we mustn't rush so that we make a fatal mistake. When the time comes, we may only get one chance to grab the princess. We must not fail."

"We won't, Master."

Daktari smiled and scratched Bane again. "Of course not. Now, tell me how the others are doing."

"I contacted Zin," Bane said. "Nord has defeated one of his two main rivals. Zin says he used Heat's Bane to good effect."

"Excellent, I had hoped he'd get a chance to practice. Continue."

"The nomads have besieged two northern towns. They've

done little damage so far. Vilos has called up the army and plans to march north."

Daktari nodded. "And the priests?"

"They reacted as planned to the dream you sent, but their champion failed."

"Good, that should build up a large chunk of resentment. What about Kent?"

"When I checked he was alone in his office."

"Well done, Bane. I'm going to pay Kent a visit. You get some rest."

Bane flew off to find a niche somewhere to sleep. Daktari couldn't remember how many times he'd offered to make a little bed for his homunculus. Bane always said he preferred to sleep in the shadows among the stalactites. Daktari shrugged and went to gather his golems.

⟶⚹

Daktari appeared in Kent's office. He'd been forced to arrive elsewhere in the city then make a second, line of sight teleport into the office. The man sat behind his desk reading some papers. He must have sensed something because he looked up an instant after Daktari appeared.

He smiled and Kent went pale. It seemed he knew with whom he dealt. Good, that would make things easier.

"You know me," Daktari said.

Kent nodded. "You destroyed the White Palace."

"Hardly destroyed. I've come to make you an offer, your brother's stone soldiers in exchange for Princess Shara."

"I don't have the princess," Kent stammered.

Daktari's smile broadened. The fool was shaking in his boots. "I'm aware of that. What you do have is resources. Use them. Find the girl."

"If I find her, I get to keep the golems?"

"Yes. In fact, you can have them now. Use them however you like. I warn you though, they will obey no order to harm me or help Vilos. Do you agree?"

Kent nodded, apparently not trusting himself to speak.

"Good." Daktari snapped his fingers. "You will find the golems in your warehouse. When you find the girl tell one of the golems. Good day."

Daktari wrapped a shield of invisibility around himself. It would appear to Kent that he had teleported away. He glided to the corner of the room. Now he'd see what Kent really planned to do. The former prince showed some patience. Daktari guessed he waited fifteen minutes before calling a wizard and a stunning woman into the room.

"He's gone," Kent said. "The meeting went as expected."

The wizard looked nervous. He cast a spell meant to detect magical eavesdropping. Daktari smiled. That spell would ignore him as he stood right in the room.

When he finished the spell he relaxed. "All clear," he said.

Kent said, "The sorcerer offered me the golems just as Vilos said he would."

Daktari's smile vanished. So, Kent had spoken to his brother. That was a surprise, considering their past.

"I agreed to look for Shara in exchange since we're doing that anyway," Kent said. "As for the golems, we can use them to guard our caravans but not help Vilos. With the nomads on the rampage they should come in handy. Yaway, make certain each caravan has three golems assigned to it."

The woman nodded and walked out.

"I'm not certain you understand the danger you face," the wizard said.

"Enough, Raven," Kent said. "I understand the risks. Your nagging won't change my mind."

Raven nodded. "As you wish. Just try not to get the rest of us killed along with you." The wizard left Kent alone in his office.

It appeared that Kent's pet wizard wasn't as keen on his plans as he might be. That could be useful. Perhaps a conversation with this Raven character would prove fruitful. Daktari teleported away with a thought, already weaving another layer into his plot.

CHAPTER 20

Four days had passed since the battle in the forest and Robert said they were nearing the edge of the Vale. Shara wouldn't be sad to leave the trees behind. While she did enjoy listening to the birds, the many shadows made her feel surrounded. After living in the desert all her life, being unable to see more than fifty feet ahead set her teeth on edge.

On the plus side, a week of walking nonstop for ten hours a day had strengthened her muscles. She now only ached a little when they stopped each night. Her shoes and dress were little more than rags and she feared they might simply fall off, leaving her naked and barefoot.

As usual, this morning found her trudging along behind the mute giant, Morden. He held the rope and she followed like a puppy. Rather undignified for a princess, but no one seemed to care.

"Hey, kid." Robert came walking back toward her. He seemed to be in a better mood than usual.

"You look happy."

"I am. This afternoon we reach Reaper's Crossing."

"Reaper's Crossing?"

"It's a little town on the edge of the Vale. All the bandit groups go there to sell plunder and buy supplies. It's neutral ground, so we shouldn't have to worry. It's also where we planned to sell you before we got ambitious."

"Wonderful," Shara said, visions of a hot bath and decent food dancing through her head. "Civilization at last."

"It might be a stretch to call Reaper's Crossing civilization. It's more like a suburb of hell. On the plus side, they have more whorehouses per acre than any town I've visited."

"How would you know that?" Shara asked, not certain she wanted to know.

Robert grinned and she felt certain she didn't want to know. "Before I met Blade, I used to take a census at every town I passed through. Father was never thrilled with my habits."

"I can imagine," Shara said.

"Don't misunderstand. It wasn't the whoring that bothered him. Father liked the ladies himself. He just thought I should be more subtle. I often thought my mother was a working girl. I try and imagine my father's reaction when he came back to see her after a year at sea and she showed me to him."

Surprised, Shara asked, "Doesn't it bother you that your mother might have been a whore?"

Robert shrugged then laughed. "Plenty of things in this life you can control, kid. Who your parents are isn't one of them. Anyway, what I came to tell you was that when we get to Reaper's Crossing stay close to one of us. We'll only be staying a day or two and we wouldn't want the locals getting any ideas."

"This town doesn't sound like the sort of place a lady should go unescorted anyway."

He laughed again. "Can't get anything past you, Princess."

They left the forest behind around noon. The trees gradually gave way to bushes, and then finally they came to an open field. A well-worn path ran through it. Calling it a road would have been too generous. It was just a place where the high grass had been trod down and turned to mud that later hardened to dirt. It seemed to extend a good way in both directions.

They turned east and picked up the pace. Everyone seemed anxious to get a hot meal. Shara's stomach grumbled in agreement.

They hadn't gone far when Shara smelled smoke. At the bottom of a steep incline sat a small town. There were perhaps a hundred buildings divided by three streets. A three-foot wall of spikes surrounded the town except for an opening at each end of the main road. A bar at each opening prevented passage. Three people stood around leaning on spears; none of them looked the least interested in guarding the gate. Robert must have been exaggerating when described the place as a suburb of hell. It didn't look so bad to her.

They walked down the hill heading straight for the gate. The whole group paused about twenty paces from the guards. Shara worked her way toward the front of the crowd just in time to see Robert heading over to the gate alone.

"What's going on?" she asked no one in particular. The only reply she got was a shrug from Morden.

She watched as Robert talked with one of the guards who trotted off a moment later. After a short wait he returned with another man dressed in slightly less horrible leather armor and armed with a sword.

Robert spoke to the new man for a minute then he waved them over. As soon as they arrived the guards raised the bar and everyone walked through. Robert and the newcomer shook hands and they left the gate behind.

Now that she got closer, Reaper's Crossing didn't look quite as bad. The muddy streets were the worst part, the buildings looked okay. Most were two stories and sported balconies. The sole purpose of those balconies seemed to be to give half-naked women a place to get a man's attention. The whores whistled and waved as their little procession passed. The men waved back and drooled.

Mud sucked at Shara's shoes as they walked down the street toward the center of town, some of it finding splits in the seams and oozing between her toes. She grimaced but kept quiet. No one was going to care about her muddy toes.

They entered an open-air market like the bazaars of the High Kingdom. Shara sighed and closed her eyes. If the air had been hotter and dryer, she could almost be standing in the market at Sultan's Oasis.

"Kind of like home, hey kid?"

Robert's voice shook her out of her reverie. She nodded. "What was the deal at the gate?"

"A fee is required to enter the town. They collect it to pay for the guards. That guy I talked to, he's the head guard. He owed me a favor so we got in free."

"What did you do for him?" she asked.

"Last time we were in town he got a little over friendly with Blade. I convinced her not to cut his throat."

"Nice of you."

"I thought so. Besides, it's nice to have people owe you. I collect favors like a miser collects gold."

"So what now? Are we just going to wander around all day?"

Robert grinned. "You got a lot of lip for a prisoner."

She shrugged. "You shouldn't have told me how valuable I was. So what are we going to do?"

"You got nerve, kid. I like that." He wandered off without telling her anything.

They left the market behind and finally stopped at a rundown three-story building. Outside hung a placard with a sickle carved in it. Underneath it said Final Rest Inn.

Inside, the common room was ill lit and empty. A dozen tables and about three times as many chairs seemed scattered around the room at random. Shara and the others clustered around a pair of tables in the back corner.

They had just gotten seated when a humpbacked old man with a cockeyed smile came hobbling out from the kitchen. He wore a grease-spattered apron and smelled like roasting meat.

"Hey, Grin," Robert said.

"What can I get you?" Grin asked.

"A bowl of whatever you have on the fire and beer, old man." Shale seemed to be in a worse mood than usual.

"Water for me, please," Shara said.

"Wine for the lady," Robert said.

Shara glanced at him but before she could say anything Blade said, "Two wines."

Shara leaned over to Robert and whispered, "I don't want wine."

"Unless you want the worst case of the watery shits you ever had, I recommend you avoid the water here."

Shara swallowed. She didn't know what the watery shits were but they sounded awful. "Wine will be fine."

The old man hobbled away.

"Listen up," Shale said. "I don't want to spend long in town. Bobby will fence our merchandise and buy supplies then we're out of here. Two days, tops. This is going to be our last brush with civilization for a while, so I suggest the rest of you enjoy it."

Everybody smiled.

"One last thing," Shale said. "I don't want to leave the same way we did last time." He glared at one of the men Shara didn't know.

The man got a pained expression, "I didn't know she was married, Shale, honest."

Grin came hobbling back with a tray so laden with steaming bowls, mugs, and small round loaves of bread it was all he could do to carry it.

"Just try not to make too much of a scene, all right?" Shale asked.

They all nodded.

After the meal the group broke up. Everyone but Blade, Scratch, and Robert left the inn. Scratch walked over to the cold fireplace and pointed. A roaring fire sprang up. He pulled over a chair and sat down with his cat in his lap.

"Can someone take these ropes off? My wrists are getting raw."

"Hey, Scratch," Robert said.

The wizard glanced over. "Yes?"

"I want to take her ropes off. You got something to keep her from wandering off?"

"I can mark her with a spell that will allow me to locate her or cause great pain. How's that?"

Robert glanced at Blade who nodded. "Sounds good."

Scratch got up and walked over to her. He traced a rune in front of her face. Each gesture caused a new line to glow in the air. When he finished he held his hand palm out and the rune struck her in the forehead. She flinched more from surprise than anything. She couldn't feel anything different.

"That's it?" Robert asked.

"That's it." Scratch returned to his seat by the fire.

Shara held out her hands and Robert untied them. "Well,

kid, I got some work to do, so I'll leave you in Blade's hands." He kissed Blade goodbye and left.

Shara massaged her wrists where the rope had rubbed them red. With nothing to do she found a seat to her liking and sat down to wait. She hadn't been there long when Blade sauntered over and sat down across from her.

"Bobby's become quite fond of you," she said.

Uh-oh. Hopefully she's not the jealous type.

Her thoughts must have shown because Blade laughed and said, "Not that way. More like a little sister."

"Oh, I'm flattered, I guess."

"He says you've got nerve. I respect that."

Blade seemed sincere. Shara decided to press her luck. "How does a beautiful woman like you become an outlaw?"

Blade leaned back and put her feet up on the table. "I was born to it, kid. My father led a crew like this. My mother was an archer in the group. I was raised around men like Shale and worse. I started learning the sword when I was four. I killed a man when I was ten."

"Heaven's mercy." Shara couldn't imagine. When she was ten all she wanted was to talk the cook out of some extra baklava.

"Don't feel too bad. The guy was trying to rape me at the time. I cut his dick off, dried it, and wore it on a thong around my neck. The others got the idea. Kind of killed my faith in men though."

"What about Robert?"

Blade sighed and Shara thought she saw the ghost of a smile playing around the woman's lips. "What about Robert? Bobby is unique. We met right here, in this room. He was on the run from some nobles and attached himself to me. Turned out he's very good at fencing things. We made a lot more gold when he took over the job. I don't have much of a knack for it."

"He doesn't seem suited to this sort of life," Shara said.

Blade smiled for real. "He isn't. Bobby hates living like this. He never complains but I can see it in his eyes. He isn't ruthless enough for the work. He tries, capturing you for example. Still, anyone else would have knocked you over the head and dragged you back to camp. What's Bobby do? He talks you into coming willingly. I don't think the man has a truly vicious bone in his body."

Shara relaxed a little. It seemed her captors weren't as bad as she thought. "Robert told me you saved him. He said before he met you he didn't care if he lived or died."

"That's partly true. What he didn't mention was that I needed him as much as he needed me. I needed someone I could trust. Being on guard all the time was wearing me out. Each of us gave the other what they needed. We couldn't have timed it better if we'd planned that meeting."

"Why are you telling me all this, Blade?"

"It's Bobby's fault. He hasn't stopped yammering about what a nice kid you are. I decided to see for myself. I'll be damned, but he's right."

"So why not let me go?"

Blade laughed. "You ain't that nice, kid. Besides, even if I wanted to I wouldn't be doing you much of a favor. There's bound to be plenty of others looking for you. Some worse than us."

Their conversation ceased when Robert came flying through the front door. He headed straight for Blade. "We've got trouble."

Blade frowned. "We've been here for an hour, how much trouble could we be in? Even those idiots couldn't get into a mess this fast."

"I spotted a hunter in the market."

Blade went dead serious. "You sure?"

"I saw his wolf medallion."

"What rank?" Blade asked.

"Silver."

"Do you think he's after the girl?"

"I doubt it. No one knew she'd be here. Still, if he knows about the bounty and sees her…"

"Good point. He won't try anything in town, though, not after last time." Blade stood up. "Time to go upstairs, kid."

"I've got some more stuff to get rid of." Robert turned toward the door. "I won't be long."

"Be careful, Bobby," Blade said.

He grinned and took his leave.

Blade led Shara upstairs. They were sharing a room with Robert and Scratch. When they were inside and had the door locked behind them Shara asked, "What was that all about?"

"Bobby spotted a bounty hunter."

"After me?" Shara shivered. Would everyone in the world be after her?

"Not likely. Don't forget the rest of us have bounties on our heads too."

Shara relaxed again. "Will Robert be all right?"

"Yeah, the hunter won't try anything in town."

"You said that before. Why not?"

Blade unbuckled her sword belt and lay down on the bed. "Last time a hunter tried to grab someone in town he was lynched."

"Lynched?"

"Everybody in town got together and subdued the hunter. They took him outside the wall and tied him down. When he woke up they split his belly open. The guy lived a day and a half. The crows started feeding way before that."

Shara shuddered. "Why did they do that?"

"The various groups of bandits may not agree on much, but we all agree that anything resembling the law is unwelcome."

Shara nodded, trying to absorb the information. While she sat thinking someone knocked. First three, then a pause. Two. One.

Blade sat up as Robert entered. "Hello, ladies."

"Bobby. What news?"

Robert went over and sat on the edge of the bed. "Could be worse. Someone stuck a knife in the hunter. Guards were dragging him out of the market when I left."

Blade slid over closer to Robert. "I guess someone decided not to wait for him to misbehave."

"Looks like. On the down side, I didn't get as much for our stuff as I'd hoped. After I buy supplies tomorrow, we'll be just about broke." Robert dropped his arm around Blade.

"We'll just have to build on it as we travel." They started kissing.

Robert paused for a moment. "Why don't you go keep Scratch company. You should be safe enough with the hunter dead."

She didn't have to be asked twice. Before Shara had left the room Robert and Blade had forgotten all about her.

CHAPTER 21

The hot season was having a last hurrah and there wasn't a cloud in the sky to help. Vilos and his men marched towards Dahan's Oasis, the first town north of Sultan's Oasis. His army stretched a quarter mile down the dirt road. Vilos still wasn't sure how his quartermaster had managed it, but in the middle of the column were a dozen wagons filled with huge water barrels. Actually, only eight were filled, the other four had been drained already. They were three days out from the capital and two more from the oasis.

The water should last.

A small cloud of dust was approaching from ahead of the army. "Cavalry, defensive formation."

The camel riders drew their swords and started to form a semicircle in front of the column. Before they reached their positions Vilos saw the approaching riders wore his white and gold uniforms.

"It's only the scouts returning, everyone back in line. Whoever's next on scout detail get up here."

Six riders detached from the main body of cavalry and rode up to Vilos. They showed little enthusiasm. Considering the heat Vilos didn't blame them.

The returning scouts raised their hands palms out to show all was clear. Their replacements rode out past them. The returning scouts stopped beside Vilos and saluted.

"What news?" Vilos asked.

"We reached the first poisoned oasis. All appeared well. A flock of blue herons drank at the water's edge. They seemed fine."

"The poison only affects people," Vilos said.

"Why?" the scout asked.

Vilos massaged his temples. He felt a headache coming on. "That's a good question, son. Thing is, the last time I saw the guy that poisoned the oases, he was busy trying to knock my house down around my ears. The whole poisoning thing must have slipped his mind. Tell you what. You see him before I do, go ahead and ask him. If you live, be sure and tell me what he said."

The young man looked sheepish. "Dumb question, Majesty?"

"You think?"

"Obviously not very well."

Vilos laughed. You had to like a kid that could make a joke at his own expense. He'd have to remember to keep an eye on that one. "Go get some water." Louder he said, "Let's move out."

The head of the column reached the oasis in about an hour. The water looked as blue and pure as any he'd ever seen. When Vilos mentioned the fact to Abin the wizard pointed out that it would be difficult to trick someone into drinking it if it looked green and cloudy.

Feeling as foolish as the scout Vilos led his camel over to

drink. When the animal had had its fill he said, "I'm going to ride ahead. Make sure everyone rests and drinks some water."

"Don't go too far, Majesty," Abin said.

Yes, Mother.

Out loud he said, "Don't worry. I just want to get to the top of that dune so I can see a ways."

Vilos remounted and kicked his camel into motion. It took only a few minutes to reach the top of the dune. The desert seemed to stretch forever. He couldn't see any signs of nomad activity.

Good.

They could drop off two hundred reservists at Dahan ahead of any trouble.

Vilos looked up into the clear blue sky. Rain should be coming soon. A few more weeks and the rainy season would begin. Granted it would only last a couple weeks, but still, it would be nice.

High above a bird circled. At first he thought vulture, but they usually traveled in groups. As the bird flew lower Vilos decided it was a falcon. The bird shrieked and swooped down. Vilos raised his hand and the bird landed on his wrist. Lucky Vilos always wore leather riding gloves.

A small scroll was tied to the bird's leg. "I thought you looked familiar."

What could the elder want so soon? Vilos untied the scroll and the falcon immediately leapt into the air. It seemed no reply was required. Vilos unrolled the scroll.

Sultan,

I have gathered all the clan leaders willing to listen to you. We will wait for you at the wild oasis between Dahan's Oasis and Silla's Oasis. We will remain at the oasis for one week after my messenger returns. Bring only one man with you.

Rao.

The old man must have been more convincing than Vilos had hoped. He had a week to reach the meeting. It would take another day and a half to reach Dahan's Oasis. Two more days after that should get him to the wild oasis. No problem.

CHAPTER 22

Daktari stood over his crystal ball. He watched as the falcon landed on Vilos's arm and he removed the scroll. Daktari adjusted the view in the ball so he could read over the sultan's shoulder. It seemed the fool still sought peace. Laudable, but peace wouldn't help accomplish his goals.

That old nomad was being too helpful. Time to remove him from the picture.

Daktari made a pass in front of the ball. The image shifted to the oasis where the clan leaders waited. There were five plus the old man. Each leader had brought only a single bodyguard.

Trusting fools. Though even a hundred guards each wouldn't make a difference.

Daktari focused on the spot, forcing the ether to concentrate enough to mark it and allow him to teleport safely. he passed his hand over the ball again and the image vanished. "Ulibo."

"Master?" The shadow demon appeared beside the sorcerer.

"We have work to do."

"I'm ready, Master."

Daktari wished he could say the same, but this had to happen for his plan to have a chance of working. He snapped his fingers and they vanished into the ether.

They emerged an instant later in the midst of the nomads. "Slay them all but leave a camel."

Ulibo didn't need to be told twice.

The demon became a mass of whirling claws.

He tore into the guards before they could draw their weapons.

Blood and flesh flew.

The shadow demon ripped men apart like a man might a piece of vellum.

As Daktari watched the carnage, a sick feeling twisting his insides, he sensed someone sneaking up on him.

A brave fool, how unfortunate.

The nomad lunged and struck a barrier of impenetrable energy. A blast of power hammered the fool to the ground and paralyzed him from the neck down.

Ulibo made short work of the remaining nomads before turning on the one Daktari had paralyzed. The sorcerer held up a hand to forestall the slaughter.

"I thought you wanted them all dead," Ulibo growled. The demon didn't like leaving anyone alive.

Daktari frowned. Ulibo was as loyal and valuable a servant as he had, but it was still a demon. Perhaps it needed a reminder of who was master.

The sorcerer clenched his fist and shadow fire swirled around it. Ulibo shrunk away. It had tasted the shadow flames before.

"Forgive me, Master. The bloodlust drives me mad."

Daktari looked around the oasis. Bits of meat lay scattered

around. The sand looked like the floor of a butcher shop. Ulibo had remembered to spare one camel, so Daktari decided to let his transgression pass.

He snuffed out the shadow fire. "Return to the cavern. Your work here is finished."

The demon seemed inclined to argue for a moment but self-preservation got the best of it. Ulibo vanished into the shadows of the palms surrounding the oasis.

With his overeager servant out of the way, Daktari turned to examine his prisoner. With a gesture the sorcerer caused the nomad to float up to eye level. So Vilos's friend Rao had survived.

Perfect. A point needed to be made and this one was the ideal person to make it.

"What will you do with me, sorcerer?" Rao asked.

Daktari ignored the old man and began to chant an ancient and powerful spell. All of Rao's knowledge and memories began to fill Daktari's mind. His body shrank and wrinkled as he took on the old man's form. In moments all that remained of the nomad was a dried husk.

Daktari grimaced at his physical weakness. That was the thing he hated most about the transference spell. The sooner he got this done, the better. He whispered a second spell, a present for Vilos when he arrived.

Now for the next step of his preparation. He found one of the more intact bodies and transformed it into a likeness of Rao before marking it with a special rune.

A shadow passed over Daktari as he let Rao's remains fall to the ground. He glanced up and spotted the falcon that had brought Vilos his message. If the falcon had seen the attack, a skilled wizard could draw the information from the animal's mind.

Daktari couldn't allow that.

He pointed at the bird and it exploded in a burst of feathers.

Satisfied that all witnesses had been taken care of, Daktari hobbled over to the surviving camel. It shied away from him as if sensing that something wasn't right.

Daktari had no patience for the beast. He reached out with a thought and crushed the animal's will. A mental command compelled the now-docile camel to kneel. He clambered aboard and urged it northeast. Rao's memories indicated that the other nomads awaited them about a day's ride away.

As Daktari bounced along on the back of the camel it occurred to him that he hadn't actually traveled in such a mundane fashion in years. He'd either flown or teleported for so long that the rolling gait of the camel felt quite relaxing. He almost dozed off but caught himself.

The old man's body he'd borrowed wanted to sleep. Out in the desert with no wards to protect his sleeping mind he'd be almost guaranteed a trip to visit Balthis and Daktari had no desire to see the imprisoned demon again.

He drew ether through his body, infusing his feeble form with energy. All urge to sleep vanished. That should hold him for the day or so he needed to get the war going in earnest.

He rode through the rest of the day mentally scanning for any danger.

The sun had just dipped below the horizon when he sensed the presence of a large group of people. That had to be the main nomad camp. Daktari muttered a spell that caused a number of cuts and bruises to appear on his borrowed body. When he was almost to the camp he slouched over the neck of his camel like a wounded man.

It didn't take long for several warriors to ride out to meet him. He sensed their presence even though he kept his head down and moaned in pain. The two men must have recognized him because gentle hands reached out to steady him.

"What happened, Elder?" one asked.

"Ambush," Daktari said, his voice barely audible. "They snuck up on us and attacked. The guards didn't stand a chance. Killed everyone. I just managed to escape." Daktari feigned unconsciousness. He heard them muttering to themselves about calling a meeting.

When he decided to open his eyes he found himself in a tent lying on a pile of cushions. Worried faces looked down at him.

"How long?" he asked.

One of the men Rao recognized as a war leader said, "Only minutes, Elder. Please tell us what happened."

"Water," Daktari rasped.

A cup of warm water was pressed to his lips. It tasted fresh. Apparently the nomads had a source of water beyond the oases. Good, they could fight all the longer.

"The sultan attacked us. Our guards were killed before they could give a warning. The cavalry hit us before anyone knew what was happening. I managed to hide under the body of Ubo. When they left, I crawled out and found a camel. I knew..." Daktari faked a coughing fit. "I knew I had to warn you. I was a fool to trust the sultan."

He let his head loll over and he put the thought that he had died into each of their minds.

It seemed they wanted to believe it because they immediately turned away to start planning the next attack. When they weren't paying attention Daktari cast a shift spell, swapping places with the body he'd prepared earlier. That would give the nomads a body to burn while they planned their revenge.

Daktari teleported away from the oasis.

As soon as he appeared in the cavern he let the old man's form fade away.

Bane fluttered down and landed on his shoulder. "Report."

"Nord marches on the last major noble. Vilos arrived at the walled town an hour ago. The wards surrounding Kent have strengthened so I can't watch him anymore."

"I'll deal with Kent's wizard later tonight. Everything else seems on schedule. Did Ulibo return?"

"Yes, Master. He's been sulking."

Daktari went over to his crystal ball which floated a couple inches above its iron holder. He pictured Kent in his mind and sent his will into the ball. As his consciousness approached where he sensed Kent to be, a swirling wall of mist filled the ball. Daktari tried to drive a mental wedge through the mist and failed.

"See?" Bane said.

Daktari shushed Bane and tried a different tactic. Instead of trying to plow through the mists he brushed them away a little at a time. After a few minutes' work he found Kent bent over his desk writing something.

Daktari gave Bane a smug look.

"Show-off," Bane said.

Daktari grinned and rubbed him between the wings.

Content that the technique worked, he turned his attention to the wizard. Even denser black fog filled the ball. That was all the evidence he needed to tell him the wizard was at the warehouse.

"Ulibo." The shadow demon appeared beside him. "I'm going to visit Kent's wizard. Want to come?"

"Can I kill him?" Ulibo asked.

"No, but you can help me scare the hell out of him." Daktari leaned over and whispered to the demon.

A slow smile spread across Ulibo's face. "I will come."

"Excellent." Daktari wrapped a shield of invisibility around himself and snapped his fingers.

They appeared a moment later in the dark warehouse. No workers were around at this unholy hour. Daktari sensed the wizard's presence in the ether and headed straight toward it.

They weaved their way through piles of merchandise silent as death. Daktari smiled when he saw one of his stone soldiers guarding the wizard's door. He waved it aside and the golem obediently stepped away.

Daktari passed an invisible hand before his eyes. A crude lightning ward crackled across the door. He negated it with a gesture. The door opened, creaking like an old man's knees. The wizard lay sound asleep on a simple cot in the far corner of the room.

Perfect.

At Daktari's signal Ulibo took the form of a huge black mastiff. The demon stood six inches from the wizard's face. Daktari wove a silence spell around the room then clapped his hands.

The wizard opened his eyes and stared into Ulibo's snarling muzzle. Daktari laughed and lowered his invisibility shield. All the blood drained from the wizard's face and he screamed.

Daktari waited until he had screamed himself hoarse then said, "Hello, Raven isn't it?"

Raven turned away from Ulibo. Daktari thought for a moment he might scream again but he mastered himself before it could escape. "You. You're, you're, you're…"

"Yes, I am." Daktari cut him off before the stammering got on his nerves. "You know why I'm here."

"I warned him not to play games with you. I tried to tell him."

"I believe your exact words were, 'Try not to get the rest of us killed too.'"

"How? How could you know that? I checked for eavesdroppers." Raven shook like a fever victim.

Daktari smiled. "You checked for outside listeners. I was standing in the corner of the room."

If it were possible, Daktari thought the dark-skinned little man would have turned white.

Raven was too unnerved to speak so Daktari continued, "I don't like being betrayed. As I see it, I have two choices. I can either let the shadow demon rip you apart as a message to anyone that would betray me." Raven swallowed as Ulibo bared its fangs and crouched like it planned to spring. "As an alternative, I would feel much better if I had someone keeping an eye on my erstwhile betrayer, someone who could let me know when he found the girl."

"Did you have someone in mind?" Raven managed to stammer out.

"What an astute fellow." Daktari reached into his robe and pulled out a small silver ring. He tossed it to Raven. "Put that on."

Raven caught the ring but hesitated. "I'm not certain I should."

Ulibo snarled and snapped at his face.

"Let me put this in the starkest manner I can," Daktari said. "Are you willing to die for a girl you've never met?"

Still Raven hesitated.

"If you prefer to be eaten alive, that's fine with me." Daktari raised his hand to give the attack order.

Raven slipped the ring on. "I accept," he said. "What must I do?"

"Nothing, until the girl is found. If Kent's agents locate her, you need only picture me in your mind. I will make contact with you and you can tell me where she is. I'll handle everything from there. The ring will vanish and you'll be free to do what you wish."

"That's it?" Raven asked. He'd managed to get his shaking under control.

Daktari nodded. "A small price to pay for your life, no?"

"Yes." Raven stared at the silver ring.

Daktari turned to go but paused by the door. "You should know that ring stores a nasty magical disease. If you get a jolt of conscience after I go, any mention of our arrangement will trigger the spell. That disease will kill you in such a slow and excruciating manner you'll wish you'd been eaten."

Daktari and Ulibo vanished leaving Raven alone to think.

CHAPTER 23

Prince Nord rode at the head of the White Tigers. They traveled through a flat plain along the main caravan road that bisected the Broken Kingdom from east to west. Six days ago they left Duke Aaron's castle to assault the keep of Duke Benwa, the only remaining noble of any power.

So far the traveling had been easy. No commander would be foolish enough to set an ambush in such open country. Tomorrow they would reach a thick patch of forest. If trouble awaited them, Nord figured that was where it would start.

Arkon rode beside Nord, scanning for potential danger. "What do we know about Benwa?" Nord asked.

"As far as defenses and fortifications go, his castle is much smaller than Aaron's. I've also never heard of him having much in the way of soldiers, just archers and a few infantrymen."

"That's it? Sounds too easy."

"Does it? In truth, Benwa himself is more than enough to handle most invaders. He's a very powerful wizard, a chaos mage, from the rumors I've heard."

"Chaos mage?" Nord said. "That's a new one to me. What exactly is chaos magic?"

"What we call magic is just the manifestation of a vast energy source called the ether. The ether is pure chaotic energy. Even without wizards it affects things at random," Arkon began. "A wizard seeks to impose order on a minute portion of that energy. The vast majority of wizards try to eliminate all potential random outcomes for a spell. When dealing with power as great as the ether, random occurrences can be lethal. Chaos mages are a splinter group that seeks to increase their power by taking advantage of, rather than suppressing, the ether's natural chaos."

Totally confused Nord said, "Huh?"

Arkon thought for a second then said, "Try this. If I wanted to destroy something, I might carefully weave energy into the precise effect I wanted, say a fireball. A chaos mage would just rip a chunk of energy from the ether and weave the desired result into it: the destruction of a particular object. He might get the fireball I so painstaking created or he might get something else. The chaos mage hopes for a more powerful effect than what he might get from a more traditional spell."

"So basically they're just lazier than the average wizard," Nord said.

"Some think so. If you ask me, I think they're insane. Lucky for the rest of us chaos mages tend to have short careers."

"Why?"

"Usually they blow themselves up."

Nord grunted. "You could say that about most wizards."

"True," Arkon said, "but chaos mages tend to die even more often than average."

"Maybe Benwa will blow himself up before we arrive," Nord said. "That would save us all kinds of time."

"Don't count on it," Arkon said. "Duke Benwa is older than you. If he hasn't blown himself up by now, I don't think it very probable he will any time soon."

They rode through that day and the next with no sign of danger, and no ambush was sprung upon entering the forest.

Now, the morning of the third day, they had only a few miles to go before reaching Benwa's keep.

"Why don't they do something?" Nord grumbled under his breath.

"Did you say something, lord?" Arkon asked.

"We've been riding through Benwa's land for a day and a half. Why hasn't he tried something, anything? I feel more nervous than a long-tailed cat in a room full of rocking chairs."

"Another of your charming northern expressions?"

Nord smiled to himself. "That was one of Father's favorites."

He sighed. Nord missed his father. Even though the old sultan had chosen his brother to succeed him, Nord still loved the old man.

He'd been close to his father, perhaps closer than either of his brothers. That made his decision to let Vilos take his place all the more painful. Nord felt certain his brother had poisoned his father against him. Once he finished his business here, Vilos would pay.

Arkon slapped his shoulder. "Nord, company."

Nord looked in the direction Arkon indicated. Sure enough four horsemen were riding toward them. Nord noted with some surprise that the lead rider carried a white flag.

"Looks like they want to talk," Arkon said, mirroring his own thoughts.

"What do you think? You sense any magic out there?"

Arkon's eyes narrowed as he focused on the approaching

riders. After a moment's study he said, "Nothing. I can't sense anything."

"No magic. What could they be up to?"

"Maybe they really do just want to talk," Arkon said.

"Assuming they didn't come out here to commit suicide, that's the only course that makes sense." The riders had stopped about two hundred yards away. "Probably shouldn't keep them waiting. Cavalry Unit One, with me."

Nord, Arkon, and twenty heavily armed men rode out to greet the messengers. As they approached Nord noticed that none of the messengers had any weapons and two were women. Nord and his men stopped about twenty feet away from the strange group.

The two women rode forward. They were a study in contrasts. The one on the left was tall and thin to the point of emaciation. She had hair as black as a tax collector's heart and eyes so pale they seemed to have no color at all. The other woman was shorter, had blond hair, and the sort of curves Nord could appreciate after almost two weeks in the saddle.

"Greetings, Prince Nord. We bring a message from Lord Benwa," the skinny one said.

Nord dragged his eyes away from the blond's curves and faced her companion. "Well, let's hear it. I'll warn you up front if this is one of those 'turn around or else' speeches you can save your breath because I'm not turning around."

The blond started giggling which created a jiggling distraction. Her companion cleared her throat, silencing her jolly companion. "Our mission is quite the opposite, Prince Nord. We have come to invite you to join our lord for his evening meal. Lord Benwa wishes to discuss your plans as the new ruler of the Broken Kingdom."

Nord and Arkon exchanged a look.

The skinny one noticed and said, "Had we wished you harm you wouldn't be sitting there wondering, you'd be rotting in a shallow grave."

Nord snorted. "The day two little girls like you can hurt me is the day I give up soldiering."

The skinny one's pale face turned red and she ground her teeth. "I'll show you just how dangerous a little girl can be."

She pointed at a clump of white birch and spat three harsh syllables. The trees rotted to the ground in an instant, leaving nothing but black scars in the earth. Even the roots were devoured by the spell.

"My turn, Skull?" the blond asked.

"Very well, Giggles, if you must."

Giggles smiled and spat toward a large pine. The glob of phlegm shot through the air with much more force than the little woman could have managed without magic. When it struck the tree it slithered up the trunk, coating the whole thing in clear liquid.

Giggles snapped her fingers. The ooze squeezed until the tree exploded, showering them splinters.

"Disgusting," Skull said.

Giggles stuck her tongue out at her companion.

Skull turned back to Nord. "As you can see, we are also Lord Benwa's apprentices. I have no idea why our lord wishes to yield to a weakling like you, but he does. What message should I take?"

"Tell him I'd be delighted to join him for dinner," Nord said.

Skull nodded. "Let's go."

She and Giggles turned their horses around to rejoin their escorts, though judging by the girls' power he figured the men were just for show. The four of them rode away leaving Nord and Arkon behind.

"No magic, huh?" Nord said. "What do you make of their invitation?"

"I think chaos mages are about as stable as active volcanoes and twice as dangerous," Arkon said. "Those girls had a point though. If Benwa wished us harm he could rain destruction on our heads with little trouble."

Nord nodded. "I agree. I had planned to offer Benwa a chance to surrender the same as I did Aaron. It seems he beat me to the punch. I can't help wondering why he'd surrender if he's as strong as those two said. You suppose he could just be faking?"

Arkon thought a moment. "There's an old saying in magic, the stronger the student, the stronger the master. If that's true then Benwa's no faker. Both those young ladies were stronger than I and they had enough control to suppress the power so I couldn't sense it."

"Guess I'll just have to ask the man himself. Let's move." Nord waved the army forward and they continued on toward the keep.

Duke Benwa's keep was indeed a much more modest affair than Aaron's. Nord and his army arrived just as the sun set. The orange sky created a stunning backdrop for the black stone keep. The keep consisted of a single large, square tower surrounded by a fifteen-foot-high wall. A single portcullis blocked the only opening in the wall. On three sides of the keep a dense forest grew.

They paused a half mile out.

"Let's make camp," Nord said. "Arkon, you're with me."

"Lucky me," the wizard muttered under his breath.

Nord chose to ignore the comment. He felt no happier at the prospect of dinner with his enemy than Arkon did. Still, if it would spare his men a battle and get them on the road south he figured he could stand it.

They rode toward the portcullis which clanked up at their approach. Nord wore Heat's Bane but had left his armor in the supply wagon. Arkon followed a little behind in his usual brown robe. When no guards appeared they urged their mounts inside and over toward the tower.

Like the wall the tower had only one door which opened at their approach. Inside stood the woman they knew as Skull. She had swapped her traveling clothes for a sheer black gown and had her hair pulled back in a ponytail.

"Leave your horses in the yard. They will be tended to," she said.

Nord and Arkon dismounted and entered the tower. When they were out of the way the door closed behind them. They found themselves in a small entry hall. Six suits of archaic plate armor polished to a mirror shine lined the path. A pale light that seemed to come from nowhere and everywhere at the same time filled the air.

"This way, gentlemen." She led them down the hall to a heavy oak door. It swung open at her gesture.

Inside was a large dining hall. A fire burned in a massive hearth along the far wall. A table of dark wood dominated the center of the room. Six chairs of matching wood were arranged around it. Another door on the left-hand wall led out of the room.

"They are here, Master."

An older man rose from the chair closest to Nord and Arkon. Nord hadn't even noticed him. The man, whom Nord assumed was Duke Benwa, looked about ten years his elder. He had salt-and-pepper hair and a gray beard down to his stomach. He wore black robes with silver trim.

"Prince Nord," Benwa said, his voice soft and melodic. "Good of you to join me. Please have a seat."

"Thank you." Nord took the chair to Benwa's right and Arkon the next chair down.

Benwa sat down. "Lady Skull, be a dear and see what's keeping my daughter."

"Yes, Lord Benwa." Skull left by the same door they entered.

"You're no doubt wondering why I've decided not to fight you," Benwa said.

"I am curious," Nord said. "I thought you wanted to rule the Broken Kingdom."

Benwa chuckled. "I have no interest in ruling anything. It takes far more time than I care to devote to anything besides magical study. My main concern is not being ruled by anyone else."

"Then why surrender to me?"

"Does the name Daktari mean anything to you?" Benwa asked.

Nord shook his head. "Should it?"

Benwa smiled. "I am a wizard of considerable power. Daktari is a sorcerer of almost unimaginable might. He is also your mysterious benefactor."

Nord nodded again as he began to see the picture.

"Were we to come to blows, even with your army, you wouldn't win," Benwa continued. "But for some reason, Daktari wishes you to rule the Broken Kingdom."

"I get it," Nord said. "You figure you can take me, but if you do you'll piss off this Daktari guy who'll come crush you between his thumb and forefinger. That about right?"

Benwa tapped his fingertips together and sighed. "A crude way of putting it, but I won't disagree. I'm willing to make a deal."

Nord grinned. Benwa sounded pretty desperate. "Seems like you'd do whatever I want to save your skin."

Arkon elbowed him in the ribs.

Benwa's eyes narrowed. "Don't push me. I may just kill you and take my chances."

Nord laughed. "I've known men like you all my life. You don't have enough nerve to try anything."

Benwa's eyes started to glow and Nord had just enough time to think he'd pushed his luck too far when a crushing weight settled on his chest.

Nord gasped and fell out of his chair.

It felt like an elephant was standing on him.

Arkon began weaving a counterspell but Benwa shot him a glare that said a quick death lay on that path.

Arkon's hands stopped moving.

Nord cursed his coward of a wizard.

Benwa looked down at Nord where he lay writhing in pain. "I'm only going to say this once. I brought you here to bargain, not to prostrate myself before you. There are only two ways out of this castle: as my ally and new ruler of the Broken Kingdom or in pieces. Choose."

"A bargain sounds fair," Nord gasped.

"I suspected it might." Benwa gestured and the elephant climbed off Nord's chest.

He sucked in a lungful of air and let it out slowly. Nord eased himself into his chair and massaged his chest. While he tried to collect himself the door opened and Skull and Giggles came in.

"I found her napping," Skull said.

Giggles leaned over and kissed Benwa on the cheek. "Sorry, Father."

Nord began easing his hand down toward the hilt of his sword. He wouldn't allow Benwa, or anyone else, to insult him.

A voice appeared in his mind. *He'll stop your heart before the blade clears the scabbard.*

Nord's first thought was that Arkon was trying to warn

him, but when he looked at the wizard he seemed not to have a clue. A quick glance at the others showed Skull staring right at him.

That's right. It's me you're hearing. If you wish to get out of here alive you'd best learn to control those violent impulses.

Mind your own damn business and stay out of my head.

Nord felt the contact break off. Despite his bluster he decided the scrawny bitch had a point. He brought his hand back on the table.

Arkon must have noticed the tension because he said, "I thought this was going to be a dinner party. I'm starving."

Benwa smiled. "Quite right. Ladies, please take your seats."

Giggles sat opposite Nord and Skull sat across from Arkon. Nord noticed Arkon offer Skull a friendly smile but he got nothing but a cold stare in return.

Benwa clapped and the unused door opened. A moment later plates laden with food began to drift in.

They ate in silence. Nord brooded. He'd thought Heat's Bane was the ultimate weapon. The fact that a wizard with a little power could render it useless was quite a letdown. Still, the blade was useful in any combat situation.

"Lord Benwa," Arkon said. "May I ask you something?"

Benwa smiled. "I've never met a wizard who could resist a chance to talk shop. Ask away."

"I had heard that you studied chaos magic but I've seen no sign of it."

Benwa nodded and took a sip of his wine. "I did study chaos magic for a while. The results were too random to be of any real use."

"That's what my teacher always said."

The wizards blathered on about the vagaries of all things magical. Nord tuned them out and tried to think how best to approach the negotiations. He devoured the plate of ribs before him without even tasting them. He'd learned long ago to eat whenever he got the chance.

When everyone finished Benwa clapped again and the plates drifted back the way they'd come. When the door closed behind the last plate Benwa said, "Shall we begin our discussion?"

"Fine," Nord said. "What do you propose?"

"I will give you my support; in exchange I ask only to be left alone. I control an area about twenty miles square and have no interest in more. Do whatever you like with the rest of the Broken Kingdom. I don't care."

"A fair offer," Nord said. "The only thing I ask in addition is that you act as my regent while I'm away."

"Away? Where are you going? You've won the war."

Nord laughed. "This was only the preliminary. As soon as I get the supplies I need, I'm marching on the High Kingdom. Once I've crushed my brother, I plan to rule a new High Kingdom that includes the old one and the Broken Kingdom."

"Interesting," Benwa said as he pulled on his beard. "This latest campaign was just to consolidate for an even bigger attack. Very well, I accept your offer. We will look after the Broken Kingdom while you're gone."

"Excellent. I in turn recognize your autonomy assuming you do nothing to oppose me." Nord stood up and stuck out his hand.

Benwa stood as well. When the wizard grabbed his hand a jolt passed through his body.

Benwa smiled and pumped his hand once.

Benwa retired shortly after that. Skull was given the task of showing them out.

When they reached the outer door Nord paused. "Why did you warn me in there?"

Skull hesitated and Nord thought she might just ignore the question.

Finally she said, "Lord Benwa didn't wish to kill you, and I didn't wish to see him forced into something by your foolish pride. My lord got what he wanted, that is all that concerns me."

The door slammed in their faces.

"Friendly, isn't she?" Arkon said.

Nord grabbed him and jerked him off his feet. "You miserable coward. What's the idea leaving me hanging in there?"

"Put. Me. Down," Arkon said. Nord heard iron in his voice that he'd never noticed before.

He lowered the wizard to his feet. "Prince Nord, I respect you, but I won't commit suicide for you. If I'd done anything besides what I did we'd both be dead right now."

"When I make a move I expect you to back me up," Nord said, his voice rising. "If you'd distracted him I might have gotten my sword free."

"And I would have been killed. When I signed up it was to provide magical support and to advise you. I will continue to do so, but if you expect me to sacrifice myself you can forget it. If that's unacceptable to you, tell me now and I'll take my leave."

"Take your leave?"

"Yes, seek other employment. No competent wizard has trouble finding work. I'll go away and you can try and find a wizard with less good sense. What do you say?"

"You're right," Nord said. It pained him to admit it. "I'd like you to stay on."

"Very well, but I don't want to have this conversation again. Any more suicidal orders and I'm gone."

"Deal."

Nord whistled and the horses came trotting over to them.

How they'd managed to remain hidden in the empty courtyard Nord didn't even want to know.

They mounted up and went to rejoin the army. Tomorrow Nord planned to head south toward Sand City, the largest city on the southern border. From there they would march on the High Kingdom and Nord would reclaim his birthright.

CHAPTER 24

Vilos left his army in town to resupply. He had three days to reach the meeting with Rao and the other elders, but he saw no reason to make them wait. At first he had planned to go alone but upon hearing his intentions his loyal advisors refused to let him. As a nod to safety, Abin rode at his side. The wizard was worth ten soldiers if they ran into trouble.

As they rode through the desert toward the oasis Abin scanned the horizon looking for potential threats. "I wish you'd brought along a few men. If we run into a force of any size..."

"A calculated risk," Vilos said. "I don't want to take a chance on scaring the elders. If we can prevent an all-out war with this meeting it will be worth it."

"Will it be worth it if both of us get killed?" Abin asked.

Vilos grinned. "If we both get killed we'll move beyond caring. How much further?"

"Another hour at least." Abin pointed to some dark shapes circling in the sky. "What do you make of that?"

Vilos shaded his eyes and squinted. "Looks like vultures. Heaven's mercy! They're circling the oasis."

He kicked his camel into a fast trot.

The stench of rotting flesh struck them as soon as they got within sight of the oasis palms. Vilos dismounted and drew his sword. Abin joined him, a slim ash wand at the ready. They tied their camels to the first bush they came to.

The smell of death almost overwhelmed Vilos as he walked closer. They entered the small clearing beside the pool of water. It seemed like a hundred vultures took flight, shrieking at having their meal interrupted. Bits of flesh and bone lay everywhere. The scavengers had cleaned up some, but Vilos could still tell a large group of people and animals had been killed.

"How long ago do you suppose this happened?" Vilos asked.

"A few days," Abin said. "What could have done this?"

What indeed?

This wasn't the work of men, Vilos felt sure. "I don't know. Let's take a look around and see if we can figure it out."

Abin walked along the left side of the pool and Vilos took the right. They'd gone about halfway when Abin shouted, "Majesty, I found something."

"What is it?" Vilos asked.

"A body."

Vilos rolled his eyes. "There are lots of bodies around here."

"A whole body, not torn up like the others."

"I'll be right there." Vilos circled around the pool and joined the wizard.

"See?" Abin pointed to a withered body.

When Vilos stepped closer to look the body started to glow an ugly purple. Vilos recognized the color. The body rose up from the ground like a puppet.

"Hello, Vilos," the corpse said.

Vilos recognized the voice. It was the sorcerer.

"I fear I had to cancel your meeting. My shadow demon didn't get along with your friends. It played a little too rough for them. It's your fault, you know. By now I have spoken to the surviving clan leaders in the form of your erstwhile ally Rao. They all believe you ambushed and killed the clan leaders. In a sense you did kill them. All I ever wanted was the girl. It didn't have to be this way. Didn't have to be this way. Didn't have to be this way."

The corpse continued repeating the final mocking line until Vilos hacked it to pieces.

"Son of a bitch," Vilos muttered. "Let's get out of here. We found what we were meant to find."

"Wise decision," Abin said.

The two men remounted and turned their camels south. They hadn't gone far when Vilos noticed a cloud of dust rising in the distance.

He stopped.

"What is it?" Abin asked.

Vilos pointed at the cloud of dust. It appeared to be getting closer. "Sand storm you think?"

"No, the shape looks wrong for a sandstorm. Look at the sky, not a cloud in sight."

"Well then, what is it?" Vilos asked.

"I haven't the least idea."

Vilos glared at the wizard. "Why don't you find out?"

"Find out this, find out that, what would you do without me?"

"You don't make with the magic, I might just be tempted to find out," Vilos said.

He didn't mean it of course. He and Abin had this discussion once a month. Vilos wouldn't have been surprised to learn that the first man to employ a wizard had had a similar argument.

Abin muttered a word of power and a small green eye appeared in the air beside him. The wizard closed his eyes and the eye streaked off toward the dust cloud.

Seconds later Abin opened his eyes and said, "We'd better hurry."

"What is it?"

"Nomads. Looks like they're coming to find their friends and they don't look happy."

"How many?" Vilos kicked his camel into motion.

"A thousand, at least."

"All right, things could be worse. We outnumber them ten to one. Is there some way you can keep an eye on them?"

"Not out here," Abin said. "When we get back to town I could whip something up."

"Good. It seems peace is now beyond my reach. So be it. Now we go on the offensive."

⁕

Vilos and Abin arrived in town just after nightfall. A sliver of moon was visible in the clear sky. Yosef paced outside a small, unoccupied building they'd adopted as headquarters.

Vilos spotted him at once and shouted, "Assemble the division commanders. We've got trouble coming."

Yosef took off. It wouldn't take long for the commanders to gather. They all bunked near headquarters for just such an emergency.

"Abin, do what you must to keep an eye on the nomads, and then contact your apprentice for updates from the other towns."

The wizard nodded and took off toward his temporary lab. Vilos smiled at his back. That's what he loved about Abin. He knew when to bitch and when to do the job. Some never learned that.

Standing alone in the dark Vilos realized he finally had a free moment. He ducked inside headquarters and looked for some food. Sure enough he found half a loaf of bread and some wine. Not the finest repast, but he hadn't eaten since morning and anything would taste good.

He finished the last bite of bread just as Yosef and the division commanders arrived. Several of them carried lanterns which they hung up to light the room. Each took a seat around the round table in the center of the room.

Vilos briefly explained what had happened at the oasis. Yosef slammed his fist on the table. "I'll see that sorcerer burn for this."

Vilos nodded. Yosef and Rao had been friends. "I know how you feel, but let's not get ahead of ourselves. Right now we have an army of nomads headed our way. Since peace now seems impossible, I hope to crush the nomads as completely as possible."

Abin slipped inside. "The nomads have started a pyre for the dead. I'd guess there are now between fifteen hundred and two thousand at the oasis. No change at the besieged villages."

"It's too soon for the forces to the north to have heard about the slaughter," Vilos said. "When a message reaches them the attacks will intensify. We have to take care of this force as fast as possible and head north. Gentlemen, any thoughts on strategy?"

One commander, Vilos couldn't remember his name, said, "We have a huge advantage in numbers, a straight-forward attack might be our best bet."

"In an equal battle I'd agree," Vilos said. "The nomads,

however, have the advantage in that they are all mounted. They could just ride away from a charge and stretch out our line leaving the flanks vulnerable to a counterattack. Yosef, you fought the nomads with my father, any suggestions?"

The debate went on until near midnight when Vilos finally called a halt. Everyone had spoken and he'd made up his mind. They all left to get some sleep before the battle.

—❖—

Dawn came too soon for Vilos. He ate, dressed, and went to the mustering area near the gate. His officers had the men assembled and ready when he arrived. Vilos noted with pleasure that they already stood in the modified turtle formation they'd discussed the night before. He spotted Abin and Yosef standing together out of the way.

Waiting for him no doubt.

Vilos walked over to join the conference. He smiled and nodded to the troops as he went. He knew he made an inspiring sight with his polished leather armor and gold circlet.

The armor was entirely for show of course. Anything that penetrated the circlet's magic wouldn't be stopped by simple leather armor.

"Gentlemen, what news?" Vilos asked when he reached the others.

"I received a message from the palace," Abin said. "You were right, the attacks have picked up in the north and a third town is besieged."

"Which one?" Vilos asked.

"Rand's Oasis, the next town north of us."

"How bad is it?"

"They were on full alert," Abin said. "The gates were sealed and no one was hurt."

"Ha, how often did they complain about the costs when my grandfather ordered those walls built? He said one day they'd be glad to have them. What about our friends from the oasis?"

"A third of them are besieging Rand's Oasis. The rest have gathered two miles north to fight us."

"They split their forces? That's crazy; we already outnumber them badly." Vilos was confused. The nomads' actions made no sense.

"The men nearby are planning a fighting retreat toward their companions at Rand's Oasis. They hope to tire our infantry then hit us hard when they join up with their comrades," Abin said.

"How do you know?" Vilos asked.

"Magic," Abin said, trying to sound mysterious. When Vilos only stared he continued, "I used an invisible eye to spy on a meeting of the war chiefs."

"Hardly seems fair," Yosef muttered.

"What?" Vilos asked.

"I said it hardly seems fair. We know what they're going to do before they do it. We can adjust our tactics and destroy them. It just doesn't seem fair to me."

"Fair or not is irrelevant. Our goal is to win the war with as few of our men hurt as possible. If the best way to accomplish that is to use magic to spy on them, so be it."

"As you say, Majesty."

The army marched forth, Vilos riding at its head. The turtle formation should protect the men from the worst of the nomads' archery fire. Each squad leader had his orders. No one was to pursue the enemy. Slow advance only to Rand's Oasis.

If Vilos's plan worked they should crush the nomads against the walls of the town.

Vilos drew his sword, an exquisite if mundane shamshir, identical in appearance and weight to Heat's Bane. "Forward."

The army started forward at a slow march. They should cover two miles an hour at that pace. The cavalry rode on either side of the infantry. Their job was to prevent the nomads from getting around the main force and attacking the rear.

They spotted the nomads milling around right where Abin said they'd be. That did wonders for Vilos's confidence. If Abin got the location right, hopefully the rest of his information would be correct as well.

The nomads spotted them a moment after they came in sight.

They raced forward in a ragged line.

The nomads pulled up a hundred yards short of Vilos's lines and fired their small bows into the mass of soldiers.

The men raised their shields and created a shell of wood and leather.

Arrows either bounced off or imbedded themselves in the wood.

Vilos heard a few screams as some found gaps in the protection.

Just as Abin had said, the nomads turned and rode away toward Rand's Oasis.

Vilos smiled as his men continued their slow, steady advance. Most of them could maintain that pace all day without getting tired. The nomads didn't go very far before they realized their tactic hadn't worked.

They wheeled around to make another run.

This time when they stopped they fired their arrows at Vilos.

He sighed as the arrows deflected off the magic shield that surrounded him. Fortunately no nomad would target a camel on purpose.

A few cavalrymen started to counterattack, but Yosef got them under control. Vilos shook his head. If the nomads had planned to goad them by attacking him all they accomplished was to waste their arrows.

So it went all morning. The nomads would lob arrows and run while Vilos's army continued its steady advance. The only change in formation was the creation of a small detachment to ferry the wounded safely to town.

It took the better part of the day but the walls of Rand's Oasis finally appeared on the horizon. Vilos figured he was down about three hundred men from the nomads' constant harassment. In the distance he could just make out the force surrounding the town.

The men could see the walls as well and Vilos could hear them growling. They were ready for some payback.

The nomads had just turned and were heading back for another attack. That should provide the opportunity Vilos wanted. They had ignored so many attacks they'd never expect a counterattack this time. When they reached three hundred yards out Vilos figured they were close enough.

"Charge!"

The cavalry surged forward behind him.

Taken by complete surprise some of the nomads tried to turn and run while others tried to get their bows up to shoot.

All they accomplished was to get in each other's way.

Vilos cut the first man he reached from his saddle with a single blow.

His new sword might not have Heat's Bane's magic, but the fine steel cut through the nomad's thin robes with ease.

The nomads were some of the finest riders in the world. It

didn't take them long to get turned around and race away from the deadly soldiers.

"Do not pursue," Vilos shouted.

The few men that had raced off pulled up short and whipped around to join the main group. Vilos looked around and figured they got about even with the nomads. He estimated at least a few hundred dead lay scattered around the battlefield.

The infantry caught up and they marched toward the town. The nomads rejoined their brethren and seemed to be preparing for another attack.

Vilos shook his head. They had no chance against his army.

What a waste.

The nomads formed themselves into more orderly lines and began to advance toward Vilos. They all had their backs to the town.

"Now, Abin!"

The wizard spoke a word of magic and pointed to the sky.

A golden light shot from his finger.

Right on cue the hundred and fifty archers lining the town wall began raking the nomads with arrows.

The first three volleys put down almost a quarter of the nomad warriors.

When they wheeled around to counterattack Vilos shouted, "Charge!"

The army raced forward at full sprint.

The cavalry soon far outdistanced the infantry.

They struck the nomads as they were half turned to attack the town. Vilos swung his blade for all he was worth.

A dozen enemy blades bounced harmlessly off his magic shield.

Like a juggernaut Vilos slaughtered the nomads around him.

All around him his men were pounding the nomads.

Their formation was starting to fall apart and he knew it wouldn't be long before they broke.

It was time to give the order. "No quarter!"

He hated himself for saying it but knew he'd never get a better chance to crush the nomads and eliminate the threat. If he played it right he might end the war in the first battle.

The fringes of the nomad formation began to turn tail and run. A quick glance showed that the infantry had managed to get in place. They had the battlefield surrounded on three sides with the town closing the fourth.

Spearmen bristled along the formation, stabbing at anything they could reach. Once a group of twenty tried to break through but the archers cut them down before they could reach the line.

The battle soon became a slaughter as the outnumbered nomads sought a way to escape the killing box.

The soldiers followed their orders and when it finally ended two thousand nomads lay dead in the sand.

Yosef rode up beside Vilos. "Was it necessary to kill them all? I fear we made no friends today."

"I tried making friends and a bunch of innocent people got killed. The sorcerer has made it quite clear that this is a war I must fight. The nomads already think I'm a monster. I plan to do nothing to dissuade them. I will fight this war in as cold and brutal a manner as I can stomach. My duty now is to my people. I must end this war as soon as possible with as few casualties as I can. The best way I can think of is to break the nomads' will to fight. If you have a better suggestion I'm willing to listen."

"I don't, Majesty. It just seems a shame. No one wanted this war."

"One person did and he's got it. I had my fill in the Crown

War. Do you know what I wanted people to remember about my reign, Yosef?"

"No, Majesty."

"I wanted them to remember a time of great peace and prosperity. Now, because of me, we're at war. My people are dying and all I can do about it is to kill even more people." Vilos felt himself close to tears but he forced them away.

He could show no weakness now.

"It's not your fault, Vilos."

The sultan smiled at his friend's attempt to make him feel better. "No, my friend. The blame lies on my shoulders. Long ago I made a bargain with the sorcerer. I sold my unborn daughter's soul for the power to end the Crown War. When the darkness came to collect I sent her away. Now my people are paying the price. Whatever becomes of the High Kingdom, for good or ill, the responsibility is mine."

After a moment's silence Yosef asked, "What now, Majesty?"

"Take the men inside and get them settled. Make sure the wounded get taken care of. We'll rest here a day or two then continue north."

Yosef saluted and went to carry out his lord's instructions. Vilos watched him go and wished not for the first time that he were just a soldier. He sighed as he thought of the old soldiers' credo: ours is not to wonder why, ours is but to do and die.

It seemed it was for him to wonder why.

CHAPTER 25

Shara trudged down the well-worn path away from Reaper's Crossing. Robert had purchased their supplies at a very good price, if his boasting could be believed. In private he explained that because everything was already stolen it was easier to find a bargain. In addition to food and weapons, he'd found a pair of heavy leather boots along with a tan tunic and trousers that just about fit her. Given the state of her wardrobe, the change was probably a good thing, even if the rough homespun was a far cry from the silk she was used to.

When everyone got together last night Robert, of course, said his haggling was the reason the prices were down. Shale glared and said that if his haggling skill was as good as his bull-shitting skill he should have gotten the supplies for free.

Everyone laughed, including Robert. One thing you could say about the guy, he was just as willing to laugh at himself as someone else. Shale said they were leaving early so everyone turned in.

Now Shara found herself leaving behind the only civilization she'd seen in over two weeks. The only good thing that had happened to her since she'd teleported from her father's throne room was her captors removing the rope that had bound her wrists more or less nonstop since they'd captured her.

Robert had argued that Scratch's spell made the rope and guard unnecessary. Shale eventually agreed with some reluctance. Now she didn't even have the silent giant Morden to keep her company.

"Hey, kid," Robert said.

Shara smiled. It seemed Robert could sense when she felt lonely. He materialized whenever she grew the least bit sorry for herself.

"It'll take us forever to reach the High Kingdom if we have to walk the whole way," she said.

"Don't worry." He flashed a larcenous grin. "The lands beyond the Vale are farm country and you know what that means."

In fact she didn't have a clue what that meant. "What?"

"Horses, my dear. First big farm we come to, we'll stop and liberate some equine transportation. After that it's about three weeks' hard ride to the Kanid Forest."

She groaned. "Not another forest."

Robert laughed. "Don't worry, the Kanid Forest is much smaller than the Vale. Of course it's also much more dangerous."

"More dangerous how?"

Robert frowned. "The Wolfen tribes live there. They make the bandit crews of the Vale look like a church playgroup. Still, there's a trade road that goes through the forest. If we stick to that we should be okay."

"What happens if we don't?" Shara had a pretty good idea what he'd say but felt the need to hear it.

"That depends. The Wolfen are extremely territorial and if they thought we were trespassing, the least they'd do is drive us out and at worst they'd kill us all."

"Great," she said.

⋅—⋆

They continued on in silence until a little after noon, when Wraith came trotting down the road. Soon the whole group had gathered around the scout.

"What is it?" Shale asked.

Wraith was breathing heavy. Between gasps she said, "About a mile ahead a little way off the road I saw a good-sized farm."

"Horses?" Shale asked.

"Some, but not enough for everyone. They had a nice-looking wagon that might do the trick."

"That might work better anyway," Robert said. "We could fill the wagon with odds and ends from the farm and continue on posing as a merchant and his guards. It would make the perfect excuse for traveling and our weapons."

"Sounds good," Shale said. "Bobby, you stay by the road with the girl. The rest of us will secure the farm."

Robert nodded and they moved out. When they reached a crude wagon trail leading off the road Robert and Shara stopped as the others passed them by. Blade paused long enough to throw Robert a wink. He smiled as she left.

"What now?" Shara asked.

Robert walked over to a shady spot under some trees and sat down. "Now we wait. Someone will come get us when it's done."

"Why don't we go watch?"

"Trust me, kid, you don't want to watch Shale at work. The guy enjoys his job way too much."

Shara swallowed the lump in her throat and went to sit beside Robert. As they sat in silence Shara once again found it remarkable how comfortable she felt in Robert's company. The man had tricked her, taken her prisoner, and planned to sell her to an insane sorcerer, yet here she was sitting in the shade next to him like they were old friends.

"I just don't get it."

"Don't get what?" Robert asked.

"What?" Shara said.

"I said, what don't you get?"

"Sorry, I didn't realize I'd spoken out loud."

"Perhaps if you tell me what's wrong I can help."

He seemed so earnest Shara had to smile. "Blade's right, you're not mean enough for this type of work."

Robert grinned. "Yeah, but I'm clever enough for three people."

"Modest too," Shara said with a laugh. "Seriously though, I just can't figure you out."

Robert sighed. "Do you remember those stories I told you about how I grew up?"

Shara nodded.

"You know what I spent most of my time doing during those trips?"

"I think you mentioned something about carousing."

He laughed. "You were listening, good. Aside from that my hobby was watching people. You know what I learned? Most people expect to get treated like dirt. They don't especially like it, but they've come to expect it. When you treat someone like that kindly it puts them at ease. They become less combative and more willing to help. I've met people who would walk across burning coals just to hear a kind word."

"Hard to believe," Shara said.

Robert nodded. "For you especially. You come from one of the two groups that don't expect to get treated like dirt."

"Which groups are those?"

"The rich and the powerful. They expect to get treated well. See, you can sometimes throw someone like that off by being brusque with them. They aren't used to it and it takes them by surprise. You see? Reading people is the key to success. Any idiot can take people's money at sword point. It takes real skill to convince someone they want to give you their money. Does that help you understand me better?"

"I guess so," she said.

Truth was she still didn't have a clue.

Robert laughed again. "No, I don't think you do. Try this; next time you see someone who looks down, talk to them. Give them a friendly ear. Once you get them cheered up and they thank you, ask them for something. Nothing big, just a little favor and some information. I'll bet a gold piece if they can help you they will."

"I'll try it," Shara said.

"Good." Robert pointed in the distance. "There's Morden, we'd better go."

Robert helped her to her feet and they went to join the mute giant.

"Any trouble?" Robert asked when they reached him.

Morden grunted and shook his head. Pretty chatty for Morden. They made good time through the flat country and soon Shara could see the farm. There was a large main house and several smaller outbuildings. People were moving around outside. No horses were visible, but they could have been inside one of the buildings.

The ground sloped down slightly toward the farm. As soon

as they got closer she could make out Blade headed toward them. She didn't look happy.

"We need to talk." Blade dragged Robert off toward the house.

"Back in a bit," Robert said as he tripped along behind Blade. "Keep an eye on her, won't you, Morden?"

The afternoon was on the wane as Shara settled down on the steps of the porch. Most of the gang was milling around outside. Near the corner of the house four guys had a card game of some sort going.

Shale appeared from behind one of the barns. He sauntered over toward her. Shara wished he'd just keep going, but it didn't seem to be her month for wishes.

Shale stopped right in front of her.

He put one foot on the step beside her and leaned in. His breath reeked. "You know me and the boys were somewhat disappointed. This worthless farmer only had boys, six sons and not a single daughter. Even the wife was dead before we got here. A shame, but then I remembered we had a cute little girl along with us all the time. I figure there's no reason Bobby should have all the fun."

No, No, NO!

Shale grabbed her arm. "Come on, girly, we're gonna go over in the bushes and you can show me all the dirty tricks a princess knows."

"NO!" Shara screamed.

She jammed her ring into his arm.

The magic burned his flesh and Shale roared in pain.

His hand flew back and she closed her eyes and braced herself for a blow which never came. She opened her eyes a bit and found Shale surrounded by sparkling motes of light.

Scratch stood beside her, his cat purring in his arms. "Keep your hands off the merchandise."

Shale's face had contorted in a look of pure rage. "Let me go, you son of a bitch. Now! By all the demons in hell I swear I'll wring your scrawny neck."

A small smile played about the wizard's lips. He set his cat down and drew a long, razor-sharp dagger. Scratch held it up and let the light from his spell play along its edge.

He pressed the point under Shale's chin. "I think you need to take a moment to consider your position before you make threats."

If it were possible Shara thought Shale's face grew even redder. "Don't forget who's in charge. I want the girl. Now."

"And I want the gold!" Scratch yelled right in his face.

He pressed the dagger hard enough to draw blood. That seemed to get the lunatic's attention.

"The sorcerer said, deliver the girl unharmed, and that's just what we're going to do. If I have to bury you to see it done, I won't shed any tears. And by the way, Shale, I know who's in charge and it isn't you."

Shale's muscles bulged as he tried to break free of the wizard's spell. His efforts had as much effect as Shara's nails would have on the stone walls of the White Palace.

Scratch offered her his hand.

"Thank you," she said as she got to her feet.

The wizard led her to the back door of the farmhouse. "From now on you stick close to Blade, Bobby, or me. No one else has the nerve to stand up to Shale."

"I will, thank you." Shara climbed the steps and Scratch bent down to pick up his cat.

"Don't thank me, kid. I was just protecting my investment."

Annoyed, Shara asked, "Why does everyone keep calling me kid? I have a name."

"You ever spend any time on a farm?" Scratch asked. "Never mind, of course you haven't. See, the reason no one calls you by your proper name is the same reason farmers don't name their cattle. Once you name something, it becomes real rather than a thing to be bought or sold."

Shara staggered against the doorjamb.

It finally sank in. "That's all I am to you people isn't it? Some prize cow to be sold to the highest bidder."

Scratch shrugged. "Bobby and Blade are in the dining hall."

He left her alone on the porch. Shara slid down to the steps and started crying.

She didn't know how much time had passed but the door finally opened and Robert appeared. "Hey, kid. Scratch told us what happened. I don't know what Shale was thinking, but of all the things he could have done, going after you the way he did was the one most likely to piss Blade off. She's going to have a talk with him now. If he lives through it it'll be miracle."

Shara hardly heard him. She had started crying again. When Robert called her "kid" she felt her heart break. She thought they were becoming friends, but now she wondered if he thought of her as nothing more than a prize cow as well.

Robert sat down beside her. "Hey, what's wrong? I told you, Blade will take care of it."

Shara couldn't hold back. Everything Scratch said came spilling out.

When she finished she looked over at Robert. "Is that how you see me, as a prize cow?"

Robert smiled, fondly she allowed herself to think, and said, "I can't speak for Scratch. He may well see you that way. I don't know him well enough to say for certain. I almost envy him if it's true. For myself, I fear I'm becoming fonder of you every day." He put an arm around her. "You're becoming like the little sister I never had."

"Then why call me kid rather than by my real name?" She sniffled and wiped the tears from her eyes.

His smile widened. "That easy. Remember when I told you about the ship's carpenter that took me under his wing? Well, whenever he saw me he'd yell, 'Hey, kid.'"

Shara nodded, starting to understand.

"When I saw our relationship becoming something similar, I thought I'd bestow my old nickname on you. Figure the others just picked up on it."

Shara hesitated. She wanted to believe him, needed to. She needed a friend if she was going to survive the trip home. Her heart said trust him and she went with it, wrapping her arms around his neck.

Robert hugged her back and said, "Let's go inside. Blade says we're staying here for the night."

CHAPTER 26

Vilos finished making the rounds of his men. They were settled in all over the little town; any place large enough to raise a tent had an occupant. Satisfied that the soldiers were as comfortable as he could make them, Vilos went to look for Abin. The wizard was supposed to be searching for the rest of the nomads.

Vilos found Abin more by smell than anything. A sharp, spicy aroma permeated the air for a hundred yards surrounding the wizard's tent.

Vilos stuck his head in the tent flap. "What's that smell?"

Abin stood over a bowl of water, eyes open but clearly seeing nothing. If he heard Vilos he gave no indication. Vilos entered the tent and sat down to wait. After a few minutes Abin came around. A deep frown creased his face.

"Bad news?" Vilos smiled as Abin jumped. "Sorry, I couldn't resist."

Abin patted his chest a couple times. "You realize that if you scare me to death, you'll need to find a new wizard."

Vilos just laughed.

"You were correct about the news, it isn't good."

Vilos gestured for him to continue.

"First the better news. The remaining nomad warriors number only a few thousand. Most of them are at the two sieges. When we've broken those two groups that should take care of the nomads."

"Go on."

"The bad news is that your brother is headed south. Our spies in Sand City say he'll be ready to invade in just a few days."

Vilos nodded. The sorcerer had told him Heat's Bane would go to Nord. It didn't take a genius to figure out what Nord would do once he got it. "How big is his army?"

"We don't have any numbers yet. Our people are working on it."

"All right. Have any of them been around long enough that Nord might recognize them?"

Abin shook his head.

"Very well, keep me posted. In the meantime we need to deal with the nomads." Vilos turned to leave then stopped. Without turning he said, "I think we've gotten rid of all of Nord's old friends in the army, but just to be safe let's keep his return to ourselves for now."

"It's going to be the Crown War all over again," Abin said.

Vilos spun around. "No, it won't. My brother has no standing. He's just another invader in need of a lesson. Is that clear?"

"Perfectly, Majesty."

"Good," Vilos said. "We move out at first light, get some rest."

I t took the better part of three days' marching before the walls of Zorn's Oasis came into view. Vilos shaded his eyes for a better look. There was nothing particularly remarkable about the place. The high stone walls enclosed a modest town of around five thousand. It served mainly as a caravan stop if he wasn't mistaken. If not for the nearly one thousand angry nomads surrounding it, no one would give the place a second look.

Vilos called a halt. The afternoon sun was well on its way out of the sky. They had at best an hour of light left.

Yosef rode up beside him. "Do we attack now or wait until morning?"

"What do you think?" Vilos asked.

"If we attack now we might take them by surprise. If we wait they're sure to spot us and maybe attack during the night."

"Agreed, let's hit them now. Abin says they only number about a thousand. We'll attack them with the cavalry and let the infantry clean up."

"Sounds good," Yosef said. "Our cavalry outnumbers theirs and we're more accustomed to fighting together. We may not even need the infantry."

Vilos nodded. "Get your men ready. I'll talk to the infantry commander."

It took only minutes to get everyone lined up. The cavalry would charge and engage the nomads. The infantry and archers would come along behind and pick off anyone that tried to escape.

Vilos drew his sword and raised it above his head. When he brought it down the cavalry surged forward, three rows deep. The infantry came behind at a steady trot.

The nomads spotted them a moment later and turned to

attack. Didn't say much for their brains but Vilos wouldn't question their courage.

The momentum of the charge carried Vilos through the first three ranks and right into the heart of the nomad's formation.

As in the first battle none of their weapons could penetrate his magic shield.

Vilos hacked and stabbed until he thought his arm would fall off.

He had no sense of how the battle was progressing. He just chopped at anything not wearing one of his uniforms.

Vilos soon found himself beyond the battle. He'd managed to fight his way through the nomads' lines. A nudge with his knees brought his camel around to rejoin the fray.

He found that unnecessary. His men had the battle well in hand. The infantry had arrived and the archers picked off any nomad not engaged.

Vilos spotted Yosef observing the battle from a little way off.

He urged his mount over next to the cavalry chief. "The battle goes well. From the stories I'd heard, I thought the nomads would have given us more trouble."

"The clan system doesn't work as well for war on this scale as ours does. Each clan has its own chief and they all have different ideas about how to run the war. We, on the other hand, fight as one unit under your direction. We have no squabbles over tactics; you decide, and then we execute."

Vilos nodded. "I'm still glad we didn't have to fight them all at once."

"Our numbers advantage was a huge plus," Yosef said. "Nothing takes an enemy's heart faster than seeing an army ten times larger than his bearing down on him."

"One town to go," Vilos said. "Then my brother."

"It'll take decades for the clans to recover." Yosef went on about the damage done to the nomads.

Vilos didn't hear a word. He was thinking about Nord and the last time he'd fought his brother.

During the Crown War he had fought a three-sided battle against both his brothers. The High Kingdom had been devastated. Nord crushed any town that dared side with either Vilos or Kent. Only in the last few years had the High Kingdom fully recovered.

And now it would begin again. At least Kent seemed to be on his side this time.

"Majesty." Yosef barged in on his thoughts. "The battle is won. What are your orders?"

"Make camp in town. We'll rest for a day and tend the wounded before we advance on the final town."

Yosef nodded and went to carry out his instructions. Vilos stared north. Only a few days away, just over the border, Nord plotted and prepared. It wouldn't take long before his brother crossed the border and returned home.

CHAPTER 27

Daktari yawned as he reclined in the magical chair he'd summoned. After slaughtering the nomad elders, he'd found little to occupy himself with beyond waiting. Luckily, a sorcerer learned patience early on. When an experiment could take a year or more to produce results, being in a rush was pointless.

Directly in front of him, a circle of flames hung in the air. The lava imp Zin filled the opening as he droned on about Nord's success in conquering the Broken Kingdom.

Nord had reached Sand City and was gathering the supplies and infrastructure he'd need to invade. It looked to Zin like he'd be ready to march in a week or less.

Daktari sent his compliments to Zin then severed their connection. "Bane."

His homunculus appeared a moment later. "Master?"

"How fare the nomads?"

"They've lost." Bane shrugged. "There may be a skirmish or two more but the sultan has won the war."

Bane didn't seem very concerned about the nomads' defeat

and Daktari agreed. They had served their purpose, tiring and weakening Vilos's army. Hopefully even now word of the uprising would be spreading to cities all over the world. Princess Shara would be all the more eager to return home when she heard.

"No matter, Nord is nearly ready to continue the battle. Come, we need to pay our ally a visit."

Daktari rose and went over to one of the tables in his lab. He grabbed a vial of opaque white liquid. Bane flew over and landed on his shoulder. With a thought Daktari teleported out of the cavern.

They reappeared in a shadowy alley that stank of garbage and worse. The sun had nearly set and true night would soon fall. A rat crawled across Daktari's foot, indifferent to the sorcerer's presence.

Daktari pointed and the rat was surrounded by a deep purple glow. It levitated up into his hand. He stroked its back and the rat hissed with pleasure. Such misunderstood animals. Despised by humanity as disease carriers, rats were killed on sight.

He smiled. Daktari had a great fondness for rats. They could survive anywhere. Few animals adapted as well as the rats. He'd make a pet of this particular specimen. He slipped the little beast into his pocket.

Time to find Nord.

Zin had said the army was camped near the southern gate. Daktari rendered himself invisible and started south. He'd never visited Sand City before, but like most large cities it featured a large market in the center of town. He ignored the few merchants still open and paused only once to pick up half a crust of bread. As soon as he dropped it in his pocket his new pet started munching.

With the market behind him, Daktari made his way

through row upon row of two-story stone houses. No one seemed to be out. No doubt having an army in town was keeping people on edge, except for the merchants selling them supplies of course.

Daktari passed Nord's first sentries about two blocks from the south gate. The two men were busy with a dice game and weren't paying the least attention to their surroundings. He could have snuck by them without using magic had he felt like it. One of the two men had a large stack of coins while the other was down to his last five.

The die was cast and Daktari gestured. The unlucky man won the roll. He wove a spell around the die that would ensure the soldier's victory on every toss after that. Daktari left them to their game with a smile on his face.

How many tosses would it take for a fight to break out? He guessed not many. That would show them what happened when you played instead of doing your work.

The main camp was laid out at random with tents pitched wherever the men felt like raising them. Daktari let his mind drift until he felt the power of Heat's Bane. He followed the sword's call through the camp until he came to a larger-than-average tent with a light glowing under the flap.

Daktari slipped inside and found Nord talking with his wizard. The wizard held up his hand to stop Nord in midsentence. "I felt something."

Daktari let the magic surrounding him fade. He found the horrified look on the wizard's face quite amusing. It seemed the man didn't realize with whom he dealt.

Nord's wizard pointed and spoke the words of a lightning bolt spell.

The bolt struck one of the many shields that surrounded Daktari at all times and fizzled.

The sorcerer frowned. "Get out."

"I don't take orders from—" the wizard began.

Daktari's eyes blazed with purple fire. "NOW!"

Having already seen his lightning bolt deflected by the sorcerer's magic the wizard seemed to decide that discretion was the better part of valor.

"I think I left a potion brewing," he muttered before hurrying out the flap.

As soon as they were alone Daktari said, "You finished your business here much faster than I expected, congratulations."

"It's all thanks to you, Daktari," Nord said.

Daktari raised an eyebrow. "Oh?"

Nord briefly described his meeting with Duke Benwa. "He could have killed me, easy. But he was more afraid of angering you."

Daktari nodded. "So this Benwa is the one who told you my name. Most people the least aware of my power fear me. It's expected. Anyway, that's not why I'm here. I assume by now you've heard of the new danger in crossing the desert."

"You mean the oases or the nomads?"

"The oases, your brother has dealt with the nomads." Daktari reached into his robe, withdrew the vial he brought, and handed it to Nord. "Take this. Put three drops into any oasis before you drink and it will neutralize the poison."

"How do you know?" Nord asked as he held the vial up to the light. "The wizards here have been trying for weeks to negate the poison."

Daktari smiled. "I have an advantage since I created the poison. I assure you the antivenom works."

Nord nodded. "So I just put three drops into the water and it's safe?"

"That's right. So simple even that idiot wizard of yours could handle it. By the way, tell that fool if he ever casts another spell at me I'll turn him inside out."

"You weren't hurt," Nord had the nerve to point out.

"That isn't the point. His attack shows a lack of respect I won't accept from anyone, much less a wizard of his piddling ability. Clear?"

"I'll relay the message, anything else?"

"Yes, your brother is now one hundred and fifty miles south of the border. If you hurry, you might be able to engage him before he returns to the capital."

An evil smile spread across Nord's face. "Excellent."

Daktari ducked out of the tent, activated his invisibility spell, and retraced his steps through the camp. He could have teleported at once but he was curious about his prank. As he rounded a turn that led to the outer perimeter, he found the two guards fighting and calling each other a cheat.

Daktari grinned and teleported home.

CHAPTER 28

Nord waited for five minutes after Daktari left then stuck his head out of the tent and bellowed for Arkon. The wizard mustn't have gone far because he appeared moments later.

Arkon ducked inside and looked all around like a trapped rat. "He's gone?"

Nord nodded then grinned. "You made yourself a new friend tonight. He asked me to tell you that if you attack him again he's going to turn you inside out. He seemed quite serious."

Arkon started trembling. "I didn't know who he was, I just reacted."

Nord laughed a great deep belly laugh. "I think that fact pissed him off even more than you trying to fry him. Mind your manners next time."

Arkon swallowed. Nord could actually watch his fear slide down his throat. "What did he want?"

Nord held up the vial. "Mostly to give us this."

"What is it?"

When he finished explaining about the antivenom Arkon said, "Do you know how valuable that is?"

"Of course," Nord said. "With this we can travel through the heart of the desert, resting and recovering at the wild oases while my brother will have to travel directly between towns. The tactical advantages are huge."

"That's not what I meant," Arkon said, his eyes glued to the vial. "The merchant's league has offered a huge reward to anyone that can make the oases safe, several thousand gold pieces in fact."

"I don't think that's what Daktari had in mind when he gave us the antivenom. Still, if you want, you can mention it to him next time he drops in."

Arkon ripped his eyes away from the vial. "That's all right. Anything else?"

"How's the resupply going?"

"Last time I checked, the quartermasters were a day or two away, why?"

"According to Daktari, Vilos is near the border. If we hurry we might catch him away from the capital and its huge stone walls. If we can hit his army hard we might score a quick victory."

"If we don't need to carry a ton of water we can probably be ready in a day," Arkon said.

"Excellent, Vilos is maybe a week away. We'll catch him by surprise and grind his army under our boots."

⁘

Prince Nord drew in a lungful of dry desert air and smiled. It felt good to be home. The White Tigers had been traveling for two days through the desert. On the horizon he could just make out the jutting palms of an oasis. Nord was running behind the schedule he'd set for himself. The men needed time to adjust to the desert heat and he'd set a slower pace to accommodate them. Even so he'd lost ten men too stubborn to part with their heavy armor.

Watching their death by heatstroke had convinced the remaining holdouts of the value of light armor.

Nord signaled the commander of his cavalry. With difficulty the man managed to get his camel over beside Nord's. "Sir?"

"Send a detachment ahead to scout the oasis. We'll camp there until morning. Remind them not to drink until I arrive."

The soldier saluted and rode away. When he rejoined his men Nord could see him barking orders. A moment later a dozen men rode out toward the oasis. None of them looked very comfortable between the two humps of their camels.

The main column arrived about an hour behind the scouts. Nord noted that the cavalrymen had the oasis surrounded and were watching for an ambush from all directions. When they finally reached the oasis Nord dismounted and added three drops of the milky liquid to the water of the well.

"Drink up, men. The water's safe now."

No one moved.

To a man they had heard the stories of slow, lingering deaths caused from drinking the water.

Disgusted, Nord cupped his hands, scooped up some water and gulped it down in two great swallows.

Everyone held their breath and watched.

A minute passed, then two.

When he didn't keel over the men charged toward the water to drink. As soon as camp was set and everyone had drunk their fill, Nord, Arkon, and the commanders of the infantry and the cavalry met in Nord's tent.

When all were seated Nord said, "Tomorrow we reach the

first town in the High Kingdom. Black Moon Oasis is small, one of the smallest towns in the land. Perhaps two hundred people call it home year round."

"If the town is so poorly defended, why don't we march on it today?" the infantry commander asked.

"We can't reach it before nightfall and I want the men well rested before the battle. If we leave tomorrow morning, we should arrive just after noon. That will give the defenders a good look at our forces and may inspire them to surrender."

"What does it matter?" the cavalry commander said. "No town that small could stop us."

"True," Nord said. "But remember, after the war I must rule these people. If I can take them with a minimum of damage, I'll earn some goodwill."

The two commanders grumbled to themselves.

Nord brought them up short. "Gentlemen, I didn't bring you here to listen to you bitch. I'm telling you how it's going to be and that's it. Understood?"

The two men straightened in their seats. "Yes, sir."

"Good. Now go see to your men and make sure all water containers are refilled. We march at first light. Arkon, I'd like a word before you go."

The two commanders filed out of the tent. When they had gone Arkon said, "Yes, my lord?"

"I want you to find my brother. I'd like to know if there's an army defending that town. If he's not there, find out how far away he is. If it looks like we can catch him, we'll bypass the rest of the towns and go straight after him."

Arkon nodded. "No problem."

CHAPTER 29

Shara sat beside Robert on the hard wooden seat of the wagon. A pair of large bay draft horses pulled the wagon along a rough dirt road. Two bandits rode in the bed along with a mishmash of junk Robert thought looked valuable enough to let them pass for merchants.

The rest of the crew rode stolen horses from the farm. They traveled in a defensive formation around the wagon with two in front, two in back and the rest divided between each flank.

They'd torched the farmhouse three days ago. No evidence, Shale had said. Somehow he'd survived his discussion with Blade, a pity that. He'd made no more moves toward her, but every time he looked her way it sent a shiver down her spine.

"What's on your mind, kid?" Robert asked.

"Nothing, Uncle," Shara said.

Robert had decided that she should pose as his niece and now insisted that she address him as uncle so she wouldn't mess up if it was ever important. The wagon hit a bump, jostling her around. Riding on the wooden seat was almost as uncomfortable as walking.

She grimaced and adjusted her position. As if one section of hard wood was better than another. "I'll be picking splinters out of my rear end for the rest of my life."

Robert laughed. "You think this is rough? One time I rode out a typhoon in a sloop about twice the length of this wagon. I've never been so scared or sick in my life, before or since."

He seemed about to say more when Blade rode up beside the wagon. "Company, Bobby."

On the alert now Robert said, "Where?"

Blade pointed up the road. "Looks like a standard patrol, seven men and an officer."

He nodded. "I should be able to talk us through this. Stay alert just in case, and keep that lunatic under control."

He didn't need to say any more. Blade knew which lunatic he meant.

"If it's going bad, I'll give you the signal to attack."

"Scratching your throat?" Blade asked.

Robert nodded.

"We'll be ready." Blade returned to her place beside the wagon.

They continued on at a slow walk toward the patrol. The soldiers wore bright metal shirts and dome-shaped hats. Shara had never seen anyone wearing metal before. The bandits all made do with leather and the warriors from home would have died from the heat in such clothes.

For a moment Shara thought they might just pass by but the lead rider held up his hand signaling them to stop. He wore a white tabard over his metal shirt and seemed to be in charge.

Robert eased back on the reins, bringing their group to a halt. "May I be of some assistance, Lieutenant?"

The soldier's eyes narrowed. "How did you know my rank?"

Robert smiled easily. "The bronze crest on your helmet—a captain would wear silver."

"Very observant," the lieutenant said, still looking suspicious. "You have a rather large entourage for just one wagon."

Robert continued as though unaware of the soldier's suspicion. "Yes, a bit of blind luck on my part. These fine soldiers were in a hurry to get to Port Saint Thomas but two of their horses came up lame. I happened to overhear their conversation at the inn where we were staying and since I was headed to the same city, I offered to let two of them ride in my wagon in exchange for protection. Since they had a ship to catch, they agreed."

"A good deal for you," the lieutenant said.

Robert grinned. "Certainly cheaper than hiring them."

Shara could see the soldiers starting to relax. Robert had that effect. She thought he could talk a charging bull into turning aside.

"Mind if I take a look at your merchandise?"

"Help yourself," Robert said. "If you see anything you like, I have a special soldier's discount."

While the officer poked through the junk in the wagon one of the other soldiers gave a closer look at the horses pulling the wagon. Robert didn't seem to notice so Shara elbowed him in the side. When he looked at her she nodded toward the soldier by the horses.

Robert smiled and said, "Fine animals, aren't they? The best deal I got on this trip. Traded a farmer up the road my old horses and two casks of honey for them."

The soldier nodded. "I thought I recognized the brand, the Grover Farm, right?"

Robert squinched up his forehead in thought. "You know, I can't remember the fellow's name. Hell of a nice guy though."

The soldier smiled. "Sounds like Eli."

"Everything looks fine," the officer said. "Sorry to bother you, sir."

"Not at all, Lieutenant, it's always a pleasure to see my tax money at work. Good day."

The patrol rode away and Robert started the wagon going. When the soldiers had gone well out of sight he sighed in relief. "That was too close. If I hadn't explained that brand things could have gotten ugly. Good eye, kid."

Shara smiled at the praise, surprised at how good it made her feel.

"So why didn't you try and get away?" Robert asked.

"What?" The question caught her off guard.

"Why didn't you try and get away? You could have told those soldiers that we kidnapped you. We're kind of a disreputable-looking crew. They probably would have believed you."

"That occurred to me," she said. In fact, she realized now that she said it that she'd thought about it and rejected the idea without even being aware of it. "If I'd said something there would have been a fight."

"Without a doubt," Robert agreed.

"I guess I didn't want anyone else to get hurt on my account." She looked up at him. "Especially not you. You're the first friend I've had outside the palace. I couldn't stand it if something happened to you."

"Thanks, kid, that's sweet."

Blade rode over next to them. "Good work, Bobby. We'd best pick up the pace. When they find that burned-out farm, we'll want as much distance between us and them as possible."

Robert nodded in agreement and urged the horses into a trot. Shara gritted her teeth. The faster the horses went the worse the bumps felt. She groaned as they went through a particularly deep hole.

It was going to be a long ride home.

—✧—

The bandits made camp that night in a clearing just off the road that seemed put there for just such a purpose. After dinner, Shara watched Robert and Blade go off by themselves. They talked long into the night, well after everyone else had gone to sleep.

Shara was given the privilege of sleeping in the wagon bed. They didn't even bother with a guard anymore, so confident they seemed in Scratch's magic.

She'd almost fallen asleep when something jumped up into the wagon with her. She flinched, at first thinking it was some sort of wild animal. A moment later she realized it was just Scratch's cat. It rubbed against her leg, demanding attention. Clearly she wouldn't get any sleep until she'd obliged. As soon as she started rubbing behind its ears, the cat started purring.

After a few minutes of attention the cat curled up in a ball and went to sleep. Shara looked at it as she tried to figure out why the animal had come to see her. She'd never seen it more than a few feet away from the wizard before.

Soon she decided she didn't care why it was there and went to sleep.

When Robert shook her awake the sun was up and her furry companion long gone.

"Good morning." Robert handed her a slice of bread with honey on it. "We have to get moving. Climb up front and you can eat on the road."

Shara glanced around and saw that everyone was packed

and mounted except for the two that rode in the wagon. They got in as soon as she climbed up front.

"Why didn't you wake me earlier?" she asked around a mouthful of bread.

"No need to. Besides, you looked all in last night."

"I was tired," she said. "The meeting with the soldiers really jangled my nerves."

"Mine too," Robert said. "With any luck we can avoid any more meetings."

Angels willing. "I almost forgot to tell you, that wizard's cat paid me a visit last night."

Robert smiled and laughed softly.

"What's the joke?"

Robert shook his head. "I suppose it's time I let you in on Scratch's secret."

"Secret?"

"Yeah, see the cat is Scratch."

"You lost me," Shara said.

"The story goes that before he joined up with Blade, Scratch messed up a shape-shift spell and trapped himself in the form of a cat. Now he's stuck until he can get some expensive magic things, I haven't the slightest idea what."

"What about the guy, the one pretending to be the wizard?"

Robert scratched his head. "I don't know. They came as a package deal. I guess since he can't talk in his cat form, Scratch uses the guy as his voice and as a protector."

"Well that at least explains his nickname."

Robert laughed. "I suppose so. By the way, when you said your father would pay a big reward for your return, were you serious?"

"Yes, why?"

"Just curious, sometimes a prisoner will say anything to try and get free."

"Oh. So how long until we reach the Kanid Forest?"

"About a week." Robert smiled nervously. "I assure you I'm in no rush."

"Why?" she asked. "I thought we had to pass through the forest to reach the Sea of Torments."

"Yeah, well, a lion tamer has to stick his head in the lion's mouth at the end of the show, but he doesn't have to be happy about it."

CHAPTER 30

Vilos sat in Abin's tent waiting for the wizard to finish talking to his apprentice. The usual stench was absent today and thank heaven for that. Vilos could still smell whatever it was in his clothes.

When the wizard finally looked up Vilos asked, "Well, what news?"

Abin cleared his throat, never a good sign. "First, there's no need to march tomorrow, the nomads besieging Black Moon Oasis have fled the field. When the sun rose this morning the wall guards said they had just vanished."

Vilos nodded, not entirely displeased. "That's just as well. I grow weary of fighting my own people. What about Nord?"

"That news is less encouraging. Your brother marched this morning at the head of an army ten thousand strong. They should reach Black Moon Oasis by the end of the week."

"Damn, that isn't enough time to set up a proper defense. What do we know about his army?"

Abin handed him a sheet of vellum. "This is all the information our people could get. They have at least one wizard and the majority of their force is infantry. They traded their horses for camels and now have a desert cavalry force about half the size of ours."

"I can read," Vilos said, waving the report at him.

"Sorry, Majesty."

"No, I'm sorry. I fear the strain is starting to show. We can't defend Black Moon. Send a message alerting them to the danger and order all soldiers to return to civilian status. When Nord arrives, tell them to offer no resistance. My brother wants to rule this land. He won't burn out a village unless they give him a reason to."

"Right, anything else?"

"After the main force leaves, tell them to make life as difficult as possible for any garrison left behind. Also send a warning to all the other villages. They need to know what's happening." Vilos left Abin to his work and went to find Yosef.

The army's temporary smithy was little more than a tent with a charcoal forge, an anvil, and a sharpening stone. The cavalry commander watched the smith run his scimitar along a spinning stone wheel with a critical eye. Sparks flew as the smith put a razor edge on the blade.

Vilos tapped his friend on the shoulder. Yosef spun and fell into a battle-ready crouch. Seeing his lord he straightened.

"We need to talk," Vilos said.

Yosef nodded. "Master Smith, have that blade delivered to my tent when you're finished."

The smith grunted without taking his eyes off the blade.

Vilos led Yosef back to his tent. Once inside he filled him in on the situation.

"Good fortune about the nomads," Yosef said.

"Perhaps they've had enough of their rebellion."

"The nomads never considered themselves a part of the High Kingdom, so I doubt they'd call it a rebellion," Yosef pointed out. "Anyway, I'm glad they've made the smart choice. Even if it was a little late in coming."

"Agreed."

Vilos hung his head. Heaven's mercy, he missed Shara. Just the sight of her could bring a smile to his face. He could use that smile right now.

"What about your brother?" Yosef asked.

"That's why I brought you here. I want you to take some cavalrymen and harass his army as they travel."

"Where will you fight the main battle?" Yosef asked.

"Main battle? I'm not certain I understand."

"Where will you confront your brother? Where will the army make its stand?"

"There will be no stand while Nord has Heat's Bane. Our armies are about equal. With that sword, my brother could wipe out a third of our forces, leaving the rest easy pickings for his army."

"Majesty, we can't just run away." Yosef began pacing around the tent.

"I share your sentiment, Captain, but now is not the time to act foolishly. If we're patient, the time to strike will come. It would be nice if we had an army available when it does. I assure you it galls me to run from Nord, but if anyone can appreciate the power of the weapon he carries it's me."

"As you say, Majesty. When do I leave?"

"As soon as you can get your best two hundred riders supplied and ready. Let me remind you that under no circumstances should you allow Nord to engage you directly, just hit and fade. Your riders should be better than his on camels."

Yosef smiled, an odd reaction Vilos thought. "Would you care to share? I could use a laugh."

"It's nothing really funny, it just struck me that the tactics you just described are the preferred fighting style of the nomads."

Vilos smiled as well. "Yes, I can appreciate the irony. Let us hope it works better for us than it did for them."

—✧—

Yosef lay flat on a low dune near the oasis where Nord's army stopped. He, along with all the men that rode with him, had traded his uniform for tan robes that let him blend in to the desert. At first Yosef couldn't imagine what Nord could be thinking camping so near the poisoned water. It would be a simple thing for someone to fall in or get splashed. His men could be killed by the dozens.

When Nord had poured some liquid into the water Yosef had been curious then stunned when Nord had taken a huge gulp. His first thought was that the exiled prince had decided to commit suicide and save them the trouble of killing him.

When nothing happened and the soldiers began splashing in the water he realized whatever Nord had poured in had negated the poison. His lord would be most interested in this news. It removed all doubt that Nord and the mysterious sorcerer were aligned. No one else could have the knowledge to negate the poison.

As soon as they began unpacking their tents, Yosef slithered back down behind the dune. It seemed they planned to rest before advancing on Black Moon. Tonight he would get his first chance to inflict some harm on the invaders.

When darkness fell Yosef selected ten men to accompany him on the first raid. He had no idea what sort of defenses Nord might have around his camp, so Yosef planned to risk as few men as possible finding out.

As they approached the oasis, Yosef saw the glow from a

few fires. He signaled his men to spread out and look around. The plan was to take out anyone they could, as fast as they could.

Yosef eased his way closer, his feet not making a sound in the soft sand. A soft cough stopped him in his tracks. In the dim starlight he could just make out the form of a sentry. The soldier was facing away from him, watching the desert without really seeing anything.

Yosef drew his curve-bladed dagger. He held it in a reverse grip, blade pointed down.

Creeping slowly closer Yosef kept an eye on the sentry for any signs that he'd been spotted.

When only a few feet separated them, Yosef took two quick steps, wrapped his hand over the man's mouth, and brought the dagger around to drive it into his heart.

It all happened in one fluid movement then the kid was dead. Yosef realized as he lowered him to the ground the sentry couldn't have been more than eighteen. He gave a grim shake of his head and ripped the dagger free. Leaving the body where it lay, Yosef went in search of further victims.

The job was bloody, but short. In five minutes Yosef killed three guards, leaving their bodies in pools of blood. He crept away from the camp toward the rendezvous point he'd set. One of his men was waiting and the rest trickled in after a few minutes. Yosef was pleased that they'd all made it back unhurt.

When everyone had arrived he led them to where their camels waited. They mounted up and headed north toward their camp. It was Yosef's hope that Nord would be less likely to pursue them if he had to retrace his steps to do it.

CHAPTER 31

P rince Nord reached for his sword when Arkon burst
into his tent. The wizard paused only a moment then
said, "Better come see."

He hurried back out as quickly as he'd come.

Curious about what could have gotten his wizard so riled
up Nord dressed and went out into the camp. In the chill,
predawn light soldiers were milling about.

He found Arkon waiting nearby. "Well?"

Arkon led him to the edge of the camp. A corpse lay on the
ground. "They found him this morning. There are nineteen
more just like him around the perimeter."

Nord swore. "When did it happen?"

"Early last night. What do you think, nomads or your
brother?"

Nord shook his head. "I don't know. Could be either,
nomads hate outlanders like us and wouldn't hesitate to cut a
few throats if they thought they could get away with it. Vilos
wouldn't be afraid to sow a little chaos either. Doesn't much

matter, either way they're dead. Bury them and let's get moving."

After a chilly start to the day it grew miserably warm. Used as they were to the cooler northern environment, his men began to wilt. They marched half the day and managed to drink all the water they'd brought from the oasis. A little after noon, the walls of the town of Black Moon came into view. There was no army in sight.

Arkon had told him Vilos wasn't there but Nord had hoped his wizard had been mistaken.

Oh, well.

"Shape up," Nord barked. The men had gotten into ragged lines as the heat wore them down.

The army formed up into neat rows, weapons held ready. Nord drew Heat's Bane and pale-blue light ran up the length of it.

"Forward."

The army marched in lockstep to the gates, ready for battle. To Nord's astonishment the gates stood open and no arrows rained down on them. Along the main street there were no signs of life.

"A curious reception," Arkon said.

"Quite. I wonder what my brother's playing at now. Steady advance. Keep your eyes open."

Nord rode at the head of his army down the street. They had marched almost to the center of the town before they saw any signs of life. At the end of the street near a large house waited an old man. The village elder, Nord assumed.

The elder bowed as low as he could manage. "Prince Nord, welcome to Black Moon Oasis."

Nord dismounted and sheathed his sword. "Tell me, Elder, why did no one try and defend the village?"

"The sultan contacted us three days ago to warn us of your coming and to say that he didn't have time to set up a proper defense. He called our garrison to join the main army and said we should do our best. We have only old men, women, and children left in town. We decided our best would be to die very quickly. When our spotters saw you coming, I ordered the gates thrown open and the people to stay inside so they wouldn't be hurt by accident. We care little who sits on the throne. Sultan's Oasis is a long way from here. We ask only to be allowed to live in peace."

Nord laid a gentle hand on the elder's shoulder. "You were wise not to oppose me. I shall reward your wisdom by harming no one. My men are tired and will camp in the square."

"Thank you for your kindness, Prince Nord."

Night had long since fallen as Nord sat in his tent studying his maps. He was well pleased with the ease of his first capture. It felt like an omen of things to come. Nord contemplated that happy thought for a moment before a scream brought him out of his reverie.

He grabbed his sword and bolted out of the tent, certain an attack was on.

He was right but not in the way he thought. The scream had come from a young village girl may be fifteen years old. One of his men had her pinned down and was tearing at her shirt. Nord grabbed the man by the back of the neck and tore him off.

"What did you think you were doing?" he demanded.

The man grinned showing several gaps in his teeth. "Just having a bit of fun, sir."

Nord backhanded him to the ground, probably creating several more holes in his smile. The man groaned but Nord ignored him. Instead he went over to the girl and helped her up.

"Why are you out so late, child?" he asked.

"I'm sorry, my lord. My grandmother was thirsty and we had no fresh water. I was going to the well to fetch some for her."

Nord smiled. "I see. Go ahead, no one will bother you."

The girl hurried off toward the well, pausing only long enough to pick up her dropped pitcher. Nord turned his attention to the fallen soldier.

He grabbed him by the throat and lifted him off the ground. "Did you not hear me say no harm would come to these people?"

"Yes, sir, I heard you."

A small crowd of soldiers had gathered. Nord thrust the man toward the nearest group. "Clap him in irons. I'll see to his punishment in the morning."

The soldiers hastened to obey, dragging their comrade off before Nord turned his anger on them.

The rest of the night passed without incident and Nord even managed to get some rest. When he woke he found Arkon sitting quietly waiting for him.

He groaned and sat up. "Well, what is it?"

"I located your brother and his army. I only made contact briefly before another wizard sensed my presence and blocked me out. They're headed southeast and look to be at least four days ahead of us."

"Southeast," Nord said. "He's headed to the capital. Sultan's Oasis is the only place he thinks he'll have a chance of beating us. He's wrong, dead wrong."

"We'll find out," Arkon said. "There's no way we can catch them at the pace we've been going."

"Yeah, and I don't dare push the men any harder or they'll keel over before we catch Vilos and save him the trouble of fighting. No, we'll take our time and fight on his ground.

Heat's Bane will more than even the odds. Can you still keep an eye on my brother?"

"I can try, but that wizard will be on the alert after this morning. I don't know how much good I can do."

Nord nodded. "Do what you can."

Arkon bowed and left. Nord dressed then went out and bellowed the assembly order and soon many voices echoed it. In a few minutes all the men had assembled.

Nord pointed at three of them at random. "Go fetch that idiot."

Everyone knew who he meant. News of the attack had spread through the camp. While the men went to fetch the prisoner, Nord addressed the remaining soldiers.

"Men," he began. "When this town surrendered they put themselves under my protection. Last night, after I said no one would be harmed, I caught one of you attacking a young woman."

The soldiers arrived with the offending man in tow. Dried blood covered his face and several more teeth were missing.

Speaking now more for the benefit of the villagers Nord knew were watching, he continued. "How can I expect my subjects to respect my orders when my own men don't? Insubordination can't be tolerated."

Nord drew Heat's Bane and drove it into the prisoner's gut. He summoned the magic and in seconds the soldier was frozen solid. He jerked the blade free and struck the icicle with the base of the hilt. A thousand pieces of frozen flesh tinkled down.

"Thus is the fate of all who defy me. Break camp, Zorn's Oasis waits."

CHAPTER 32

Vilos ate the last bit of his breakfast. Soon they would leave camp and continue the long march to Sultan's Oasis. He'd made up his mind that the only place they had a chance against Nord was the capital. Sultan's Oasis had the highest walls and most defensible design of all the town and cities of the High Kingdom. To make his stand anywhere else would be folly.

Vilos drained his wine as Abin entered. "Majesty," the wizard said. "I have Captain Yosef's first report."

"Excellent, let's hear it."

Abin gestured and a little mote of light drifted in, no bigger than a marble. Vilos realized the light came from an impossibly small winged creature.

"Abin?" Vilos said.

"Sorry, Your Majesty, let me introduce Skydancer, the wind sprite to whom I've entrusted the task of carrying messages between us and Captain Yosef."

"I see," Vilos said. "Go ahead."

Abin nodded. "Tell him, Dancer."

The sprite relayed Yosef's message, describing in a high thin voice the successful attack on the guards at the oasis. When the sprite got to the part about purifying the oasis Vilos listened with particular attention. If they could get that vial they could purify the rest of the oases.

When the sprite finished Vilos said, "Thank you, Skydancer." The light bobbed up and down in what could only be called a curtsy. "Tell Captain Yosef well done and to keep doing what he's doing."

The light bobbed again and vanished. Vilos leaned back in his chair.

"What are you thinking, Majesty?" Abin asked.

"I'm thinking I'd like to get my hands on that vial."

"Perhaps when we've dealt with your brother we can take it from him."

Vilos smiled. "Feeling optimistic today?"

Abin smiled back. "When you brought me out to fight this war I didn't think I'd last this long. Since I'm still alive, why not be optimistic?"

"Why not indeed?"

CHAPTER 33

A dark forest loomed in the distance. Though the sun was at its highest a shiver ran down Shara's spine. After all the stories Robert had told her of the Kanid Forest, the actual sight of it made them seem all the more real.

The week had passed with little to mark it save two meetings with merchant caravans. Robert had spoken with both groups and done a little trading. Neither group had passed through the forest, so they could offer no information. Of the patrol that questioned them earlier they'd seen no sign. If the soldiers suspected them of burning the farm, they hadn't managed to catch up yet.

"Grim sight, huh?" Robert asked when he caught her staring at the forest.

Shara swallowed the lump in her throat and nodded. "The light seems funny around it."

"The tall trees cause shadows to fall across the road like that. Don't worry about it, we'll be fine."

Shara looked down at the crossbow he'd assembled the day before then back to him.

He shrugged. "You can worry a little if you want, but don't overdo it."

Shara laughed. It sounded a little hysterical, but she felt better afterward.

"Will we be alright?" she asked, a slight quiver in her voice.

Robert put a comforting arm around her. "Listen, every year hundreds of caravans pass through the forest. Less than a dozen of them are attacked. As a gambling man, I'd say our odds of getting sunk in a storm on the Sea of Torments are better than our odds of being attacked."

"We gonna keep going or what?" Shale demanded.

Shara realized Robert had let the horses slow to a walk. "We were just discussing if we should go now or after lunch," Robert said with a solemn face.

He managed to hold it for a few seconds before breaking into a broad grin.

Shale snorted in disgust and kicked his horse forward.

"Before lunch I guess," Shara said.

Robert gave her one last squeeze, then urged the horses to a quicker pace. As they passed into the shadows the horses shied, perhaps sensing their rider's fear.

Shara glanced over her shoulder. The shadows near the entrance of the forest appeared to create a barrier, almost a wall of shadows. Even though she knew they could turn around and ride out if they wanted to, it appeared the way was cut off.

Her breathing grew fast and ragged.

The world was closing in on her.

Everything started spinning.

Robert's hand fell on her shoulder. "Steady, kid. You're alright."

Shara took slow, steady breaths until the dizziness passed. It was all in her head. She had to be strong. Every turn of the wagon wheel brought her closer to home. She shuddered. And the sorcerer waiting for her.

They traveled through the dark forest. Huge trees towered over them. None of the animal noises she'd noticed in the Vale seemed evident here. All she could hear was the creaking of the wagon.

The silence was getting to her. "Talk to me, Robert."

"Sure, kid. What do you want to talk about?"

"Anything. Tell me about the forest. It seems different from the Vale."

"It's not that different," Robert said. "Once upon a time I heard they were both part of one big forest that included all the ground we've covered and then some. The land was gradually cleared for farms and towns. That's the way it goes most everywhere I've traveled."

Unable to imagine a forest that large Shara asked, "Why weren't the Vale and Kanid Forest cleared as well?"

"The Vale survived because it provides a buffer between two kingdoms that really dislike each other. The Kanid Forest is still standing because the Wolfen decided they didn't want it cut down. Anyone with a saw would do well to steer clear of this forest, unless they fancy becoming a Wolfen's dinner."

Shara shivered at the thought.

Robert smiled and chuckled to himself.

"What's so funny?"

"Don't you think it's odd that with all the things in the world to be scared of, the thing that gets most people is the thought of getting eaten by some big-toothed critter? Ask any sailor what scares him and I guarantee you the most common answer you get won't be storms or pirates. Sharks are what sailors fear most."

"I don't think it's funny at all," Shara said. "Aren't you afraid of getting eaten?"

"Sure, you'd have to be out of your mind not to be, it's just that I fear some things even more."

Shara was about to ask what when he hauled back on the reins. "Did you hear that?"

Shale rode up beside the wagon. "What now?" he asked.

"I heard something, over there." Robert pointed to the left side of the road.

Swords cleared scabbards and in an instant everyone was armed. They waited, tension filling the air. You could hear a butterfly sneeze it was so quiet.

After a minute or two where nothing happened Robert shrugged. "Must have been an animal."

Everyone sheathed their weapons and they continued on. Robert looked at Blade again and Shara thought she saw a nod pass between them. She wasn't certain and decided not to mention it.

The rest of the day passed without incident and near dark they made camp in a small clearing beside the road. They made no fire and set a double guard.

Shara had just finished her cold jerky when Robert came over and sat beside her. "How you holding up, kid?"

She smiled weakly. "I'll feel better when we've left this forest behind."

"With any luck tomorrow night we'll camp beyond the forest. We'll be safe then, at least from the Wolfen."

"How can you be certain?" she asked.

"No Wolfen has ever been seen beyond the borders of the forest."

Robert left her and headed toward the edge of the clearing near the forest.

Shale stopped him. "Where do you think you're going?"

"I've got to piss. You want to come along and shake off the excess?"

Shale spat at Robert's feet then wandered off.

Despite her anxiety, Shara soon drifted off to sleep.

—⁕—

I t seemed to her only seconds had passed yet someone was shaking her awake. "Time to get up."

Shara rolled over, not bothering to open her eyes. "I just fell asleep."

"Open your eyes," Robert said.

Shara opened her left eye and bright morning light stabbed it. She closed it again.

"We're leaving in five minutes. If you don't want to spend another night in the forest I suggest you get up."

Shara sat bolt upright, her eyes wide open. "I'm awake."

Robert grinned and bared his teeth in a mock snarl. "I thought that might get your attention."

She stuck her tongue out at him which only made him smile more. She tossed her blanket off and took the water skin he offered. The skin was halfway to her lips when she paused and looked down at the blanket. She hadn't had it last night.

She looked over at Robert but he was busy fussing with the wagon. Shara finished her drink, folded up the blanket and brought it over to him. "Thanks."

Robert stowed the blanket in the bed of the wagon. "Climb aboard. There's a bag of food on the seat, help yourself."

The little group soon got underway. The morning sun filtered down through the leaves creating strange patterns on the ground that swirled in the breeze. They hadn't gone far when Blade drew her sword. Everyone else did the same, looking on both sides of the road for the threat.

When nothing appeared she muttered something about the wind and sheathed her sword.

The rest of the morning passed without incident. As they ate lunch Shara said, "You and Blade seem awfully jumpy."

"This forest tends to encourage the feeling. Do you trust me?"

The question caught her off guard. She thought for a moment and realized she did. "I trust you, why?"

He lowered his voice so she could just hear him above the creak of the wagon wheels. "If anything happens, I need you to do what I say, no argument. Promise me."

She found the intensity with which he spoke a little scary. "I promise."

He grinned and the feeling passed. "Good girl."

Not long after their chat Shara heard a branch snap. "Did you hear that?"

"Yeah, hang on tight, kid, things are about to get ugly."

When Robert saw that Shara had a tight grip on the seat, he said, "I heard something, over there."

Robert pointed to opposite side of the road from the noise she'd heard.

No one reacted until half a dozen hairy forms burst from the tree line.

Shara screamed.

The Wolfen looked like true monsters. Most stood as tall as Morden and were covered in thick gray hair. Their heads resembled wolves but from the neck down they had the bodies of men. The only difference Shara could see besides the hair was that their hands ended in two-inch claws.

The first Wolfen hit Morden and sunk its claws into the big man's side, tearing him from his saddle.

Morden roared and struck the Wolfen in the chest, forcing it back.

Robert glanced over his shoulder and Shara turned with him. The two bandits in the wagon bed had gotten to their feet. Robert flicked the reins and sent the men sprawling on the ground.

Robert snapped the reins again and the horses took off.

"Blade!" he yelled, reaching out for her.

Blade rode at the front of the group and no Wolfen had attacked her yet.

She kicked her feet free of the stirrups and grabbed Robert's arm as the wagon thundered by.

Their momentum jerked her off the horse's back and Robert lifted her into his lap.

With Blade safely aboard Robert urged the horses to even greater speed. They soon left the other bandits behind.

Shara looked over her shoulder. A huge black Wolfen was chasing them and actually managed to gain a little on the horses.

"Robert! Behind us!"

Blade disengaged herself from Robert and slid into the wagon bed.

She reached back and grabbed the crossbow off the seat and leveled it at the Wolfen chasing them.

The weapon twanged and the bolt embedded itself in the Wolfen's hip.

It fell to the ground unable to run.

Blade reloaded the crossbow and set it on the bed of the wagon beside her.

"Nice shot," Shara said.

Blade looked at her and Shara saw a deep sadness in her eyes. She doubted shooting the Wolfen had anything to do with it.

When they'd put some distance between them and the fight Robert slowed the wagon. "Take a look, kid."

Shara had been watching behind them for signs of pursuit. She faced front when Robert spoke. Ahead a bright light flashed between the trees. A broad plain spread out before them. The evening sun colored the land pink.

The sight cheered Shara a great deal.

They stopped to make camp a couple miles from the edge of the forest. While Robert busied himself making a fire Shara noticed Blade sat away from them, not saying a word.

Shara went over to Robert and asked, "What's with Blade?"

Robert sighed and put another piece of wood on the fire. "Those guys had been a big part of her life since she was a kid. By choosing to come with us, with me, she left everything she's ever known behind."

"Heaven's mercy, Robert, what about the wizard? He put a spell on me, remember? He could cause me pain so I wouldn't be able to move."

Robert grinned. "Don't worry, that was just bullshit. In his current form Scratch doesn't have enough control over his magic to cast a spell like that."

Shara slapped him on the shoulder. "You jerk. You made me think that if I misbehaved that wizard would hurt me."

"Exactly, it didn't matter if the spell worked as long as you believed it would." Robert had a good fire going. He put a pot of water on to boil.

Shara felt relieved and annoyed. "So Scratch can't find me either?"

Robert grimaced. "That's another matter. The beacon spell is quite simple and well within his ability."

Shara threw up her hands in frustration. "So what's to keep him from hunting me down?"

"The Wolfen with any luck." The water started boiling and Robert added meat and vegetables for his stew.

Shara shuddered as she remembered those huge, hairy forms boiling out of the forest. "How did you know the Wolfen would attack?"

Robert looked up from his stew. "When we made camp last night, I scarred half a dozen trees near the camp. The Wolfen consider themselves guardians of the forest. I figured a little vandalism would anger them enough to get the job done."

"What if it hadn't?"

"It did. Let it go, kid. What's done is done."

CHAPTER 34

"Where is my brother?" Nord thundered.

His army had just marched into a third village, and they had yet to see a hint of resistance or any sign of Vilos's army. The only real trouble they'd encountered was the occasional night raid by a small group of nomads.

Twice he'd dispatched riders to deal with them but they'd never managed to catch up with the more skilled riders.

Arkon waited until Nord had calmed a bit before speaking. "My lord, all the information I've managed to gather says he's headed for the capital."

"Your information has precious few details." Nord dropped into a chair.

He'd grown sick of living in a tent, so he'd commandeered a house for the duration of his stay in this town, he couldn't even remember its name.

"My apologies, the wizard working for your brother is quite skilled. The information I've given you is the best I can manage with that power opposing me."

Nord massaged his temples. Trying to figure out his brother was giving him a headache. "Why, Arkon? Why is he running? At the very least he should try and engage us in a running battle to wear us down."

"Strategy isn't my area of expertise, my lord. All I've been able to think of is perhaps he hopes to arrive far enough ahead of us to set up a trap."

Nord tapped his chin as he thought over Arkon's idea. It made sense. Given enough time Vilos could build traps both magical and mundane. The roofs of the city buildings would also provide fine sniping positions. But Vilos should still be doing something to slow them down.

The truth hit Nord like a battle axe. "He doesn't have to slow us down. We're doing the job for him."

"Excuse me, my lord?"

"Tell the commanders starting tomorrow we're heading straight for the capital." Nord rose and clapped Arkon on the shoulder. "Good thinking, wizard."

CHAPTER 35

Vilos and his army arrived at Sultan's Oasis near dusk. The city seemed subdued to Vilos. The streets were empty and the few taverns they passed silent.

News of the invasion must have reached the city. As they marched through the near-deserted streets the army began to break up. The soldiers were heading home for the night. At dawn, the battle preparations would begin.

Vilos, Abin, and the palace guard continued on to the White Palace. Repairs had continued at a good clip during his absence. Most of the exterior damage had been fixed. There were no servants camped in the garden, so he figured the inside must have been good enough for them to move back in.

Once they were safely behind the walls Vilos dismissed the guard who returned to their barracks. Vilos and Abin continued on alone to the palace.

"Looks almost as good as new," Abin said.

"Yes, it looks like they finished just in time for Nord to smash it."

The two men walked up the steps toward the palace doors.

Waiting just outside was Sashen, his majordomo. Vilos had left him in charge of rebuilding the palace. It seemed he had done a good job.

"Welcome home, Majesty." Sashen bobbed up and down as was his habit.

"Hello, Sashen. The palace looks great, as always a job well done."

Sashen beamed. "We all worked hard. May I show you all the repairs we've made?"

"I've been riding for ten days. All I want to see is my bed." Seeing the crestfallen look on Sashen's face Vilos added, "I'll look at the repairs in the morning."

Sashen smiled. "As you wish, Majesty."

⋅—⋇⋅

Bright light streaming through his window woke Vilos. The sun had risen well above the horizon. Cursing to himself Vilos threw on his clothes and headed downstairs. He'd given orders that someone wake him at sunrise. There was a great deal to do and very little time in which to do it.

The smell of fresh-baked sweet rolls drew him to the dining room. Sashen was there with a mug of warm, spiced wine. "Morning, Majesty. Breakfast will be out in a moment."

"I thought I said to wake me at sunrise." Vilos took a sip of the wine, letting it slide down the back of his throat. It tasted wonderful and reminded Vilos how much he'd missed being home.

"That you did, but the royal magician said I should let you sleep."

Vilos frowned at him. "Since when do the wishes of the royal magician outweigh those of the sultan?"

"Only when the royal magician is correct," Abin said. He

appeared at the door in the far end of the dining room. The wizard walked over and took a seat beside Vilos. "You were exhausted last night. We need you at your best, so I suggested Sashen let you sleep."

Vilos knew when Abin said "suggested" he meant he used his magic to make Sashen do what he wanted.

Since he could do nothing about it now Vilos said, "Thanks, but if you ever countermand one of my orders again, I'll start looking for a new wizard. Understand?"

Abin winced. "Perfectly. On another subject, Skydancer arrived this morning with a message. Nord has turned straight south. He's heading directly here, no longer bothering to capture towns along the way."

"How long until he arrives?"

"If he pushes, three days. If he wants his men in any condition to fight more like five."

Vilos nodded. "We'll be ready."

.—✕⊱

For the second time Vilos's army gathered in the city square. In the feeble morning light Vilos looked over the brave men that would defend Sultan's Oasis. They had spent the last four days preparing the city for the upcoming battle. Despite all those preparations, he knew many of these men would not live through the day.

He had divided the army into two groups, each numbering about five thousand. The left-hand group consisted of the cavalry, which would be of little use in the tight streets, and about one-third of the infantry. This group would head south and join up with Yosef who would lead them on to Haydrien where Vilos would rejoin them if forced to abandon the city.

The right-hand group held the rest of the infantry and

archers. Vilos would lead this group in defense of the city. "Soldiers of the High Kingdom, hear me." Vilos's voice thundered over the gathering bringing the chatter to a halt. The soldiers all looked at him. "I know the last weeks have been difficult. Withdrawing before an enemy is a hard thing for proud warriors like us. Today we run no more. The time has come to make the invaders pay."

The assembled soldiers roared and brandished their weapons. Vilos raised his arms to silence them. "I know some of you aren't happy about leaving, but should we fail, it will go to you to avenge us. My scouts say the enemy will reach the gate by noon. Those of you that are leaving should get moving. I want you out of sight before the enemy arrives. The rest of you know your positions, get to them."

The various sergeants began barking orders, getting men and material where they needed to go. Vilos left them to their work and followed along behind the cavalry toward the main gate. Abin was there working on a surprise for Nord's troops.

Vilos had covered half the distance to the main gate when he spotted a group of priests approaching him from a side street. He counted twenty of them and they looked determined to talk to him. The ten guards that followed him everywhere moved to block the little group but Vilos waved them back. Perhaps he could deal with them quickly and return to work.

"Sultan, we would speak with you."

Vilos groaned. The leader of the pack was the priest of the Binder that had challenged him earlier. The rest just seemed to be following in his wake.

"How can I help you most holy sirs?"

"Sultan, we demand that you fight the battle outside the city." Again the priest of the Binder spoke for the group.

Vilos frowned but held his calm. "I have considered that option but deemed it unworkable. Was there anything else?"

The priest began to sputter then turned red. "I command you in the Binder's name. You dare not disobey."

Vilos reared back and swung a roundhouse right that caught the priest in the side of the head and sent him sprawling to the ground. The other priests gaped at their fallen leader then back to Vilos.

"It would seem the Binder favors me once more this day. Unless you gentlemen want to fight, I suggest you get out of the way. A hospital has been set up at The Lady of Mercy's temple. Perhaps you can be of some use there." Vilos walked away leaving the priests staring at him.

Vilos smiled as he rubbed his knuckles. He'd been wanting to flatten that sanctimonious prick for years. If he died, at least he'd go with the satisfaction of leveling that uppity priest.

The last of the cavalry had entered the city when Vilos arrived. Abin was overseeing the sealing of the gate. Twenty feet from them four ballistae sat pointed at the slowly disappearing opening. Whoever came through first was in for a nasty surprise.

CHAPTER 36

N ord's army paused half a mile from the walls of Sultan's Oasis. Nord hoped the sight would intimidate the soldiers guarding the city. For almost five days they'd seen no sign of Vilos's army. He'd felt certain someone would try and harass them as they got ever closer to the capital. Perhaps his brother feared him more than he'd first thought.

Nord drew Heat's Bane and motioned his army forward. They advanced at a steady march toward the main gate. Nord saw no sign of any archers along the wall. Not that that meant anything, they could be hiding ready to spring up when the army got within range. At the last town Nord had taken, they prepared a ram similar to the one they'd used at Aaron's castle. Nord planned to take care of the city gates the same way he'd dealt with Aaron's.

He motioned his army to stop then rode to within a hundred yards of the gate. No archers appeared so Nord blasted the gates with the sword until they were coated with ice. At his signal a dozen men charged forward pushing the ram.

Behind them came two hundred of his best infantrymen. They would seize the area surrounding the gate.

Nord smiled as they passed him. It appeared his brother planned to give him Sultan's Oasis as well.

The ram struck the gate which exploded in a shower of wood chips. The infantry charged through the opening and an instant later four six-foot spears came flying out.

One missed Nord's head by a foot. The others were less fortunate. The ballistae bolts struck with such force that they drove through three, sometimes four men before stopping.

A score of men lay dead or dying around the gate when Nord entered. The entire ram crew lay on the ground moaning in pain. None of them appeared injured.

"Arkon," Nord bellowed.

The wizard rode up beside him. "Yes, my lord?"

"What's wrong with those men?" Nord gestured toward the ram crew.

Arkon dismounted and looked the men over. He made several passes over them then picked up a piece of wood from the broken gate. The wizard spoke a brief incantation and the wood vanished in a puff of smoke.

"Poison," Arkon said.

"Poison? How in the nine hells did they get poisoned?"

Before Arkon could explain an arrow embedded itself in the chest of one of the soldiers standing nearby. Men screamed as arrows rained down on them.

"Take cover," Nord yelled.

The order was unnecessary since everyone was already scrambling around trying not to get hit. The only cover was behind the outer wall. Before everyone managed to get back through the gate half the initial entry force was dead or wounded.

"Anyone see where those arrows came from?" Nord asked.

No one answered and Nord swore. The bulk of the army had advanced down near the edge of the wall. They had to get in and establish a foothold.

Nord looked around for something he could use. He spotted the wagon that had held their ram. The bed still looked pretty solid.

"You men." Nord pointed to a group of half a dozen soldiers that looked a little bigger than the rest. "Grab that wagon and we'll use it for cover. Gray Company, get in behind them."

Nord took a spot near the front of the soldiers as the big men hefted the wagon bed.

When they indicated they were ready Nord said, "Go!"

The whole group surged around the wall and through the shattered gate. Several arrows thunked home into the wood. Then they stopped.

The archers knew they couldn't get to them.

"Keep moving," Nord said.

No sooner had he spoken than there was a loud thwack and a ballista bolt smashed through the wagon bed killing three men.

A second bolt smashed through inches from Nord's head, killing the man next to him.

The last two bolts blasted the wagon to splinters and killed six more men.

With no cover left Nord decided to let rip with a blast from Heat's Bane.

He didn't aim; he just sprayed the area in front of them with killing magic.

The man in front of him went down with an arrow in his throat.

His view clear, Nord saw no sign of bodies.

He'd hit no one.

All he managed to do was destroy the ballistae.

Arrows rained down on them. Nord saw dozens of archers positioned on rooftops all around them.

"Fall back."

Nord was in a frothing rage when they finally reached the safety of the wall. He'd lost better than a hundred men with nothing to show for it.

"These half-assed measures aren't getting us anywhere. When I give the order, the whole army will charge. We'll drive right through to the palace."

"Is that wise?" Arkon asked. "Bunched up in those streets we'll make easy targets for their archers."

"I saw only a few dozen archers defending the gate. If we move fast enough we can make it to the palace in fifteen minutes. The faster we get through the streets the better. At the rate we're going they'll just pick us apart."

"True enough." Arkon drew a slim black wand with a silver tip from his robe. "Perhaps I can give those archers something to think about."

"Now you're talking." Nord clapped him on the shoulder. Louder he said, "Alright, we're going to charge. Don't stop until we reach the palace wall."

Everyone nodded.

"Let's go."

Wave after wave of soldiers poured through the ruined gate, Nord and Arkon in the lead.

Arrows began raining down on them.

None of them got close to Nord.

He figured Arkon must have worked some spell to protect him.

When an arrow headed straight toward the wizard then

veered suddenly away he decided maybe he was just getting a side benefit of Arkon's own protection.

The wizard raised his wand and pointed at an archer. Streamers of red light streaked out and cut the man to ribbons. Nord's own archers tried to run and shoot at the same time with little success.

Arkon raised the wand again and the red light streaked out.

Before it reached its target the light vanished in a flash.

"What the hell was that?" Nord asked.

"Your brother's wizard negated the spell. I'm afraid I won't be of much use now. His power is equal to mine."

"You'll be able to counter his attacks as well though, right?"

"Absolutely," Arkon said.

They moved past the first group of archers and into a densely built-up portion of the city. Multistoried buildings and narrow side streets surrounded them.

Perfect place for an ambush.

CHAPTER 37

V ilos stood atop the flat roof of a two-story building and observed the initial attack and retreat of his brother's forces with grim pleasure. The ballistae had given them a real shock.

When the main rush came he knew that playtime had ended. Abin was flying, invisible, over the battle keeping an eye out for Nord's wizard. It was time for Vilos to join his men.

He climbed down from the roof and hurried toward the two thousand men waiting for him. His guards fell in silently beside him.

The main group of soldiers had taken up position in an evacuated bakery. Nearby, along the main avenue of approach, fifteen men armed with special weapons waited atop a building. When those weapons went off, Vilos's men would prepare for the attack.

As they milled around waiting for the signal Vilos heard one of them mutter, "How are we supposed to scare them when we all smell like fresh baklava?"

Vilos grinned. The initial attack had done wonders for

morale. After weeks of running the men had needed to take out their frustrations. He was about to say something when the back door swung open.

Everyone drew their weapons thinking they'd been discovered. When nothing appeared they all relaxed.

When Abin spoke Vilos almost jumped out of his boots. "I've neutralized their wizard, Majesty. Both your brother and the wizard march at the head of the army."

"Very good," Vilos said. "That should make the ambush more effective. Keep watch on them, I'll handle things here."

"Yes, Majesty," Abin's disembodied voice said. A moment later the bakery door shut and the wizard was gone.

Abin hadn't been gone long when Vilos heard the first explosion. The screams came soon after.

CHAPTER 38

Nord surveyed the narrow stretch of road. His initial plan had been to charge straight through to the palace, but it didn't take long for him to reconsider. It would be incredibly easy for them to charge straight into a trap. Now that no one was shooting at them, Nord decided to slow down and be cautious.

"Do you sense any magic?"

Arkon closed his eyes for a moment then shook his head. "Nothing."

Perhaps the location was too obvious. The army started forward.

They hadn't taken ten steps when the first enemy soldier appeared atop a nearby building. The man lobbed a small item at the center of the densely packed column before ducking down again. All around them more men appeared and lobbed similar items.

The first one struck the center of Nord's army and exploded in a ball of sound and fire.

They had little time to react before the second firebomb exploded.

A dozen more explosions mingled with the sound of screaming and the hungry crackle of flames.

In moments his well-trained army collapsed into a frenzy of men running every which way trying to escape the killing flames.

Those on the opposite side of the fire scattered into the side streets and back the way they'd come.

"To me, men!" Nord bellowed, trying to regain control of his disintegrating army.

The noise was such that only the nearest companies heard him. They put some distance between themselves and the dying.

"I thought you said there was no magic."

Arkon studied the sooty black smoke and said, "That isn't magic, it's alchemist's fire."

"What the hell is that?"

"A volatile liquid that explodes on contact with air, purely mundane, no magic at all."

"Terrific, how do we stop it?"

Arkon looked at the sword in Nord's hand.

"Of course." Nord leveled the sword and let rip with a blast of chill magic.

An icy sheet of energy hit the inferno. He watched as the flames died down revealing the charred bodies of hundreds of his men.

Behind them there was no sign of the rest of his soldiers.

He swore. That one attack had cost him nearly half his army. There was nothing to be done about it now. "Let's move out. The palace waits."

They left the stench of charred meat behind and headed deeper into the city. The closer they got to the palace the more lavish the homes became. As they passed a particularly well-built mansion Arkon held out his arm. "I sense magic."

Everyone came to a halt. "Where?" Nord asked.

"The center of the road; there's about three feet of safe space on either side. The danger zone looks about twenty feet long."

"Everyone hear that?" Nord asked. The soldiers murmured their understanding. "Arkon, take half the men along the left side. The rest of you come with me."

Nord led his men along the right edge of the road, Heat's Bane glittering icy blue in his hand. He went about ten paces before he felt confident enough to step away from the wall of the building. When nothing happened he turned to watch the men's progress.

About half of them were safely beyond the trap when the first spear thrust through the window of the house. The spear struck a man through the gut and pushed him into the spell field.

Nord braced himself, waiting for an explosion.

Nothing happened.

As the men gaped in surprise, a score more spears struck home on both sides of the road. When a dozen bodies fell and nothing happened the soldiers moved away from the buildings and into the middle of the road.

"Come on," Nord yelled. "They're just trying to slow us down."

He pointed Heat's Bane and summoned a wall of ice to protect his men.

They left the trap behind and continued down the main road. They'd gone maybe three hundred yards when Arkon stopped them again. "I sense another spell field."

"Like the last one?" Nord asked.

Arkon nodded. "Exact same size and shape, designed to make us travel close to the buildings."

"How stupid do they think we are?" one of the sergeants asked. "We ain't gonna fall for the same trick twice."

He stepped right into the spell field and exploded in a shower of blood.

Nord wiped his face. "I think we should go around."

No one argued.

He pointed Heat's Bane and threw up walls of ice to stop any soldiers inside the building from attacking them. When everyone had made it safely past, Nord said, "My brother is cleverer than I thought."

"Then you perceive his true intention?" Arkon asked.

"He's trying to sow confusion and slow us down."

"That's part of it," Arkon said moving closer to Nord. "There's more though. Every trap has something in common. To pass safely you have to call on the sword's magic. Your brother's trying to drain your power before he confronts you directly."

Nord frowned as he considered Arkon's words. He could feel the truth in them. Vilos always did favor a sneaky approach.

He might try but Nord would be damned before Vilos's tricks stopped him from claiming what was his.

CHAPTER 39

Vilos drove his sword through the chest of one of Nord's soldiers. The dead man fell to the ground and Vilos pulled his sword free. This first skirmish ended quickly as his force outnumbered the small group of fleeing soldiers five to one.

"Report, Captain."

Vilos's second-in-command for this battle offered a nervous bow. "Three dead, six wounded, sir."

"Alright, get the wounded to the healers. Everyone else, let's go hunting."

Vilos led them through the streets toward the ambush site. Three other groups scoured the streets for invaders that had fled the ambush. He hoped it wouldn't cost too many lives rounding up the stragglers.

As they approached the main street the scent of death assaulted them. The sight as they stepped onto Sultan's Way was even worse. Hundreds of bodies burned beyond recognition lay scattered about. Abin had told him the alchemist's fire wasn't pretty; effective, but not pretty.

Vilos certainly couldn't argue.

One of his men had dug out a pipe and was getting ready to light it with a smoldering finger bone. The others laughed until they saw the look on Vilos's face.

He slapped the bone from the soldier's hand. "They may have earned their death when they marched through our gates, but now that they've passed into the next world, you will treat them with respect."

The soldier pocketed his pipe and hung his head. "Sorry, Majesty."

Vilos laid a hand on the man's shoulder. "It's all right. Just remember, we mustn't lower ourselves to the level of our enemies or we risk becoming what we fight against. Understood?"

The last question was addressed to everyone.

"Yes, Majesty," came the unanimous reply.

"Good, now let's go find their buddies and send them to join their friends."

Vilos led them down a side street then paused when he heard the sound of fighting. "This way."

They thundered to the right and found a large group of invaders fighting one of his other bands of hunters.

Vilos roared and charged.

The nearest man turned just in time to get his skull split in half.

Unfortunately the force of the blow caused Vilos's sword to get stuck in the bone.

A massive axeman didn't waste the opportunity.

He swung his weapon with the idea of separating Vilos's head from his shoulders.

The look on his face when the weapon bounced off Vilos's neck brought a grin to the sultan's face.

It also bought him the second he needed to jerk his sword

free and spill the unlucky soldier's guts onto the street.

The shock of Vilos's attack brought the skirmish to a quick end.

He was about to lead his men off in search of another battle when he heard Abin's voice. "Majesty, your brother has reached the palace gates."

"Damn. Captain, I'll leave you in charge of the cleanup." Vilos tossed him a rune-covered stone. "Should the palace fall, I'll send a message through the stone. Get everyone hidden, understood?"

"Yes, Majesty," the captain said. "I won't let you down."

Vilos clapped him on the shoulder. "Good man. Abin, get us to the palace."

The wizard muttered a few words then tapped Vilos on the shoulder. His feet lifted off the ground and his stomach lurched.

He hated flying. Abin had assured him he knew just how long the spell would last and they'd be on the ground well before then.

Abin canceled his invisibility spell and they rose up into the air and shot toward the palace. At least Vilos assumed they shot toward the palace. He couldn't be certain since his eyes were clamped shut.

He felt the wind on his face then after a few seconds Abin said, "We're here."

Vilos opened his eyes and found himself hovering about an inch above the ground. Two thousand men stood waiting to fight the invaders.

"Why am I still floating here?"

"Sorry." Abin snapped his fingers and they settled back to earth.

A deep pounding echoed through the garden. "What is that?" Vilos asked.

"Your brother is trying to chop his way through the gate," one of the soldiers reported.

"Why doesn't he use the sword?" Vilos hoped blasting through the gate would use up the last of its power.

"Perhaps he's figured out your plan," Abin said as if reading his mind.

Vilos marched toward the gate. "Someone get me a crossbow."

When he arrived, a loaded heavy crossbow waited for him. The wood shuddered under the impact of an axe. Vilos took the weapon and put it to his shoulder. There was a small slot the guards used to look over visitors.

Vilos pointed at one of the soldiers. "Open that slot."

The man gingerly reached over and slid it open. Vilos spotted his brother's ugly face and fired.

The bolt scored a bloody line across Nord's cheek.

Vilos tossed the crossbow to a nearby soldier. "Everyone back."

"What did you do?" Abin asked.

"I just scratched Nord's pride." Vilos grinned at his friend. "He'll be coming, even if it takes every drop of power left in Heat's Bane."

A moment later the gates exploded in a blast of chill air.

A screaming clot of men poured through the sundered gate.

"Attack!" Vilos drew his sword and led the defenders on a fierce counterassault.

Vilos spotted his brother on the left side of the battlefield. Having no great desire to face the power of his sword he headed right.

Nord's men were skilled fighters and Vilos soon found himself hard pressed by a pair of warriors fighting in tandem. One had an axe and would attack aggressively then when Vilos tried to counter the swordsman would move in to guard his partner.

Finally Vilos was forced to allow the axeman to land a blow.

The distraction of his failed attack gave Vilos the second he needed to run the swordsman through.

Without his partner the axeman fell soon after.

Temporarily free, Vilos surveyed the battle. His men were getting pushed back. Nord's army was too large. The defense was going to break.

"Retreat to the palace," Vilos roared.

The defenders began a fighting retreat. Nord's men pushed hard but paid a steep price for every foot. They weren't the only ones paying, though. Vilos saw more than a few of his own men lying on the ground.

All of a sudden a blast of frigid air struck Vilos. He turned toward the source and saw a chunk of his flank frozen on the ground.

A hand fell on his shoulder.

He wheeled around ready to strike.

Abin was there. "The palace is lost. You must escape, Majesty. I'll send the message to our men in the city."

Vilos wanted to argue but Abin cut him off. "The people need their sultan alive. Think of Shara."

Vilos swore but knew the wizard was correct. "Alright, let's get to the portal. Sound the surrender and get the others out of sight."

Abin muttered a word of power and made some gestures in the air. "It's done, let's go."

They turned and ran from the battlefield, heading straight toward the palace. As they approached the doors Abin gestured and they flew open. The pair ran through the main hall toward the throne room.

The doors lay open before them. Vilos hurried behind the throne while Abin watched the door for signs of pursuit. After a moment's search he found a slight indentation and pressed it.

A hidden panel slid open revealing a stone tunnel that went deep into the earth.

"I got it, come on."

Abin joined him and conjured a sphere of light. Once they had entered the tunnel Vilos touched another indentation and closed the panel behind them. They followed the twisting path for several hundred yards until it emerged in a cavern about fifty feet across and twenty feet high. Two black stone pillars about eight feet apart rose ten feet in the air from the center of the cavern floor. Twisted runes covered every inch of the pillars.

Vilos stepped up to them and said, "In the name of the Sultan of the High Kingdom I command the path to open."

The runes began to glow with silver light. Soon the cavern was filled with so much light that Abin let his fade. When the space between the pillars finished filling with swirling silver light Vilos said, "Time to go."

Abin nodded and the two men stepped through side by side.

A jolt of power coursed through Vilos.

He felt like his body was being torn apart.

The sensation lasted only an instant, then they were standing in a cavern similar to the one beneath the palace.

The silver light faded and soon they were standing in total darkness. After a few moments Abin summoned a light. A small tunnel to their right led toward the surface.

Vilos went first up the tunnel, setting a slow pace. His head spun from the aftereffects of the teleportation spell.

He slammed his fist into the stone wall. "How many times has that gate been used?" he asked.

Before Abin could answer he continued, "Damn few, I know. Many of my ancestors died rather than flee an enemy."

"While you live the people have hope," Abin said. "Think of your daughter. Perhaps Kent has some word of Shara."

Vilos took little comfort in his words, but little comfort was better than none. At the top of the tunnel they exited into a quiet alley. When Vilos looked back he saw only a stone wall.

Abin saw the look on his face and smiled. "Illusory wall. One of my predecessors put it there to keep out unwanted visitors."

Vilos laughed. A salty breeze struck him and he drew in a deep breath. It had been too long since he'd seen the sea.

"My brother's office is near the docks. Let's go find him."

CHAPTER 40

Nord snarled in pain as the bolt ripped into his face. "Out of the way!" he bellowed.

He leveled Heat's Bane at the gate and blasted it to splinters. His men rushed in and were met by a mass of defenders. Nord kept his distance, feeling weak from using the sword's magic.

His men pushed the defenders back but at high cost. Nord closed his eyes and delved deep into Heat's Bane's magic. Little remained, but he felt a wisp of power. Enough, he hoped, to turn the tide quickly.

His right flank was starting to weaken. Nord raised his sword and summoned the last of the sword's magic.

Icy magic swept over Vilos's right flank killing scores of men.

The attack lost momentum as the defenders reeled.

Nord's men renewed their push.

They forced the defenders on to the palace steps then without warning they threw down their weapons and surrendered.

Thoroughly sick of fighting for one day, Nord accepted the surrender without question. His men rounded up the survivors and went to set up a temporary prison.

"You've won, my lord," Arkon said.

Nord looked at the wizard as blood dripped off his chin. "Hardly. Vilos escaped and my army is in ruins. I have the capital in name only. With the men I have left we can't even patrol the streets. I have no doubt my brother left plenty of men behind to cause trouble. We control the palace and that's it. Once everyone is secure I want you to contact Duke Benwa. Have him send more men south. Then we will finish off my brother."

CHAPTER 41

"There it is, King's Port." Robert made a grand sweeping gesture to encompass the entire city. He had brought the wagon to a halt on a small hill looking down over the city.

King's Port was an oddly sprawling city with a huge waterfront. Ships of all sizes, from massive galleons to three-man sloops crowded the docks. What made the city look odd was that it sprawled along the coast but only went about half a mile inland.

Gentle waves lapped against the shoreline. It looked perfectly calm to Shara. "Why do they call it the Sea of Torments?"

"Because one of the nastiest creatures on the planet calls this sea home, the Black Widow Shark. It gets about fifty feet long and some have been known to swallow small ships whole."

"Why is it called the Black Widow Shark?" Shara asked.

"Because it's all black and has a red hourglass-shaped mark on its belly, just like the spider."

Shara shuddered. "I hope we don't meet one."

Robert smiled and Blade slapped him across the back of his head.

"Tell her the real reason," Blade said.

"Real reason?" Shara was confused.

Robert rubbed his head. "I was only kidding about the shark. They call it the Sea of Torments because there's a whirlpool at the center that moans like a tormented man. Don't worry, everyone just sails around it."

"Then there is no Black Widow Shark?"

"Nope, just sea dragons and giant octopi. We'd better get going." Robert flicked the reins and they started down the rough dirt road toward the city.

Sea dragons and giant octopi, that's much better than giant sharks. Shara shook her head as they rattled down toward the city.

She grabbed the side of the wagon when they hit a bad bump. Since they'd left the other bandits behind, Shara had gotten relegated to the back of the wagon like cargo.

For the most part, the trip had been quiet, lacking the usual chatter between Robert and Blade. When they got a moment alone Robert had told her that Blade felt down because she'd left a big part of her life to the wolves, literally. For the last week Robert had done his best to bring Blade around. He'd do or say just about anything to get a response out of her, even if it was just to tell him to shut up.

His efforts had started to pay off two nights ago when Blade had started working out with her sword again, weaving and dancing through a complex routine.

When she'd finished she'd gone to lie down beside Robert to sleep, the first time she'd done so since the battle in the forest.

Then last night she'd cried.

Shara had actually heard her sobbing into Robert's shoulder. If anyone had told her the woman was capable of crying, she'd have called them a liar. Yet Shara had heard it.

When the sun came up Robert and Blade acted as if nothing had happened and Shara followed their lead.

They came to a stop just outside the city. Unlike most towns Shara was familiar with, King's Port had no wall surrounding it. Instead groups of four bored-looking guards stood at regular intervals to inspect the incoming merchants.

Robert drove right up to one such group. He reined in the horses when one of the guards raised his mailed hand.

"Purpose of your visit?" he asked in a bland monotone that suggested he didn't really give a damn.

"We're paying a visit to an old friend, Argus Hamilton," Robert said.

The guards immediately straightened up and looked serious. "You're a friend of Lord Argus?"

Robert and Blade exchanged glances. "Last time I saw him he wasn't a lord, but yes, Argus and I go way back," Robert said.

The guard that had spoken gave their wagon a superficial glance then waved them into the city. "Give my best to Lord Argus," the guardsman called after them as he took his poleax from his partner.

Robert smiled and waved.

He turned to Blade. "How does a guy with a leaky caravel become a lord of the city in five years?"

Blade shrugged. "You'll have to ask him. Does this change our plans?"

"No, if anything it helps us. Someone with a lot to lose is easier to blackmail."

Blade made a face. "I wouldn't know."

"Look, I'm not crazy about blackmail myself, but we have

little time and less money. If Argus doesn't want to help, we don't have much choice."

"Is anyone else hungry?" Shara asked.

Robert grinned. "You bet. Let's find an inn then I'll go find Argus."

The inn was a typical design with a large common room downstairs and rooms above for rent. A score of tables were scattered about the room and a wooden bar ran half its length. Behind it hung several nautical-looking items like a harpoon and sextant. On the right-hand wall was a large fireplace with a pair of cutlasses hanging over it.

They had arrived between meal times so the common room was almost empty. The only other people in evidence were a pair of men at the bar and the bartender.

Shara and Blade found a table while Robert went to talk to the bartender. He returned after a couple minutes with a key and three glasses of wine.

Blade took her glass and smiled. "At least the help is cute."

Robert dropped into the third chair with a grin. "Remember that when you leave the tip."

The bartender brought their food over after a few minutes. The fish chowder wasn't the best-looking food Shara had ever eaten, but after weeks of trail rations it tasted like heaven.

When they had finished Robert said, "I'm going to look up Argus. See you back here tonight. We're in room two."

He handed the key to Blade and walked off, leaving the two women alone.

Shara said, "Doesn't it seem like we spend a lot of time waiting for him?"

"Sure does." Blade stood up and stretched. "I don't feel like sitting around here for three or four hours. Let's get out of here. King's Port has a ton of little shops, or so Robert claims."

Shara smiled in surprise. "I didn't take you for the shopping type."

Blade looked down at herself in disgust. "This armor's about had it, and my sword could stand a visit to a smith."

"Sounds good to me, but I thought we were low on funds."

Blade winked at her. "I have a little stash of my own."

Shara and Blade left the inn and headed toward the sea. The shopping district lay just inland from the docks.

They walked at a leisurely pace and the closer they got to the docks the more crowded the streets became. It took about fifteen minutes to reach the shopping district. Stores lined both sides of a broad boulevard. It appeared the city planners had put all the businesses in the city in one area. A good idea, Shara thought. If everything was in one place shoppers would be more likely to go to more than one store, thereby increasing business.

Shara looked in the window of the first store they passed. Coral jewelry was displayed in a variety of settings. The pinks, blues, and greens looked beautiful. She didn't have much time to browse as Blade continued on without pause. They passed half a dozen more shops before Blade spotted what she was looking for.

"Over here," Blade said.

Shara left the window of a silversmith and joined Blade. The shop where she stood didn't have a large window like all the others. Hanging over the door was a sign with a shield drawn on it.

"This is the best armorer in town. I should be able to get what I need here."

"How do you know it's the best?" Shara asked. "It looks like a dump to me."

"See that mark above the shield?" Blade pointed to a small carving of a pair of crossed swords. "That's the mark of the mercenary's guild. My father once told me that every major city had a weapon and armor shop with that mark. It means the owner makes the best equipment and won't try and cheat you."

"I see." Shara followed Blade inside.

When she got home she'd have to make a point of looking around Sultan's Oasis for similar marks. It would be interesting to see how far such customs traveled.

Inside the shop were a score of wooden stands. A number of different styles of armor hung from them for a prospective buyer to look at. Leather and chain were the most common though Shara spotted a heavy steel breastplate near the rear of the shop.

At the front a fat man in a leather apron stood talking to a trio of other men dressed in filthy clothes. All three carried shortswords.

While Blade studied a suit of black leather armor, Shara noticed the three men staring at them. Blade seemed oblivious so Shara nudged her. "Blade, those men…"

"I see them. They could be trouble. Just ignore them unless they make a move."

Shara nodded and continued to watch them out of the corner of her eye. They kept pointing at Blade and snickering. She swallowed the lump in her throat and prayed they wouldn't do anything foolish. Blade finally chose a suit of armor and Shara followed her up to the counter where the three men stood.

"Who owns this place?" Blade asked.

"I do," the fat man said.

Blade set the armor on the counter. "How much?"

"I never had much use for women wearing clothes, much less armor, how about you, Juck?" one of the filthy men said to his companion.

"Me neither," Juck agreed.

Blade's eyes narrowed and Shara winced. This was going to get ugly.

"Me and my buddy will make you forget all about that armor, girlie." The first man grabbed Blade by the shoulder and spun her around.

Blade lashed out with her right hand, the fingers held straight and rigid.

She struck the man in the throat with enough force to drop him to the floor gasping for air. Before Juck could react Blade had her sword drawn and the tip resting against his Adam's apple.

"Please don't kill them, miss," the fat man said. "Both these louts owe me money and it's hard to collect from a corpse."

"True enough."

Blade drew back and hit Juck between the eyes with the hilt of her sword. He collapsed on the ground next to his friend. The third man raised his hands and backed away, seeming to have taken the hint.

"How much for the armor?"

"Seven gold pieces," the shopkeeper said.

"A fair price, do you not wish to bargain?"

The merchant eyed Blade's naked sword. "I'm not in the mood."

She shrugged. "As you wish."

Blade reached down the front of her shirt, pulled up a small leather pouch, and counted out seven coins. The merchant pocketed them with a smile.

"Where can I get my sword sharpened?"

"Three doors up, miss."

Blade nodded, sheathed her sword, and swung the armor over her shoulder. She started toward the door when the first man she'd hit groaned. Blade walked over and kicked him in the side of the head. Smiling, she left the shop behind.

When they were outside Shara said, "That was most impressive."

Blade snorted. "Those two were so drunk you could have taken them."

"No, I don't know anything about fighting," Shara said.

They walked down the street to the smith's shop. Blade paused outside the door. "Do you want to know one of the secrets to winning a fight?"

Shara nodded. She didn't really, but if Blade felt like talking she could listen.

"Never do what your opponent expects. Take those two idiots back there. They expected a meek reaction when they confronted a woman. Therefore I attacked aggressively. Such a simple tactic wouldn't work against a truly skilled opponent, but against many it will end a fight in a hurry."

"I'll keep that in mind," Shara said.

"Good." Blade led the way into the weapon shop. It took about ten minutes for the burly smith to regrind the edge of Blade's sword.

It was near dusk when they set out for the inn. Long shadows filled the streets. Blade wore a happy smile as she carried her new armor over one shoulder.

Shara yawned. It had been a long day and even a dirty bed would feel good tonight.

They were about halfway back to the inn when six men stepped out of the shadows of an alley. They all held cocked and loaded crossbows. Blade didn't even try for her sword.

"Hold very still," said a voice from the shadows. "Princess Shara, you will come with us."

Shara started. How could they know her name? "What about my friend?"

"If she does nothing foolish she won't be harmed. Now, come here."

Shara looked at Blade who nodded ever so slightly. She sighed. It didn't seem she had much choice.

Shara followed the voice into the right-hand alley. As her eyes adjusted to the dim light she saw a small man leaning against one of the buildings. Petite was the only word to describe him. He stood an inch shorter than her and couldn't weigh much more. Still, he held himself with the calm assurance of a man used to being obeyed.

The little man sketched a bow. "Princess, your Uncle Kent sends his regards. If you will accompany me, a safe house is waiting."

Uncle Kent? How could these men know her Uncle? "What about my friend?"

"Have no fear, my men will stay with her for a few minutes to make certain she doesn't try and follow us. Once we have a good lead they'll leave her, unharmed." He added that last bit as if it was just an afterthought.

The little man started down the alley and Shara followed. She didn't have many choices that didn't involve half a dozen men with crossbows, and if she tried anything they might hurt Blade. They came to the end of the alley and turned left, away from the sea.

"How is it you know my uncle?" Shara asked.

"Know might not be the correct word," the little man said, slowing his pace just a fraction. "I've never had the pleasure of meeting Lord Kent. I'm just an employee, a spy for lack of a better word. One day though I hope to distinguish myself enough to earn a meeting with your uncle."

Shara stopped and leaned against the building. "Look, I'm tired. Can we rest a minute?"

"Certainly, Princess, if you were tired you should have said something." The little man walked over beside her. "I want you to understand we are here to protect you. We will do everything in our power to ensure your health and wellbeing."

"Including kidnapping me?" Shara asked.

The spy held his hands out to the sides. "I apologize for the method of our introduction. Had you arrived alone, I would have simply approached you myself, quietly. However we had no idea what your relationship with that rather stern-looking woman might be, so we assumed she was your captor rather than your friend. Considering the bounty on your head it seemed prudent. If you like I can arrange for a message to be sent to her and the gentleman with you letting them know you're unharmed."

Shara nodded. What the man said made sense. She certainly couldn't fault his logic.

"Thank you. I'd appreciate it if you let them know."

"As you wish. If you're feeling rested we should get going. The safe house isn't far and the streets can be dangerous."

"No kidding," Shara said.

CHAPTER 42

Robert left the inn and headed toward the docks. Argus had a warehouse on the waterfront; at least he'd had one the last time Robert had visited. It was early yet and he figured the old smuggler would still be working. As he made his way through the busy streets Robert considered the best way to approach Argus.

He devoutly hoped Argus would remember him and the favors his father had done for him. The best possible outcome would be willing assistance.

Not likely, but certainly best. He hated using blackmail, but getting Shara home safe was his main concern. If he had to play rough to get the job done then heaven knew it wouldn't be the first time.

Argus's warehouse was a huge dilapidated structure with a sagging roof and crumbling pillars. It looked for all the world like a swift kick would send it tumbling into the sea. Robert knew it was just an illusion meant to fool the city assessors into lowering his taxes. He walked up to the small side door and knocked.

A surly looking fellow with an eyepatch opened the door. "Yeah?"

"I'd like to speak to Argus, please."

The doorman spat on the floor. "How do I know the boss wants to talk to you?"

"You don't. Tell him Robert, son of Julian Longridge, would like to speak to him. I assure you he'll remember my father." Robert crossed his arms trying to look confident.

The doorman grunted and slammed the door in his face.

Robert leaned against the side of the warehouse and whistled a dirty sailor's tune. A pair of seagulls squawked at him and Robert smiled. Everyone was a critic.

The doorman returned after a few minutes. "Right this way, sir."

The surly man had become the perfect majordomo.

The inside of the warehouse was nothing like the outside. Rows of sturdy shelves filled the main room. Two longshoremen were busy loading a wagon with goods. Along the wall was a staircase that led up to the office. Robert followed his guide up the steps. They paused just outside the door.

"Please don't mention my rudeness earlier," the doorman said. "I meant no disrespect."

Robert clapped him on the shoulder. "Forget it."

The doorman smiled. "Thank you, sir."

He opened the door to the office.

Inside, Argus was seated behind a huge wooden desk. Paper covered every inch of its surface. "You should hire a secretary, Argus. In a year or two you might even see the top of your desk again."

Argus stood up to his full six-and-a-half-foot height. A thick red beard hung down over his huge belly. Biceps bigger than Robert's thighs bulged as he pushed himself up out of his chair. "Bobby? Little Bobby, is that you?"

284

"Long time, Argus," Robert said with a smile of genuine pleasure.

"Too damn long." Argus came around the desk and hoisted Robert up into a crushing bear hug. Argus set him down and took a step back. "Torment my eyes, but you've grown into a man since I last saw you."

"I'm not the only one who's grown." Robert poked his friend in the gut.

Argus patted his belly. "Aye, been livin' too much of the good life on land. I ain't spilled a man's guts in years."

"I suppose all lords must sacrifice."

Argus grimaced. "Heard about that did you? Wasn't my idea, my wife wanted to mix with the nobles so becoming a lord was necessary."

"You got married?" Robert tried not to sound incredulous and failed.

"Who'd have thought, hey Bobby?"

"That must cut back on your wenching quite a bit," Robert said.

"I gave it up," Argus said.

Robert stared, stunned. He'd once heard Argus bedded ten women in one night. "The hell you say."

"I'll swear by any demon you care to name. I haven't touched another woman since I met my Marie. If you're looking for some action I know a few places."

Robert felt his face flush. "No need."

Argus grinned. "Got a little woman too, haven't you?"

Robert thought of Blade's reaction to being called a little woman and smiled. "Sort of, though nothing official."

Argus gave him a knowing look then turned serious. "So, what is it you need from me?"

The moment of truth had arrived. "I need transport to the High Kingdom for myself and two companions."

"That's no problem; any of a dozen ships could take you. So why come to me?"

"I'm just about broke," Robert said.

Argus nodded. "I see. I'll look into it, on one condition."

Here it comes. "What is that?"

"That you and this woman with whom you have no official relationship join me and Marie for supper tomorrow."

Robert let out the breath he'd been holding. "An excellent deal, we'll be there."

"Splendid, we live in the nobles' quarter to the north. It's a white house surrounded by an iron fence. You can't miss it, there's an old ship's wheel over the gate."

Robert got to his feet. Blade and Shara would worry if he didn't get back soon. "Thank you for everything, Argus."

Argus walked Robert to the door. "No promises, Bobby. I don't do a lot of business with the High Kingdom."

The men shook hands. "Whatever you can do will be much appreciated, old friend."

"Until tomorrow night then."

Robert nodded and retraced his steps through the warehouse. He waved to the doorman as he left. Outside the cool night air felt refreshing. It was almost dark but the sun still held on by a thread.

Robert took a deep breath of the salt air. He felt relieved and more than a little surprised that Argus had decided to help of his own free will. Maybe getting married had mellowed him. Robert really liked the old sailor and would have hated to have to ruin their friendship.

He made his way to the inn keeping to the shadows. As he moved between two buildings he suddenly felt silly. No one in King's Port was looking for him. As it was he stood to draw more attention to himself acting like a thief than if he just walked along like an honest citizen.

He had just decided to follow his own advice when he heard a harsh, familiar voice. "What do you mean turn back the other way? I thought you said she was this way."

Robert could hardly credit his ears. That sounded like Shale. Couldn't be, of course. The Wolfen should have killed them all.

All the same, Robert decided to play thief a little longer. He crept through the shadows toward Shale's voice.

"I know you can't just tell her to hold still," Shale said. "You know, forget it. I'm beat. Let's find an inn and continue searching tomorrow."

Robert poked his head around the corner of a building and sure enough in a shaft of dying light stood Shale. His face looked pretty cut up, but Robert recognized him. Standing beside him was a familiar cat. It appeared Scratch had lost his voice. Shale held the crystal rod that would lead him to Shara.

Shale tucked the rod away and started down the street. Scratch just sat in the road and stared at him. Shale stopped and turned around. "I don't care if you want to keep looking. I'm tired. Go ahead and look on your own if you want. Maybe I'll get lucky and some bum'll kill you and have you for his supper."

Shale continued on his way and Scratch followed, tail drooping. Robert trailed them for the better part of fifteen minutes before Shale found an inn to his liking. It looked like the cheapest one in the city. The roof sagged in the middle and the windows bore a coat of grease and soot so thick Robert couldn't see through them.

Man and cat entered the building and Robert lingered for a few more minutes to make certain they didn't come out again. When he felt satisfied that they were settled for the night, he retraced his steps to his inn. He had to tell Blade that Shale survived.

Robert hurried through the streets no longer concerned about being seen. Other than the occasional doubletake no one paid him the least attention. He stopped to catch his breath outside the door of the inn.

When he'd composed himself he entered and spotted Blade sitting by herself near the fire. He saw no sign of Shara, probably upstairs sleeping. Blade stood as he approached.

"We've got trouble," they both said.

They stared at each other for a moment. Blade looked as confused as he felt. "You want to go first or shall I?" he asked.

"I will. Your news couldn't possibly be any worse than mine."

He gestured for her to proceed. If Blade thought the news was bad it had to be.

"I lost her, Bobby," she said.

"Lost her?" He suddenly felt sick.

She nodded. "Six men with crossbows jumped us. I never had a chance. A seventh man took her away while the rest kept me from following."

"Son of a bitch! Well, you're right. Your news is worse than mine. On the way back from the warehouse I spotted Shale and Scratch."

"You did?" Blade looked pleased.

"Yeah, you seem happy. That wasn't the reaction I was expecting."

"Are you kidding? This is the best news I've had all night."

Half an hour later, Robert and Blade were crouching in an alley across from the filthy inn where Shale was staying. They spent the entire night watching to make certain their former comrades didn't leave under cover of darkness.

Blade kept watch the first part of the night then woke Robert from his garbage-pile bed to handle the morning watch. She was asleep now, leaning against one of the buildings, her bare sword on her lap. Robert kept his crossbow cocked and loaded.

When Blade had been happy to hear about Shale's arrival Robert couldn't have been more surprised. It hadn't taken Blade long to explain her plan. She intended to use Shale to lead them to Shara. Once she'd explained, Robert had found the irony delicious.

The sun was just starting to color the horizon when Shale came out the door. He held the crystal rod in his left hand. The tip glowed in the dull morning light.

Robert bent down and touched Blade's arm. Her eyes popped open.

"They're on the move," Robert whispered.

Blade hopped to her feet and sheathed her sword. Shale was headed north. Robert and Blade followed along behind trying to keep out of sight. They hardly needed to do anything special as Shale rarely looked up from the crystal.

They finally stopped in front of a two-story stone building. There was no activity outside.

Robert looked at Blade. "I'd have thought there'd be guards posted outside."

"Might too obvious," Blade said.

Robert didn't feel inclined to argue. Shale tried the front door which opened with no problem. "Don't tell me they decided not to lock the door too."

"Something's definitely wrong," Blade agreed.

CHAPTER 43

S hara sighed and stared up at the ceiling. When they'd arrived at the grim two-story house hours ago her petite captor had led her upstairs and locked her in a bedroom. Soon after that an attractive young woman about her age had entered carrying a bucket of steaming water and a clean lavender dress. It had been so long since Shara had washed that even the thought of a sponge bath appealed to her.

She'd tossed her filthy clothes in a pile and bathed while the silent young woman stood with her back turned. Once she'd dried off she dropped the dress over her head. The silk felt wonderfully soft against her skin after the rough homespun cotton shift Robert had given her. The servant left then with the bucket and her dirty clothes.

Heaven only knew how long ago that was and she hadn't seen anyone since. Shara hopped off the bed and walked around the room again. There was no window, so she had no idea what time of day or night it was or where in the city she might be.

She was about to lie down and try to sleep when someone

knocked on the door. It opened a moment later and her tiny captor entered.

He sketched a bow. "Princess, we've contacted your uncle. It seems your father has gone south for a visit."

She took a deep breath. Father. Though she'd never really admitted it to herself she'd feared he hadn't survived the confrontation with the sorcerer. "My father was well?"

"Yes, I believe so. Your uncle's wizard said nothing that would make me think otherwise, why?"

Before she could answer someone screamed downstairs. "Stay here, Princess." The little man pushed the door shut and Shara heard a click as he relocked it.

"Where do you think I'm going to go?" she asked the empty room.

She started pacing. Three trips across the room and someone else screamed. She stopped and moved closer to the door so she could hear.

From the hall beyond came the sound of steel on steel. The sounds grew louder as the battle moved closer to her room. Gradually the battle came to an end.

Moments after the last thump of sword striking flesh a crash sounded. She took three steps away from the door. The decision proved wise when an axe-head burst through her door right where her head had been a second before.

In seconds the door was reduced to kindling.

A figure in a gray cloak entered, brushing aside the few splinters of wood as he passed through the opening. A gold wolf's head medallion hung around the intruder's neck.

A hunter. Shara remembered Robert mentioning the bounty hunter group back in Reaper's Crossing.

"Princess Shara, I presume," the hunter said, his voice deep and commanding.

"Yes." Shara stood straight with her chin raised like her father had often told her she should.

"You have been captured by the Hunters' Guild. The bounty specifies no harm be done to you. I would prefer to allow you to walk out of here but I will carry you bound and gagged if I must."

Shara sniffed in disgust. "I will walk."

"As you wish." The hunter gestured her through the door. "This way."

Outside her ruined door stood three more gray-robed men with silver wolf's head medallions. One let her pass and the other two preceded her down the steps. They led her to a rear entrance.

Outside dawn was just coloring the horizon. They crossed the street and went down a dark alley.

Kidnapped again. This really wasn't her night.

CHAPTER 44

R obert and Blade watched from across the street as Shale drew his sword and went inside a stone building with Scratch at his heels. They waited about thirty heartbeats before following.

The pair raced across the street then paused by the doors. Robert put his hand on the door and found it still loose. When Blade nodded he pushed it open and she stepped inside. Robert followed right behind, crossbow at his shoulder ready to fire.

They found the guards just inside the door. Both men were lying in puddles of blood, their throats cut ear to ear. Blade reached down and touched one of the puddles.

She rubbed the blood between her thumb and forefinger. "Still fresh. These men were killed recently."

Robert's eyes darted around the room. "This isn't terribly encouraging."

"Yeah, let's hope we find her before who did this does."

Red footprints led away from the bodies. They followed them to a staircase then up to the second floor. The blood must have worn off because the footprints started to fade halfway up the stairs before vanishing altogether.

At the top of the stairs was a short hall with a door on each side. Both doors had been smashed down.

Blade pointed to the door on the left.

Robert nodded and pointed to the door on the right.

They eased along with their backs to the wall before stopping beside their respective doors. Blade leaned over and peeked inside. When she pulled her head back she shook her head.

Robert nodded and peeked in his room. He found Shale rummaging through some papers. As far as Robert knew, Shale couldn't even read.

He waved Blade over beside him.

Barely whispering he said, "He's in there."

"I'll go in first," Blade said just as softly. "Shale's mine, you take care of the wizard."

Robert gave her a thumbs-up and after a moment's hesitation she stepped into the room. Robert followed a step behind. He scanned the room for Scratch but couldn't see him.

Not good.

"Where's the girl, Shale?" Blade demanded.

Shale spun around at the sound of her voice, sword held ready. "I assumed with you. Seems I was mistaken."

Shale charged hoping to knock Blade off balance.

She batted his sword to the left then spun right, away from the force of his charge.

Shale staggered slightly when the expected impact didn't come.

Blade lunged, her sword diving straight for Shale's heart. Shale just managed to turn the blow aside enough to save himself though Blade cut a nasty groove in his side.

She withdrew quickly and parried his weak counter.

As the battle continued back and forth Robert spotted Scratch sneaking up behind Blade, his yellow eyes glowing.

Not wasting any time, Robert fired a bolt that took Scratch through both lungs.

He died in an instant.

The pained look on Shale's face revealed his plan. He'd been trying to hold out long enough for the wizard to save him.

An evil smile spread across Blade's beautiful face. "Just you and me now."

Blade launched a furious assault that forced Shale back on his heels.

She was so much faster than him that he couldn't land a counter or even block most of her attacks.

It wasn't long before he was bleeding from a dozen shallow cuts.

Shale raised his sword over his head and charged.

Blade sidestepped and delivered a backhand slash across his neck as he passed.

Shale's head came free of his body in a shower of blood.

"You all right?" Robert asked.

Blade nodded, not even breathing hard. "I never did like him."

She bent and removed the crystal rod from his pocket and slipped it into hers.

"Me either." Robert reloaded his crossbow. "Let's go find Shara."

There were two more rooms down the hall, both with intact doors. Blade kicked down the first one and Robert went in crossbow ready. The room was empty. Not even a piece of furniture to show someone had been there.

Morning sun was streaking through the window. Robert slid it open to let in some fresh air. As he looked out he spotted a flash of light. In the alley across the street a man was trying to hide. The flash came from something shiny on his chest.

"Blade, take a look at this." Robert waved her over to the window. "See that guy down there? Can you make out what's shining?"

Blade shaded her eyes and stared. "Looks like a silver medallion."

"Hunters," Robert muttered. "That makes sense. Who else could have found her? Let's go ask him where she is."

"Wait, if we go charging down there, he'll run as soon as he sees us."

"Good point." Robert raised his crossbow to his shoulder. "I assure you he won't run anywhere with a foot of steel in his hip."

Sighting down the length of the bolt Robert took careful aim at the hunter. It wasn't a long shot but the angle from the second-story window made it awkward. He eased the trigger down until the bolt leapt forward and struck the hunter in the upper left thigh.

"A little low," Blade said.

The man was on the ground grasping his leg.

"You shoot him next time. Come on, before he crawls away."

They went through the building and hurried over to the alley where the hunter lay writhing in pain. "Grab his arm," Blade said.

Robert did so and they dragged him deeper into the shadows of the alley. When they were a little better hidden Robert took a closer look at the kid. He didn't look more than twenty and had a smooth face never touched by a razor. On his chest was a silver wolf's head medallion.

Robert sighed in relief. At least he hadn't shot an innocent bystander.

"All right, boy, where is she?" Robert asked.

"I don't know what you're talking about," the hunter said through clenched teeth.

"Then let me be more specific. The young lady that was in residence across the street was a friend of mine. I'd like to know where your companions have taken her. I'm in a bit of a rush, so why don't you just tell me so I can go get someone to look at your leg?"

"I can't."

"A pity."

Robert put his index finger on the nock of the bolt sticking out of the hunter's leg. He started moving it in a circle, slowly tearing the wound wider. The kid started to scream but Blade clamped a hand over his mouth stifling the worst of it.

Robert stopped. "Are you certain you wouldn't like to reconsider? This is only going to get worse."

The hunter nodded. Blade drew a dagger and put it to his throat. "Don't yell," she said in a harsh whisper before removing her hand.

"The chapter house," the hunter said softly. "They took her to the chapter house for safekeeping."

"And where is that?" Robert asked.

"South, near the edge of the city. It's a single-story wooden building across from the Prancing Pegasus tavern. You'll never free your friend. There are thirty hunters in residence."

Robert nodded, only half listening. Blade thumped the hunter on the head to silence his moaning.

"He's right you know," Blade said. "There's no way we can storm a chapter house filled with hunters."

"Quite right, but to collect the bounty they'll have to deliver her to the High Kingdom, no?"

"Yes, those were the terms of the contract."

"Then they'll need a ship for transport."

"Yeah, so?"

"Let's get back to the inn. Did I mention we have a dinner engagement tonight?"

CHAPTER 45

R aven groaned as the flashing of his crystal ball jolted him awake. He'd only rarely left his lab since Daktari had enlisted his services. His absolute terror of missing something the sorcerer might deem important kept him chained in place.

The crystal glowed steadily now. Someone was trying to make contact. Please don't let it be Daktari.

He touched the sides of the ball and established the psychic connection required for the magic to function. A moment later an unshaven, red-eyed face appeared in the ball.

"Morning, Raven," the unshaven wizard said, his words slurring together. Raven imagined he could smell the stink of spilled ale.

"What is it?" Raven asked with ill-concealed impatience. Stupid wizards shouldn't play with crystal balls when they were drunk.

"We got that girl the boss was looking for."

The princess.

Suddenly less annoyed and more nervous Raven asked, "Where is she?"

"King's Port, sir, we've got her at safe house three."

"Well done. I'll tell Kent. I'm sure your team will receive a bonus."

The other wizard started to thank him but Raven broke the connection. They had the princess. Now he had to decide whether or not to honor his deal with Daktari.

Raven got up and started pacing around the small lab. He could just neglect to contact the sorcerer. Daktari would never know the princess had been found. If the great sorcerer asked, he'd just deny it.

Raven snorted, disgusted with himself. Like there was any way he could keep a secret from a sorcerer of Daktari's power.

He settled down before the crystal ball and steeled himself for the unpleasant task. His fingers touched the cool surface of the crystal and he summoned Daktari's face to his mind. Almost as quick as thought he felt the weight of the sorcerer's will settle upon him.

"Speak," Daktari commanded.

"The princess has been found. Kent's men have her in the city of King's Port."

"Where in the city?"

Raven concentrated, picturing the safe house in his mind. "There should be only half a dozen guards."

"There could be half a hundred for all the difference it would make."

"Of course. About your promise not to harm me if she was found…"

Daktari's image in the crystal frowned and Raven thought he was a dead man but then the sorcerer chuckled. "You have five minutes to get as far from Kent's warehouse as you can."

Daktari broke the connection.

Five minutes, perhaps he could yet redeem himself.

Wasting no time Raven tapped his crystal ball which shrank to the size of a marble. He slipped it into his pocket and grabbed his spell book. Those were the only two items in his lab that couldn't be readily replaced.

The stone soldier that guarded his door was still there. Its eyes glowed with a bloody light.

Not good.

Raven sprinted through the warehouse and over to Kent's office.

"You can't go in there.' Kent's assistant stepped in front of him.

He spoke a word of power that put her on her rear end.

"Sorry, my dear, but I'm in a bit of a rush," Raven said as he stepped over her and through the office door.

Inside the office Kent was speaking to his brother, the sultan, and a third man Raven didn't know. "Sorry to bother you gentlemen but in four minutes something very unpleasant is going to happen."

"Explain," Kent said.

"I've betrayed you, I'm afraid. Daktari knew you didn't plan to honor your agreement. The night after he spoke to you he came to me. I was given the choice of spying on you or dying in a very slow, painful manner. I didn't find my decision very difficult. All he wanted was for me to alert him when he found your niece. I have just done so."

"You son of a bitch!" the sultan roared. "You've just sold my daughter's life."

"I'm sorry for your loss, Your Majesty, but as the saying goes, better her than me. Now I suggest we get out of here before Daktari's revenge arrives."

"Why should we trust a spy?" the third man asked.

"I don't care if you trust me or not. If you're so anxious to pass over to the next world, I suggest you stay right here. I've already wasted half my head start, so I'll bid you all good day. Kent, you may consider this my resignation." Raven turned and ran out the door without a backward glance.

CHAPTER 46

Daktari smiled. At last the girl had been found.

In a few minutes one of his golems would blow Kent's warehouse apart and the rest smash through the city before exploding in turn. A fitting punishment for the disloyal swine. He'd never had much faith in humanity, but lately, the betrayals were coming at a record pace.

Now to King's Port to collect his prize and finally conclude his bargain with Balthis.

"Bane."

"Yes, Master?"

"Fetch the world map."

Bane flapped into the lab with a rolled-up map in his arms. The large parchment was almost more than the homunculus could handle. Daktari snatched it from him and spread it across the stone table. He started scanning the coasts looking for the port. He'd never been to King's Port, so it wouldn't be possible to teleport there directly. Instead he'd have to find the nearest place he had visited and fly the rest of the way.

"Found it, Master." Bane pointed to the city marked King's Port.

Directly across the Sea of Torments, so she wasn't that far away after all. A hundred miles north was the city of Queen's Port. He'd visited there a few times. It wouldn't take long to fly south and pick up the girl.

Bane alighted on his shoulder and Daktari snapped his fingers.

They appeared three hundred yards above the ground. Daktari fell a few feet before activating his flying spell. Bane circled around his floating master.

"Better hang on to me, Bane," Daktari said.

When he felt Bane's claws get a good grip on his robe, Daktari willed them forward. Without his shield he had no doubt the acceleration would have broken his neck. As it was, he felt barely a whisper of wind as he streaked through the morning sky. At this speed if anyone saw them they would register as nothing but a dark blur.

It took less than a minute to reach King's Port. Daktari slowed above the city and wove an invisibility spell around himself and Bane. He called up the image of the building he sought along with its location to the front of his mind.

Soon enough he spotted the building and settled on the ground beside it. Three men dressed in uniforms stood across the street, but of course they paid no attention to the invisible sorcerer.

Daktari pushed the doors open and found two dead bodies lying on the floor. He pushed his will out, seeking any signs of life and finding none. Daktari drifted up the steps, finding several more bodies. He checked the entire second floor and found even more bodies, none of them belonging to Princess Shara.

"She's not here."

How could that be? He'd only taken minutes to get here after Raven contacted him. He shook his head at the irrelevant thought. The how didn't matter.

Daktari spun in a slow circle, fists clenched. "SHE'S NOT HERE!"

With the full weight of his frustration and magic behind them, the words manifested as a physical force lashing out in every direction, blasting the second floor of the building to smithereens.

He levitated out the top of the ruined building. The guards were staring up at him and the destruction he'd caused.

One of them cleared his throat and said, "You there, you're under arrest. Come down here this instant."

Daktari narrowed his eyes. The unmitigated gall of the presumptuous insect astonished him. It appeared guards were getting stupider by the day.

He didn't seem to be alone in his assessment. The two other guards stared at their companion like he'd grown a second head.

As Daktari descended he conjured an aura of dark fire to surround his body. The fool guard was standing with his arms crossed and left foot tapping the ground as if impatient for Daktari to land.

His companions were looking about for a place to hide.

One suddenly seemed to get a bright idea and slammed the blunt side of his halberd into the back of the stupid one's head.

The guard collapsed, unmoving, to the dirt.

The guard that struck him waved at Daktari and said, "Just kidding."

Daktari smiled and started to laugh. He laughed so hard his whole body shook. When he finally got control of himself he wiped the tears from his eyes and banished the dark fire.

Laughter had cooled his rage and cleared his mind. Clearly

Raven had delayed his report long enough for the princess to be relocated or, judging from the number of bodies inside, captured by another group.

She could be anywhere in the city or even on a ship out of it if the delay had been great enough. With Silvermane's ring still protecting her, he had no choice but to wait for another chance.

Daktari was getting extremely sick of waiting.

CHAPTER 47

Vilos watched as the wizard turned and fled the office. His anger almost overwhelmed him. He wanted to chase the man down and strangle him barehanded. Vilos forced his fists to unclench. He knew few people would place a stranger's life above their own.

"We'd best get moving."

"You're not going to take the word of a spy, are you, Majesty?" Abin asked.

"It looks that way," Vilos said.

Kent was staring dumbfounded behind his desk.

"Kent, better order your people out of the warehouse."

Kent stared at him not comprehending.

Vilos reached across the desk and cuffed him upside the head. "Snap out of it! You need to order the warehouse cleared."

Kent nodded. "Right."

The three men left the office. Once they were outside Kent yelled, "Everybody clear out, now."

The men were used to obeying Kent's orders even if they

didn't understand them. The ten men shifting merchandise around dropped what they were doing and went for the doors.

Abin tapped Vilos on the shoulder. "Take a look."

The wizard pointed at one of the stone soldiers. Its eyes glowed with a bright red light.

"Move!" Vilos yelled. He pushed Abin toward the door and grabbed Kent's arm. "Come on!"

He pushed Abin out the door ahead of him and dragged his brother along behind. The workers were in the street already.

Vilos waved at them. "Keep going."

They came to a stop about fifty yards from the warehouse. "How many stone soldiers were in the warehouse?" Vilos asked.

"Twelve." Kent seemed recovered from Raven's betrayal.

Kent had barely answered when a tremendous explosion turned the warehouse into kindling. One of the workers went down with a seven-inch dagger of wood in his shoulder. No one else appeared injured.

"That could have been worse," Abin said.

The dust started to settle revealing what remained of the warehouse. The walls had been reduced to a few jagged boards. The foundation had scores of cracks running through it and the pilings were just barely hanging on. The only things still in one piece were the other eleven golems.

All of them turned their glowing eyes toward Vilos and the others.

"It's worse," Vilos said.

The stone soldiers started toward Vilos.

One by one they broke off, each heading in a different direction. If they exploded like the one in the warehouse, there was no telling how much damage they could do.

"We have to warn as many people as we can," Vilos said.

"It's impossible," Kent said. "A quarter million people live here. We'll never warn them all in time."

"Maybe not, but we're going to try just the same." He pointed to the workers. "You men, fan out. The three of us will try and draw them away. Hopefully they'd rather get us than a bunch of innocent people."

The workers scattered, yelling at the top of their lungs for everyone to clear out. Hopefully some would listen.

"Over here!" Vilos waved, trying to get their attention. "Come on."

The wizard sighed as if resigning himself to his lord's lunacy, pointed at one of the golems, and spoke a word of power.

A bolt of fire leapt from his finger and splashed against a golem with no visible effect save to get it to turn in their direction.

"Good, blast as many as you can. The more that follow us the better," Vilos said.

"Right," Abin said with a marked lack of enthusiasm. He spread his fingers like a fan and worked another spell. This time ten bolts of fire shot from his outstretched fingers to hit all of the remaining golems. All but two turned toward them and began to advance. The last two continued into the city.

"We got their attention, now what?" Kent asked.

"Now we run like hell," Vilos said.

The three of them headed toward the city gates just fast enough to allow the golems to keep them in sight. For their part the golems trudged along behind, crushing anything unfortunate enough to get in their way.

As they went down the street toward the north gate people stopped and stared at them.

Vilos waved at them. "Get inside. Stay out of the way."

As if to punctuate his words the nearest golem exploded

sending jagged shards of rock in every direction and blowing away half of the nearest building.

People screamed and those still capable of running did so.

Vilos was staggered as one of the pieces of rock cut his cheek. As they hurried on he reached up and touched his bloody face. The enchanted stone had passed through his crown's magic without slowing.

He shuddered as he thought what would happen if the next piece hit him square. In the distance one of the other two golems exploded. He silently prayed everyone had the good sense to flee the stone soldiers.

They reached the north gate without any of the remaining golems exploding.

"Open the gate," Vilos shouted. It took only seconds for the massive wooden doors to swing open but the delay was enough for the stone soldiers to catch up and form a semicircle around them.

They started to glow.

Vilos grabbed his brother and Abin and pushed them through the narrow gap in the doors.

He dove through right behind them just as the golems exploded.

Vilos landed on his stomach beside Abin and Kent. His ears rang from the roar of the blasts.

He rolled onto his back just in time to see the thick stone wall come crumbling down on top of them.

Vilos raised his arms in a futile effort to save himself. After a few seconds, when he hadn't been crushed to death, he lowered his arms and found himself surrounded by a ring of broken rock.

Kent sat beside him, unharmed.

Abin stood over the two of them, his arms raised. As Vilos watched he lowered his arms and collapsed.

By some miracle, Abin landed between two rocks that would have split his skull just as sure as hell.

Vilos crawled over to him. "Are you alright?"

When Abin didn't respond Vilos slapped him on the cheek.

Abin's eyes fluttered open. "You are safe, Majesty?"

"Thanks to you, old friend. How did you manage to stop those stones?"

Abin managed a weak smile. "Magic."

Vilos laughed. "Heaven save me from wizards with a sense of humor."

Abin massaged his temples. "I managed to draw enough power from your crown and expand it to surround us. It was a near thing. I just managed to hold the magic together long enough."

"Lucky for us." Vilos turned to his brother. "Where are the other golems?"

Kent paled. "I sent them to guard four caravans. If they blew up like these…"

"Do you know where the caravans should be now?" Vilos asked.

"There were almost a hundred of my people in those caravans. All dead."

Vilos gave Kent a shake. "Snap out of it. Should any of them have reached a town yet?"

Kent shook his head. "They left only two days ago."

"That's something anyway. I'm sorry, Kent, but it's better if they blow in the open desert away from any large populations."

Vilos clambered to his feet and offered Abin a hand up. The wizard still looked wobbly but managed to stay upright. "You going to be alright?"

Abin nodded. "I shouldn't use my magic for a while though."

"How about you?" Vilos asked as Kent got to his feet.

"I'll be fine," Kent said. "We should go see how many were hurt."

They picked their way through the rubble of the city wall. For fifty feet in each direction the wall was little more than shattered stone. It would take weeks, maybe months, to rebuild.

Inside the city where the golems had stood was a crater thirty feet in diameter and ten feet deep. A guard house that had overseen the gate was just gone. Vilos didn't hear anyone yelling. He didn't take that as a good sign as it probably meant everyone in the area was dead.

In the distance toward the northeast gate an alarm horn sounded. A few seconds later it sounded again. Two soundings meant something serious.

"I'd better go see what's happening. You two keep looking for survivors." Vilos walked quickly toward the gate to see what new trouble had arrived to bedevil him.

CHAPTER 48

R obert and Blade walked up the slate path to Argus's house, though house was probably too pedestrian a description for it, mansion was more accurate. It had a two-story central building with single-story wings to either side. The entryway was framed by six pillars, three on each side of the heavy oak doors. The fence that surrounded the property had been unlocked.

The same disagreeable doorman from the warehouse opened the gate for them. Tonight he wore a proper black servant's uniform and a bland servant's smile to match. He didn't speak, instead directing them toward the main house.

As they approached the doors Robert noticed the iron door knockers were shaped like mermaids.

They stopped in front of the doors.

"I look ridiculous," Blade said.

Robert turned to face her. She had on a plain, knee-length black dress and boots that stopped just below the hem. The only jewelry she wore was a silver necklace they'd found in the wagon. She'd wanted to wear her sword but Robert had dissuaded her. They had compromised on a dagger in each boot. That seemed to alleviate some of her discomfort.

"You look beautiful," Robert said. She did too. He'd never seen a woman as lovely.

She looked away, embarrassed Robert thought. "Tell me, Bobby, if you had a say, is this how you'd want me to dress all the time?"

Robert took her chin lightly in his hand and turned her face back toward him. "There's something I've wanted to tell you for a long time."

A look of fear crossed her face, just for a moment, but it was there. It was the first time Robert had ever seen even a hint of fear in her.

"What?"

"I love you, Blade. I love you in that dress or the nastiest, most sweat-stained suit of leather armor you've ever worn." He kissed her and held her close.

"I love you too, Bobby," she whispered in his ear.

Robert smiled as they separated. "We'd best not keep the lord of the manor waiting." He reached up and clanged the door knocker twice.

Someone must have bèen standing on the other side of the door because it opened almost as soon as the second knock sounded. A bored-looking man in a black servant's uniform said, "Sir Robert and companion?"

"That's us," Robert said. Blade shot him a funny look when the butler said sir but he just shrugged.

"This way, sir, the master is waiting for you in the dining room." They followed the butler into the house. The entryway was a large room with a cathedral ceiling and glass chandelier. There must have been a dozen candles burning in it. A staircase in the center of the room led to the second floor. The butler led them to the right and through an ornately carved door made of some wood Robert didn't recognize.

The dining room was half again the size of the entryway and was dominated by a table long enough to seat forty people. Argus was seated at the far end of the table, holding a glass of wine. Spheres of light illuminated the room.

Argus rose as they entered and smiled. "Welcome, my friend," he said. "This must be the lady with whom you have no official relationship."

Robert winced when Blade looked his way.

"Just my way of saying we aren't married. Blade, let me introduce Argus Hamilton, an old friend of the family. Argus, this is Blade."

Argus came around the table and Blade held out her hand. Argus ignored it and picked her up in a bear hug that enveloped her lithe body. Blade looked ready to reach for her daggers by the time Argus set her down.

"Pretty little thing," he said. "You always did have good taste in women, Bobby."

"I prefer to think I have good taste in men," Blade countered.

Argus roared with laughter. "This one's a keeper, Bobby."

Robert smiled, happy to see them getting along. "Where's your wife, Argus?"

"In the kitchen. You'd think with the money I pay that damn cook she'd let the man do his job without fussing over him like a mother hen, but no. She doesn't think anyone can do anything right without her looking over their shoulder."

"Maybe she just wants everything to be perfect for our visit," Blade said.

"I used to think that," Argus said. "But she fusses when it's just the two of us. I think it's just her nature."

"You should be grateful, you hairy oaf, that you have a

woman that cares enough to fuss over your supper." Standing in the doorway behind Argus was a heavyset woman with graying blond hair dressed in a blue gown. Rings glittered on her fingers and a diamond necklace was almost swallowed up in the folds of her neck.

"I'm afraid to turn around," Argus said looking a little rueful.

Before Robert could comment, the woman said, "You ought to be."

"Marie, let me introduce my old friend Robert and his, ah…" Argus looked at Robert. "Help me out here, son."

Robert bowed and put his hand on Blade's back. "My lady, Blade."

"Smooth-tongued devil," Marie said.

Argus laughed again. "Aye, I believe Bobby could talk a starving rat out of its last bite of cheese."

Blade looked surprised for a moment then smiled. "I've been called a lot of things over the years but this is a first for 'lady.'" She shook hands with a slightly flummoxed Marie. "Nice to meet you."

"Likewise, I'm sure," Marie said sounding a little unsteady.

"Where's supper?" Argus asked.

"A few more minutes, dear." Marie left them to return to the kitchen.

"It could be hours and that woman would say just a few more minutes." Argus sighed, fondly Robert thought, and gestured at the seats to his right. "Come and sit down, we can talk for a while."

Robert sat beside Argus and Blade sat beside Robert. "So did you find out about the ships?" Robert asked.

"Like I told you before," Argus said. "There aren't many ships going to the High Kingdom from here. You lucked out though. There are two ships leaving this week, the *Desert Fox* and the *Mermaid's Smile*. The *Fox* is owned by a High Kingdom merchant. They only have one bunk available for passengers, the rest were reserved."

Robert glanced at Blade who nodded. "How many bunks were available to begin with?" Robert asked.

"Six, why?"

"Just curious," Robert said.

"Where's she docked?" Blade asked.

"Pier twenty-seven, near the south end of town. Look, I told you guys she's full up."

"I know," Robert said. "But there might be a cancellation or two. Never hurts to cover all the options. When does she sail?"

"Tomorrow evening. All passengers are to be on board by noon."

"Thanks, what about the other one?"

"The *Mermaid's Smile* is a free trader from the north. They had four bunks and I booked three of them."

"Excellent, how much do I owe you?" Robert asked.

"That's the best part," Argus said. "They didn't figure anyone would want to travel to the High Kingdom, so when I offered to book the rooms they agreed to my first offer which was half the going rate for a trip of that length, forty gold pieces each."

"There are some odds and ends I can liquidate but at best I might get a hundred. I'll have to owe you the rest."

"Forget it," Argus said. "I've got more money than I'll ever spend. Pay me when you can."

Robert smiled in relief. "Thanks, I will pay you back. I promise."

Argus waved off his offer. "The *Mermaid's* docked at pier two and she sails the day after tomorrow."

"Dinner's ready." Argus's wife came through the door with a servant on her heels.

Marie sat beside her husband and the servant set a plate of appetizers down on the table. They looked like little cups filled with some kind of white paste.

"What are those?" Blade asked.

Argus grabbed one and popped it in his mouth. After he swallowed he said, "Mushroom caps filled with ground lobster. They're quite good."

Robert and Blade each took more cautious bites.

"They are good," Robert said.

Blade finished hers without comment.

"So, did you two hear about the excitement this morning?" Marie asked.

"I'm afraid not," Robert said. "I'd love to though."

"Well," Marie said, needing no further encouragement. "I heard at the market that a wizard appeared in the city, blew up a building, and attacked three members of the guard. One of them was hurt before the other two managed to drive the wizard off."

"How awful," Robert said. "Did anyone get hurt in the explosion?"

"Several dead bodies were found in the ruined building. The guardsman will recover, thank heaven."

The rest of the meal passed quickly with meaningless chatter and little substance. About two hours later Argus and Marie walked with them to the door. They paused just outside and Blade shook hands with them both. "Thank you for everything," she said.

Argus and Robert embraced. "Don't be a stranger, Bobby."

"I won't. Thanks again." He leaned over and kissed Marie on the cheek. "Goodbye."

Robert and Blade left the grounds of Argus's home. As they walked to the inn Robert said, "Something's up."

"What do you mean?" Blade asked. "I thought everything went well."

"I thought so too, but then Argus said not to worry about paying him back. In all the years I've known him, he's never been so casual about a debt. With Argus it was always business is business and friendship be damned."

"Are you sure?" Blade asked.

"No. The way I see it there are two possibilities. One, Argus has changed so much over the years since I'd seen him last that I just can't believe it or he's got something unpleasant planned for us. While I wish the first option were true, I fear it's much more likely we've got a nasty surprise coming."

"So what do you want to do?"

"I'll tell you when we reach the inn. First thing we need to do is change into our working clothes."

CHAPTER 49

S hara sat on the hard, thin mattress of her prison bunk. The hunters had thrown her in there almost immediately after they arrived at the dirty little building that served as their base. They had delayed just long enough to try and remove her ring. She'd taken considerable pleasure in the pained look that crossed the young hunter's face when the jolt of magic struck his hand.

He'd yelped and jumped back like a bee-stung puppy, then sworn and thrown her in the cell without a word.

She looked around the cell. The only furniture was the uncomfortable cot upon which she sat. A door with thick iron bars was locked with a sturdy-looking padlock and chain. The accommodations weren't nearly as nice as her first kidnappers' hideout. The next group that grabbed her would probably take her to the sewer.

Shara never heard the gray-robed hunter approach. She closed her eyes for a moment and yelped in surprise when she found him standing in front of her door.

"Someone should put a bell on you. Didn't your mother teach you that it's rude to sneak up on people?"

The hunter smiled. "Feeling feisty, are we?"

Shara glared at him. "Nothing like being stuck in a cage to improve your mood."

"You won't be there for long. Tomorrow you begin your journey home."

Shara felt like telling him she'd begun her journey home weeks ago but decided she didn't feel like it.

"We'll be leaving by ship in the morning," the hunter continued. "Do you know, with your capture my pack will be assured the alpha position for the next year? Never has a pack from a city as small as King's Port held that distinction."

"I'm thrilled for you," Shara said, her voice dripping with venom.

"I don't expect a mark to understand. It's a matter of pride, of honor. There are packs in every city in the world. Whichever brings in the most gold each year gets to hold the rank of alpha for the following year. We gain no wealth, only the acknowledgement of our peers that we are the best. I hope you can take some solace in the fact that you made this possible for us."

"When I'm getting tortured by that lunatic sorcerer, I'll be certain to keep that in mind."

The hunter laughed and left her alone in her cell.

CHAPTER 50

Nord pounded his fist on the table. He sat at the head of a long table in the palace war room with Arkon on his right and the only surviving officer of his once-great army, a Jalin something, on his left. While it felt good to be home, Nord couldn't exactly relax and enjoy it.

"They wiped out the entire patrol?" Nord demanded.

"Not all of them, my lord. They left one alive to report back," Jalin said.

Nord fought with all his might to keep from drawing Heat's Bane and striking the fool down where he stood. With so few men remaining every warm body was valuable, even stupid ones. "Get out."

With no further prompting Jalin scampered out of the war room like a scared rabbit. When he was gone Arkon asked, "What do you want to do?"

"We need more men," Nord said. "Try and contact Duke Benwa again and tell him to send whatever troops he can raise south as soon as possible."

"Perhaps it would be best if you told him yourself. I can arrange for you to speak to him directly."

"You're afraid of him," Nord said.

"Damn right," Arkon agreed.

"Fine, do what you must. I'll handle Benwa."

Fifteen minutes later in the crude lab Arkon had set up, Nord sat before the wizard's crystal ball. A thin blue light connected Nord to the crystal. Benwa's face floated in the sphere. "Close your eyes, my lord, and you'll be able to speak to him."

Nord did as he was bid and closed his eyes. Benwa's face appeared in his mind's eye.

"Duke Benwa?" Nord said hesitantly.

"Good day, Prince Nord. What can I do for you?" Benwa asked.

"I need you to gather as many soldiers as you can and send them south to reinforce my position. They should be on their way in a week at most."

"I don't think so," Benwa said.

"What?" Nord demanded.

"I believe you heard what I said. I've been watching your efforts with considerable interest. It appears to me that Daktari takes less interest in your wellbeing than I originally thought. I simply can't imagine the great sorcerer would allow you to fail so miserably if he cared about the outcome of your efforts. If Daktari doesn't support you, then I see no reason I should. I will send no troops south, and should you consider returning north I can assure you, you won't find a pleasant welcome waiting." Benwa snapped his fingers and the connection broke.

Nord shuddered slightly as the mind link vanished. Benwa wouldn't help and any attempt to return north would be suicide. Arkon made a slashing gesture and the blue light that connected him to the crystal ball vanished.

"You heard?" Nord asked.

Arkon nodded. "What now, my lord?"

Nord ran his fingers through his hair and laughed. He sounded more than a little hysterical even to his own ears. He couldn't imagine what Arkon thought.

Then again maybe he could. The boss is going mad. Maybe I should disappear while I'm still in one piece.

But no, Arkon was loyal. As long as his life wasn't in any immediate danger he'd stay. "My friend, it's time to survive. Cease all patrols. We'll keep our people inside the palace walls. Perhaps if we can last long enough, fate will deal us a better hand."

CHAPTER 51

Vilos stood atop the city wall beside the sentry that had sounded the alarm. Approaching from the north was a column of men, soldiers judging by the weapons that glittered in the sun. Given the gaping hole in the wall, holding them off would be a problem.

"Can you make out their flag?" Vilos asked.

"No, Majesty."

Vilos shaded his eyes against the glare. It couldn't be Nord's men, and his own forces weren't due for two more days. He squinted. Nomads didn't march with that much discipline.

Who the hell were they?

A rider urged his camel ahead of the main force. The sentry bent down and picked up the crossbow lying at his feet.

"Steady," Vilos said. "We won't start anything."

The sentry lowered his weapon but still held it ready. As the rider got closer Vilos almost sagged in relief. He recognized the uniform first, then his face. It was Yosef, two days early and a sight for sore eyes.

"Open the gate!" Vilos said. When he heard the wooden

gates start to creak he climbed down to meet Yosef. Yosef was just dismounting from his camel when Vilos reached him. He straightened and saluted.

Vilos returned the salute. "Captain, good to see you in one piece."

Yosef grinned. "Likewise, Majesty. How'd you fare in the battle for the capital?"

"Well enough," Vilos replied with a shrug. "Abin says we have my brother bottled up in the palace with less than ten percent of his fighting force remaining."

"Wonderful, when do we ride in and retake our home?"

"It may be that the people here need our help more for the time being." Vilos briefly filled him in on what had happened. "How did you manage to get here so fast? I didn't expect you for another two days."

"I pushed the men a little harder than usual. When they told me how big your brother's army was, I got worried. It seems I need not have bothered."

Vilos smiled. "No you didn't need to, but I appreciate the thought."

Seeming eager to change the subject Yosef said, "So, your daughter's alright. That's wonderful news."

The two men moved away from the gates as the rest of his command began pouring through. Two hundred soldiers wasn't a huge force, but Vilos would take what he could get.

"As of a few hours ago at least. If the sorcerer got his hands on her..." He shook his head as despair started to seep in and forced the feeling away, just enough so he could function. The despair never left. He could feel it crouched and ready to pounce if he started to think about Shara. "I'm assuming she's all right until I know for certain otherwise."

"Company." Yosef pointed behind him.

Vilos turned to see Abin approaching. "What's the damage?"

"Bad, the last two golems exploded in the middle of the city. The majority of two blocks have been leveled. The survivors are being taken to the House of Healing Winds. Plenty of others are trapped beneath the rubble."

"Lucky we just got some volunteers. Let's go dig those people out."

CHAPTER 52

Robert and Blade made their way through the quiet night streets. They'd stopped at the inn just long enough to change into their traveling clothes and pack their gear. Robert now carried his crossbow and six quarrels. Blade wore her old armor and sword. The new armor she'd bought creaked too much for sneaking around.

As they made their way toward the Prancing Pegasus tavern, Robert felt dozens of unseen eyes on him. Happily, no one was foolish enough to get in their way. The grim look on Blade's face more than saw to that.

Near the south edge of the city they stopped in an alley beside a tavern with a winged horse sign in front. Across the street was a sturdy-looking single-story building. Just like the kid had said.

"Think she's in there?" Blade asked.

"That looks like the building, but the hunter could have sent us on a wild goose chase. You're the one with the magic, you tell me."

Blade took the crystal rod out of the satchel she wore. She

hesitated a moment then handed the rod to Robert. "You do it. I don't like magic."

Robert shrugged, took the rod, and pointed it at the building. It began to glow almost at once.

He grinned. "Looks like she's in there. I wasn't sure the spell would still work after Scratch died. Did I ever tell you when I was a kid I always wanted to learn magic?"

"No," Blade said. "Why didn't you?"

"My father was like you. He didn't trust wizards and said he'd be damned before any son of his would study magic. We also spent so much time traveling I wouldn't have been able to find a teacher even if I'd dared go against him."

"When this is over and we get the reward from Shara's father, I think you should give it a try," Blade said.

"I might just do that," Robert said. "Think you could stand being married to a wizard?"

"Married?" Blade said softly.

He looked at her, smile gone. "What do you say?"

She looked around the filthy alley. "Hardly the best place for a proposal."

He grinned. "We seem to be doing a lot of skulking lately. Somehow it seemed appropriate."

She made a face. "I'll have to wear a dress."

"Says who? It's your wedding, wear whatever you want. That new armor you bought looks pretty good."

Blade wrapped her arms around his neck. "You're on," she whispered in his ear.

They spent the rest of the night taking turns watching the hunters' chapter house. It was a long miserable slog, not unlike the previous night, made tolerable only because they had each other for company. No one stirred until the sun was well up and the sounds of the city coming awake filled the streets.

Robert opened his eyes when Blade shook him.

He groaned. "What?"

"They're on the move. A group of five just left the building."

Robert clambered to his feet. "Is she with them?"

"I can't tell, they're all wrapped up in cloaks." She handed him the crystal rod.

Robert poked his head out of the alley. The group of hunters was walking at a steady pace down the street. Four of them surrounded a fifth. They all wore billowing gray cloaks that concealed their features. Robert pointed the crystal at the one in the middle and it started to glow.

He grinned, how predictable.

"They've got her. Shara's in the middle. Let's see if we can get ahead of them."

They ran north parallel to the street the hunters had taken. It was still early enough that the majority of the population wasn't out and about yet. The few that were gave them a curious glance that vanished when they reached for their weapons. The general consensus seemed to be that if a couple of heavily armed people wanted to run through the street, who cared.

They ran five blocks north of the hunters' chapter house then cut across to the street the hunters had taken. He couldn't see their prey, but when Robert pointed the crystal down the street it started to glow.

"Did we get too far ahead?" Robert asked between gasps.

"No," Blade said. "We want to be far enough away that they can't call their comrades for help. Come on. Let's find a place to set up."

Robert followed Blade further up the street without comment. She'd been setting up ambushes since she was a kid, so Robert felt content to follow her lead. When they reached a four-way intersection Blade stopped. On the left was a half-loaded wagon and across from it a shadowy alcove.

"This looks like the best we're going to find," Blade said without much enthusiasm. "Get behind the wagon. When the hunters come into view take out one on my side."

"Right, be careful." Robert kissed her then took his place behind the wagon.

Blade ducked into the alcove, her dark armor blending with the shadows so that he could barely see her. Robert loaded his crossbow. He'd only get one chance. He had to make it count.

After a nervous few minutes Robert spotted the group approaching. He took out the crystal rod again to make certain Shara was still in the center of their formation. He let out a sigh of relief when it started to glow.

As they passed between him and Blade, Robert drew a bead on the front hunter on Blade's side of the street.

He held his breath and squeezed the trigger.

The bolt leapt from the string and struck the hunter in the side of the head, killing him instantly.

The moment the crossbow twanged the remained hunters turned to face him.

They drew their longswords and two of them advanced in his direction.

Robert put his foot in the crossbow stirrup and pulled the string up. When they turn to face you look scared, Blade had said.

No problem there.

Robert managed to get the string seated in the firing mechanism. He picked up a quarrel but fumbled it.

Look frantic, Blade had said. Make them think you don't have a clue what you're doing. Get them to lower their guard.

A quick look up showed the hunters still had their swords raised but they were both smiling. Robert wasn't certain if that was a good sign or not. Probably not good for him at any rate.

They were almost within reach when the second hunter

screamed behind them. Robert couldn't see through the two hunters advancing on him but he had a pretty good idea what had happened. With any luck Shara was now free.

The remaining hunters turned toward their stricken comrade. When they did they parted just enough so that Robert could see Blade standing over the dead hunter and another gray form racing away.

She's safe, thank heaven. The two remaining hunters charged Blade, no doubt hoping to kill her quickly and reclaim their lost bounty.

Stupid.

Robert quit fumbling and reloaded his weapon with the speed of long practice. Never leave an enemy behind you.

He put a bolt between the shoulder blades of the left hunter.

He collapsed, dead or dying, Robert didn't care which.

The remaining hunter challenged Blade without his friend to back him up. Not a prudent decision if you desired a long life.

The hunter barged in obviously hoping to use his superior size to bowl Blade over.

He was fighting just about the same as Shale.

It seemed all they could see was a woman that couldn't possibly be a match for someone twice her size.

He learned the folly of that thought when Blade side-stepped and drove her sword through his ribcage impaling both lungs.

The hunter breathed blood and died.

Blade pulled her sword free and cleaned it on the hunter's gray cloak. "Nice shooting," she said.

"Thanks, you all right?"

"Yeah, I've never fought hunters before. I was hoping for a better workout."

Robert kicked over the hunter he'd shot. He had a silver pendant around his neck. A quick search revealed the others were low-level members as well. Ever practical, Robert quickly rummaged through their pockets and helped himself to their coin pouches and silver pendants.

"There's your problem," Robert said as he finished lifting the last hunter's valuables. "They're just a bunch of kids. I guess they figured once they had her, even this lot could keep her."

"No," Blade said. "What they figured was no one would dare interfere with them. Did you ever notice how people react to hunters?"

"Yeah," Robert said as they started down the street after Shara. "Kind of like how a deer reacts to a wolf."

Blade nodded in agreement. "When most people see a hunter they cross to the other side of the street. They're scared to death of them."

"Why is that, do you think?" Robert asked. "The odds of the average person having a bounty on their head are so small it's almost a joke."

"True," Blade agreed. "The problem is everyone can remember someone they've pissed off in the past and when they see hunters they wonder, has that person decided the time has come to get even? The hunters have come to rely on that fear. They play on it to get what they want. Unfortunately for the hunters, they can hardly remember a time when the majority of people weren't afraid of them. That leaves them feeling arrogant and wide open for an attack like this one."

Robert smiled. "You've been giving this a lot of thought, haven't you?"

"Not that much," Blade said. "Most of it came to me when I was trying to think of the best way to rescue Shara."

"Speaking of Shara, where did you send her?"

"I told her to wait for us at the next intersection. There she is."

CHAPTER 53

S hara stood at the intersection a block from the ambush. The morning had already started to warm but she felt herself shivering in spite of the fine cloak the hunters had told her to wear. When the first of her guards had gone down she'd thought she was about to get kidnapped again, then Blade had appeared and cut down the hunter guarding her.

She almost collapsed in relief. When Blade told her to run and wait for them at the next intersection she'd just stared stupidly until the two remaining hunters had turned back toward them.

Then she'd run.

Five minutes had passed by her guess and she was getting nervous. Robert and Blade should have caught up by now. She was thinking seriously of going to look for them when she finally spotted them strolling down the street, chatting like they hadn't a care in the world. Relief flooded over her. She waved and ran over to them.

"Hey, kid. Miss me?" Robert asked.

Shara threw herself into his arms and hugged him. After a few moments she stepped back and put her hands on her hips. "Where have you been? Since I last saw you I've been kidnapped twice."

Robert gave Blade a despairing look. "How do the knights in the bards' tales do it? You rescue a princess and two minutes later she's nagging you. If it were me I'd let the dragons keep the princesses and find a nice quiet tavern wench to settle down with."

Blade grinned and Shara cuffed him on the shoulder. Heaven's mercy it was good to see them again. She felt tears rolling down her face. Twice she'd been captured at sword point and hadn't cried. Everything seemed to catch up to her at once now that she was safe.

"I thought I'd never see you again," Shara managed to say between sobs.

Robert held her for a moment then whispered in her ear, "We're not out of the woods yet, kid. You've got to hold it together until we get to the ship, okay?"

She wiped her eyes and blew her nose on the cloak the hunters had forced her to wear. That seemed an appropriate gesture. She would have liked to spit on it as well but decided that would be a little too disgusting.

"Better get rid of that cloak, it's too obvious," Blade said.

Shara shrugged out of it. Hell with it. She spat on the thing for good measure. As they started down the street Blade walked on her left and Robert on her right. They set a maddeningly slow pace.

"Shouldn't we hurry?" she asked.

"Never run from the scene of a crime," Robert said. "Nothing stands out like someone running. As far as anyone knows we're just three friends out for a morning stroll."

"One with a crossbow and the other a longsword?" Shara sounded dubious.

"Good point," Robert said. With a couple quick movements he broke the crossbow down into its component pieces and stowed them in several large hidden pockets on his cloak. "There, no more crossbow. As for the sword, no one goes around without a weapon of some sort."

They continued on down the streets toward the docks. A guard patrol came running around the corner. Shara gripped Robert's arm a little tighter, but they passed without giving them a second look. Robert gave her an "I told you so" look. Shara smiled in relief, more than happy to be wrong.

It took another fifteen minutes to reach the docks. A hundred feet from the sea waited a line of dingy bars and brothels. Before heading down the docks, Robert led them to an alley between the third and fourth bar to their left. A large pile of garbage lay rotting between the buildings. Robert took a deep breath and reached behind the garbage pile. He came back holding two packs and Blade's new armor.

"Couldn't you have found a better place to hide them?" Shara asked.

"We were in a rush," Robert said. "Where was that ship docked again?"

"Pier twenty-seven," Blade said.

They moved away from the bars and went over to the nearest piling. A brass plaque said twenty-four. "We came too far north," Robert said.

They walked south along the wharf. Each piling they came to had a brass plaque with a number. When they reached pier twenty-seven they found two ships tied up.

"Which one?" Shara asked.

Robert looked the ships over. They were both caravels. The first one had a triton armed with a trident as its figurehead.

The other had a camel with one hump attached to its prow. It looked like someone had cut a camel in half and glued it to the front of the ship.

"That one." Robert pointed to the ship with the camel.

"Are you sure?" Blade asked.

"Who but a captain from a desert kingdom would have such an ugly figurehead on his ship?"

Shara swatted him on the arm. "Watch what you say about camels. They're the second most valuable animal in the High Kingdom."

"Sorry, kid, but being valuable doesn't keep them from being ugly. Come on, let's see if anyone's on board."

They walked down the pier and stopped by the gangplank. "Ahoy on deck!" Robert yelled.

A few moments later a dark-skinned man in loose-fitting black pants and a white shirt appeared at the rail. "Can I help you?" the sailor asked.

"We've booked passage to the High Kingdom and request permission to come aboard," Robert said.

"We've been expecting you," the sailor said. "Just a minute and I'll get the captain."

The sailor returned shortly with a gray-haired man dressed in blue trousers and shirt. His right eye was missing and had been replaced with a large fire opal. He bounded down the gangplank in two great leaps.

"Captain Haram, at your service." He stuck out his hand and Robert gave it a firm shake. "I was told there'd be five members in your party."

"The others were dispatched on an emergency assignment," Robert lied without missing a beat. "I assumed someone had told you."

The captain was eyeballing them real close. Shara feared he hadn't believed Robert's story.

As if to prove her right Captain Haram asked, "How do I know you're really my passengers?"

Robert looked around to make sure no one was watching them. When he was satisfied he reached into his pouch and took out one of the amulets he'd taken from the dead hunters. "I trust you will require no further proof."

The captain paled a little. "No sir, just had to make certain. You understand?" The last two words came almost pleadingly.

Robert smiled and put the amulet away. "Of course, we appreciate you doing such a fine job."

The captain looked relieved. "I wouldn't have questioned you except I thought you folks always wore those little baubles."

"You appear to be an honorable man," Robert said. "So I'm going to take you into my confidence. Our mission is very important, so important that we're traveling without advertising who we are. It is vital no one finds out. Can I rely on your discretion, Captain?"

The captain was smiling now and Shara couldn't help but marvel at how Robert had played the man. "You understand I can't offer a refund for the men that couldn't make it."

Robert frowned, causing the captain's smile to do a slow fade. Then he shrugged. "As you wish. I still expect full use of the cabins we paid for."

"Of course, of course."

"May we come aboard now?" Robert asked.

"Yes, right this way. One of my men will show you to your cabins."

Shara stumbled up the gangplank behind Robert and Blade. The bobbing of the ship made her a little queasy and she had trouble keeping her balance. She stumbled but Blade was there to grab her arm.

"Take it slow," she said. "We wouldn't want you falling overboard before you even get aboard."

Shara smiled. "I'll be careful. Have you ever been on a ship before?"

"Before this I'd never been beyond Reaper's Crossing, much less to the sea."

"He seems happy." Shara nodded toward Robert who was chatting with the sailor leading them to their quarters.

Blade smiled softly at Robert's back. "Bobby spent most of his life traveling. He must have told you about it."

"A little," Shara said. "He must love you a lot to have given up something that means so much to him to stay in a tent in the woods. I wonder if I'll ever find anyone that cares that much for me?"

"I hope you do. Being rich and beautiful will at least give you a large pool to choose from. I figure I got damn lucky when Bobby walked into my life. I got even luckier that he put up with me until I figured out what I think he knew from the start, that we were meant to be together."

They followed the sailor down a flight of steps near the rear of the ship. Shara had to duck to avoid a low-hanging lantern. She noticed several others hanging along the narrow corridor and thought that it must be awfully dangerous having lit lanterns on a ship. A closer look at the next one they came to revealed that the flame was really a small globe of light that gave off no heat.

"The witch light is much safer." Their guide had stopped when he noticed Shara's interest in the lantern. "Some ships still use oil lanterns and every so often they burn up."

"Seems like it would be safer to do without the extra light," Shara said shuddering at the thought of being aboard a burning ship in the middle of the sea.

The sailor smiled, revealing that his two front teeth were

missing. "Some do just that. Others cut holes in the deck and put crystals in them to reflect the sunlight below deck."

"Have you sailed on many ships?" Robert asked.

"Two before this one, sir," the sailor said. He gestured toward two doors a little way ahead of them. "Those are your cabins. If you need anything just ask for Ako."

Robert shook hands with him. "Thank you."

Shara followed Robert and Blade into the left-hand cabin. It wasn't very big, maybe ten feet square. Two hammocks hung along the far wall, one above the other. Two sea chests sat beside a bench with a chamber pot under it. Not much in the way of furniture.

"We should probably stay below deck until we're out to sea," Blade said.

"Good idea." Robert yawned so wide Shara thought his face would rip in half. "Those hammocks look pretty comfortable."

Blade drew her dagger and used it to wedge the door shut. "You want the top or bottom?"

"Bottom," Robert said. "I'd probably break my neck getting out of that top one."

"You're going to sleep?" Shara said. "It's the middle of the day."

Robert collapsed into the bottom hammock. "Kid, we haven't slept four hours since we arrived in King's Port. Right now a nap sounds like just the ticket."

"Don't open the door for anyone," Blade added. She hopped up into the top hammock with no trouble.

"But…" Shara started to ask another question but both her companions were already asleep.

CHAPTER 54

Nord swore when Arkon finished his report. It was just the two of them in the throne room. Nord sprawled on the throne, enjoying the irony of having the seat, but nothing else to show for all his efforts.

Two more men had deserted during the night. That made five in the last two days. Not a lot, but if they kept losing men at this rate, his five hundred would soon be just two. Still, he didn't know what he could do about it. He and Arkon couldn't be everywhere at once.

If Vilos's men outside would kill and hang up the bodies of the deserters outside the gate he could get them to stay, but that didn't happen. Whoever his brother had left in charge was smart enough not to do anything to discourage his men from giving up.

"You have any suggestions about how to end the desertions?" Nord asked.

"No, my lord, under other circumstances the threat of corporal punishment might do it, but now we'd be more apt to push more men to try and escape with such a threat. I just don't know."

"Damn that sorcerer! If he hadn't pushed me to move so fast I could have consolidated my power in the Broken Kingdom and left someone trustworthy in charge. Then I could get the reinforcements I need."

Nord hung his head, feeling dejected. All his plans, his grand vision, lay in ruins. "I was never a religious man, but right now I can't see much beyond divine intervention getting us out of this alive."

"I fear you are right," Arkon said.

Nord offered a cynical smile. "How long until you leave me too, old friend?"

"You want the truth, my lord?"

Nord nodded.

"I'll stick with you until I'm in serious physical danger. When that happens you're on your own."

Nord laughed. He knew he sounded insane but he no longer cared. "Fair enough."

The mad laughter echoed through the palace.

CHAPTER 55

Robert stood in the prow of the ship as close as he could get to the railing. The *Desert Fox* crashed through the waves, sending cool seawater spraying over him. The day was fine and clear. The sun glittered on the water, making it look like an ocean of gems.

They'd been at sea for two days now and Robert had spent most of those sleeping. His body felt rested and his mind clearer than it had in days.

He took a deep breath, savoring the salt smell in the air. He was reminded again how much he loved the water. The snap of the ship's flag drew his gaze up to the three hundred yards of cloth pulled taut by the wind. Three masts creaked at the strain. If the wind held, they might make the crossing in less than a month.

He looked down at the water. The only thing missing that would make the day perfect was a few dolphins to watch.

"Morning, sir."

Robert turned to see Ako headed toward him. "Good morning, Ako."

"I do not see your fine companions this morning. Sleeping in?"

Robert smiled. Blade and Shara were definitely not sleeping in.

"No, this is their first time sailing and they haven't gotten their sea legs yet."

He didn't add that besides the beautiful weather the main reason he was on deck was that he couldn't stand to listen to the ladies throw up any longer.

"The cabins were satisfactory then?"

"Perfectly."

"Not too small?"

Robert laughed. "I've never been on a ship that had big enough cabins. As ship's cabins go, these are better than most."

Ako was wringing his hands and fidgeting. It seemed painfully obvious he wanted to ask something but couldn't work up the nerve.

Finally Robert asked, "Something on your mind, sailor?"

"The young lady with you is very beautiful," Ako said then quickly added, "So is the older lady. I meant no offense."

Robert chuckled to himself. "Best not let Blade hear you call her the older lady. She's apt to cut your liver out and fry it for her supper."

Not that she could keep it down at the moment.

The young man smiled weakly and managed a halfhearted laugh. "I will keep that in mind, sir."

Robert let his smile fade. "I'm not kidding, son. Best control your tongue around Blade."

"Yes, sir, but the other girl, I was wondering if it would be all right for me to talk to her."

"Sure, but I wouldn't get your hopes up. She's already spoken for. Her intended is a wizard, and the worst kind at that."

Ako looked crestfallen. "What kind is that?"

"Excuse me?"

"The wizard, you said he's the worst kind, I wanted to know what kind that was."

"Oh, he's the jealous kind. Unless you fancy a short life as a frog, I recommend you be on your best behavior around the young lady."

Ako had turned a sickly shade of green, no doubt contemplating life as a frog. "Thank you for the warning, sir."

"Not at all, my fine young friend, and call me Robert. Sir just doesn't fit. Now, on to a more pleasant subject. Do you suppose anyone would object to my taking a turn in the crow's nest? I haven't climbed a mast in years. I'd like to see if the view is as splendid as I remember."

"You love the sea," Ako said.

Robert nodded, looking wistfully out over the water. "I was raised on a ship. I've spent more of my life walking a ship's deck than on solid ground. It's been five years since I've had the pleasure of sailing. Now I find it's everything I remember and more."

"I know what you mean. I've only been sailing for four years, but I can't imagine a life away from the water."

"Why so many ships?"

Ako blushed. "I was wondering when you'd ask. I noticed the funny look you gave me when I mentioned it. Don't worry, I'm not a troublemaker. I parted on good terms with the other captains I've sailed with. The problem is they all sail in just one little part of the world and I wanted to see more. So when I got bored, I'd leave and try another ship. This is my second crossing of the Sea of Torments and I'm already getting bored."

Robert smiled good-naturedly at the boy. "I understand. I've sailed all the seas but two, the Sea of Ice in the north and the Dead Sea. I hope to cross them both someday."

Ako smiled back. "Me too, Robert."

"Well I'd best check on my companions. If I'm up here too long, they'll think I'm having fun while they suffer. Fair winds, my young friend."

"Smooth water, Robert." Ako started away then turned back. "I'll ask the captain about the crow's nest."

Robert waved his thanks then disappeared belowdecks.

CHAPTER 56

Shara groaned as the ship hit another wave. She was seated on the cabin bench with the chamber pot between her feet. Her stomach was in revolt and had been since they set sail two days ago. The ship lurched suddenly and her stomach heaved. The only good thing she could think of was that she'd emptied her stomach hours ago so she only had to endure dry heaves.

She looked up from the floor and watched Blade move gracefully through a complex unarmed combat routine. She said it helped her get used to the bobbing of the ship. It seemed to be working. Blade hadn't thrown up in hours. Shara had tried a more basic version of the movements yesterday, but they only made her feel worse.

Someone knocked on the door, three knocks followed by a pause then one more. Robert had returned.

Blade opened the door and he stepped inside. He was smiling as usual, the rat.

"How are you two feeling?" he asked.

"Better," Blade said.

"Lousy," Shara countered.

"Well for those feeling better I have a snack." Robert took a small sack from behind his back and removed an orange, two apples, and some brown bread. Shara longed for the food but her stomach had other ideas as they bobbed up and over another wave.

"Maybe later," Shara said between groans.

Robert put a comforting hand on her shoulder. "Don't worry, it will get better. I almost forgot. It seems you have an admirer. Our young guide seems quite smitten with you."

Blade sighed. "That's all we need."

"Don't worry, I told him Shara was engaged to a jealous sorcerer. Once that story gets around no one will bother her."

"Isn't that a little close to the truth?" Shara asked.

"Well, yeah, but in this case the truth suits our needs. Besides, I haven't had many opportunities to tell the truth lately. I thought the practice would do me good."

Shara laughed. He was absolutely incorrigible. Father would like him.

"How long until we arrive?" she asked.

"If the good weather holds about three more weeks, if not, maybe four."

Shara groaned again. "Three more weeks? Heaven help me."

He patted her shoulder again. "You'll be fine in a couple more days, don't worry."

CHAPTER 57

The next day when Robert went up on deck Blade joined him. She had gotten used to the movement of the ship and now showed no signs of ever having been sick at all. Robert put an arm around her waist and they went to his favorite spot in the forecastle. It was another perfect day with only a few high puffy clouds dotting the sky.

"I told you it was beautiful out on the open sea," Robert said.

"For once you didn't exaggerate." Blade offered him one of her rare smiles. Her dark hair was blowing in the wind. Robert thought she had never looked lovelier.

She turned to face him. "How did you ever give all this up to live in a tent in the woods?"

"You left out the most important part of the question, the part that explains everything. I was living in a tent in the woods with you. From the moment I saw you I knew I wanted to be with you. If that meant living in the forest so be it. Nothing lasts forever. I knew our situation would change eventually."

"You couldn't know how it would change. We both could have been killed any number of times. To give up a life like this —" She made a gesture that seemed to encompass the whole ship. "To give up this freedom on the hope that everything might work out okay? I think you must be a little crazy."

Robert grinned. "You're just now figuring that out?"

She gave him a playful slap on the shoulder. "I'm serious."

"I know. I suppose when it comes right down to it some things are worth taking a chance for, and for me, you most certainly were."

Blade looked away. Robert reached out and gently turned her face back toward him. He caressed her cheek.

"I don't know exactly when it happened, but somewhere along the line I fell in love with you and not even my first love could lure me away."

"I...I don't know what to say," Blade said softly.

Robert kissed her. "You don't have to say anything. I just thought you should know, you know, in case anything happens."

"Nothing's going to happen," she said with a fierceness that surprised him.

Robert nodded. "I know. How's the kid doing?"

"Better," Blade said seeming pleased to leave the emotional stuff for the moment. "She managed to keep down a little bread and water. Hopefully she'll be okay in a day or two."

"Excuse me." Ako had snuck up on them without their noticing.

Blade frowned at him. The boy shuffled back a few steps.

"What's on your mind, Ako?" Robert asked.

"I spoke to the captain. He said anytime you wanted to climb up it was all right. Just shout up and let whoever's up there know you're coming."

"Thanks, Ako."

The boy nodded, shot a sideways look at Blade, and hurried off.

"What was that all about?" Blade asked.

"I wanted to climb up to the crow's nest. The views are spectacular."

"Is that the boy you told the tall tale to?" Blade asked giving him an arch look.

"Sure is, why?"

"What else did you tell him?"

"What do you mean?"

"Don't give me that innocent look. That sailor looked at me like I was planning to bite his head off. Now spill it."

Robert grinned, unable to help himself, and told her what he'd said.

When he finished Blade shook her head and sighed. "You're right, you do need practice telling the truth."

"It's all part of the plan," Robert said. "If they're afraid of us, it will make it easier to convince them to go along with our requests later."

"What requests?" Blade asked.

"I've been thinking about it, and it doesn't make much sense to just sail into port with the crown princess in tow. Someone's bound to recognize her then we'll have ten flavors of hell to pay."

"But she's the princess," Blade said. "Couldn't she just order them to do what she wants?"

"Maybe, but if that sorcerer has any idea what he's doing, he'll have someone or something watching the ports. I would, anyway."

"I never thought of that," Blade said.

"I figure we'll borrow one of their skiffs and land a few miles up the coast from the city. Then I'll walk in alone and get our supplies."

"Sounds risky," Blade said.

"It is," Robert agreed. "But I don't see any other options. If you have any suggestions I'm more than interested. In the meantime how about we climb up to the crow's nest and check out the view?"

Blade looked at the little basket at the top of the mast sixty feet up. "You go ahead. I'll go check on Shara."

Blade headed toward their cabin and Robert started climbing the rigging. He smiled to himself as he climbed up the thick hemp rope. Just like the old days. When he was about halfway up he shouted, "Ahoy in the crow's nest. I'm coming up to join you."

"Hold a moment, mate. Gonna be a bit crowded up here with two of us." The sailor carefully climbed out of the basket. He waved down at Robert. "All yours, mate."

Robert clambered up the rest of the way and joined the sailor on the top rigging. "Do you have a farseer?"

The man shook his head. "Only one on the ship and the captain keeps it with him at all times. If there's something worth checking out just let him know. I'll head down now. When you're ready to come down just holler for Paco."

"Will do." Robert climbed into the crow's nest.

The view was even more spectacular than he'd remembered. For miles in every direction he could see nothing but blue water. A mile off the port side a whale breeched, sending a fountain of water into the air. From what he could see he guessed the whale was at least as long as the ship, perhaps a bit longer. He shook his head in amazement as it dove. Hate to get one of those critters mad at him.

He saw nothing of note to starboard or dead ahead. He turned to look behind them. At first he thought it looked clear then he saw a white speck on the horizon. He narrowed his eyes and shaded them from the sun. It looked like a sail. Probably just another merchant headed south.

He spent the next hour enjoying the view and watching the whale breech off and on nearby. He checked on the ship behind them.

It was gaining.

He could make out two masts on her now, though he could see little else.

"Paco!" Robert yelled. The sailor appeared a moment later on the deck below him. "I'm coming down."

Paco waved and began to climb the rigging. Robert spotted a rope tied to the railing and shinnied down it. He dropped the last few feet to the deck, landing easily. He found the captain at the helm holding the oversized wheel.

Robert made his way around a group of sailors mending a net. As soon as the captain saw him he called over one of his men to take the helm. He met Robert at the top of a short flight of stairs.

"Good day, sir. I trust all is well," the captain said. "Nothing wrong with the cabins, is there?"

"The cabins are fine. I was just up in the crow's nest—"

"Did you enjoy the view, sir?" the captain interrupted him.

"It was great, listen—"

"Something else I can arrange for you, sir?" the captain again interrupted him.

Robert rolled his eyes. "Could you please shut up for a minute?"

"Sorry, sir, it's just you people make me nervous."

"You know what makes me nervous, that ship following us."

"Are you certain it's following us? Many ships start out in this direction before turning toward other ports."

"I'm not sure it's following us, but there's something odd about it. That I am sure of."

"Please explain." The captain suddenly seemed all business now that his ship might be in danger.

"It's probably nothing," Robert said. He felt very grateful that the captain seemed to be over his stammering spell. "I noticed she only had two masts and about seventy-five feet less cloth out than us, but she's still gaining. That just doesn't seem right for a fully loaded cargo ship."

"It certainly doesn't." The captain reached into his pocket and took out a short tubular object. He extended it to three times its length and held it to his good eye. After scanning the horizon for a few seconds his hand steadied. He studied the other ship for half a minute muttering to himself.

"Have a look."

Robert took the farseer and brought it to his eye. It took a moment to find the ship but when he did the first thing he noted was a ballista mounted in the forecastle. Just below the ballista was the figurehead of a mermaid.

Robert swallowed. Maybe it wasn't the same ship, after all mermaids were popular for figureheads. He looked up to the top of the main mast to see what colors she was flying. He found a black flag with a set of white manacles painted on it. He took the farseer from his eye and handed it back to the captain.

"Does that flag mean what I think?" he asked.

"If you think it means that ship is full of slavers then yes," Captain Haram said. Robert thought he sounded worried. He looked Robert square in the face. "I'd like to know, do you think they're after you?"

Robert hesitated, trying to decide what he should tell the captain.

Before Robert could make up his mind Captain Haram said, "It doesn't make any difference mind you. When I agreed to take you people on as passengers I was told there'd be risks.

I took the money and the chance. I said I'd get you to the High Kingdom and I will. I just wondered if my luck's gone south or there's something more behind that ship."

Robert sighed. "The plain truth, Captain, is I just don't know. Let's say it's possible. Not many knew we'd be aboard this ship but if someone talked…"

Robert threw up his hands leaving the thought unfinished.

Captain Haram nodded his understanding. "Fair enough, sir. I think you've been honest with me and that's all a man can ask."

"How soon do you think they'll catch us?" Robert asked.

The captain thought for a moment. "If the weather holds, we have a day at most. If the weather gets ugly, who knows."

Robert nodded. "I'd better go tell Blade. If we can do anything to help just ask."

The captain clapped him on the shoulder. "I appreciate it. If they catch up it's gonna get ugly and any help'll be welcome."

"Do you know that ship?" Robert asked.

"Only by reputation. She's called the *Bound Hope*. Worst bunch of pirates and slavers a man could hope to meet. They take at least three ships every year around here. If they manage to board us, well, my men are all good lads, but we're no match for those pirates."

Robert left feeling slightly sick and no longer enjoying the nice weather in the least. He'd known Argus was up to something, but handing them over to slavers? That seemed a bit much even for his old friend. Though if they had something to do with his rise to a lordship, Argus might have had debts of his own to repay.

He'd just have to pay with someone else's hide. Robert's plan didn't include ending up shackled in the hold of a slave ship.

CHAPTER 58

Robert and Blade stood in the rear of the ship watching as the slavers drew ever closer. Blade had donned her new armor and wore her sword at the ready. During the night, the *Bound Hope* had cut the distance between them in half. It was just after dawn and the wind had let up a bit. The day was clear and Robert had abandoned all hope of a storm dissuading the pirates from attacking, slim hope though it was.

The sailors working on deck now carried cutlasses in their belts. Heavy crossbows had been placed in strategic locations around the ship. With any luck they could get off a couple volleys before the slavers boarded.

"What do you think?" Blade asked.

Robert sighed. "I think it would be a terrible irony to lose the kid now to a bunch of half-assed slavers after everything we've been through."

"They won't take her," Blade said. "How soon till they catch us?"

"We should be in ballista range by noon. An hour after that, we'd best be ready to repel boarders."

Blade shook her head. "With that ballista they could thin us down enough that we won't have enough people to resist when they board."

"That's not too likely. They'll want to take as many of us alive as possible. Corpses don't make very good slaves after all," Robert said.

"Once they board the fun really begins." Blade had a fierce smile.

"What do you mean?" Robert asked. He wasn't certain he liked the look she gave him.

"I've fought slavers before. Often times they'll pass up a killing blow that might end a fight quick because they don't want to damage their merchandise. It makes the job of fighting them much easier since I don't have any problem with killing them."

The captain ordered an early lunch prepared. No one wanted to eat but most forced themselves to choke down a little. Once the battle started no one knew when or if they'd get another meal. The slavers' ship was now so close they could make out individuals climbing in the ship's rigging.

Robert sighed, not long now.

He descended the steps to their cabin. He carried two bowls of soup; behind him Blade carried a third bowl and a small loaf of bread. Robert kicked the door of their cabin. "Lunch time, kid."

Shara opened the door and accepted one of the bowls from him. "How close?" she asked.

"Too close," Blade said as she tore the bread into three roughly equal chunks and handed them out.

Robert and Blade sat on either side of Shara.

Robert noticed Shara tore into her food with considerable

enthusiasm. He took that to be a good sign. "How you feeling, kid?"

"Scared," she said. "A bunch more people are going to get killed because of me."

"Not because of you," he said. Shara was staring at the floor as he spoke. "Look at me."

She slowly looked up at him.

"This isn't your fault."

"You're just saying that to make me feel better. None of this would be happening if not for me."

"Don't say that and don't think it. No one but us and the hunters know you're on this ship. The hunters wouldn't tell a bunch of slavers you were on board, they'd just have a pack waiting in port to grab you. I figure when we didn't arrive to board Argus's ship, he told his slaver friends which one we were on. It's just coincidence you're here, nothing more."

"But the others, so many have died over the last few months." Shara started sniffling softly.

Robert tried to think what he could say but nothing came to him.

Finally, Blade said, "Those who came after you chose their path. They saw the bounty on your head and tried to claim it. When you live by the sword you take the risk that your opponent may be better than you. If you stay at it long enough, it's a sure thing. Trust me, kid, I know."

Shara nodded though Robert couldn't tell if she felt any better. He slurped down the rest of his soup. As he started to sop up the rest of it with his bread something thumped against the hull.

"Was that what I think it was?" Robert asked.

"Afraid so." Blade swallowed the last of her soup and dropped the bowl. "We'd best get up on deck."

Robert kissed Shara on the forehead. "Stay down here where you'll be safe."

"Be careful," Shara said.

Blade paused by the door. "Don't worry. We look out for each other."

Robert grinned. "Actually she looks out for me and I try and stay out of the way."

Shara laughed slightly and managed a weak smile.

"That's a girl, chin up. This will be over before you know it." Hopefully with all of us still in one piece, Robert added to himself.

Robert caught up with Blade at the top step. "Be careful," he said.

"You too." They kissed and Robert went to take his position in the rear castle where he'd have the best field of fire.

The *Bound Hope* was about a hundred yards to starboard and fifty yards behind them. Robert could see individual faces in the crowd along the ship's rail. They were a gruesome-looking lot, many lacking a piece or two of their anatomy. Most were armed with thick wooden clubs.

Robert smiled to himself; Blade was right, they did mean to take as many of them alive as they could.

At the front of the slavers' ship the ballista crew was busy loading a second bolt. Robert picked up his borrowed cross-bow, sighted on the artillerist, and fired. It was likely he'd miss at this range, but at least he could give them something to think about.

The bolt streaked away. He'd done his best to allow for the bobbing of the ships but still missed low by two feet.

The bolt struck one of the ballista crew in the lower back, dropping him to the deck.

Better than a clean miss anyway. He began reloading his

weapon. Taking their cue from him other sailors began plinking at the ballista crew and slavers lining the rail.

Soon the ballista sported so many bolts it looked like a porcupine. The sailors cheered when the slavers abandoned the weapon and took cover below the rail. Robert just shook his head and took one last shot.

It was still way too soon for cheers.

The enemy ship drew alongside the *Fox*. As planned, most of the sailors drew their cutlasses to repel boarders while the rest reloaded their crossbows and waited for a clear shot.

When the slavers' ship was almost even with the *Fox* a row of men bearing heavy rope popped up above the ship's rail.

The crossbowmen fired, dropping four of them.

The remaining men threw lines tipped with iron hooks that sailed out toward the *Fox*.

Eight hooks landed over the rail.

Blade led the sailors toward the rail, sword raised. They hesitated just long enough for the slavers to pull the ropes tight then sword and cutlasses came down.

Only the line Blade hit cut through cleanly. The others continued hacking but every second the enemy got closer.

Robert finished reloading his crossbow and watched as the sailors struggled to cut the thick ropes. Where their blades hit something shiny appeared. Wires, the slavers had woven wires into the rope to make it harder to cut and to dull the weapons of their enemies.

Very clever.

The sailors managed to cut all but three of the ropes.

It didn't matter; the *Bound Hope* was now only six feet away. Two heavy planks with iron spikes on the underside fell from the slavers' ship. The spikes hammered through the deck locking the two ships together.

"Fall back," Blade yelled.

The sailors backpedaled away from the planks as slavers stormed across.

Blade led fifteen sailors against twenty-five slavers.

Not a very even fight, but Blade was worth at least five slavers so that made it close.

Only two sailors, the best shots, remained with him in the rear castle. Their job was to put a bolt in any slaver that presented a clean target and protect the captain where he manned the helm.

Easier said than done. As the melee spread across the deck, telling friend from foe grew harder by the moment.

Robert held his crossbow tight and ready. Try as he might, he couldn't take his eyes off of Blade.

As long as she survived, nothing else mattered.

CHAPTER 59

Blade awaited the first wave of slavers. She stood near the center of the *Desert Fox*'s defenders, so she could respond to whatever the enemy tried.

Two men separated themselves from the mob and came toward her. One lacked an eye and the other had a peg leg from the knee down. As with many others they approached her with their weapons low, obviously smelling easy prey.

She took a step back letting them think she was afraid.

For a moment they looked away from her and grinned at each other.

That was all the opening she needed.

With a single lightning slash she opened both their throats spilling a river of blood on the deck.

She had no time to celebrate the small victory. To her right she spotted a young sailor go to his knees under heavy assault from a huge slaver.

The attacker looked like he weighed at least three hundred pounds, all of it muscle.

With a savage blow he knocked the young man's cutlass away and probably broke his arm as well.

Blade raced over as he raised his arm for the knockout blow.

Before it could fall she slashed across the back of his knees, severing tendons and dropping him to the deck.

A quick stomp crushed his throat.

Blade leaned down to help the sailor up.

A look of fear filled his face.

She thought for a moment Robert's stupid story was causing her trouble then she sensed someone behind her.

She whirled but there was no way she could get her sword up in time to block the man's club.

Before it could fall he shuddered and a crossbow bolt appeared in his chest.

The slaver collapsed and Blade glanced toward the rear castle.

Robert shot her a little salute and began to reload his crossbow.

She smiled to herself, just for a moment reveling in how good it felt to have someone worry about her.

The moment passed quickly and she rejoined the battle.

Blade looked around. Instead of one big melee the battle had broken up into half a dozen small skirmishes. The slavers had a slight numbers advantage and were pressing the sailors hard. Only the lack of lethal weapons on the slavers' side allowed the men any chance.

Blade swore as a pair of pirates broke away from the melee and headed toward the stairs that led belowdecks.

She ran toward them sword ready.

They must have heard her coming because they both turned to face her.

These two didn't rush blindly in, instead they separated, one going left and the other right.

She couldn't let one get behind her.

She lunged at the one on the left forcing him back then quickly spun to deflect the second slaver's attack.

Her arm went numb under the force of the blow.

Blade spun left and slashed at her opponent's leg hoping to put him out of the battle before his comrade could recover.

He anticipated her attack and jumped over her sword.

The ship lurched and he stumbled, falling to the deck.

Before Blade could finish him, the second slaver came roaring back into the fray.

She retreated a step and let his hard overhead swing pass by her and slam into the deck.

Not allowing him to recover she stepped on the club pinning it down.

The slaver let go and retreated.

He drew a short curved dagger from his belt but hesitated.

Behind her Blade heard the patter of feet. The other fighter must have recovered.

She reversed the grip on her sword and leapt thrusting behind her. The sword bit deep into the man's body.

She threw her head back into his face for good measure, crushing his nose with the back of her skull.

A backward roll brought her to her feet, ripping her sword free in the process.

The man with the dagger was staring at her.

"Sure you want to continue with that little knife?" she asked with a wicked grin, almost willing him to attack.

The slaver looked at his weapon, then at her, and then ran toward his ship.

She smiled; he wouldn't be back.

Just to be safe she watched as he crossed the deck, hopped up on the boarding planks and ran across to the other ship.

He was met on the other side by a man dressed in a pirate costume. That was all Blade could think of. He looked like the pirates described in the bad tales told by bards for drinks in Reaper's Crossing: billowing pants, an open vest showing off his hairy chest, and leather boots.

The only thing not amusing about him was the heavy curved cutlass he carried.

He raised the weapon and the slaver started to retreat. He moved two steps before the pirate captain, for that was what Blade assumed he was, lopped his head off.

He looked over toward Blade as his gold hoop earrings flashed in the sun.

He smiled, grabbed a rope, and swung over to land on the *Fox*'s deck a few feet from Blade.

"You must be captain of that ship," she said.

He smiled again and she noticed one of his teeth was gold. That would make an interesting souvenir of her first sea journey.

"I am." He swirled his cutlass with a flourish and bowed to her. "I believe when I've killed you all the fight will go out of your shipmates."

Blade laughed in his face. Cocky bastard. "You mean if you kill me."

"I've been fighting for more years than you've been around. I mean when, not if."

Blade smacked the flat of her sword on her gloved hand. It made a wet sound as the sticky blood splattered on her gauntlet. "Let's find out."

The pirate roared and slashed at her head then thrust at her midsection before reversing direction with another high slash.

Blade batted them all aside with three quick flicks of her sword.

He took a step back from her and she yawned. "Decided to try and bore me to death instead of using your sword? A wise change in strategy."

He ground his teeth in frustration then smiled. All around them the other battles had stopped and the combatants turned to watch the duel.

"You'll not goad me into a rash attack, wench."

"Any attack at this point would be welcome. Are you hoping I'll die of old age?"

He only smiled and beckoned her forward. If she wanted to end this fight any time soon, it appeared she'd have to take the initiative.

She feinted left then lunged at his right leg.

He shuffled aside then countered with a slash that would have taken her head if she hadn't rolled under it.

She sprang to her feet, sword at high guard.

The pirate came at her again.

He wielded his cutlass with a speed she didn't think possible for such a heavy weapon.

He was good.

The force of his blows drove her toward the center of the ship.

Blade parried the incessant attacks, unable to get a blow of her own in.

She had to think of something soon or his superior strength would eventually break her guard.

As they approached the main mast she got an idea. Blade continued to block and move away. The pirate captain had fallen into a rhythm, four slashes followed by a thrust to her head. He'd followed the same pattern twice now.

Blade parried the thrust then began to count. When the

fourth slash came in she batted it aside and felt behind her with her left hand. The main mast was only inches away.

Perfect.

The thrust came.

She dropped straight down into a split. The cutlass parted her hair and stuck in the mast.

Before he could react, Blade thrust her sword up under his ribcage and into his heart.

A disbelieving look came across his face as he fell to the deck, dead.

"Anybody that wants to live had best drop their weapons," Robert bellowed. Blade looked up toward the rear castle and saw Robert and five sailors with leveled crossbows.

"You don't have enough shots to take us all," one of the slavers said.

Robert pointed his crossbow at the man's chest. "You're right, but I guarantee you'll be one of the dead ones unless you convince your pals to surrender. Anybody else want to take a chance?"

"How do we know you won't just kill us once we surrender?" another slaver asked.

The captain appeared beside Robert. "You have my word, anyone who surrenders will be spared. I imagine that's a better offer than you planned to make us."

The slavers looked at each other and slowly lowered their clubs to the deck.

"A wise decision," the captain said. "You men watch those prisoners."

Blade made her way to the rear castle to talk to Bobby and the captain. Her arms ached from the heavy blows of the pirate captain's cutlass. It was with great pleasure that she sheathed her sword. As she staggered up the steps Bobby was waiting for her.

"You all right?" he asked.

She smiled at the concern in his voice. "Fine, just tired."

"Young lady, that was the most impressive display of swordsmanship I've ever seen," Captain Haram said. "We owe you our lives. If my crew or I can do anything for you, just ask."

"Thanks." Robert and Blade exchanged glances. "I may take you up on that offer later."

"We've got things under control up here," Bobby said. "Why don't you go below and rest. The kid will be wondering what's happened."

Blade worked her head from side to side. There were several audible snaps. "I think that might be a good idea. Join me as soon as you can."

Blade heard several of the nearby sailors chuckle. Robert nodded and she left them to their work. When she reached their cabin she knocked twice. "Open up, kid, it's me."

After a moment's pause the door opened. "Is it over?" Shara asked.

Blade brushed past her and dropped into one of the hammocks. "Yeah, it's over."

"How'd we do?"

Blade managed a weak grin. "Better than they did. I don't think anyone was killed. A few broken bones and plenty of bruises, but that's about it." Blade draped an arm over her eyes. "Bobby will know more when they finish up topside."

CHAPTER 60

Robert and Captain Haram descended from the rear castle to interrogate the prisoners. A group of ten sailors formed a very nervous ring of steel around the slavers.

"Who's ranking officer here?" the captain asked.

A scarred sailor stepped hesitantly forward. "I'm second mate, sir."

"All right, sailor, do you have any slaves belowdecks?"

"No, sir, we were fresh out of port when we spotted you. Captain, what are you going to do with us?"

"Good question." The captain gestured for Robert to step away with him. "What do you think? I don't have room to transport a bunch of prisoners and I can't just let them go."

Robert thought for a moment then said, "Here's what I think. Let me take some men over to their ship and check for slaves. When we've cleared the ship we'll lower their longboat and load it with food and water. Then we'll scuttle the ship and they can take their chances in the longboat. Given our space limitations, I think that's the best we can do. The only other option is to put them to the sword and I have little taste for that."

"Aye, I'm with you there. I gave my word that they wouldn't be harmed and I'm loath to break it even to dogs like these. Take what men you need and search the ship. We'll watch this lot."

"As you wish, Captain," Robert said.

Robert got six volunteers and crossed over to the *Bound Hope*. On deck they found a handful of dead and dying men with crossbow bolts sticking out of them. They were dumped overboard without ceremony. Sharks had to eat after all.

He chose two men at random and pointed at the cabin in the rear of the ship. "You two check in there, the rest of us will head below deck."

The sailors nodded and walked cautiously over toward the cabin, weapons at the ready.

Robert and the rest of his party found a set of steps that led down into the hold. Below, two-thirds of the hold was divided up into cells, all empty just as the slavers had said. The smell that filled the closed space was an obscene combination of sweat and excrement. Not exactly first class accommodations.

One of the sailors was muttering under his breath, probably praying.

"Come on, guys. Let's finish up and get the hell out of here." The sailors seemed eager to comply.

At the rear of the holding area was a heavy wooden door. Robert picked the largest sailor in the bunch and pointed at the door. The man put a boot into the middle of the door.

It cracked but didn't fall.

A second blow sent it into the room with a crash. Light from a pair of crystals embedded in the deck above illuminated the cargo area. Boxes of preserved food and barrels of fresh water filled the room. The only items of note were three axes and a score of spare grappling hooks.

"Grab those axes, and some food and water," Robert said.

The sailors quickly divided up the items and they retraced their steps up to the deck. The other sailors were waiting for them.

"Find anything?" Robert asked.

"Just this." One of the sailors opened a coffer filled to the rim with gold coins.

Robert grinned. "We'll keep that for our trouble. Three of you guys load those supplies in the longboat then lower it and secure it to the *Fox*. The rest of you take those axes below and scuttle this heap."

The longboat was lowered and secured in short order. The remaining sailors came up on deck after a couple minutes, their clothes soaked below the waist. The *Bound Hope* started to list.

"Everyone back to the *Fox*." Robert waved them across the planks that still joined the two ships.

Captain Haram was waiting. "It's done," Robert said.

The captain nodded and a pair of sailors with crowbars ripped the planks free of the deck. "All right, let them go. If I see you swabs again there'll be no mercy, understand?"

The slavers ignored the question and climbed a rope to the longboat. When everyone was aboard the rope tethering it to the *Fox* was cut. They immediately turned the longboat north away from the *Desert Fox*.

Robert and Captain Haram watched the *Bound Hope* sink slowly beneath the waves. Robert doubted he'd ever know for sure if Argus set him up or if it was just bad luck.

Not that it mattered. They'd made it through the danger in one piece and that was enough.

CHAPTER 61

V ilos stood in a guard tower overlooking the site of the explosion. His decidedly modest army was busy digging through the rubble. For the last week they had done little but pull out bodies and the rare survivor. It was hard work and Vilos was only taking a break. In another hour or so he'd rejoin his men in the effort. He rolled his shoulders, trying to work the kinks out. The many aches and pains reminded him that he wasn't getting any younger.

He sighed. No one expected him to do any real work, but it helped ease the guilt he felt. Though others might argue, he knew this mess was his fault. If he'd just told that damn sorcerer to go to hell all those years ago, none of this would have happened.

"You're thinking dark thoughts." Abin appeared in the doorway at the top of the tower.

"It's rude to read your lord's mind," Vilos said.

Abin smiled. "It takes no magic to read your mind, Majesty. One look at your face reveals all. Why don't you rest and let the others finish the cleanup?"

"Every day you ask me that and every day I tell you the same thing, I need to do it."

"No one blames you for this," Abin said.

"Can't you understand? I blame myself. It doesn't matter what anyone else thinks. I know the truth. This is my fault."

"Suppose you're right. What would have happened if you hadn't accepted this sorcerer's help? How many more people would have died during the Crown War? Would you have blamed yourself for their deaths because you didn't take help that was offered? What's done is done. We must look to the future."

"Right you are, my friend. Why don't you tell me what my disagreeable brother is up to?"

"At the moment he's up to very little. According to our people in the city, his men have been fleeing in small groups for the last few days. Our men have grabbed them and incarcerated them in a warehouse in the outer ward."

Vilos grinned. "Nord must be fit to be tied."

"I couldn't say. Nord's wizard must have noticed my spying and cast a shielding spell. I can't find a trace of them."

Vilos waved his hand. "It doesn't matter. How long before we have the worst of the rubble searched for survivors?"

"We haven't found any survivors in the last two days," Abin said. "I doubt we'll find any more now. The rest of the cleanup could take months."

"Months we don't have. Tomorrow we'll switch the men to working on the wall. We'll fix up their defenses the best we can then go settle with my brother."

"A wise decision, Majesty. When should we plan on leaving?"

Vilos thought for a moment. "Ten days at most. That'll give us a week to patch the wall and three days to rest. The men will be no good if they arrive exhausted."

Agreed," Abin said. "I'll contact our people in the city and let them know your plan."

Vilos nodded and turned back to the window. Ten more days and he'd be face to face with Nord again. He sighed and remembered the last time they'd faced each other.

Father had just died and Nord and Vilos were escorting the last of the nobles out of the palace. When they had gone Vilos said, "I hope I can count on your support when the time of selection comes."

Nord laughed. "You can't be serious. Why would I support you?"

Vilos had been puzzled at his brother's words. "It was Father's wish that I succeed him. Is that not enough?"

Nord managed to suppress any further laughter with great effort. "If he had made a public announcement, maybe, but as it is only we three know what he wanted. No, brother, the throne belongs to whoever is strong enough to take it. I trust you noticed Kent talking with the wealthy merchants that came to the funeral. He's already making alliances."

"There'll be war," Vilos had said softly.

"Yes." Nord had a vicious gleam in his eye. "For the first time in generations the strongest will rule, not the one with the good fortune to be born first. It will be glorious."

"It's insane. Thousands will be killed. The High Kingdom could tear itself apart."

"This sort of thing happens all the time in nature. The strong kill the weak. That's the way the world works."

Vilos stared at his brother. He spoke calmly enough for a madman. "We're not animals, Nord. We don't have to settle things with claws and teeth."

"You're wrong. We're no different than the lions that stalk the oases. Ignore that truth at your peril." Nord had stomped off into the palace and Vilos hadn't spoken to him again.

Vilos shook away the unpleasant memory. It seemed very little had changed for Nord since that day twenty-one years ago. It was a pity. Kent had managed to change over the years, but then he always was the smartest of the three of them. No one would ever debate that.

Nord it seemed never would change. When they faced each other next Vilos feared he might have to kill his brother.

CHAPTER 62

Robert, Blade and Captain Haram stood in the prow of the *Desert Fox* and watched a pod of dolphins swimming in front of the ship. They almost seemed to make a game of seeing which one could get the closest to the keel without getting hit. They leapt and played on the spray like kids on a beach. Robert smiled and wished Shara could risk a trip up on deck to see it.

Turning away from the show Captain Haram said, "We'll reach port tomorrow. I'd like to thank you again for your help."

"It was our pleasure," Robert said for what seemed the twentieth time in the last three-plus weeks.

After the slavers had sailed their little boat away, the crew had found and repaired the minor damage done by the ballista bolt. They had gotten lucky that it hit above the water line. Six men had been injured in the battle, only one seriously enough that he couldn't work.

"Perhaps you could do us a favor in return."

"Of course, my friends, anything in my power."

"We'd like to borrow one of your longboats and land a few miles away from the city. There may be some unpleasantness if we show up there. You understand?"

"Of course, I know a place sometimes used by smugglers." The captain cleared his throat. "Just tavern talk mind you."

Robert smiled knowingly. "No doubt. Your men will take us there?"

Captain Haram nodded. "There may be trouble. The smugglers don't trust newcomers."

Blade cracked her knuckles. "Don't worry about the smugglers."

Captain Haram swallowed nervously.

Robert smiled. His sweetheart certainly had a way with words. "Let us know when we're to disembark. We'll be below packing our things."

When they had moved out of earshot Blade asked, "What things? Everything we own is in two packs."

Robert waved his hand. "That was just an excuse. We need to fix up a disguise for Shara. I don't want anyone to get too good a look at her. No one paid much attention when we boarded, but a second look might jog their memories. When we reach the High Kingdom, we'll need a disguise even more. I imagine everyone there is looking for her."

"Good point. What did you have in mind for a disguise?"

"I don't know. We haven't got much to work with. A cloak with a deep cowl will probably be the best we can do. I'll try and find something better in the city."

They reached the bottom of the steps and turned down the little hall. "What do you plan to do for money?" Blade asked.

Robert grinned and reached inside his tunic to the hidden pocket and pulled out three gold coins. "They have friends."

"Where'd you get those?"

Robert knocked on the cabin door. "We found a coffer of

them over on the slavers' ship. I took a handful for our trouble. The sailors didn't mind when I mentioned some of it was for you."

Shara opened the door for them and they stepped inside.

"Hey, kid. In a few hours you should be on your home soil, or sand as the case may be."

Shara closed her eyes and sighed. "At last."

"I thought you'd be pleased. Now we need to fix you up a disguise." Robert looked around the cabin and his eyes finally settled on the thin green blanket on the floor next to the bench. It wasn't much but at the moment they had little choice.

He picked up the blanket and gave it a shake. No mouse droppings went flying which he took as a good sign. Robert glanced at Blade. "Can you sew?"

She raised an eyebrow.

"Didn't think so," Robert said staring at the blanket. "Well I used to patch sails, so I guess the job's mine."

"Excuse me," Shara said staring at him. "If you need something sewn, I know how. That was one of the things a proper lady must be able to do. Father insisted I learn even though my aunt swore Mother couldn't sew a stitch."

"Thank heaven for a classical education." Robert went over to his pack and retrieved an oilskin pouch. He tossed it to Shara. "You should find everything you need in there."

Blade gave him a funny look as Shara pulled out a needle and thread. "You carry a sewing kit with you?"

Robert shrugged. "How did you think the tent got fixed every time we found a new leak?"

Blade smiled and began putting her things in order.

It took about two hours before someone knocked on their door. "The captain is ready for you."

Shara draped her crudely made cloak over her shoulders and brought the deep cowl up over her head. "Ready."

"Okay, remember to keep your head down and don't talk."

"Don't worry," Shara said. "I won't do anything stupid."

"I know," Robert said giving her a reassuring pat on the shoulder. "But it makes me feel better if I remind you."

Blade opened the door and Robert groaned when he saw Ako standing there. The kid probably wanted one last look at his dream girl. All they needed was a curious kid trying to get a peek at Shara's face.

Robert shouldered his pack. "Lead on."

He followed Ako up on deck. Shara came behind him and Blade brought up the rear. Robert spotted the captain and half a dozen sailors standing beside the longboat. Ako led them quickly over to the others. The coast was visible about half a mile out. Between patches of large jagged rocks was a small beach with what looked like two boats flipped upside down above the water line.

"Are those the smugglers' ships?" Robert asked.

Captain Haram nodded. "More than likely. I checked with the farseer and couldn't make out anyone in the vicinity."

"Probably hiding out of sight," Blade said.

"No sense waiting any longer." Robert shook hands with the captain. "Thanks for the ride."

Captain Haram pumped his hand vigorously. "Not at all, and thank you for everything. We would have been in poor shape when those slavers attacked without your help."

You probably wouldn't have been attacked at all if it weren't for us. Robert kept that thought to himself.

Captain Haram shook Blade's hand as well. "I wish you safe journey the rest of your way. May the angels watch over you."

Robert grinned and stepped over the rail into the longboat. "They haven't so far, but it can't hurt to ask."

Robert held out his hand to help Shara into the boat. When she reached out to take it Ako darted forward and grabbed her hand. He fell to one knee. "Lady, you are the most beautiful woman I have ever seen. I know you are pledged to another but please tell me your name. I beg you."

Shara gently removed her hand from his grasp. In a voice barely above a whisper she said, "You ask for more than I can give."

Robert helped her into the boat and Blade came right behind. The four-man crew got in last. The longboat was lowered into the water then two of the sailors unhooked it. Two of them manned the oars while a third got in the rear and took the rudder. The last man stood in the prow and watched for rocks or coral that might punch a hole in the hull.

The sailors bent to their tasks and soon the longboat was pulling hard for shore. Robert kept his eyes riveted on the beach. He couldn't see any sign of movement but that didn't mean much. The smugglers could be hiding anywhere.

"Adjust to starboard," the spotter called out. The man at the tiller obliged and a few minutes later the prow of the boat struck the soft sand of the beach.

Robert and Blade jumped out then turned to help Shara. When they were safely out the spotter said, "Safe journey."

Robert waved. "Safe journey."

The rowers heaved and the boat slid free of its tenuous grip on the sand. Robert watched as they faded from sight.

He sighed. "We're on our own again. Let's get moving before the owners of these boats show up."

The two boats suddenly flipped over and four men armed with wicked curved daggers stood up. They were a nasty-looking quartet that appeared to be cut from the same cloth as the slavers, though none of them lacked any extremities.

"Too late I'm afraid," said one of the men, a broad-shouldered fellow with rotten teeth.

"This here's our beach. You want to use it you gotta pay us," one of the others said.

Robert pulled Shara behind him. "We're in a bit of a rush, gentlemen. Perhaps next time we're in the neighborhood."

"Yer gonna pay or we'll kill ya and take our pay out of your pretty friends' hides."

Blade's eyes narrowed and Robert swallowed a sigh. Of all the things the son of a bitch could have said, that was the one most apt to get him killed.

"I wish you hadn't said that."

Blade whipped her sword out and in the same motion slashed across Rotten Teeth's eyes, turning them both to jelly.

She kept her momentum going and cut low on the man beside him, severing the tendon above his knee.

He fell to the ground screaming.

She leveled her sword at the other two who stared at her like she was a devil from hell come to claim their souls.

Rotten Teeth was screaming and blood leaked out from between his fingers where they covered what remained of his eyes.

"Why don't you two throw those knives away and run along before she gets really pissed off?" Robert suggested.

The knives hit the sand and the two smugglers vanished like a bad smell.

"What about those two?" Shara asked.

"Let them bleed." Blade sheathed her sword. "Perhaps their friends will return for them. If not it's no great loss. Where to next?"

"Good question," Robert said. "I've never been to this part of the country. Any ideas, kid?"

"Sorry," Shara said. "I didn't travel much. Father thought it was too dangerous."

Robert ran a hand through his hair. "Let's head further inland. Maybe we'll come across something."

They left the beach and headed east. About an hour's travel brought them to a grassy plain. This close to the water, Robert figured there must be more rain than further inland where desert dominated everything. In the distance he could see rolling hills that turned into true mountains. Most of the storm clouds were probably stopped by those mountains.

They walked for another hour before they hit a path. It resembled the cart path that led to Reaper's Crossing except not as well used. It was basically a shallow rut worn in the ground. Still, this was the first sign of life they'd seen since leaving the beach.

"What do you think?" Robert asked. "Do we follow the ruts or strike out on our own?"

"Let's follow the tracks," Shara said. "Maybe we'll find an inn. I could really use a bath."

Robert lifted his arm and sniffed. Turning his head quickly away he said, "Sounds good to me. Blade?"

"After a month on sea rations, I could stand a decent meal. I say we follow the tracks."

That settled things and the little group headed north on the wagon tracks. As far as Robert could see in either direction was nothing but grass and the occasion clump of stubby trees. They trudged on for hours without seeing a soul.

Finally Robert asked, "Is it always this dead?"

"This is the cool season," Shara said. "Traditionally the merchants do most of their desert travel this time of year. It's the only time the desert can be crossed in anything approaching comfort. Travel along the coasts will pick up later along with the temperatures."

Dusk had almost arrived when they finally spotted a wisp of

smoke rising ahead of them. Feeling hopeful, Robert forced his tired body to move a little faster. As they got closer the source of the smoke became visible, it was a large building with three chimneys. The place was built like a fort with an eight-foot wall surrounding a three-story main building. Robert could make out at least four people marching around the top of the wall.

"Looks more like a border fort than an inn," Blade said as if reading his mind.

"A necessary evil," Shara said. "Our towns are built to be as self-sufficient as possible so my father doesn't have to send out regular patrols. The lands between towns can be quite rough, so when a would-be innkeeper builds his place, he builds it like a fortress. This gives the merchants a place to rest in safety and the guards a chance to unwind without having to keep watch."

"I bet they charge for the privilege too," Robert muttered.

"Consider the expense of building a place like that," Shara said. "Just importing the wood costs a small fortune."

"Looks like the best we can do," Blade said.

Robert nodded. "Let's check it out."

They walked on toward the inn and as they got closer Robert could make out the crossbows the guards walking along the wall carried. The guards noticed them as well. When they reached the main gate a pair of them came over and pointed their weapons down at them.

"State your business," one of the guards said.

"We're travelers looking for a place to stay for the night," Robert said.

"Let's see your coin," the guard ordered.

Robert reached into his pocket and pulled out a gold coin. He let it flash in the dying light. That seemed to satisfy the guard who hollered down for the portcullis to be raised. It clanked and squeaked but managed to get high enough for them to enter without ducking.

Inside the wall there was a large empty space surrounding the inn. Two tents were pitched near the right-hand wall. The inn itself was built of rough-hewn logs and looked like it could withstand damn near anything. Two more guards in leather armor and carrying cudgels flanked the door to the inn.

As opposed to the grim warriors on the walls these guards smiled and held the door open for them.

"Welcome to the Bubbly Wine Inn," the guard on the left said.

"If you need a room just ask the big bartender," the guard on the right added.

Robert nodded and led his two companions inside. Despite its massiveness the inn appeared to be laid out like most other inns Robert had visited. The ground floor consisted of a large common room and kitchen. A bar ran the length of the far wall, and behind it stood two bartenders. One towered over seven feet, while the other's head was just visible.

"I see why they call him the big bartender," Shara said.

They approached the bar and the giant came to meet them. "Can I help you?" he asked, his voice a deep bass rumble.

"We'd like a room please," Robert said.

"Just one for all three of you?"

Robert nodded. "With a fireplace if possible."

A slow smile spread across the giant's face. "You want a little romance." He gave Shara and Blade a look and the smile broadened. "You're a lucky man. We have one room with a fireplace. It's five gold pieces for the night and includes breakfast. There's also a tub if you want a bath."

Robert plunked down seven gold coins, half his treasure from the slavers' ship. "Please send up some meat, bread, cheese, and fruit in about an hour."

"Of course." The giant snatched up the coins and dropped

them in a box behind the bar. He also grabbed a brass key and handed it to Robert. "Room ten. Top of the stairs, turn right."

He leered at them but refrained from making any further comments.

Robert and his companions went upstairs. He could feel the bartender's eyes on them the whole way. He unlocked the door to their room and ushered the others in.

The room was well-appointed with two beds, a desk and chair, and the fireplace Robert had wanted along with a bucket full of black coal. In a separate room off the main room was an iron tub. A small pile of clean towels was stacked beside it.

When they had the door locked behind them Shara said, "That bartender thought the three of us were, you know."

Robert nodded. He and Blade began checking the walls for hidden doors and peepholes.

As they made their way around the room Shara asked, "Why didn't you tell him he was wrong?"

Robert shrugged. "It doesn't matter what he thought. If I'd kicked up a fuss, he might have been more apt to remember us, this way we're just another group out in the country for a little fun."

"I'm more interested in why you went to the extra expense of getting a room with a fireplace," Blade said.

"I'm going to do a little smelting this evening. I need the fire to do it."

"Smelting?" Blade and Shara said at the same moment as if unable to believe their ears.

"Yeah." Robert heard a hollow sound under his dagger. "Found something."

Blade moved to join him. "What have you got?"

She started tapping her dagger along the wall. It took them about a minute to define the boundary of the hidden door.

"I don't see a peephole," Robert said.

Blade probed the bottom of the door and found a slight crack. She got the tip of her dagger in it then kicked the hilt twice, driving the blade deep into the wood wedging the door shut.

"Let's see anyone sneak in now."

"Who wants the first bath?" Robert asked.

Shara scampered toward the tub. "Me."

⸙

Robert dried his hair and gave a contented groan. Never a fiend for cleanliness, he still felt better after washing off about a month's worth of sweat and grime. The tub was most fascinating. It was enchanted so that it would fill on command with hot water then drain at a second command.

Robert tossed his towel in the pile on the floor and dressed in his cleaner clothes. After riding around in his backpack it wouldn't be fair to call them clean, but they were a considerable improvement over his filthy, bloodstained outfit. He left the bathroom and entered the main room just as a knock sounded on the door.

Blade hopped to her feet from where she was reclining on one of the beds and grabbed her sword.

Robert waved at her. "That'll be our dinner."

He opened the door and sure enough there stood a burly fellow carrying a heavy covered tray. Robert took it from him. "Thank you, would you mind returning in an hour or so to get these dishes?"

The waiter grunted and turned to leave.

"I'll take that as a yes," Robert called after him.

He uncovered the tray and found a steaming platter of roast meat, a pyramid of cheese and a loaf of crusty bread. Robert smiled and helped himself to a piece of meat. He was a little disappointed at the lack of fruit but everything else looked great.

A bite of the meat sent juice running down his lips. After weeks of jerky it tasted wonderful.

"I guess you get what you pay for." He smacked his lips.

"Why don't you tell me about this smelting business that cost us seven gold coins," Blade said.

Robert reached into his pack and dropped one of the hunters' medallions on the table. "These are solid silver and probably worth three times as much as the gold we had combined before I bought the room and meal. Unfortunately, as they are now, they're only worth about half their true value."

"Why is that?" Shara asked around a mouthful of sandwich.

Robert beamed. "Excellent question. You see no merchant in his right mind would accept a hunter's medallion as payment, so I'd have to sell them to a fence who'd only give me about half what they're worth. If I melt them down myself, I can get their fair value. That's why I wanted the fireplace."

They finished their meal and Robert saved some bread and cheese. When the knock came on the door he answered it.

The grumpy waiter was standing there. Robert handed him the tray and empty platters. "Would you mind bringing us up a small pot? We've got some cheese and bread left and I thought we'd make a fondue."

The waiter grumbled until Robert held up a silver coin. "Please."

The now-smiling waiter hurried off to get the pot. When he returned, Robert flipped him the coin and took the small steel pot. It only looked big enough to do one medallion at a time, but Robert figured the steel would hold up better than iron or copper so it was probably best.

"Now I'm going to need an assistant," Robert said.

Shara raised her hand. "Me, pick me."

"Okay."

Blade rolled her eyes. "Terrific, you can teach her to be a fence just in case the whole princess thing doesn't work out."

Robert grinned and began building up a pile of coal. When the fire was burning steadily he handed Shara a small bellows. "Blow on the base of the fire until it gets going good." While Shara was tending the fire Robert removed one of the drawers from the desk and ripped the back off. He carefully carved two rectangular depressions about half an inch deep by four long and two wide. By the time he'd finished, the coals were glowing cherry red.

"That looks good." Robert took one of the medallions, put it in the pot, and set it on the coals. "Okay, kid, make with the bellows."

Shara pumped and soon the bottom of the pot turned bright red. She kept at it and Robert watched as the silver began to soften. He smiled and wiped the sweat off his face. By the time they finished everyone would probably need another bath.

"That's enough." The silver had liquefied now.

Robert wrapped the handle in leather and gingerly took the pot off the coals. He'd judged the size of his molds pretty close and only a few drops of silver remained when he'd filled them both.

When they finished the last medallion it was nearing midnight and only a handful of coal remained in the bucket. Robert grinned as he looked at the small pile of ingots sitting on the floor beside him. Not a huge amount of wealth, but if he acted prudently, it should get Shara home.

He looked over at her where she slept. It was hard to believe anyone could wish to harm such a sweet kid.

Robert stripped off his sweaty clothes and crawled into bed

beside Blade. The cool silk sheets felt wonderful against his flushed skin.

"All done?" Blade whispered in his ear.

"Yeah, I'm going into the nearest city in the morning. With any luck I'll be able to get what we need and be back in a day or two."

"The only luck we've had has been bad."

"Don't remind me," Robert mumbled.

"Bobby." Robert felt Blade's foot slide along his calf. "When this is over we should come again for a private visit."

Robert smiled in the dark. "It's a date."

<hr />

Robert woke as the first rays of dawn were filtering through the window. He wiggled carefully out of bed so as not to bother Blade. She groaned a little but rolled over and went back to sleep.

He looked down at her and smiled. When she slept, all the tension went out of her face. She looked even more beautiful than usual. Though he would have loved nothing more than to spend the rest of the morning looking at Blade he had more pressing matters to attend. Robert threw on his clothes and left the cozy little room, locking the door behind him.

Downstairs in the common room, the smell of fresh bread filled the air. A score of men clustered around three tables. Most of them looked like warriors but two of them wore fine robes.

Robert headed over to the bar. The giant was absent but his small associate hurried over to see what Robert wanted.

"Can I help you, sir?" the little man asked.

Robert placed his order and the bartender went to the

kitchen. A few minutes later he returned with a platter of sweet rolls, some bacon and honey, and a pitcher of mead.

"There you are, sir."

"Thanks." Robert nodded toward the group gathered in the common room. "Caravan?"

"Yes, sir, they got in about an hour after you."

"Where they headed?"

The bartender looked around the room, not wanting to meet Robert's eyes. "Well…"

Robert reached into his pocket and produced a silver coin. "Well?"

"They're headed to Port Dalton. The merchant said something about picking up a load of copper pans."

Robert flipped the bartender the coin. "Thanks."

As he carried the food up the steps he thought sneaking into the city would be much easier as part of a caravan. He'd never visited the city with his father, so it must be one of the smaller ports. That suited his needs perfectly.

When he reached the door to their room he realized he wouldn't be able to open the door with his hands full.

"Hey Blade, open up." He gave the door a crack with his foot.

The door opened and Shara said, "Shh, you'll wake the neighbors. Ooh, sweet rolls."

She helped herself to one of the gooey treats.

Robert set the platter down on the table. "Where's Blade?"

"Washin' up," Shara said around a mouthful of roll.

Robert grinned and helped himself to a strip of bacon. "Your manners are going straight to hell."

Shara eyed her next victim without comment.

Robert was nibbling his second strip of bacon and Shara her third roll when Blade emerged from the bathroom.

"Just in time," Robert said. "If you'd taken much longer the kid would have finished all the rolls."

Shara scrunched up her nose at him and shoved the rest of the roll in her mouth. Blade ignored the chatter and poured herself a mug of mead. "When are you leaving?"

"A caravan rolled in late last night. When I finish up here, I'm going to see if I can ride in with them. I figure it'll provide a good cover." Robert took all but two of his remaining gold coins and gave them to Blade. "This should cover you until I get back."

"You should keep these. I've got enough to hold us."

"If something should happen I'd rather you had a little extra."

"Nothing's going to happen," Shara said.

Robert gave her a reassuring smile. "I know, but I'll feel better knowing you have it." He grabbed his pack and said, "Wish me luck."

Blade wrapped her arms around his neck and kissed him for long seconds. Her lips tasted like honey.

She pulled away. "Good luck."

"Good luck," Shara echoed.

Robert nodded and left them alone. He didn't know why he worried. Blade was better able to take care of Shara and herself than he was. Still, he worried just the same.

Down in the common room the merchants and their guards were still gathered around the table. Robert took a deep breath and headed over to the group.

"Excuse me," he said addressing one of the merchants. "The bartender mentioned that you were headed to Port Dalton and I was wondering if you had room for one more."

The merchant looked at his partner then said, "We can't afford to hire another guard."

Robert relaxed. If money was their only objection he was

all set. "That's all right, I'm not looking for a job. I'm headed to the city myself and I figured there'd be safety in numbers. I'm a fair shot with a crossbow."

The merchant shrugged. "It's only a day's journey. I doubt you could cause much trouble. We leave in fifteen minutes. Welcome aboard."

· ⁙

I t took the little caravan a day and a half to reach Port Dalton. Robert rode beside a grizzled old teamster, a borrowed crossbow cradled in his arm. The wagon ride was rough, but it beat walking. The teamster, who said his name was Orik, chattered the whole way about the new grand-daughter he was finally going to meet after this run.

Robert figured the trip took about thirty hours and the old man only paused his narrative to drink from a flask of pungent whisky, sleep, and eat. Robert had at first wondered why he'd gotten such an easy job. He guessed no one else could sit next to the old man for long without strangling him.

Robert sighed with relief when the walls of the city came into view. Soon he'd be able to leave his new companions, get the supplies he required, and return to Shara and Blade.

As they approached the gate three guards emerged from a little shack in front of the massive wooden doors. Two guards carried crossbows and the third wore a scimitar at his belt and appeared to be in charge. One of the merchants—they were brothers according to the ever-chatty Orik—climbed down from the lead wagon and approached the guards.

"Trouble?" Robert asked.

"Nah," Orik said. "Just routine questions. If we had cargo they'd look it over, but since the wagons are empty the bosses just have to pay a three-gold-coin entry fee."

As if to confirm this, the merchant counted out three coins to the guard and hurried back to his wagon. The lead guard motioned and the gate creaked open. When it stopped the guards waved them through. Orik nodded to the guards as they passed.

The city was laid out with one broad street paved with flat stones running from the main gate down to the docks. All the other streets branched off from it. Shops of all sorts lined the main street. As they made their way toward the docks Robert said, "Would you mind dropping me off at a tavern?"

"Sure, the Traveler's Rest is about halfway to the docks. It's clean and not too expensive."

"Much obliged," Robert said. For all his talk Orik wasn't a bad guy, annoying, but not bad.

They rode through the slowly darkening city before finally coming to a stop in front of a small two-story building with a sign featuring a bed in the center and a foaming mug on either side.

"This is it," Orik said.

The rest of the caravan stopped as well.

Robert unloaded his borrowed crossbow and eased the tension of the string. "Thanks for the loan," he said handing it back to Orik. "Glad I didn't have to use it."

"Me too," Orik said and the two men shook hands.

Robert clambered down off the wagon seat, his legs stiff after sitting on the hard wooden bench for so long. He made his wobbly way over to the door of the inn and was joined by the two brothers.

"I appreciate the lift into the city," Robert said. He reached into his pocket and drew out two silver coins. "These should cover my share of the entry fee."

One of the brothers, Robert couldn't remember their

names, shook his head. "Consider the entry fee our way of paying for your services as a guard."

Robert pocketed the coins. "Thank you again, and best of luck with your copperware."

The brothers smiled and climbed aboard their wagon. Robert waved as the caravan got underway again.

On his own, he entered the Traveler's Rest and walked up to the bar. The common room was deserted. That suited Robert fine, the fewer people that saw him here the better.

"Ale please," he said to the sweaty bartender.

The bartender plunked a frothy mug down in front of him. "You from around here?" he asked.

Robert took a sip of the warm ale and winced. It was the bitterest swill he'd ever tasted. No wonder the common room was empty.

"No, I'm actually on my way north and I need some supplies. Any recommendations?"

"Sure, there's about a dozen places around should be able to fix you up. You can probably get a damn good deal too, not many caravans headed north these days."

"Why is that?" Robert asked.

"Been a lot of fighting up that way. Nomads were up in arms about poisoned oases, then some warlord led an army down from the Broken Kingdom. Hell of a mess. If you can get through, your goods should bring a fine price."

Robert took a last sip of the ale, more to be a good sport than because he wanted any more. "Where can I find these suppliers you mentioned?"

"Most of them are in the North Ward. If you have trouble finding them just ask a guard, they'll point you in the right direction."

"Thanks, how much for the drink?"

"Three coppers."

Robert plunked a silver coin down. "Keep the change."

The bartender snatched up the coin. "Thank you, sir, stop by again anytime."

Robert smiled as he left the inn. He wouldn't be stopping by for another drink that was certain.

While he had been busy gathering information, darkness had settled in over the city. He had no desire to be out on the streets after dark. Fortunately the main street was lined with inns. He chose one on the opposite side of the street and two doors up from the Traveler's Rest. It would be interesting to see if anyone came looking for him. It seemed unlikely, but he decided safety was the prudent course.

· —✧·

F ully rested after a decent night's sleep, Robert left his room and headed north through the city. He hadn't gone far when the smell of cooking meat caught his attention. He followed his nose east and found an elderly woman with a push cart offering grilled sausage.

"How much?" he asked.

"Two coppers each," said the white-haired woman.

Robert handed her his last silver coin. "Two please."

The old woman looked away. "My apologies, sir, I have only two coppers for change."

She looked like those two coppers were her last judging by the frayed, dirty smock she wore. "You can keep the difference."

Her eyes widened a little. "That's very generous, young man." She stuck two sausages on a long wooden skewer and handed them to him.

As Robert leaned down to take the skewer he noticed a flash in the corner of his eye. He smiled and took his breakfast.

He brought the meat up to his lips and glanced toward the flash.

Damned if there wasn't a hunter walking down the street opposite him. The glint from his silver medallion had gotten Robert's attention.

The sausage caught in his throat. There was no way they could know he was here.

When he finally managed to swallow he said, "Very tasty."

Robert walked further up the street but the hunter didn't pay him the least attention.

Despite a distinct lack of appetite, he forced himself to finish the sausage. Depending on how things went, he might not get another meal soon. Setting himself back on course, Robert headed toward the North Ward. The sooner he got the supplies they needed, the sooner he could return to the inn.

It didn't take long for him to get totally lost. When he finally stopped it was in the middle of a residential area. As far as he could see there was nothing resembling a supply shop within five blocks. For the last half hour he'd been walking generally north. He couldn't be that far off.

He spotted a small woman bundled in robes hobbling her way down the street. Robert walked slowly over so as not to frighten her.

"Excuse me," he said. "Can you tell me if I'm near a caravan supply shop? I was told there were several in this part of the city."

The woman looked startled at first, probably not used to strangers. She relaxed after a moment; no doubt his charming smile put her at ease. "You're too far east, young man. All the caravans buy their supplies at one of the shops near North Gate. Head west and you'll find them."

"I see, thank you. Could you give me directions to these shops?"

She gave him a disgusted look. The one the old reserved for those younger than themselves.

She pointed toward the massive stone wall looming in the distance. "Go that way. When you reach the wall follow it west. You can't miss North Gate. When you reach the gate you won't be able to miss the shops."

The old woman was right. As soon as he reached the gates he spotted the shops. Actually smelled was probably more accurate. The stench coming from the camels was incredible, no doubt because so many were packed into such a small place. The entire area looked devoid of customers.

Robert shrugged and selected the most prosperous-looking shop, in this case the one that had bothered to whitewash its walls. As soon as he entered, a little man with greasy hair slicked back from his forehead scurried over to greet him.

"Welcome, sir, welcome. I am most happy to serve you."

Robert looked around the empty store. All manner of dry goods were stacked to the ceiling. "I'll bet you are. I'm putting together a small caravan. I need four camels, food for four people and the animals for two weeks, five ten-gallon water skins and a large tent."

"Ah, I see my wise customer has heard about the poisoned oases. A very good idea is bringing extra water with you. May I ask your destination?"

"Sure," Robert said without elaborating.

He wandered around the shop selecting several boxes of dried food, a length of rope, and two heavy tarps. He carried the supplies over to a large table in the front of the shop. "I'll need saddlebags for the camels as well. How soon can you have my animals packed and ready to go?"

"They could be ready in an hour, sir. As you see, we are not so busy. How will you be paying?"

Robert reached into his pack and plunked down four silver bars. "This should cover it."

The merchant licked his lips as he stared at the silver. "Alas, that is insufficient. I will need at least three more bars like those."

Robert dropped one more bar on the table. "Take it or leave it."

The little merchant trembled, obviously wanting more.

"It's not like you have customers beating down your doors," Robert pointed out.

"Quite correct. Very well, I accept. I'll prepare your animals and you can be on your way."

CHAPTER 63

Shara sat on the edge of her bed and watched Blade sleep. They'd swapped their expensive room for a cheaper one. This one only had two beds and a chamber pot. No desk, chair, or magic tub.

On the other hand, they got it for three nights and it only cost one gold coin. Blade didn't seem to care that the beds were lumpy. After a lifetime of sleeping on the ground any bed probably felt good to her.

She sighed. The room wasn't what was bothering her. She was closer to her father than she'd been in months, but rather than feeling happy she felt nervous. Her father, of course, wasn't the cause of her nervousness. The sorcerer was.

She felt like she was walking right into his arms. That was ridiculous of course. As long as she wore her ring, he couldn't find her. She tried to relax but found sleep long in coming.

They spent the next several days in their room. After the disaster in King's Port, Blade didn't seem inclined to take any chances and Shara didn't argue. That night Shara tossed and turned until morning. When she woke up after a miserable few hours' sleep she found Blade already dressed and packed.

"Bobby should be back today," Blade said.

"Can we wait in the common room?" Shara asked. She didn't add that if she didn't get out soon she'd scream.

Blade seemed to feel the same. "Sure, just keep your hood up. We don't need any questions just now."

Shara eagerly dressed and pulled on her crude cloak. They went downstairs and found the common room almost empty. Blade chose a table near the window looking out over the yard. She indicated Shara should take the chair facing out. Blade sat opposite her watching the room.

A serving girl came over and took their order, honey cakes and wine. She hadn't been gone long when Shara heard Blade mutter under her breath.

"What's wrong?"

"Hello ladies," a deep voice behind Shara said. "Mind if I join you?"

Blade got to her feet. "We mind, take a hike."

"I noticed your friend left. Perhaps you two would like to keep me company tonight."

"I said take a hike."

A huge fist slammed into the table beside Shara. "No woman denies me in my own inn."

Blade darted around the table and drew her sword.

There was a thump.

Shara turned around to see what was happening and found Blade with her boot on the big bartender's chest and her sword at his throat.

The big man was actually trembling, though with fear or anger Shara couldn't tell.

"Since you can't seem to take a hint," Blade said. "Let me be blunter. Leave. Us. Alone."

"Sorry, miss. I meant no offense."

Blade took a step back, sword still held ready. "Of course not."

Blade waited until he was behind the bar to sit down.

"That was incredible," Shara said. The serving girl returned with their food and set it on the table. "He was four times bigger than you. How'd you do it?"

"Strike fast and don't hesitate, just like I told you." Blade took a honey cake. "The problem with big men is they're slow. I could have killed him as well as knocked him on his ass. I figure we don't need the hassle. Bobby should be back soon and we'll leave this idiot and his inn behind."

They spent another hour or so lounging around the common room sipping wine and keeping a close watch. Finally the gate opened and a column of four camels entered the compound. Atop the lead camel was a figure wrapped in the robes common to nomad traders.

"Blade, I think this might be him."

Blade took her eyes off the common room long enough to glance out the window.

"I think you might be right." She signaled the serving girl. When she arrived Blade asked, "How much do we owe you?"

"No charge, miss. What you did to Lugo was enough."

Blade smiled and reached into her pocket. She let the half a dozen silver flakes they'd scraped out of the fondue pot fall onto the tabletop.

"Here's your tip," Blade said. "Come on, if that's Bobby the sooner we get out of here the happier I'll be."

Shara followed Blade out of the inn. She could almost feel the eyes of the giant bartender following her. Blade seemed to sense it too and she stopped in the doorway.

Slowly Blade turned and shot him one of her excellent

narrow-eyed glares. Lugo immediately looked away and began polishing a glass. Blade smiled an evil smile and walked out the door. Shara followed close behind.

CHAPTER 64

They were only two days out from the inn and Shara already felt miserable. Of all the lands they'd traveled through, she found it ironic that the one she hated most was her home. They had left the coastal plain behind yesterday and entered the desert. A constant, steady breeze blew sand into her hair and left her itching all the time.

The meager robes Robert had purchased for them provided little protection from the sand, though they did keep off the worst of the sun. Riding as she was between Robert and Blade, she didn't have to keep track of what she was doing so she let her mind wander.

The last time she'd traveled through the desert was on a short trip with her father about three years ago. She smiled as she remembered. On that trip she'd ridden in a covered howdah and hadn't gotten sand in her hair. They'd returned to the palace before dark so she had no idea what the deserts were like at night.

They didn't dare approach an oasis because they were

poisoned. Their tents were sturdy enough but there wasn't a silk pillow or soft mattress in sight.

She didn't bother to complain though, after all Blade and Robert were risking their lives to get her home. She was about to heave another great sigh when Robert reined in his camel and waved them up to join him.

"What is it?" Blade asked.

Robert pointed. In the distance three twisters of sand kicked up a dust storm.

"Sand devils," she said.

"Sand devils?" Robert echoed

"Air elementals that live in the desert. I read about them. They aren't evil. They just like to play with sand, making whirlwinds and things like that."

"So they won't bother us?" Blade asked, fingering her sword.

Shara hesitated. "Well, if they see us, they may want to play. I don't think they'd hurt us, not on purpose anyway, but they might stick us in a sand storm."

"Let's swing out wide around them," Robert said. "Maybe we'll get lucky and they won't notice us."

"Luck is one thing we haven't had in abundance of late," Blade said.

"That just means we're due," Robert countered.

Blade smiled and shook her head.

· —❊-

The wind screamed around them as they huddled in a hastily raised shelter. The sand devils had spotted them an hour ago and made a beeline in their direction. As soon as the devils turned toward them, Shara had insisted they dismount and set up a shelter.

That had turned out to be a wise decision as they could no more outride the devils than they could the wind. Four camels now anchored a heavy tarp over their heads. The tarp whipped and snapped as the devils tugged at it. Every so often a cackle of glee could be heard.

"So we're due for good luck?" Blade said in disgust.

"Just because we didn't get it doesn't mean we're not due," Robert said in his defense.

Shara shook her head in amazement as she listened to them banter in the middle of the storm. Nothing seemed to faze them. She, on the other hand, was shaking so bad she couldn't see straight.

"What now, kid?" Robert shouted over the howling devils.

"Now we pray they get bored before they manage to rip the tarp off us."

"Wonderful," Blade muttered.

The devils continued to howl and giggle though for how long Shara couldn't guess. Suddenly there was a loud snap. One corner of the tarp had come out from under the camel sitting on it.

Robert and Blade both lunged for it as sand gushed in choking Shara and causing her eyes to water. They finally managed to get the tarp pulled back down, though not before the devils managed to deposit a foot of sand underneath.

After a while the wind let up, and then it stopped all together. They waited another few minutes before pushing the tarp up to look around.

Robert got to his feet and brushed off his robe. "That wasn't so bad."

Blade shot him a baleful look.

"What?"

He offered Shara a hand up. While Shara and Blade dusted themselves off Robert fetched a water skin from their pack camel. He rinsed his mouth and spat out a mouthful of brown water. The next mouthful he swallowed then passed the skin to Shara. Shara and Blade rinsed their mouths and drank while Robert cleaned off the tarp and repacked it.

When everyone had drunk their fill they remounted and got underway. Shara shielded her eyes and could just make out the sand devils playing in the distance. Pity they couldn't fly around like that.

Much to Shara's delight, the next week passed without much excitement. It was just after dawn on their ninth day out from the inn that they spotted the gleaming white walls of Sultan's Oasis. Home at last. Shara's throat tightened and tears ran down her cheeks. She had finally made it. It seemed like a lifetime ago when she vanished from the throne room. Now she was back and soon she'd be with her father.

"What the hell is that?" Blade asked pointing off in the distance.

Shara and Robert shaded their eyes to try and get a better look. There was a huge cloud of dust and she could see small figures moving in it.

"Looks like an army," Robert said. "I heard in Port Dalton that there had been some trouble up this way."

"The question is, are those the good guys or the bad guys," Blade said.

"We should get to the palace," Shara said. "If that's the invader's army, we can make our stand with my father. If it's his army we can celebrate."

"Whoever it is," Blade said. "I don't care much for getting caught out in the open when they arrive. It looks like we have a mile or two lead on them, let's make the most of it."

They rode hard toward the city, Robert and Blade in front with Shara half a length behind. They reached the gates well ahead of the army. Unfortunately, the gates they'd planned to hide behind had been blown off their hinges.

"This looks bad," Robert said.

Blade shot him a no-kidding look and turned to Shara. "What do you think?"

"If my father's here he'll be at the palace. I have to see."

Blade nodded and they started down the street. All along the main road bodies lay desiccating in the bright sun. Buildings were burned out, some still smoking.

As they approached the scene of a particularly large battle a flock of vultures flew up and perched on a nearby building. Their hideous bald heads turned to follow Shara and her friends. No doubt they were wondering if they were going to get some fresh meat soon.

They had hardly left the battle site when she heard the flutter of wings as the vultures settled back down to feed. It took all of Shara's self-control not to turn around and chase the ugly animals out of her city.

"Does something seem wrong about all this?" Robert asked.

Shara choked on a sob. "Everything seems wrong."

"That's not what I mean. Shouldn't the survivors be out cleaning up and rebuilding? Whenever this battle took place it wasn't recent and nothing looks disturbed."

"I don't see any sign of activity," Blade said.

Shara thought she sounded a little nervous.

"Let's get to the palace," Shara said more anxious now than ever. "Whatever answers there are, that's where we'll get them."

They rode through the ghost city, fighting their camels the whole way. The smell of death was everywhere and whenever the wind swirled the camels got a fresh whiff and shied, trying to turn around and run. Shara didn't blame them. She wanted to run from the horror that her beautiful city had become.

When they entered the nobles' district, the damage seemed

less evident. There were plenty of smashed buildings, but nothing burned and fewer bodies lay rotting in the street.

"A quarter million people lived here. Someone must still be alive," Shara said.

"Considering everything that's happened, the survivors are probably still hiding from any strangers they see, just in case," Robert said.

"I suppose," Shara said not believing it for a second.

No guards challenged them as they approached the white marble walls of the palace. The huge double doors lay in ruin just like the gates that led into the city. Bodies were scattered about. Many wore the uniforms of the palace guard.

Shara bit her lip. Whoever attacked the city had made it into the palace. What a horrible twist of fate to find her father dead before she could see him again.

She forced the tears away. Assuming the worst wouldn't do any good. They would search the palace and if there was no body, then he was still alive. Robert and Blade were talking softly to each other.

"What is it?" she asked.

"I smell food," Robert said.

"How can you think about food at a time like this?" Shara demanded.

Blade raised a finger to her lips. "It means someone's still alive around here. We should be cautious."

They continued up the path toward the palace. The once-magnificent gardens were in ruin. Signs of battle were everywhere. Arrows were embedded in trees; delicate ferns had been trampled and stained with blood.

Shara sniffed. "These gardens were Father's joy. Sometimes, when there was a lull in court, he would walk for hours out here. Now it's all ruined."

Robert stopped and went to her. He laid a reassuring hand

on her shoulder. "Gardens can be fixed. So can cities. When we find your father the two of you can set things right, but if you don't pull yourself together, we won't live long enough to find him."

Shara swallowed the lump in her throat. Robert was right. She had to keep her wits if she was going to find her father. She could cry later when they were finally together.

"I'll be all right," she said trying to sound convincing. "Let's go."

Robert nodded and smiled. "That's the way, kid."

They reached the palace and found the doors intact but thrown open. Blade had her sword out but no guard challenged them. "Where should we check first?"

"The throne room is straight ahead," Shara said. "Let's check there first."

The inside of the palace was almost exactly as Shara remembered. There was some minor damage but nothing like the rest of the city or even the garden. The statues that had lined the wall were gone, but that was the only major change. At the end of the hall was a set of closed double doors. Blade tapped them with her foot and they swung silently inward.

They entered cautiously but no one seemed to be home. Where could her father be?

"Father, are you here?" Shara shouted.

A blinding light flashed.

Shara threw her arm across her eyes.

Robert and Blade snarled in pain as the light seared their eyes.

"I'm sorry," said a deep, vaguely familiar voice. "Your father isn't here. He fled before me like the coward I always knew he was."

Shara lowered her arm. A swarm of spots swirled in front of her eyes. As her vision cleared the first thing she saw was a loaded crossbow floating a foot from her face. A quick glance showed a dozen more weapons surrounding them.

"You all right, kid?" Robert asked.

"Other than seeing spots before my eyes I'm fine. How about you?"

"Fine," Blade and Robert said at the same time.

"I'm thrilled to hear you're all feeling well," said the voice.

Heaven's mercy it sounded familiar, but Shara couldn't put a name to it. "If you wish to continue feeling well you should drop your weapons."

Surrounded as they were by loaded crossbows, Blade didn't have much choice but to let her sword fall to the floor. Shara heard the clang but never took her eyes off the spot near the throne where the voice originated.

"Good." Two men suddenly appeared. One looked completely unfamiliar and wore the robes of a wizard. He was obviously the one controlling the crossbows.

The second man looked like a more heavily muscled version of her father. His blond hair was cut short and he wore a sword on his belt, her father's sword she realized with a start.

"Well, my beautiful niece, I assume you recognize me."

Shara nodded. There was only one man he could be. "Uncle Nord, where is my father?"

"My miserable excuse of a brother fled rather than face me." With a rueful glance around him Nord added, "I'll admit he did a good job decimating my army. Now that I have you though, nothing else matters. Soon I will rule the High Kingdom as is my destiny."

"You were never meant to rule," Shara said. "My grandfather chose my father to succeed him."

"A foolish decision made by a doddering old man." Nord clapped his hands and eight guards armed with spears entered the throne room. "Escort my niece's companions to the dungeon. They can keep Vilos's soldiers company."

Robert and Blade were driven at spear point out of the room leaving Shara alone with her uncle and the wizard. "I think we can dispense with the crossbows, Arkon," Nord said.

"As you wish, my lord." Arkon waved his hand and the crossbows floated over to the wall and lined up in a neat row.

"How is it you think having me will gain you a kingdom?" Shara asked.

Nord smiled, not a pleasant sight from where Shara stood. "Simple, I'm going to trade you to that crazy sorcerer for an army of demons. Then my brother will be destroyed."

Shara went numb as she realized two things. First, her uncle was a lunatic and second, she couldn't hide from the sorcerer if he told him where she was. "You're mad. My father made a bargain with this sorcerer and look what he got."

"Vilos broke the deal and got what he deserved. All I plan to do is renegotiate my current arrangement."

CHAPTER 65

aktari!

Nord's mental voice rang in the sorcerer's mind as he sat trying to study a tome in his lab. He frowned and looked up from the book. What could that fool want now? After his pathetic failures to date Daktari was tempted to kill the man just to rid the world of him, an act of charity on his part.

What?

He sent the thought with enough force that he felt Nord's mind recoil in pain. After weeks of frustration that bit of pain brought him great pleasure.

I have the princess. We are in the throne room of the palace now.

Daktari marveled. Perhaps he'd spare Nord after all.

I will be there shortly.

The sorcerer summoned a shield of invisibility and teleported to collect his prize.

Daktari arrived a moment later, invisible, in the throne room. An instant after that, he felt the weak mental probe of Nord's pitiful wizard. With a blast of mental energy, he bludgeoned the weakling into near unconsciousness, leaving just enough awareness to keep him standing.

Turning his attention to Nord he found the would-be king standing behind the princess with a dagger in his hand.

It seemed Nord had treachery in his heart. Just like every other member of his worthless family apparently.

A thought and gesture made the princess's skin as impenetrable as iron. Now to see what the fool was about. He allowed the invisibility spell to fade and appeared before Nord.

"I see you do indeed have the girl," Daktari said as Nord tried to recover from his sudden appearance. "Very good. Give her to me and I'll be on my way."

Nord brought the dagger up to Shara's throat. "Not so fast. I think we need to renegotiate our deal. My army has been wiped out and I require a replacement. You will summon an army of demons to serve me or the girl dies."

Daktari frowned. "There will be no renegotiation. Turn the girl over to me this instant and you may live to draw another breath."

"You had your chance."

Nord dragged the blade of his dagger across Shara's throat. When the flesh didn't yield in the slightest he tried to stab her. The force of the blow bent his dagger blade.

A razor-thin smile creased Daktari's face. "You had your chance as well."

The sorcerer flicked his index finger at Nord and a blast of magic lifted him off his feet and flung him ten feet through the air.

As soon as Nord was airborne, Shara took off toward the door. Daktari gestured again and this time a gentle force levitated her three feet in the air. Kick and struggle though she might, Shara couldn't move an inch.

"Be still, Princess, I'll be with you shortly."

Turning to Nord as he struggled to his feet Daktari said, "We had a deal. If you captured the princess, you were to hand her over at once. There was no ambiguity. Yet still you felt you could try and betray me. Foolish."

Nord ripped Heat's Bane from its sheath and charged.

Daktari shook his head and pointed.

Nord stopped in his tracks, unable to lift his feet from the floor.

Heat's Bane began to glow ice blue. Inch by inch ice spread over Nord until he was a giant icicle from the neck down.

Daktari snapped his fingers and Nord shattered. His head landed with a crunch on the broken ice. When the binding spell ended, Nord's head screamed. His soul was still bound to his head and would stay bound for an eternity of suffering.

Heat's Bane drifted obediently over next to Daktari. He spoke a word of power and the sword vanished.

Anguish radiated from Nord's head in waves that washed over Daktari. He needed to leave before it strengthened the corruption lurking in his body so much that he couldn't control himself.

Losing control in his current mood would be a disaster for everyone.

CHAPTER 66

Robert preceded Blade out of the throne room. Surrounded as they were Robert knew they wouldn't have a chance even if Blade had her sword. They were ushered down a short, unadorned hall then down a flight of steps. At the bottom were two doors. One led down another hall and the second to a room filled with cells. The dungeon was lit only by two torches, one at either end of the row of cells.

The lead guard opened one of the cells, the third on the right Robert noted with little interest. The remaining guards prodded them into the cell. As soon as they were inside the door shut with a final-sounding clanging. After all their efforts all they managed to do was lead Shara back into captivity.

Robert sighed. Sometimes it just didn't pay to get out of bed.

"Who's there?" asked a voice in the dark.

"My companion and I are merchants. We were hired to bring a package to the palace."

"Let me guess, that no-good bastard upstairs took your package and dumped you down here?"

"You got it. And who might you be?" Robert asked.

"I am Azim, a humble foot soldier in my lord's army. I was taken prisoner when the palace was overrun and have been alone in this cell for I don't know how many days. It feels good to have company even if I can't see you."

"It's always good to be needed. Now, how do we get out of here?"

"We don't," said the dejected soldier.

CHAPTER 67

Vilos and Abin stood before the illusory wall in the alley where they'd first arrived in Haydrien. Yosef had sent word that he would arrive in the city in a few minutes. The prisoners had to be set free before the attack began.

"Ready, Majesty?" Abin asked.

Vilos adjusted his gold circlet and nodded. They passed through the wall and into the underground. At Vilos's command the portal rippled into being. They shared a glance then stepped through. After a gut-wrenching moment they were through to the palace.

"Remember, your brother's wizard will certainly have sensed our arrival. We must move fast."

Vilos drew his scimitar. "Let's go."

They mounted the steps and ran to the top. The dungeon waited one floor up.

When they reached the hidden door at the top Abin held Vilos back.

"Your brother knew about the portal as well, there may be guards waiting." The wizard closed his eyes and concentrated. "All clear."

Vilos stepped through the opening, sword ready just in case. The hallway was clear. The dungeons were on the opposite side from the secret door. Vilos charged down the hall and turned right down a connecting passage, Abin following right behind him. They stopped about ten paces from the door to the dungeon.

Vilos drew a ragged breath. "I'm getting too old for this foolishness."

"How do you think I feel?" Abin said between wheezes.

"What about guards?" Vilos asked.

Abin closed his eyes again. After a moment he said, "There are at least a hundred people in there. I can't tell our men from the guards."

"Guess we'll have to find out the hard way. You blast the door down and I'll go in first."

Abin summoned a sphere of energy and hurled it at the door.

The spell detonated against the door and blew it off its hinges and ten feet into the room. Vilos followed right behind. One guard was groaning under the remains of the door. The second guard leveled his spear and charged from the other end of the room.

Vilos braced himself and took the blow full force in the chest.

The spear snapped in half when it hit the magic barrier that surrounded him.

A backhand slash left the guard dying in a pool of blood.

Vilos bent down and picked up a set of keys from the dead man's belt.

It took only minutes to free the captured soldiers. Vilos noted with pleasure that they all seemed reasonably healthy if thinner. Along with his men was a strange couple that, according to his men, had been brought in that day.

"What brings you two to my troubled land?" Vilos asked the strangers.

"Well," the man said. "We were hired to deliver a package to the palace. My name is Robert, by the way, and this is my companion, Blade."

"What manner of package were you hired to deliver, and who hired you?"

"Well," Robert said. "The person who hired us was your daughter and she was the package. She said if we brought her here you'd be generous."

Vilos only vaguely heard what the stranger said after he mentioned Shara. She was here. Not in the dungeon so where?

Nord.

"She's with my brother."

Robert nodded. "That's probably a safe bet."

Vilos turned and ran out the door without a word.

If the others followed he didn't care.

Shara was all that mattered.

With Nord in league with the sorcerer, he had little time.

Vilos charged up the steps that led to the throne room.

A sharp kick knocked the door open.

Inside, Vilos discovered his worst nightmare come true. The sorcerer stood facing away from him about ten paces into the room and Shara floated beside him, helpless.

"Shara!" Vilos roared, dragging his sword from its sheath.

"Daddy, no!" Shara yelled.

The sorcerer turned and smiled. "Vilos, I had feared I wouldn't get to see you again."

The sorcerer gestured and he slammed into an invisible

wall. He pounded his fists against it to no avail. "Let her go, damn you."

"I don't think so. However, since I have what I've wanted from the start, I will allow you to live. Goodbye, Vilos."

Vilos blinked and they were gone.

CHAPTER 68

Shara was still floating when they appeared in a gloomy cavern. The cavern was filled with stone tables, all but one of which was covered with bubbling tubes and beakers. Something fluttered down from the ceiling and at first she thought it was a bat. When it landed on the sorcerer's shoulder she could see that it had arms and legs in addition to wings.

The creature cocked its head and looked at the sorcerer.

He nodded and said, "Yes, Bane, that's her. Finally I can complete my pact with Balthis."

"What are you going to do with me?" Shara demanded.

The sorcerer smiled. "You are to be the guest of honor in a ritual that will set an elder demon free from a prison that has held it for thousands of years."

Shara shuddered at the cold way he spoke. "You're going to kill me."

"Yes, but not in the way you seem to think. I don't plan to cut your heart out or anything like that. You're intended to be the host for Balthis's new form. That has been your destiny since before you were born. Over the course of about a year the organism will live within you and slowly drain your life energy. When the year is up it will emerge, weak, but free from the prison that has held it for ages. You, unfortunately, will die in the process."

"Who are you?" Shara asked.

Her arms and legs felt like lead weights and she could barely look at her captor. Everything she'd gone through to get home and this is how it ends.

"I have been known by many names over the years, I have now chosen Daktari." The sorcerer snapped his fingers and she settled gently down to the stone floor. "Please have a seat. I can't begin the ritual until the sun sets. We have several more hours."

A year and several hours to live. She sighed and sat on the edge of the empty stone table. Daktari leaned against empty air.

"What did you mean when you said this was my destiny since before I was born?" Shara asked.

"I don't fully understand what makes you so special. Balthis learned that your father's firstborn child was the key to a ritual that would free him from his divine prison. As I said when we first met, during the Crown War, I made an arrangement with your father. In exchange for his firstborn child, you, I would help him defeat his brothers and end the war. You were to be turned over to me on your eighteenth birthday."

"I still don't believe it," Shara said. It hurt too much to think of her father and this ghoul bargaining over her fate before she was even born.

"Believe it or not, I don't care, but know that it is the truth. Your father was willing to sacrifice one life in the future to save thousands then. I admit, not claiming you at birth was a poor idea on my part, but I had no desire to waste eighteen years raising a child. Vilos became too attached to you, especially after your mother died. Still, I kept an eye on you through my stone soldiers. Having that boy's arm ripped off was enough to dissuade others from interfering with you."

"You did that?" Shara asked, horrified.

"Oh yes, hardly a day passed when I or one of my minions wasn't watching you. Once your ring activated, that became impossible."

Shara held up her hand and gazed wonderingly at the ring that had protected her for so long. Fat lot of good it was doing her now.

"Is that the little bauble that has so vexed me?" Daktari asked.

Shara nodded and held out her hand. She forced herself not to smile when he reached out to touch it.

Serve him right if he got a shock.

When he grasped it the ring flashed, but rather than jerk his hand back like everyone else that had ever tried to touch it he just ignored the shock.

A drop of dark fire appeared on the tip of his finger where he touched the ring. The fire burst forth and surrounded the ring. When it faded, nothing remained save a few ashes that fell to the cavern floor.

Daktari smiled at the surprised look on her face. "You hoped to give me a shock. I assure you it would take magic a great deal stronger than that to harm me."

Shara stared down at the floor. "Why? Why are you doing this to me?"

"I'll show you." Daktari turned his back on her and walked over toward a large stand.

As soon as he turned away Shara began frantically searching the tables for a weapon. Her eyes landed on an obsidian dagger. She grabbed it and ran toward him ready to plunge it between his shoulder blades.

It probably wouldn't kill him but maybe she could make him mad enough to kill her now rather than waiting to complete the ritual. At least she could stop the demon from being freed.

If Daktari was aware of her running toward him he showed no sign.

Three feet from his back she lunged with all her might.

The dagger struck an invisible shield that blasted her through the air.

As she came crashing down what felt like a gentle hand caught her and carried her over beside the sorcerer.

"That was a very silly thing to do," Daktari said not sounding the least upset. "You have a strong spirit. No wonder Balthis chose you as his host. As I was saying, the reason I agreed to help Balthis escape his prison is this."

Daktari stepped away from the stand revealing a book about three feet long by two feet wide. The cover was stretched hide of some creature she couldn't identify. The book was about four inches thick and seemed to shimmer in and out of sight.

Shara stared up at the sorcerer. "A book? You did all this for a book?"

"Not just a book. This is the Book of Shadows. Lost for a thousand years, sorcerers and wizards have spent lifetimes searching for it. The most powerful magic in the world is contained within its pages."

"Do you think it will give you enough power to survive when you let this demon loose on the world?"

"I have no intention of waiting around once I have completed the ritual. When our pact is complete, I shall walk between the worlds to a new planet with new magic for me to master."

"New planet, what are you talking about?"

Daktari smiled. "Despite what the priests may tell you about our importance in the universe, this rock is of little consequence. The Creator forged a multitude of worlds, many eons more advanced than this one. Our world is utterly meaningless. If Balthis destroys it, there are billions more drifting throughout the universe."

"It matters to the people living here," Shara said.

"I imagine so."

Shara was still floating, unable to move. "Could you let me down?"

"I don't think so," Daktari said. "Your belligerent attitude makes it quite possible you will try some other foolish stunt to try and stop the ritual. I'm afraid I can't allow that."

CHAPTER 69

The wall that had held the sultan back vanished along with his daughter. Robert watched the sultan seethe with frustration as he stalked through the throne room.

Robert felt pretty crappy too. As bad as he felt, he couldn't imagine what a father felt when he saw his daughter vanish before his eyes.

A groan drew his attention to a head lying in a slowly melting pile of ice. He looked closer. The head's mouth opened and another soft groan emerged.

Robert's first thought was, how did a head without a body groan? His second, more important, thought was that the head appeared to belong to the crazy gentleman that captured them.

The sultan seemed to notice the head as well and walked over for a closer look. Robert and Blade joined him, curious to see what was happening. None of the guards made any effort to stop them.

"Who is he?" Robert asked.

The sultan glanced up as if to see who would be so impertinent as to speak without being spoken to then shrugged. "My brother."

Vilos didn't sound too broken up to see his brother burnt to a crisp.

A short fellow dressed in shimmering robes hurried over to join the discussion. Robert knew a wizard when he saw one.

"What happened to him, Abin?" Vilos asked.

Abin chanted, touched the head, and described the altercation between Nord and Daktari. "It seems your brother followed in your footsteps and tried to alter his arrangement with the sorcerer."

When it appeared the sultan had no more questions Abin broke the connection.

The sultan began pacing around the throne room. Everyone seemed reluctant to approach him.

Robert whispered to Abin, "How is it that guy can still be alive, seeing as he doesn't have a body?"

The wizard swallowed. "Daktari used a spell that bound his soul to his flesh before decapitating him. That way no matter what happened, Nord would live and suffer. Unless we can find a wizard powerful enough to free his spirit he may well spend eternity that way."

Robert turned to Blade. "Remind me not to make any bargains with crazy sorcerers."

Suddenly the door to the throne room burst open and about a hundred soldiers came streaming through. Robert and Blade moved back to back ready for a fight.

"Be at ease," Abin said. "Those are the sultan's men."

One of the men approached the sultan and bowed. "Majesty, we encountered no resistance on our way to the palace. Our forces in the city joined us halfway through town. We have no word yet on the city battalion's losses."

"Thank you, Captain. You may release the men and thank them for a job well done."

"What about your brother, Majesty?" the captain asked.

The sultan nodded his head toward the still-moaning head. "My brother is no longer a concern."

Robert saw the captain's Adam's apple bob as he swallowed. Finally he nodded and led the other soldiers out of the room.

After they had gone Robert hesitantly approached the sultan where he stood staring at his brother's remains. "Uh, excuse me, Your Highness, but shouldn't we be gathering a rescue party or something to go after Shara?"

The sultan turned and favored him with a tired look. "That's what we should be doing, unfortunately we have no idea where Daktari took my daughter and even if we did unless he's within a day's ride we'll probably be too late to stop whatever evil plan he has in mind."

Robert scratched his head. "Well, I don't know about traveling arrangements, but I figure Shara's somewhere in the Chaos Hills. At least that's where this sorcerer guy said she should be brought if you wanted to collect the bounty."

"How did you know about the bounty?" the sultan asked.

He sounded a little suspicious. "On our way here we had to rescue her from some hunters. Blade persuaded one of them to tell us why they were so interested in your daughter. That's when we first heard about the bounty and where to collect it."

The sultan nodded, stroking his chin. He seemed to buy Robert's story. "I'd heard about the bounty but no one saw fit to mention the Chaos Hills. It is a good guess."

Blade and Abin had come over to join them. "Majesty," Abin said. "I believe I have a way to get a small group to the hills quickly. Let me check my lab to make sure Nord's wizard hasn't discovered my hidden magic."

"Quickly, wizard, we have little time."

Abin hurried away.

The sultan said, "Why don't you two tell me about your journey here."

Robert and Blade had finished their tale, edited to make them look better at the start, when Abin returned carrying a black iron rod and three steel flasks. "I was fortunate. It seems Nord's wizard didn't get a chance to check my lab. Everything was where I'd left it."

"What do you have?" the sultan asked.

Abin held up the rod first. "This device holds a teleport spell that will transport four people touching it anywhere on the planet."

"Only four," the sultan said. "I was hoping to take the entire palace guard. I suppose I'll just have to ask for volunteers."

"That won't be necessary," Robert said. "Blade and I will go. We didn't see her this far just to let her go now."

Blade walked over and picked up her sword. She checked both edges then sheathed it. "When do we leave?"

The sultan looked at the two of them but before he could object Robert said, "There's going to be trouble. If there is, you'll want Blade along, and I'll be damned if I'm going to sit around and let something happen to the kid."

Vilos nodded. "You both did well to see my daughter home safely. I will trust you to finish the job. Abin, when can we leave?"

"Soon, Majesty." The wizard handed each of them a steel flask. "Inside these flasks is magical oil that will provide a temporary enchantment for your weapons. Don't apply it until we arrive as the effect won't last more than a few hours."

"Speaking of weapons, can I borrow a shortsword?" Robert asked.

"Of course," the sultan said. "Let's go to the armory and get properly equipped for battle."

The royal armory was about what Robert expected but on a much larger scale. It looked about fifty paces wide and twice that long. Every manner of weapon he could imagine was lined up in racks. There were some weapons Robert had never even heard of.

He helped himself to a fine shortsword and a crossbow. Blade took a pair of daggers and tucked them into her boots. The sultan didn't add anything to the scimitar he already wore.

"Is everyone ready?" Abin asked. When they all nodded he raised the iron rod. "Okay, grab hold."

When they had all taken a firm grip Abin spoke a word and Robert found himself falling in a terrible void filled with swirling, chaotic lights.

The feeling lasted only a moment then they were standing in a patch of grass surrounded by low rocky hills. The sun hung low in the sky, causing the mountains to cast weird shadows. The rod disintegrated leaving their hands covered with iron powder.

"One-way trip it seems." Robert loaded his crossbow.

"I'm afraid so," Abin said. He removed a slim piece of dark polished wood about a foot long from the inside of his robe and began a spell. When he finished he turned a slow circle until the tip of the wand started to glow. "This way."

They headed north and a little east. Everyone was tense with weapons held ready.

Always curious Robert asked, "So what does that spell of yours do?"

Without looking away from the wand Abin said, "It seeks out magic. I believe if we find the magic, we'll find the sorcerer."

"Great. I don't suppose when we find this guy he'll just give up Shara if we ask nicely?"

"You can try if you want, but I think it would be a waste of time."

"I figured. So just how strong is this sorcerer anyway?"

"Imagine an ant," Abin said.

"Okay, but I'm not liking how this metaphor is starting out."

"It gets worse. Now imagine an elephant standing next to the ant. Finally imagine the elephant stepping on the ant. Needless to say the sorcerer isn't the ant. Any more questions?"

Even if Robert had wanted to ask another question he found that his mouth refused to work. Considering the fact that that had never happened to him before he took it as a bad sign.

They continued through the mountains for about a mile or so before they reached the mouth of a cave. The entrance was remarkable in that it was perfectly smooth. Robert could see no sign that a pick or shovel had ever touched the rock.

"This is it," Abin said.

"Are you certain?" the sultan asked. "I would have thought there'd be guards."

Robert grinned. "I suppose when you're the most powerful sorcerer in the world, you don't get robbed very often."

The sultan snorted, making Robert smile all the more. Blade laughed softly and came over to him. She wrapped her arms around his neck and kissed him.

Robert reveled in the warmth for a moment before she pulled away. "See you on the other side."

He nodded. "You know it."

"I suggest you anoint your weapons with the oil," Abin said. "Once we enter, anything is possible."

CHAPTER 70

Daktari set the final item he would need to complete the ritual on the unused stone table. The once-empty table bore four black diamonds, one at each corner, and a large shadow stone in the center. Daktari had sunk the shadow stone flush with the top of the table and it now pulsed with flickering, purple light. The final item was a knife infused with corrupt magic that resonated with Balthis.

"What's all this stuff for?" Shara asked. She still floated above the floor.

"They are simple foci that will allow the necessary transfer of energy to happen more easily."

He gestured and she floated up and turned so she was lying on her back looking up at the ceiling. She gently settled down on the tabletop. "The sun has almost set."

Daktari flinched as one of his wards was triggered. Someone was just outside the tunnel entrance. "Ulibo."

The shadow demon separated itself from the darkness. "Yes, Master?"

"We have company. Go introduce yourself."

"May I kill them, Master?"

"By all means, just don't let them interrupt the ritual."

The demon hissed with glee. "I will bring you their hearts."

"Fine, just get going."

"What's happening?" Shara asked.

"We have uninvited guests."

"Father."

"Probably," Daktari said. "I would have let him live if he just had the sense to leave me alone. Now he has come all this way only to die. Pity. But no matter, the sun has set, and now we shall begin."

Allowing for the very small possibility that Vilos would get past Ulibo, Daktari summoned a dome of invisible energy that would prevent anyone from disturbing him. Next he picked up the knife and raised it over Shara's stomach. The girl shivered but otherwise couldn't move.

"Be still," Daktari said. "I won't cut you."

With great precision he sliced away a square of her dress revealing her navel and about a square foot of flesh. He flicked the fabric away and set the knife down. With the tip of his right index finger he drew a circle of black flame in the air. Red flames shot from his left hand filling in the circle. As soon as the flames had completely filled the circle a savage wind ripped through the cavern swirling Daktari's black robes around him.

Daktari thrust his left hand into the flames and set his right on Shara's bare skin. In a moment Balthis's energy began to fill him.

His back arched and he groaned in pain. A ruddy light oozed out from around the fingers of his right hand as the demonic energy entered the princess's body.

Balthis's rebirth had begun.

CHAPTER 71

Robert and his companions made their way deeper into the mountain. Blade led the way, her sword glowing slightly from the magical oil. The sultan followed behind her then Robert and Abin brought up the rear. Over their heads, an orb of light illuminated the tunnel for about thirty feet in both directions.

In the distance Robert thought he heard something. "Did you hear that?"

Abin staggered. "He's cast a very powerful spell. The psychic wave was incredible."

"We have to hurry," the sultan said.

Blade led them at a quick walk. The sultan kept trying to push past her but she wouldn't allow it. In the end that's what saved them.

As Blade turned around to restrain Vilos, a shadowy claw shot out where her head had been an instant before.

She leapt back as a shadowy form separated itself from the darkness ahead. The creature appeared to be composed entirely of shadow. It towered above them. The tips of its wings brushed the ceiling. It had two diamond-shaped slits for eyes and a jagged hole for a mouth. All in all, not the most pleasant-looking creature Robert had ever seen.

"Welcome to your graves, mortals." Monster hissed.

The creature lunged toward Vilos but Blade batted its claw aside with her sword.

It hissed and drew back

"I see you have a sting, little one." It shifted its form into a giant scorpion. "Now I have as well."

A loud crack filled the tunnel as a lightning bolt tore along the beast's side shearing off four legs. Abin stood with his hands raised and smoking, a smile of triumph on his face.

"You will not best us, shadow demon."

The shadow demon snarled and changed form again, this time choosing a humanoid shape with four arms. "If you think you can beat me, human, you are sadly mistaken."

A tendril of darkness shot out from one of the demon's hands, wrapped around Abin, and slammed him against the wall.

The demon held him pinned for a moment before Blade severed its tendril with an overhand slash.

The wizard fell to the floor with a grunt.

Vilos hurried over to his injured friend while Blade tried to drive the demon away.

"We have to get past it," Vilos said. "Can you do anything?"

Abin coughed up a drop of blood. "I can get you past it, Majesty, but that's all. The rest of us will have to stay behind to keep it from coming after you. Once we finish it, we'll catch up with you."

Finish the demon? Robert laughed to himself. Who the hell was he kidding?

Robert turned to watch Blade who was trying her best to do exactly that.

Robert was torn between wanting to help and not wanting to get in the way. She seemed okay for the moment, so he decided not to interfere.

The demon roared as Blade scored a cut across its chest.

"That's twice you've hurt me, human." It shifted form again, this time becoming an amorphous blob with eight tentacles.

One of them shot out and wrapped around Blade, lifting her off the ground. "Now I'll crush you to a pulp."

"No!" Robert roared. He lunged forward, dodging a pair of tentacles, to drive his sword into the tentacle holding Blade.

The demon snarled and dropped her.

"You okay?" he asked.

Blade grunted and got to her feet.

The demon lunged toward them, but before it could strike, a white globe of light struck it and drove it shrieking backward.

Robert turned to see Abin back on his feet arms raised. He muttered something then touched Vilos on the shoulder.

The sultan vanished.

While the demon was still blinded by the light Abin motioned them to come to his side. "The sultan has gone ahead to try and help his daughter. We must hold the demon here to give him a chance."

"Great plan," Robert said. "Any idea how we manage it?"

"You've seen that your weapons can hurt it. We just need to cause some more damage."

"Is that all? Well what was I worried about? You forgot about the part where we survive."

"All that matters is rescuing the princess," Abin said. "If we die, so be it."

"Speak for yourself, wizard," Robert said. "I like Shara, but I plan to get Blade and me out of this in one piece."

"It's coming," Blade hissed.

Abin's white light was fading and the demon looked angry and unhurt.

Blade charged not giving it a chance to fully recover.

She slashed, severing any tentacles that got too close.

The little bits of shadow flesh vanished in a puff of acrid smoke.

Abin raised his hands again and this time half a dozen spheres of white light streaked away striking the demon in the face and causing it to roar in pain.

Blade took advantage of the distraction to lunge in and drive her sword deep into the mass of shadow flesh.

The demon shook her off and she went flying into the wall.

It oozed over toward her, intent on crushing the life from her stunned body.

Robert charged and leapt on to its back.

He drove his shortsword in up to the hilt.

The demon shook again, but he held on, determined not to let it reach Blade.

The demon surged back, trying to crush him against the other side of the tunnel.

Robert leapt clear and landed with a grunt on the stone floor.

The demon struck the wall with such force that the tunnel shook.

The force of the blow drove the sword in even deeper and the demon howled with pain and began writhing on the ground shifting from one form to the next almost faster than the eye could register.

Blade regained her feet, marched over to the demon, and began hacking at it. Her left arm hung limp and useless. Abin came over beside her and motioned her aside.

She glanced at him but did as he asked.

The wizard pointed both palms at the demon and whispered a spell.

There was a blast as sheets of white fire shot forth consuming the wounded demon.

In moments nothing remained of it but a few wisps of shadow flesh and Robert's charred sword.

CHAPTER 72

Vilos thundered down the tunnel. Abin's invisibility spell had allowed him to sneak past the demon with no trouble. He hadn't gone far when the tunnel opened into a huge cavern with a high ceiling studded with stalactites. Near the rear wall glowed a ruddy light.

The sorcerer stood near the light source, a disk of red flame, and had one hand plunged into the fire. Sprawled on the table in front of him was Shara. The sorcerer had his other hand on her stomach.

All sense left Vilos.

Only one thought existed in his mind.

He had to save his little girl.

He charged toward them, sword lifted above his head.

He weaved around stone tables covered with alchemical paraphernalia.

Ten feet away he slammed into an invisible wall like the one Daktari had used at the palace.

Vilos hammered at the shield until he was out of breath and could barely hold his sword.

It did no good.

Now that he was closer he could see red light leaking out from between Daktari's fingers where he rested them on Shara's belly.

"Shara!" he screamed.

Neither the sorcerer nor his daughter showed any sign that they heard him.

Cursing the angels and himself, Vilos slammed his sword into the barrier once more.

He may as well have beaten it against the walls of the cave for all the good it did.

He heard a sound behind him and spun around.

From the tunnel entrance Abin, Robert, and Blade eased into the cavern. The three of them were quite a mess.

Robert was limping badly, Blade had one arm hanging by her side, and he knew Abin already had broken ribs.

"You three look like hell," Vilos said.

Robert grinned. "You should see the other guy."

Vilos laughed. He rather liked this Robert fellow.

"What about the princess?" Abin asked.

Vilos pointed to where she and Daktari waited behind the shield. "I can't get to her. I beat my sword dull against his shield and it didn't even make a bit of difference that I could see."

"Help me over there," Abin said. "Perhaps I can bring the shield down."

Vilos took his injured friend by the arm and helped him over next to the shield. Abin placed his hands on it and closed his eyes.

When he opened them he sighed. "The shield is incredibly strong. I can try and breach it but I don't hold much hope. Stand back, please."

Vilos moved a few paces away and heard Abin muttering

under his breath. A moment later there was a flash of light and he had to raise his arm to shield his eyes from the glare. When he brought his arm down the light was gone and Abin was flat on the ground unconscious. Vilos hurried over to Abin's side. He carefully reached over, felt for the shield, and found it still intact.

"Sorry, Majesty, I wasn't strong enough." Abin rasped through blood-flecked lips.

He passed out again.

Vilos lifted him gently and carried him away from whatever foul magic Daktari was brewing.

Abin had given his all, Vilos could ask for no more.

Vilos rejoined Robert and Blade next to the shield. Whatever the sorcerer was doing, it seemed to be getting worse. The red light was getting brighter and Shara had begun to squirm under the sorcerer's hand.

"So what do we do now?" Robert asked.

Vilos shook his head. "There's nothing we can do."

"I'll tell you what we're going to do," Blade said. "We're going to wait for the barrier to come down then I'm going to cut that sorcerer's heart out."

Robert shot Blade a funny look but declined to comment. Robert sat down on the edge of one of the stone benches. He winced as he lifted his foot off the ground.

Vilos sat beside him. "How you holding up?"

Robert grimaced. "I hurt in places I didn't even know I had, how about you?"

"I'll live. It's her I'm worried about."

Both men looked at Shara where she lay still under the sorcerer's hand. The light seemed to be getting brighter all the time. Soon it grew so bright they had to look away or get their eyes burned out.

When they looked back the light was gone except for the

still-glowing circle floating in the air. The sorcerer was looking at them. His eyes glowed with an inner fire.

"So you made it past my demon, an impressive accomplishment for the four of you. Though you do look a little worse for wear."

Blade was glaring daggers at him, her sword clenched in her good hand.

"My dear, you look a little upset," he said. Behind him Shara sat up. Where her dress had been cut, a symbol was visible around her navel. It looked like a key with a solar halo.

The sorcerer turned to face her. "How are you feeling, child?"

She got to her feet and rubbed her stomach through the hole in her dress. "Better than I expected."

"Shara." Vilos ran over to the barrier and pressed his hands against it.

She smiled, tears in her eyes. "Daddy."

She ran right through the barrier and into his arms. Vilos held her close, not the least interested in how she managed to get through the shield.

"DAKTARI!" A voice thundered through the cavern. "What are you doing? You must protect my host until my new form is born."

Daktari turned to look into the circle of flame. "No."

"WHAT!?" the voice demanded.

"Our bargain, Lord Balthis, said specifically that once I performed the ritual our pact was complete." As Daktari spoke to the demon he didn't notice Blade sneaking up behind him. "I have now completed the ritual. What happens to the girl and your new body is of no concern to me."

An inarticulate roar of rage filled the cavern.

Daktari snorted and snapped his fingers. The circle of flame vanished taking the noise with it.

In that moment Blade struck.

She leapt into the air bringing her sword down on Daktari's collarbone apparently planning to cut him in half.

What happened, however, was a blast of magic shattered her sword and sent her flying ass over elbows eight feet through the air to land with a dull thump on the stone floor.

Robert and Vilos both raised their swords ready to die defending their loved ones.

Daktari sighed. "You've got to be kidding."

The sorcerer pointed and a beam of dark fire shot out towards them. The beam split just before it reached them and struck their weapons. In an instant both men's weapons were reduced to slag.

"Now what, sorcerer?" Vilos demanded.

Daktari levitated about ten feet off the ground. "Now nothing, my bargain with Balthis is fulfilled. I'm free of his miserable presence forever. As for you, I'm tempted to kill the lot of you for the difficulties you've caused me, and make no mistake, if I wished it, you'd be dead just like that."

The sorcerer snapped his fingers.

"However, considering the damage I've done to your kingdom I believe I've made my point about making bargains you don't plan to keep. As for your daughter, any reasonably competent priest should be able to exorcise the demonic essence from her body. The sooner the better though, because it will only grow stronger over time."

"Excuse me," Robert said. He suddenly seemed to realize he was still holding the melted sword and tossed it away. "Wasn't this a lot of trouble to go through if you weren't planning to actually bring the demon here?"

Suddenly Daktari looked tired and old. "Boy, in the universe there are powers that dwarf my own even as mine dwarf yours. When a sorcerer like myself makes a bargain with a creature from the pit, there are ways to bind us both into completing our respective sides of the bargain. Once Balthis had delivered on his end, I had to do the same, anything else would have been suicide."

Robert scratched his head. "Yeah, but doesn't it break the deal if you just abandon him after completing the ritual?"

Daktari smiled. "It breaks the spirit but not the letter of the contract. Now, if you fools will shut up and get the child to a priest, Balthis should remain bound in his prison for the fore-seeable future."

"Why?" Everyone looked at Shara. "Why would you help us now? If you hate this world so much why not let Balthis destroy it?"

Daktari smiled at Shara, fondly if Vilos was any judge. "I'm not a monster and I have no desire to see a being as powerful and thoroughly evil as Balthis let loose on the universe. I imagine there are more than a few archangels that wouldn't thank me for undoing their work as well. It is time for you to get exorcised. Be well, child."

Vilos led the silent group outside. Only when the stars twinkled above them did anyone speak.

"That went better than I'd feared," Robert said as he leaned against Blade's good side. "You okay?"

Blade groaned. "I never thought I'd say this, Bobby, but even I've had my fill of fighting."

Robert grinned. "You said it, gorgeous. When we get back to civilization, I'm not moving for a month. How about you, kid, how you holding up?"

Shara arched an eyebrow. "I've often heard it said that being pregnant gives a woman a special glow. I didn't think they meant hellfire red."

Robert laughed and Vilos gave his daughter a strange look. "Where did you learn sarcasm?"

"Ask him." Shara nodded toward the still-laughing Robert.

"All joking aside," Blade said. "Any thoughts on how we get back to civilization?"

Vilos thought for a moment. "There's a village south of the hills. I'd often considered having it evacuated because of the large garrison needed to defend it from constant raids. Now I'm glad I didn't. At a guess I'd say it's about ten miles. If we can avoid any of the really nasty monsters, we should be okay."

Robert nodded. "We'll need to rig a stretcher for Abin, and I'll need a cane or something to lean on."

They spread out and searched. A dead tree yielded the staves they needed for a stretcher and walking stick. Robert and Vilos sacrificed their tunics for the rest of the stretcher.

They were a rather pathetic-looking group as they set out for the ten-mile hike. Vilos was dragging Abin along on the stretcher. Trailing behind him came Blade with her broken arm, Robert with his twisted ankle, and Shara.

Between them they had a pair of daggers and his crossbow. The moon was still high in the sky, not much past midnight Vilos thought. If the angels were merciful, perhaps they could make it to safety without running into anything too disagreeable.

The angels did indeed smile upon them and they reached the village just after sunup. Abin was still breathing and they hadn't run into anything bigger than a cliff viper.

As the ragged little group approached the village a gate guard on the wall hailed them. As soon as he learned who was waiting the gate was opened and they were escorted to the finest and only inn the village had to offer.

The only healing potion in the whole town was poured down Abin's throat. He woke up almost at once and took a deep breath. He winced but it appeared that his broken ribs were mostly healed.

"We're still alive?" he asked.

"Daktari didn't feel like killing us," Robert said from where he sat, one arm around Blade, on a small couch.

"Why?" the wizard asked.

"He wants us to clean up the mess he made." Blade nodded over toward where Shara slept on another couch.

"So he never intended to summon the demon to our world. He put us through a lot if he didn't plan to go through with it."

"I'm just glad we came out of it alive," Robert said.

CHAPTER 73

Robert sighed with pleasure as he leaned on the down-filled silk pillows. They had been resting in Sultan's Oasis for a month and Shara was demon free. Robert smiled as he remembered how Vilos had gathered the high priests of the various temples together and informed them of the task they would have to perform.

The priest of the Binder, whom Robert gathered Vilos had some history with, tried to demur, but Vilos had explained any priest that refused to help would have his temple burned to the ground.

The sultan seemed to take a great deal of pleasure in making the threat. Of course, once the situation was properly explained, everyone was delighted to help.

That conversation had happened the day after their return. He and Blade had been given one of the splendid rooms generally reserved for diplomats and nobility. After the exorcism, Shara had slept for almost two days. The priests said it was because she had already lost quite a bit of life energy to the demon inside her. She was now fully recovered as were he and

Blade thanks to the generous donation of several healing potions.

"Enjoying your last day wallowing in luxury?"

Robert looked over his shoulder to see Blade emerge from their bath chamber. She had taken a fancy to the local fashion and was currently wearing a black silk nightgown that clung just right to every curve. He smiled and thanked whatever angel had put her in his path for the millionth time.

"Are you sure we can't stay here for a couple more years?"

She stood hands planted firmly on hips. "Positive, if I don't get some action soon, I'm going to go crazy."

He offered a speculative look. "I can help you with the action thing."

She made a fist and waved it at him in mock fury. "If you don't start getting dressed in the next five seconds, this is the only action you're going to get."

He sighed. Heaven's mercy, he loved that woman. "Okay Blade, you win."

She nodded. "Good, we're supposed to meet Shara and her father in the throne room."

"Yeah, do you suppose we'll get our reward?"

"Don't pretend you helped that girl just to get a reward at this late date."

"I'm only saying I wouldn't mind a little something for our trouble, that's all."

Blade groaned. "Just get dressed."

When he and Blade entered the throne room, Vilos, Shara, and Abin were waiting for them. There were no guards which seemed a bit odd, but then again they had pretty well proven their loyalty.

They carried all their meager possessions in two worn leather packs.

"Hey, kid," Robert said as soon as they entered.

Vilos winced at the informality, but Shara smiled and gave him a hug. While Shara hugged Blade Vilos descended from his throne and shook Robert's hand. "I can't thank you enough for what you did for my daughter, but I will try."

Robert clapped him on the back. "It was our pleasure, right Blade?"

She smiled and put an arm around Shara.

"Never the less," Vilos went on. "Please accept the first half of your reward."

He clapped and a guard entered from a side door carrying a sword in a scabbard. The guard bowed and presented the weapon to Blade. She drew the sword and the keen edge glittered brightly in the light.

"That sword is forged from silver steel, one of the hardest metals on the planet. I hope it serves you well."

She sheathed the sword and bowed. "It's magnificent, Your Majesty, thank you."

Abin approached Robert and handed him a small book. "I heard you wish to learn magic. This book contains thirty simple cantrips as well as about fifty pages of magical theory. When you have mastered them all you will be well on your way as a beginning wizard."

Robert beamed as he accepted the book. It wasn't the gold and jewels he'd expected, but a chance to learn magic was a gift he couldn't pass up. "I thank you as well."

"Splendid," Vilos said. "If you will follow me, we'll go take a look at the rest of your reward."

The five of them went behind the throne room and for a moment Robert had the perverse feeling they were going to the dungeon. They went right past it however and descended to a stone chamber where Vilos opened a gate for them.

"Where does this go?" Robert asked.

"To Haydrien," Vilos said. "My brother, Kent, will meet you with the rest of your reward."

"Speaking of brothers," Robert said. "What happened to the other one's head?"

"I'm looking into that," Abin said in a tone that didn't invite further questions.

They followed Vilos through the portal and emerged in an identical room. At the top of a set of stone stairs they emerged in an alley. No one seemed to notice them as Vilos led them through the busy streets toward the docks.

"So what's the reward?" Robert asked Shara.

She offered an impish grin. "It's a surprise."

Robert shrugged. As long as there wasn't a gallows waiting at the end of this trip he'd be happy to take whatever the sultan and his brother offered. When they reached the dock ward another tall blond man met them. Even at a glance it was obvious the sultan and this man were related.

As if reading his mind Vilos said, "Robert, Blade, let me introduce my brother Kent."

They all shook hands and Kent said, "A pleasure to meet you. If you'll come this way, please."

They followed him past fifteen slips before stopping in front of a sleek caravel. "This is it," Kent said.

"Very nice," Robert said. "Is this the ship we're taking out of here?"

Vilos smiled. "In a manner of speaking."

"Read the name," Shara said.

Robert and Blade both looked at the side of the ship. Chiseled into a board was *The Grateful Journey*. They both looked back at Vilos and the others.

"It's yours," Shara said throwing her arms around Robert's neck.

"It's been loaded with the finest trade goods my brother's

warehouses had to offer. You should do quite well selling them in any port you decide to visit. The crew has been paid for six months. I trust you like the second part of your reward."

"Very much," Robert said. "'Thank you' doesn't seem adequate. For as long as I can remember I've wanted a ship of my own." He looked at Blade. "So where do you want to go?"

"South," Blade said. "The island of Tao has gladiatorial games. I think I'd make a good gladiator."

"The island of Tao sounds good to me." The little group walked over to the gangplank. "It's been a pleasure, most of the time."

"In your cabin you'll find a crystal ball," Abin said. "The princess insisted she have some way to talk with you. The means to use it are in that book I gave you."

"Thanks." Robert put his hand on Shara's shoulder. "Well kid, it's been interesting."

Shara was crying. "I'll miss you, Bobby."

Robert held her close and stroked her hair. "Hey, it's all right, don't worry. We'll be around this way again."

She sniffed. "Promise?"

"You bet."

"All right."

Blade took her turn getting a hug. "Don't worry, I won't let him forget. If you ever find a prince worthy of you we'll return for the wedding."

"Bye, Blade."

He and Blade climbed the gangplank and went to the back of the ship. As the Grateful Journey slowly left the harbor behind the giant turtle magically bound for that purpose, they waved goodbye to their friends.

A ship of his own and a new adventure. Much as he'd miss the kid, Robert was eager to see what the wide world had to offer.

CHAPTER 74

Daktari sat at his desk in the cool, gloomy cavern, his mind awhirl. The mark on the princess's stomach nagged at him. He'd seen it somewhere, but where exactly eluded him. His best guess, an ancient reference book, sat ignored in front of him. There was no sign of the symbol anywhere in its pages.

He turned a fraction and looked for the hundredth time at his reflection in the polished surface of his crystal ball. The skull marks on his cheeks were gone and the anger that constantly filled him slowly fading. With his pact complete, Balthis's influence over him would soon be reduced to nothing.

It was a welcome change. He still shivered when he thought about some of the things that unnatural rage had driven him to do. Not that he would have changed anything. The knowledge held by the Tome of Shadows was so valuable, no price was too high to acquire it.

He ran a hand over his bald head and stood. There was one other book he could check.

As he crossed the workshop to his bookcase Bane flittered down and landed on his shoulder. "Are we leaving soon, Master?"

"No, Bane. Something has caught my interest. The ritual awakened a power in the girl. What, I don't yet know. But I will."

"Why do you care, Master?" Bane asked.

"It's magic and it's a mystery. Is that not reason enough? I feared there was nothing left to interest me on this world. I'm delighted to be wrong."

Daktari selected a second book and flipped through it. There were only fifty pages and none of them held an image like the golden key on Shara's stomach.

Once the lack of information would have angered him beyond reason, now he felt excited. Without the demon clouding his judgement, his mind felt clearer than ever.

The book went back on the shelf and he snapped his fingers. Silvermane dealt with angels and judging from the design, that mark had something to do with the forces of Heaven. Perhaps the old witch's soul would be able to answer his questions.

And if she couldn't, he'd try something else. He was free at last and he intended to make the most of it.

F rom the doorway of a crumbling stone temple deep in the heart of the jungle, Kweeg screeched and shook his bone staff as the last half dozen members of his tribe disappeared into the undergrowth. Barely over three feet tall, Kweeg was short even for a goblin. His wrinkly green skin sagged and his puss-yellow eyes looked near to bugging out of his head.

Abandoning their shaman was wrong and Kweeg would be certain to call a curse down on the fools' heads. Of course that would work better if he could actually use magic. Despite endless prayers in front of the monstrous statue in the heart of the temple, no power had seen fit to answer.

He suspected that, along with the miserable hunting in the area, was what prompted the last of the holdouts to abandon him.

With a sad shake of his head, Kweeg retreated to his temple. Somewhere inside a stone came crashing down. The temple was in worse shape than the tribe if that were possible.

The entry hall ended in a huge cathedral at the center of

which was a statue of a demon. At least Kweeg assumed it was a demon from the fang-filled mouth, bat wings, and huge gut. The belt of skulls also argued against an angel.

He knelt in front of the statue and touched his head to the stone. "Why won't you speak to me, Master? Is my poor soul of no value to you?"

Another rumble and Kweeg feared he might end up buried alive. Instead a voice so deep and powerful it made his bones ache said, "I hear you, little goblin. I hear and grant your wish. My name is Balthis and you will serve as my agent in the world. Touch your statue and receive my gift."

Kweeg, enraptured to finally hear the voice of his master, hastened to lay his hands on the statue's feet.

Power and purpose filled him. He knew now what Balthis required and he would do anything to see the task complete.

AUTHOR NOTE

And so we come to the end of the first book in The Divine Key Trilogy. Though she survived her trials, fate isn't finished with Princess Shara. Her adventures continue in book two, For The Greater Good.

If you'd like to get new and updates about my writing you can sign up for my newsletter on my website, www. jamesewisher.com You'll also get a free electronic copy of the novella Lizzy's First Bearer set in my Soul Force Saga world.

Thanks for reading and I'll see you next time,

James

ALSO BY JAMES E WISHER

The Divine Key Trilogy
Shadow Magic
For The Greater Good
The Divine Key Awakens

The Portal Wars Saga
The Hidden Tower
The Great Northern War
The Portal Thieves
The Master of Magic
The Chamber of Eternity
The Heart of Alchemy
The Sanguine Scroll

The Dragonspire Chronicles
The Black Egg
The Mysterious Coin
The Dragons' Graveyard
The Slave War
The Sunken Tower
The Dragon Empress
The Dragonspire Chronicles Omnibus Vol. 1
The Dragonspire Chronicles Omnibus Vol. 2
The Complete Dragonspire Chronicles Omnibus

Soul Force Saga

Disciples of the Horned One Trilogy:

Darkness Rising

Raging Sea and Trembling Earth

Harvest of Souls

Disciples of the Horned One Omnibus

Chains of the Fallen Arc:

Dreaming in the Dark

On Blackened Wings

Chains of the Fallen Omnibus

The Complete Soul Force Saga Omnibus

The Aegis of Merlin:

The Impossible Wizard

The Awakening

The Chimera Jar

The Raven's Shadow

Escape From the Dragon Czar

Wrath of the Dragon Czar

The Four Nations Tournament

Death Incarnate

Atlantis Rising

Rise of the Demon Lords

Aegis of Merlin Omnibus Vol 1.

Aegis of Merlin Omnibus Vol 2.

The Complete Aegis of Merlin Omnibus

Other Fantasy Novels:

The Squire
Death and Honor Omnibus

The Rogue Star Series:
Children of Darkness
Children of the Void
Children of Junk
Rogue Star Omnibus Vol. 1
Children of the Black Ship

ABOUT THE AUTHOR

James E. Wisher is a writer of science fiction and fantasy novels. He's been writing since high school and reading everything he could get his hands on for as long as he can remember.

To learn more:
www.jamesewisher.com
james@jamesewisher.com